Praise for

THE LAST GIFT

"Finally, a volume that reprints Freeman's Christmas fare. Her seasonal stories are inventive and experimental, emphasizing the emotional and practical complexities of the holiday, with profound implications for gendered labor, class inequality, the building of community, and the pleasures and perils of consumption. The impressive introduction frames the stories within the history of the holiday and Freeman's delight in its intrigue."

—**STEPHANIE PALMER**, coeditor of *New Perspectives on Mary E. Wilkins Freeman: Reading with and against the Grain*

"Celebrated in her own time not only as a New England regionalist but also as a writer of popular Christmas stories, Mary E. Wilkins Freeman challenged the genre's sentimental limits by questioning the relationships between charity and obligation, theft and gift, and transgression and redemption which her characters experience at Christmas. As Thomas Ruys Smith argues in his excellent, lively, and comprehensive introduction to these twenty-five stories, some published for the first time since their original appearance, Freeman's unjustly neglected Christmas stories reveal a new understanding both of the genre's significance and of Freeman's career as a professional writer."

—**DONNA CAMPBELL**, author of *Bitter Tastes: Literary Naturalism and Early Cinema in American Women's Writing*

THE LAST GIFT

THE LAST GIFT

The Christmas Stories of

Mary E. Wilkins Freeman

Edited, with an Introduction, by

Thomas Ruys Smith

Louisiana State University Press

Baton Rouge

Published by Louisiana State University Press
lsupress.org

LSU Press Paperback Original

DESIGNER: Mandy McDonald Scallan
TYPEFACE: Ingelborg, text; Aquatory Vintage, display

COVER ILLUSTRATION: *Red School House (Country Scene),* 1858, by George Henry Durrie. Courtesy Metropolitan Museum of Art, New York, Bequest of Peter H. B. Frelinghuysen, 2011.

Library of Congress Cataloging-in-Publication Data

Names: Freeman, Mary Eleanor Wilkins, 1852–1930, author. | Smith, Thomas Ruys, 1979– editor.
Title: The last gift : the Christmas stories of Mary E. Wilkins Freeman / edited, with an introduction, by Thomas Ruys Smith.
Description: Baton Rouge : Louisiana State University Press, [2023] | Includes bibliographical references.
Identifiers: LCCN 2023004073 (print) | LCCN 2023004074 (ebook) | ISBN 978-0-8071-8016-7 (paperback) | ISBN 978-0-8071-8064-8 (pdf) | ISBN 978-0-8071-8063-1 (epub)
Subjects: LCSH: Christmas stories, American.
Classification: LCC PS1711 .L37 2023 (print) | LCC PS1711 (ebook) | DDC 813/.4—dc23/eng/20230620
LC record available at https://lccn.loc.gov/2023004073
LC ebook record available at https://lccn.loc.gov/2023004074

for my family

CONTENTS

Stolen Christmases, Uninvited Guests

Introduction

"Christmas is tomfoolery, anyhow," says he.
"That's as you look at it," says I.
—MARY E. WILKINS FREEMAN,
"The Revolt of Sophia Lane," 1903

IN HER OWN LIFETIME, Mary E. Wilkins Freeman was internationally renowned as one of the most important and beloved American writers of the late nineteenth century. Her portraits of New England life—in poems, novels, children's literature, drama, essays, and most significantly, short stories—delighted readers across the world. In 1891, a reviewer for the *Bookman* magazine captured the sensation generated by her "fresh and original" arrival on the literary scene: "Miss Wilkins's stories are realistic in the true sense of that much misused word. They are not mere collections of facts, more or less unpleasant, but a faithful chronicling of such details of human affairs as have a real meaning [. . .] and in all, whatever may be the setting, she sees those things which are of perennial interest—the pathos and beauty of simple lives. Here is true excellence, native born, uncopied and untaught." In particular, the *Bookman* noted, "it is in her pictures of middle-aged women that Miss Wilkins excels, and she has done what no other writer has ever dared to do in making them the heroines of her stories."[1] By any measure, she was a major celebrity for the next few decades, at the top table of American literary culture—sometimes literally. When *Harper's Weekly* threw Mark Twain a swanky seventieth birthday party at Delmonico's Restaurant in 1905, Freeman was conspicuously seated at his right hand.

Mary Wilkins Freeman sits to the right of Mark Twain during his seventieth birthday celebrations at Delmonico's Restaurant in 1905—an image published in a special souvenir edition of *Harper's Weekly* on December 23, 1905, as *Mark Twain's 70th Birthday: Souvenir of Its Celebration* to mark the occasion.

As fashions changed, Freeman's art slowly fell out of favor with critics, if not readers. What had been the terms of her praise became the tools of her marginalization. Her focus on New England led to her dismissal as a parochial writer of merely regional interest. And it was precisely her concern for the "small trials, the little heroisms and silent sorrows of old maids," that contributed to her own neglect for much of the twentieth century.[2] As Mary Reichardt has summarized, "Trivial, trite, not worth much attention, because women, or at least these kind of women, were not worth much attention: this opinion continued to dominate Freeman criticism until the mid-1960s."[3] Still, she retained her partisans. In a sketch of a literary gathering in America in the 1920s, first published in the *New Yorker* in 1966, the British writer Sylvia Townsend Warner mused, "If I had had the courage of my convictions [. . .] when everyone was talking about Joyce and Pound [. . .] I would have said, 'Why don't you think more of Mary Wilkins?'"[4] Thankfully, a new generation of feminist scholars did just that, rediscovering Freeman's extraordinary power as a writer and recognizing in her work searching explorations of "gender attitudes and relationships, women, the tension between the individual and a coded society, class, work, and other elements long neglected."[5] Today she retains a position in the American canon, even if that status hardly reflects her extensive popularity or significance in her own moment.

Until now, though, one element of Freeman's work has remained resolutely neglected. Throughout the decades of her long, prolific, and celebrated career, Freeman crafted a treasure trove of Christmas stories that remain unrivalled in American literary history. Her vision of the season was a constant presence in the lives of readers at precisely the moment that the holiday was taking its modern form. Across dozens of stories, poems, and sketches—for young and old, on both sides of the Atlantic—she demonstrated an extraordinary ability to repeatedly reimagine the significance of Christmas, always grappling with its emotional and practical complexities, imbuing the festival with humor and poignancy in equal measure. But you wouldn't know any of that from Freeman's current place in the American literary conversation, in which her seasonal writing—a very significant portion of her published output—has been left out in the cold. So here, for the first time, a rich selection of her Christmas stories are brought together in one place; most of them have been uncollected since their first, scattered appearances in print over a century ago; one of them, until now, has been entirely lost to readers and scholars alike. Taken together, they reshape our sense of both Freeman as a writer and the literary landscape of Christmas.

Yet why have these Christmas stories remained a missing part of Freeman's literary legacy? At least in part, because some of her most significant cheerleaders have also been most at pains to disappear this defining element of her career. Through all the periodic revivals to which she has been subject, a certain queasiness over the apparently commercial motivations lurking behind the centrality of the festive season in Freeman's body of work have caused a litany of editors, scholars, and biographers to wage their own war on the Christmas stories that threaded through her career like a sparkling strand of tinsel. It was a process that started early. Influential editor and writer William Dean Howells often praised Freeman's stories ("good through and through," he judged her first collection in 1887).[6] Indeed, she was the inaugural recipient of the William Dean Howells Medal from the American Academy of Arts and Letters in 1925. Yet Howells was constitutionally opposed to the Christmas stories that flooded the pages of newspapers and magazines every December: "a whole school of unrealities so ghastly that one can hardly recall without a shudder those sentimentalities at second-hand."[7] Freeman's handiness with a Christmas sketch was, perhaps, one of the reasons that Howells also felt compelled to publicly pronounce that in matters literary, "Miss Wilkins [. . .] cannot always be trusted," and to note of her stories, "Sometimes they ring false, sentimental, romantic."[8] (Even then, in one of his numerous diatribes against seasonal stories, he acknowledged that Freeman's ability to draw "graphic situations" was an example of the "art [. . .] at its highest.")[9]

Later commentators followed Howells in their suspicion of seasonal stories. Freeman's most important biographer Edward Foster dismissed her festive sketches as "inconsequential trifles [. . .] by no means the worst of this sentimental *genre* but sticky enough."[10] When explaining her rationale for selecting which stories would feature in her own anthology of Freeman's uncollected pieces, Mary R. Reichardt—one of the leading voices in Freeman scholarship—similarly dismissed most of Freeman's Christmas work: "The quality of these stories is extremely uneven. Many end disappointingly with a platitude appropriate to the season despite development of otherwise realistic situations and themes; others, poorly plotted from the outset, seem forced." A small handful Reichardt deemed palatable "in spite of the overt holiday intent."[11] Elsewhere, she has labeled Freeman's seasonal work "formulaic and trite," again allowing that some of the stories "succeed despite their holiday themes."[12] Perry Westbrook damned Freeman's Christmas stories with the faintest of praise: "sentimental in plot [. . .] the stories are at worst harmless and at best heart-warming"; at least, he admitted, they largely avoided being "downright mawkish."[13] Bah, humbug, indeed. Like the oblivious Hiram Snell in Freeman's story "The Revolt of Sophia Lane," such critics seem keen to dismiss Christmas as inconsequential "tomfoolery," worried that its popularity as a subject might undermine our sense of Freeman as a writer to be taken seriously. We might reply knowingly, like Sophia herself, with her full awareness of the profound implications that the apparent fripperies of the season can hold: "That's as you look at it." Until we embrace her Christmas work, our sense of Freeman as a writer will always be partial; attempting to hide these stories away in the literary attic like so many dusty Christmas decorations simply because of their seasonal focus is to implicitly agree with the judgments of those critics who sought to dismiss her in previous decades.

Happily, a handful of scholars have begun the task of rehabilitating this major theme that runs throughout Freeman's entire body of work—even though this valuable undertaking has been made more difficult by the way that Freeman's Christmas stories have been dispersed widely, sometimes completely forgotten, and, until now, largely unavailable in major reprints of her writings.[14] Indeed, decades ago, Charles Johanningsmeier made the forceful case that far more attention needs to be paid to these stories: "Documenting all of Freeman's holidays stories is important because they represent a vital part of the context in which Freeman conducted her professional career." Without them, and other forgotten aspects of her work, we are left with "an incomplete picture of Freeman's career and her audience, which in turn makes it more difficult to accurately assess her cultural influence among readers."[15] Very recently, Stephanie Palmer has offered the prompt that Freeman's "holiday stories are [. . .] worth examining as an oeuvre."[16]

So what happens if, rather than seeing these stories as succeeding "in spite" of their treatment of Christmas, we put Christmas at the center of the frame—as Freeman herself so often did—and pay close attention to one of the most important motifs in her career without dismissing it as mere seasonal window dressing? Foster was at least right when he described the Christmas story as a genre. As early as 1943, Katharine Allyn See had rightly made this judgment, declaring the American Christmas story to be "an independent, minor literary genre unto itself."[17] And like any genre, the Christmas story is constructed from repeating themes, conventions, props, and devices that authors can use, abuse, and, at best, play with in fresh and surprising ways. By any rights, Freeman and her apparently endless seasonal invention should be lauded as its leading proponent, at the head of a competitive field that jostled for space in magazines and newspapers every December. Year after year, Freeman proved amazingly adept at finding new ways to deploy festive tropes in ways that struck right to the heart of their meaning in American lives.

This was no easy task. By the time that Freeman started to make the season her own in the 1880s, modern Christmas celebrations already had a significant literary heritage, on both sides of the Atlantic. Indeed, popular literature framed around seasonal celebrations had undoubtedly encouraged America to overcome its long-standing religious resistance to the holiday—the persistent Puritan suspicions that still linger in some of Freeman's stories. Washington Irving's glowing portrait of Old English

Christmas traditions in *The Sketch Book of Geoffrey Crayon* (1819) helped to reestablish the popularity of the season on both sides of the Atlantic.[18] The ubiquity of Charles Dickens's *A Christmas Carol* (1843) was also vitally important, even if Americans were slightly slower to embrace it than their British counterparts. Dickens had upset them with his criticisms of the New World in his travel book *American Notes* (1842), but his Christmas ghost story helped to thaw out the relationship. As the *Broadway Journal* put it in 1845: "We said a good many severe things, even malicious, about Dickens, as soon as he left us; but we seized on his Christmas Carol with as hearty a good will as old Scrooge poked his timid clerk in the ribs the morning after Christmas."[19] Undoubtedly, his influence on Christmas literature echoed (and still echoes) down the decades. It is perhaps telling that Freeman herself described her first published short story—"Her Shadow Family" (1882)—as either a "passable" or "poor" imitation of Dickens, depending on her mood.[20] By the middle of the nineteenth century, the popular icons of domestic Christmas celebrations were well established, if not yet universally embraced: gift giving, Santa Claus, stockings, Christmas trees—and a flood of seasonal printed material that entered the literary marketplace every December. Indeed, before long, the sheer volume of this Christmas literary fare attracted censure and accusations of creative exhaustion. In 1866, a critic for the *London Times* lamented, "Regularly as the year draws to a close we are inundated with a peculiar class of books which are supposed to be appropriate to the goodwill and joviality of the season. Most of these publications are quickly forgotten; and [. . .] deserve no better fate."[21] In America, Howells was at the forefront of the realist turn against the seasonal sketch, but perhaps no one expressed this mood more succinctly than his friend Mark Twain, when he stated bluntly, "I hate Xmas stories."[22]

Still, despite such denunciations, Christmas numbers of newspapers and magazines remained the biggest-selling editions of the year. Established authors could name their price for a seasonal sketch, and aspiring writers sought to tap into this lucrative market; editors were inundated with Christmas content. In 1898, the *Writer* magazine instructed its readers in the basics of publishing "'Timely' Articles': "A great deal of Christmas matter comes into editorial sanctums when all December forms have gone to press, and even when the Christmas papers are in the mail." Instead, ambitious writers needed to "sit under the shade of a tree" in summertime, ignore the heat, and "write about [. . .] December snows." After all, that was the time when "such articles as skates, sleighs, and snow-shovels" were made.[23] Still, such industry was no guarantee of success. In 1893, the editor of the *Yale Literary Magazine* wrote of "absent-mindedly filling the waste-basket with rejected Christmas stories."[24] Selling seasonal stories was a tough business. For many writers, these market demands were a profound burden. Perhaps no one gave fuller expression to these frustrations than British novelist Anthony Trollope, who complained in his autobiography in 1883:

> Nothing can be more distasteful to me than to have to give a relish of Christmas to what I write. I feel the humbug implied by the nature of the order. A Christmas story, in the proper sense, should be the ebullition of some mind anxious to instil others with a desire for Christmas religious thought, or Christmas festivities,—or, better still, with Christmas charity. Such was the case with Dickens when he wrote his two first Christmas stories. But since that the things written annually—all of which have been fixed to Christmas like children's toys to a Christmas tree—have had no real savour of Christmas about them. I had done two or three before. Alas! At this very moment I have one to write, which I have promised to supply within three weeks of this time,—the picture-makers always require a long interval,—as to which I have in vain been cudgelling my brain for the last month.[25]

For decades, Freeman met the challenge—not just supplying Christmas stories for a wide variety of powerful editors and prominent publications or simply attaching her stories to Christmas "like children's toys to a Christmas tree" but tangling anew each year with the meaning of the holiday as it played out in the lives of her characters and readers, reinvigorating the form at the moment that it seemed imaginatively spent.

Even for Freeman, succeeding in the Christmas market required her, like the reformed Scrooge, to keep Christmas in her heart the whole year round—though if she found that process as arduous as Trollope, little trace of it is evident in her letters. Nevertheless, negotiations with journal editors about Christmas stories were continual. What remains of this correspondence shows that as much as her attention to the seasonal market was a commercial consideration for Freeman, a very uncynical concern for craft was ever-present too. Early in her career, for example,

Freeman wrote a New Year's message on January 9, 1887, to Mary Louise Booth—the editor of *Harper's Bazar* (as it was spelled until 1929), one of Freeman's most important publishing outlets. She informed Booth, in self-deprecating terms: "I have some stories nearly ready to show. I am trying to produce a good Christmas one for Mr. Alden [the editor of *Harper's New Monthly Magazine*], but I dare say I won't succeed very well." ("I had some pretty Christmas presents," she happily added.) In March 1887, she again wrote to Booth: "I am delighted that you like the Christmas story, and also that Mr. Alden and Mr. Ford like the other two, thank you ever so much for telling me." By 1890, others were already lobbying her directly for the kind of seasonal content she could provide, and Freeman was learning her market value. "I will be much pleased to write the Christmas story for you," she wrote to editor Jeannette Leonard Gilder in September 1890, "and will let you have it in time." In November that same year, Freeman was writing to Samuel Sidney McClure about a Christmas story that had gone missing in the mail: "It must sooner or later be found, unless stolen." To Arthur Stedman, in June 1894, Freeman apologized: "I have not begun your Christmas story yet. I am going to take time for it, and do my very prettiest." By October, the story had been submitted, but still Freeman fretted that she "did not know I would have space for 4,000 words, as I think the story would have been improved by not cramming so at the end."[26] The story in question was likely to have been "Serena Ann," included in this volume, so you, too, can judge if Freeman did her "very prettiest" after all.

To Henry Loomis Nelson, editor of *Harper's Weekly,* Freeman also promised a Christmas story in 1897: "I am not quite sure, myself, as to whither they will fare," she wrote of the characters she had created, "except into some sort of a Christmas situation." "I am rather experimenting," she informed him, a clear sign that Freeman did not see literary innovation as incompatible with her seasonal stories. Yet even when she was a very established voice, Freeman still had to find ways to negotiate a path through the Christmas market. In July 1906, she wrote to Hayden Carruth, editor of the *Woman's Home Companion,* with a Christmas story that had been rejected by Harper's because "they had already accepted three Christmas stories this week, and had two already on hand, making five in all." Because it was "'second fiddle,' and not written to your order," Freeman suggested, unusually, she would let it go for less than her usual market rate. Carruth was happy to accept. That story was "The Gift of Love," also included in this volume. Customarily, Freeman was adamant about the commercial value of her work. When Elizabeth Garver Jordan, the new editor of *Harper's Bazar,* approached Freeman for a Christmas tale in 1910, Freeman made it clear that she wouldn't work for less than five hundred dollars a story (easily over ten thousand dollars today): "I would love to write stories for the dear old Bazar, for nothing at all, but the money does seem essential in these days of high prices, and I do have many requests." Sometimes, though, even she was defeated. By September 1906, she had to apologize to Hamilton Holt: "I am very sorry, but I am unable to supply you with a Christmas story this year. The extreme heat of the summer interfered with my work, and I have all that I can do to fill other orders."[27] These, and countless other negotiations about her work with a wide variety of editors, dominated her professional life; while her Christmas stories were only a part of her output, they loomed large, and the festive labor never stopped.

As such, it would surely be surprising to Freeman's contemporary readers that her literary legacy has been skewed in this way. From the late 1880s until the early twentieth century, every December would bring with it announcements of at least one, and often more, of Freeman's forthcoming Christmas stories (as evidenced, for example, by an advertisement for

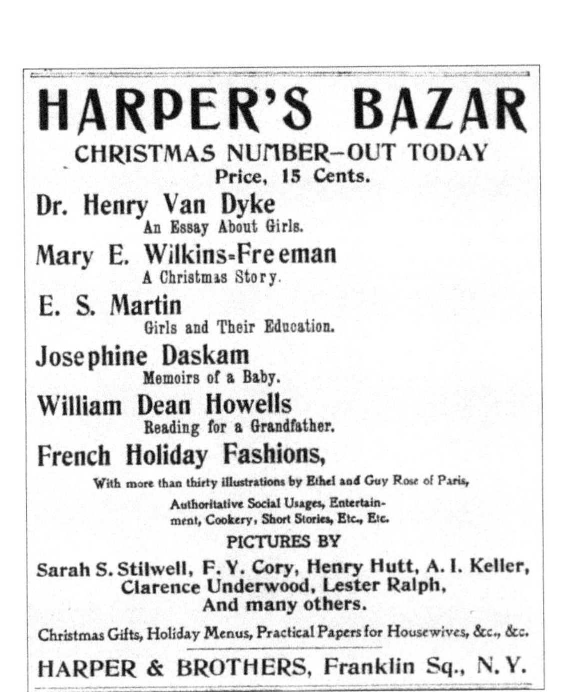

An advertisement for the Christmas edition of *Harper's Bazar* in 1903, with the promise of a "Christmas Story" from Mary E. Wilkins Freeman. *Washington (DC) Evening Star,* November 14, 1903, 9.

the Christmas number of *Harper's Bazar* in 1903 in which she is given billing over William Dean Howells). While much of Freeman's work appeared in Harper & Brothers' publications, her prolific seasonal output could also be found in magazines and newspapers syndicated across America and beyond, as the stories in this volume demonstrate. Yet that syndication is also a reason why a number of these stories have been hidden from view since their first publication. As Johanningsmeier has elucidated, Freeman worked with two newspaper syndicates who "would buy individual stories from Freeman with the understanding that they would sell the first serial rights to between 20 and 140 newspapers for near-simultaneous publication across the United States."[28] Despite their far-flung reach in their own moment, the ephemeral nature of these newspaper stories means that without a definitive first point of publication and even a definitive text—subject as they were to the whims of local editors—they remain haphazardly sprinkled across newspaper archives. It also explains why one story collected here, "Harriet Ann's Christmas" (1898), has been lost since the moment of its first publication—perhaps the most profound demonstration of the neglect of Freeman's Christmas material.[29] Hiding in plain sight, I have found copies of this significant addition to her bibliography

.. THE HOLIDAY ..
EXPRESS

Being the regular issue of **The Illustrated Buffalo Express** for December 18th, will contain many special features of the highest attractiveness.

Extra Pages in Color

"The American Girl"

She who makes the Holidays, portrayed direct from Nature for The Express by its amateur friends.

Mary E. Wilkins

Most popular of American story writers, will contribute a new story, entitled

"HARRIET ANN'S CHRISTMAS"

An advertisement for Freeman's previously lost story "Harriet Ann's Christmas," billing her as the "most popular of American story writers." *Buffalo (NY) Morning Express,* December 17, 1898, 10.

THE ALTON DEMOCRAT, SATURDAY, DECEMBER 17, 1898.

HARRIET ANN'S CHRISTMAS.

By MARY E. WILKINS.

Copyright, 1898, by the Author.

I PEEKED IN, AND THERE WAS SAMUEL RUMMAGING IN THE CHEST.

NEW-YEAR'S DAY-IN-SCOTLAND

The long lost "Harriet Ann's Christmas" as originally published in the *Alton (IA) Democrat. Alton Democrat,* December 17, 1898, 5.

in publications spanning America, sometimes more than a decade apart: the *Bellows Falls Times* in Vermont, the *Lowell Sun* in Massachusetts, the *Asbury Park Daily Press* in New Jersey, the *Wellsville Daily Reporter* in New York, the *Denison Review* in Iowa, the *Sterling Evening Gazette* in Illinois, the *Salt Lake Desert News* in Utah, the *Fresno Morning Republican* in

California, and the *El Paso Daily Herald* in Texas—and more, an aggregation of readers from communities big and small, surely counting in the millions, united in their enjoyment of a Christmas story by Mary E. Wilkins Freeman that has been invisible since that moment—and now we, too, can join them.

Nor should we think of these stories as only having an American audience. As Stephanie Palmer has illuminated, Freeman's appeal was deeply transatlantic. British audiences experienced a profound "craze" for Freeman's works after the publication of her first collections; British reviewers "compared her artistic achievement to George Eliot and Jane Austen and did not find her wanting."[30] Her Christmas stories were clearly part of this popularity; syndication networks stretched across the Atlantic, and newspapers distributed throughout Britain, metropolitan and provincial, published a number of the stories contained in this collection, sometimes over a number of years. For example, "Found in the Snow" seems to have been published more widely in Britain than America: among others, it appeared in the *Northern Echo Christmas Budget* and *Young Woman* magazine in 1899, the *Buckingham Advertiser* and the *Biggleswade Chronicle* in 1900, and the *Totnes Weekly Times* in 1901.[31] And it had a wider appeal still, also featuring in Toronto's *Saturday Night* magazine in 1899 and the Irish *Kerryman* as late as 1909.[32] "Santa Claus and Two Jack-Knives" appeared in the *Cambridge Independent Press* in 1901 and again in the *London Daily News* in 1906—and who knows where and how many more times in between?[33] Taken together, it may well be the case that the Christmas tales that have been least studied by scholars, and least available to readers in recent years, might have been the very stories that were distributed and consumed most widely in Freeman's own lifetime. A clear fixture of the season, the arrival of her new Christmas sketches each December must have served as a popular marker of the holiday as surely as Hallmark movies and Starbucks' red cups do in our own time.

As Susan Koppelman has judged, regardless of any financial motivation, the sheer number of seasonal stories that Freeman crafted suggests that she "must have had a love for Christmas that transcended such considerations."[34] What glimpses of Freeman's personal relationship with Christmas we can glean from her letters and other writings provide hints that beyond professional commitments, she did have a deep fondness for the season that lasted throughout the vicissitudes of her personal life. Despite growing up in New England at a time when the celebration of Christmas was still a little unusual, even theologically and morally suspect—a situation explored in a number of the stories in this volume—Freeman apparently experienced happy Christmases as a child in which the relatively new traditions of the season were enthusiastically embraced by her family. In December 1913, the *Mother's Magazine* asked a number of commentators to respond to the question, "Shall We Banish Santa Claus?" Freeman's answer to that question is given here in full:

> I believed in Santa Claus, when I was a child, in a curious way. I knew perfectly well that my parents gave me the Christmas presents, but, at the same time, I believed in Santa Claus, reindeer and all. It seems to me that most reasonably intelligent children must be able to grasp symbolism at an early age and derive real enjoyment from it, with no injury to their morals. I think children are not given enough credit for common sense. I remember listening with the greatest delight to my mother's stories of Santa Claus driving madly over the roofs en route for our particular chimney, and I really do not think I was much harmed. I rather think Santa Claus stands at the back of my mind during the holidays now. I think that myths are good for children and adults—a sort of mental candy which sweetens the world—and yet I do not think that sensible children really believe them to be precisely true. They emblazon the truth, make it more decorative and pleasing. I can see less harm in Santa Claus than in a surplus of presents. I can judge only from personal experience. I am sure Santa Claus did not injure me, and I am glad I did not miss him.[35]

Certainly, Freeman was able to capture the childhood magic of Christmas, especially as it contrasted with the adult stresses and strains of the season. In her novel *The Portion of Labor* (1901), for example, she depicted the "little prospective paradise" created by her young heroine: "Christmas was only a week distant, she was to have a tree, and the very next evening her mother had promised to take her down-town and show her the beautiful, lighted Christmas shops." Such a prospect "seemed to overgild her own future and all the troubles of the world."[36] A similar sense of care and attention to the inner workings of Christmas can be seen in an article that Freeman wrote for *Success* magazine, "The Art of Christmas Giving," in which she dwelt at length on the underrated "science" of buying presents for others—another theme that runs through many of the stories in this collection:

> I am not by any means decrying the joys of Christmas and Christmas giving. I consider that it is the sweetest and holiest holiday of the year; but I do think it has gradually acquired, among a certain number, a strenuous, almost forcible, nature which detracts from its real glory. People give because other people have presented them, the preceding Christmas, with things for which they had no manner of desire, and sometimes, when the gift has really delighted them in one way, it has placed them under a painful obligation. It almost amounts to a blow on the other cheek to an insult given and returned, rather than a gift,—that is, of course, in some cases. Christmas is still Christmas to many honest souls, who study the needs of those whom they love, and give and deny themselves for the love of them and the love of Christ, which is, after all, the true essence of all giving.[37]

Freeman did not shy away from the celebration of Christmas in her own adult life. Her correspondence contains a variety of seasonal greetings to her acquaintances and expressions of gratitude for presents received ("The little book is darling," she thanked her friend Harriet Randolph Hyatt Mayor on December 23, 1908, having to also confess that she had opened the gift early in her excitement). In 1900, Freeman made this passion public when she sponsored a Christmas tree for the children who attended a Sunday school in Braintree, Massachusetts. "Made Happy by Miss Mary E. Wilkins," the *Boston Daily Globe* headlined its coverage of the event: "They had a beautiful Christmas tree, loaded with gifts, due to her kindness." A program of carols and recitations followed, and Santa Claus distributed the presents, "to the delight of all."[38] This was precisely the kind of situation that Freeman used as a setting for a number of the stories contained in this collection.

Yet Freeman's correspondence also suggests that Christmas had a deeper resonance in her own life, in ways that are also reflected in her stories—an abiding awareness that the season was profoundly enmeshed in people's inner lives in ways that could unleash complicated emotions. Famously, Freeman's own personal circumstances underwent periodic revolutions. She was born in Randolph, Massachusetts, in 1852; moved with her family to Battleboro, Vermont, in 1867; moved back to Randolph after the failure of her family's business in 1873; and in 1883, after the death of both of her parents, lodged at the home of her childhood friend Mary J. Wales. At this pivotal moment, Freeman had already published a number of poems for children, like the one that opens this collection, but it was after her arrival in the Wales household that Freeman began to write professionally—stories, largely, of the kind of New England towns that she had known all her life. For nearly the next two decades, her relationship with Mary Wales was the most important in Freeman's life. Freeman wrote, and Wales supported her physically and emotionally. In an

MADE HAPPY BY MISS MARY E. WILKINS.

MISS MARY E. WILKINS.

An account of the Christmas tree that "famous author" Freeman donated to the Sunday school children at Trinity Episcopal Church in Braintree, Massachusetts, in 1900. *Boston Daily Globe,* December 26, 1900, 4.

1887 Christmas letter to editor Mary Louise Booth, who shared a similar domestic arrangement with her companion Anne W. Wright, Freeman gave a glimpse of their life together:

> Yesterday Mary and I took a novel way to celebrate, and I tried hard all day to think that I really was celebrating, but grew more and more doubtful, especially when night came and I felt very nearly ill. Mrs. Wales is away spending Christmas with some relatives in Bristol, and Mary and I are house-keeping, and we took a fancy that it would be nice to make Christmas-cakes and send around to some people who would not have had many Christmas presents. So we made ten cakes between twelve o'clock and four, and tried to think that we were enjoying ourselves, and that the people would like them, and not wonder why we did it. The cakes were a great success, and I do love to cook, but ten are considerable to make at one time.

The next day, the pair were "going to Boston for some shopping. I have some few more Christmas things to buy"—though she also noted that "Christmas has been sad for me this year, for my dear Grandmother died two weeks ago." Freeman signed off with the hope that "you and Mrs. Wright have had a good Christmas."[39] In miniature, these were themes that Freeman would extend across her Christmas stories: the sense that Christmas could bring companionship and kindness but also hard labor, physical and emotional, and consumption, both its pleasures and costs, and inevitable sadnesses wrapped up with joy.

It's also clear that Freeman had an understanding that the demands that Christmas brought had a highly gendered quality. To her friend Kate Upson Clark, she maintained in December 1889 that "as far as the signs of the time go, I do not see any reason to apprehend that I ever shall be married." She explained that a litany of things needed her attention, including the demands of Christmas itself, and that marriage would only add to the burden of the coming weeks: "It is so much trouble to run one's self in all the departments! Talk about getting married! If I had to see to a man's collar and stockings, besides the drama and the story and Christmas and the new dress, in the next three weeks, I should be crazy."[40] Yet in the late 1890s, rumors began to spread that the woman who was often likened to the committed spinsters who populated her stories was going to marry after all. Indeed, it was a subject that even became the subject of some newspaper scrutiny: "Is Mary E. Wilkins, the novelist, going to marry Dr. Charles E. Freeman, or isn't she?" speculated the *Boston Globe* in July 1901.[41] In a message to Harriet Randolph Hyatt Mayor in December 1901, Freeman gave her answer: "This is to wish you most lovingly a Merry Christmas and happy New Year [. . .] I shall be married very quietly [. . .] I am wondering if I will make a good wife and my husband will be happy. I shall try, but it is dealing with unknown quantities and sometimes I feel afraid." She was married on New Year's Day, 1902. Whether or not she spent many merry Christmases with her husband is a matter of speculation; certainly, their marriage did not have a happy ending. After Charles Freeman descended into alcoholism and drug addiction, they separated before his death in 1923. One thing is clear, though: marriage brought new demands that Christmas stories still helped Freeman to meet. In July 1906, she wrote to Hayden Carruth after she had received payment for "The Gift of Love" with concrete news of its intended purpose: "Thank you very much for the check for the Christmas story. Ground is broken for our new house to day, and I think that will go aways toward the kitchen chimney, for the Christmas turkey, ultimately."[42] Christmas stories helped build her marital home in Metuchen, New Jersey, as well as putting food on the Christmas table—a vivid example of the way in which the season still threaded through her married life and tied together her professional and domestic labor.

As the years passed, Freeman's mind turned more frequently to her youth and the period of her life that she had spent in Brattleboro, a time particularly characterized by memories of winter. In a Christmas message to her friend Allie Morse in 1911, she reminisced, "I know just how the mountain looks with its winter colors of rose, and blue, and mauve, and I wish I could see it." For a Brattleboro newspaper in December 1925, Freeman wistfully developed that image, clearly important to her: "The mountain in winter with sunshine on ice and snow was a crescendo of jewels. I used to stand (I think at the head of High street) and look at that mountain and its brethren along the horizon, giving to all who were willing to receive, colors wonderful enough to transform lives, no matter what troubles were in store for them, and it is something to be thankful for." She signed off with "Christmas greetings to the beautifully beloved town." To Allie Morse in December 1929, the last Christmas before her death, she declared again, "I love the winter landscapes." She also included "a little Christmas gift"—three Christmas boxes sent to the Brattleboro Home for the Aged, where a number of her childhood acquaintances, Allie Morse included, were then living. "My room is northeast," she informed her old friend, "and I think exactly suited to Santa Claus."[43] She died in March 1930.

• • •

The stories selected for this anthology have been chosen to demonstrate the full range of Freeman's Christmas vision. They have been grouped together to highlight the inventive and experimental ways that she played with the familiar themes and icons of the season while instilling the holiday with her distinctive style and the fresh flavor of other genres. Bringing them together in one setting underscores the degree to which Christmas was not merely a commercial hook for Freeman and was never a mere backdrop. While these stories often wear the joyful trappings of the genre of which they are a leading part, they also demonstrate Freeman's profound ability to subtly subvert the expectations of generic convention—what Kate Gardner has described as the characteristic "curious twist" that makes her stories simultaneously "familiar and strange."[44] The constraints of genre could clearly be liberating too. What Alfred Bendixen concluded in relation to the engagement of women writers, like Freeman, with the genre of the ghost story in this period is telling: "Supernatural fiction opened doors for American women writers, allowing them to move into otherwise forbidden regions. It permitted them to acknowledge the needs and fears of women, enabling them to examine such 'unladylike' subjects as sexuality, bad marriages, and repression."[45] So, in their often deceptively jolly way, do the forgotten Christmas stories that make up this volume. As Jana Tigchelaar has noted, these stories recurrently focus on "protagonists at odds with conventions."[46] Taken together, they demonstrate the vivid strengths of Freeman's best work—her humor, her eye for character and ear for dialogue, her emotional richness. Religious reflection is largely absent. More secular and domestic in her concerns, Freeman's Christmases are frequently moments of dramatic tension and intense emotion that amplify the themes discernible in her other work. Very often in these stories, Christmas is a point of crisis for Freeman's characters, particularly women—the time at which the demands, desires, and deprivations of the season force simmering frustrations, long-held yearnings, and deep needs to demand expression. They exemplify what Leah Blatt Glasser has described as the essential conflict in Freeman's work "between defiance and submission, self-fulfillment and self-sacrifice."[47]

In an attempt to redeem the Christmas story in his eyes, William Dean Howells instructed American writers to "turn to human life and observe how it is really affected on these holidays, and be tempted to present some of its actualities. This would be a great thing to do, and would come home to readers with surprise."[48] Whether or not Freeman took this cue directly, her stories also exemplify Howells's desires. At the moment that it seemed to be creatively drained, Freeman breathed new life into the festive sketch. In turn, the apparently familiar decorations of the season—gifts, Christmas trees, stockings, Santa Claus himself—are imbued with profound significance in her work, taking on a series of powerful and ambiguous meanings. And if these stories often end happily and carry a clear sentimental legacy, we can both enjoy the snatched seasonal joys they offer and recognize what Julia Tutwiler understood in 1903: that in Freeman's stories a happy ending is often "the price of rending anguish, or the happiness itself a tragic commentary upon life's denials and tyrannies."[49] Often they cloak subversive instants of rebellion, the uncanny, and even overt acts of crime. And if they are variations on a theme, their variety is remarkable.

In 1920, Blanche Colton Williams perceptively noted: "You will observe that the season Mrs. Freeman favors is usually one of snow. Her country is cold and barren; but from it spring flowers clean and rare, like those on all high and stony places; over it is the bracing mountain air, and throughout its length and breadth a homely sympathy."[50] This perspective places Freeman in interesting creative company: we might think of her constant return to Christmas as akin to the work of American artists like George Henry Durrie and John Henry Twachtman, who obsessively painted snowscapes at the same moment that Freeman was shaping her seasonal stories. Eliza Butler has written of Twachtman that he "painted snow to emphasize its transformative quality and force the viewer to look at it carefully [. . .] to reflect its fleeting, constant changes"; snow provided him with "opportunities for experimentation that he did not find in other subjects."[51] George Philip LeBourdais has read Durrie's New England snow scenes (like the one on the cover of this book) as "complex depictions of human desire" that "could preserve a nostalgic past, or unleash an avalanche of potentialities."[52] We might well apply both claims to Freeman and her snowy stories of winter that hold Christmas at their heart.

Turning to those stories, the opening section of this collection features, appropriately, a series of first encounters with the festive season. It begins with an early Freeman poem that meditates on the prehistory of Christmas in America. While "The Puritan Doll" (1882) makes it clear that colonial New England "never made merry on Christmas Day," still Freeman imagines a mother and daughter creating their own simple seasonal joy against the communal grain and in the face of patriarchal disapproval. It is followed by a series of stories in which other characters experience Christmas for the first time—or, at least, attempt to do so. As a group, they highlight the degree to which the Puritan prejudice against the holiday lingered well into the nineteenth century and how the familiar trappings of Christmas were still a relative novelty for many. In 1883, George William Curtis could meaningfully describe Christmas as a "universal holiday" in America, but the example that he used was itself telling: "Even the New England air, which was so black with sermons that it suffocated Christmas, now murmurs softly with Christmas bells."[53] These stories themselves were part and parcel of the continuing process of coming to terms with the holiday, and in them, we can see an American Christmas still taking shape. Here, too, as elsewhere in Freeman's work, Christmas becomes a chance for characters to step outside of their usual habits and social norms and stage their own moments of rebellion, however apparently minor. In "Christmas for Once," Nancy is an archetypal Freeman heroine: her wish to "have Christmas for once [. . .] jest for the sake of sayin' I had" puts her into conflict with her overbearing sister, Maria, who "ain't had no time for extra kinks that ain't mentioned in the Ten Commandments." In common with the traditional inversions of power that Christmas celebrations brought, the weaker sister ends up victorious, bathed in the light of a "glittering Christmas tree." The other two Christmas neophytes featured here are children, both living in the days when "Christmas-keeping was not yet much in fashion in New England": Serena Ann, who plaintively laments, "I never hung up my stocking since I was born"; and Josiah, who has "arrived at the age of five years and had never heard of Santa Claus and his reindeer team, nor stocking-hanging." One of them, at least, gets to experience "one of the pleasantest memories" of their life.

The next section features a selection of stories framed around various acts of gifting. Alexandra Urakova has perceptively noted that, frequently, "Christmas giving in Freeman's stories borders on risky or dangerous."[54] As Freeman herself made clear in "The Art of Christmas Giving," she well understood the high emotional stakes that were invested in the exchange of gifts and the frequency with which they seemed to express sentiments quite counter to their overt meaning. A misdirected or thoughtless gift could seem akin to violence: "To give where no need exists is an injury," she wrote, "to give where no desire exists is worse, almost an insult, since it implies that the wishes of the recipient have not been in the least studied." The necessities of false gratitude were no less fierce: "The bitterness of deceit must rankle in the very soul." And the practicalities—even for those who could afford them—were frequently intolerable for the women obliged to meet them: "She is burdened and bored, and angry, but give she must. She struggles amidst the sharp elbows of the shopping crowd."[55] These sentiments are so palpable in her stories of gift giving that at least one newspaper saw her as the figurehead of a movement pushing back against the purchasing demands of the season: "An effort to check the injudicious giving of Christmas presents is in the air. Mary E. Wilkins Freeman began the protest."[56] That many of her stories appeared in seasonal issues of popular periodicals next to advertisements encouraging conspicuous Christmas consumption adds another layer of significance to this motif. Certainly, the demands of giving and receiving gifts drive more than one of Freeman's heroines over the brink. "Christmas is the one time of year when we ought to think of other people and not of ourselves," declares Honora Crosby in "The Pink Shawls," before she is embroiled in a series of misadventures in which the perils of gift giving—and regifting—are mostly played for laughs. In "For the Love of One's Self," however, Amanda Dearborn's obligation to send presents to her distant relatives, despite her own financial straits, leads her to despair: "Why should I drudge all my life and go without, in order to send Christmas presents to these cousins of mother's whom I have not seen more than two or three times in my life, and who send me things I don't want, like so many machines?" But Freeman also understood the power of a meaningful present—what Tigchelaar has described as "cycles of gift exchange that promote empathy and community well-being"—and a simple box of candies redeems Amanda's sense of the season.[57] Sophia Lane, on the other hand, takes matters into her own hands in dramatic fashion after her niece receives a succession of thoughtless gifts: "It did seem as if everybody that gave us Christmas presents sat up a week of Sundays tryin' to think of something to give us that we didn't want." Trampling over conventional niceties with gleeful abandon, she packs up her sleigh and, like an anti-Santa, bluntly returns gifts to their givers in a way that still seems bracing: "I wasn't a mite ashamed of it," she concludes, "I guess they got a good lesson."

Rather different kinds of gifts also feature in this section. In today's media landscape, Hallmark and its imitators have positioned romance firmly at the heart of Christmas culture. So, too, do many of Freeman's Christmas stories revolve around gifts of love. The marriages that are made at this time of year, however, are not without their complications, and Freeman frequently seems more interested in the acts of self-sacrifice and disappointment that generate them as she is in the romantic love stories themselves. In two of these stories—perhaps echoing her own experiences—Christmas marriages are as much about the breakup of female relationships as about the union of men and women. In "The Gift of Love," Caroline attempts to covertly rekindle an old romance while her sister, Julia, is away "bossing the Christmas-tree" in the church vestry; one of them is left with "such loneliness and desolation as she had never known." In "Friend of My Heart," Elvira is driven to despair, like other Freeman heroines, by thoughtless presents from others: "Somehow, this Christmas [. . .] I have lost all courage [. . .] I seem to look ahead and see nothing but [. . .] things I don't want, on all my Christmas-trees, the rest of my life." Her friend Catherine contrives to provide her with "the Christmas present she wants"—but at what cost to herself? Less fraught is the delightfully gossipy narrator of "The Christmas Sing in Our Village," who lets us vicariously enjoy an event that "seemed to bring much happiness to our village."

The Christmas icons that still sit at the heart of today's celebrations take center stage in the next section. It begins with a trio of Christmas trees, each infused with its own significance in the life of its characters. The Christmas tree was clearly a resonant image for Freeman. As late as 1923, she published a poem in the *Ladies' Home Journal* that was a poignant and powerful meditation on the brief glory of the beloved seasonal totem.[58] Some readers clearly took this poem as a protest against the regular denuding of American woodlands that the new holiday fashion had caused. For example, the editors of the *Marysville (OH) Evening Tribune* reprinted the poem in full, alongside a letter from a reader who used it to launch a plea for their town to "plant a community Christmas tree": "Its brave sentiment must express the thought of a good many people who for several years have watched wonderfully strong and beautiful trees borne rootless and sapless to the platform from the glory of their native heath."[59] But Freeman's poem seems far more ambiguous than that reading sug-

The Christmas Tree

By MARY E. WILKINS FREEMAN

MY MOTHER was a singing wind I never knew;
My father was a tall and stately pine;
Beside his majesty I slowly grew
Through God's great seasons for this fate divine.

I glory in my triumph, which has slain
My life among my comrades of the trees;
I cannot greet with them the spring again,
Tuning my leaves—the jocund glees
Of homeward birds are not for me; I kept their nests
in vain.

The keen ax cut my roots; I fell mid spray
Of glittering snow-wreaths; and my nests were torn
By clinging brambles as I crashed away,
Slain like a king who is by death reborn
To splendor past his reach of earthly day.

They placed me where His little ones could see;
They hung my boughs with lamps of lovely fire;
They sang for joy to symbolize proud me,
Who gave them gifts for all the year's desire. . . .
Thrown to the flames! Who cares? . . . *I was the
Christmas Tree.*

"The Christmas Tree," published in *Ladies' Home Journal.*
Ladies' Home Journal, December 1923, 178.

gests: the Christmas tree who narrates the poem—like some of her heroines or even perhaps Freeman herself—seems willing to pay a fiery price for living a life different from its rooted comrades.

The trees that feature in these stories certainly have their own powers of transformation. "The Balsam Fir" provides temporary relief in the life of Martha Elder, who is "sick and tired of livin'" when she protests against a neighbor's attempt to chop down a Christmas tree growing on her land. In so doing, she unlocks "secret longings." Conversely, chopping down a tree serves as a point of redemption for the remarkable Hannah Stone, with her reputation for being "strange" and "mean," when she surprises her community with a "splendid hemlock, as straight and evenly pointed as if a special gardener had tended it on purpose, and it was loaded down with presents." Perhaps it was no coincidence that this story was published in the same festive season that Freeman sponsored the Sunday school Christmas tree in Braintree. Yet Freeman also clearly understood that the communal nature of such public celebrations could starkly highlight the disparities between rich and poor. In "General: A Christmas Story," the eponymous hero has to find an inventive way to save face when his mother is unable to contribute financially to the community's celebration: "If it had been an apple year I might have managed it, but it ain't an apple year and I haven't got enough money for another Christmas tree unless I run in debt or mortgage the place."

Santa and his helpers, big and small, also feature. Freeman's childhood affection for the figure who had already come to dominate the season in the minds of the young is evident in her children's story "Jimmy Scarecrow's Christmas," a representative of the large (and equally neglected) body of work that she produced for young readers. This tale of a kind scarecrow who finds a new occupation at the North Pole clearly struck a chord with readers in its moment and beyond. In 1919, the "Story Tellers League" of Harrisburg, Pennsylvania, invited "every child in the city to attend one of [. . .] three Christmas story matinees." At Edison High School, Miss Kate Craven performed "Jimmy Scarecrow's Christmas" for the assembled children.[60] In 1922, Frederic Taber Cooper included the story in his article for the *New York Herald:* "What Are the Great Christmas Stories and Why."[61] Yet in his other appearances in this section, Santa causes as much confusion as resolution. In "The Usurper," a "mysterious Santa Claus" baffles the children and teachers of the schoolhouse of District № 2, while the discovery of some unexpected stocking stuffers in "Santa Claus and Two Jack-Knives" makes for a troublesome Christmas morning for two boys and their parents. "I'd rather believe in Santa Claus than to think my dear precious Tommy could steal," sobs one mother. All of these different strands come together in "Christmas Jenny," one of Freeman's most compelling portraits. Descending from her solitary mountain home at Christmas time "laden with evergreen wreaths," caring for the weak and broken, the titular heroine emerges as a resonant seasonal spirit to rival Santa Claus.

The final section groups together stories that play with other genres in a Christmas setting, changing both as a result. Frequently, Freeman drew on her abilities in crime writing and the supernatural to take her seasonal stories in unexpected directions. In 1895, Freeman wrote a prize-winning detective story, "The Long Arm," and while there are no murders contained in these pages, there are certainly a number of petty crimes. What might be even more surprising is the degree to which Freeman seems to subversively endorse the thefts that her characters are driven to commit by seasonal circumstance. Tommy and Loreny, the forlorn orphaned protagonists of "Found in the Snow," are hardly master criminals, but their discovery of some simple treasures on their way home puts them into a moral quandary that has significant implications. The itinerant preacher of "The Last Gift" is more willful in his transgressions. Feeling "the full bitterness of having absolutely nothing to give," spurred on by the "festive significance" of Christmas Eve, Robinson Carnes is driven to offer up his "last gift" to help a family in need. The "squat, shabby, defiant old" heroine of "A Stolen Christmas" is also driven to extremes by her desire for her dead daughter's children to "have things like other folks"—and by her rage that those of her neighbors who "'ain't never begun to work so hard" can still afford "lace curtains an' Christmas trees." Yet perhaps most eye-opening of all is "The Gospel According to Joan," in which a young girl sells back some stolen Christmas gifts to their original owners to feed her abandoned brothers and sisters and receives an approving blessing for the illicit act: "There she goes, little anarchist, holy-hearted in holy cause, and if her way be not as mine, who am I to judge?" The profound sedition on display in these stories has, perhaps, been hidden by their Christmas wrapping. Conversely, in "Harriet Ann's Christmas," when the eponymous twelve-year-old heroine is left in charge of her younger brothers and sisters and a secret drawer full of money, the arrival of a stranger "smiling with such a pleasant smile" is the beginning of a moment of peril. For the first time since its initial publication in 1898, readers can discover the suitably seasonal manner in which resilient Harriet Ann foils his plans.

The Christmas ghost story remained a staple of British literary culture in the years that Freeman was working; as a writer who often experimented with supernatural themes, it is perhaps inevitable that Freeman permeated some of her own Christmas sketches with a sense of the strange and mysterious. A succession of her characters are visited by unsettling uninvited guests. Jane White's moments of "supernatural terror" in "The Christmas Ghost" are the closest that Freeman comes to traditional seasonal spookiness. Who is the spirit who keeps sneaking into her house to perform "kindly deeds"? In the sublime "The Reign of the Doll," sisters Fidelia and Diantha find their lives turned upside down by the arrival of an uncanny doll with an "inscrutable" smile. "A Christmas Pastel" serves as a curious coda—an enigmatic, impressionistic, experimental sketch featuring another mysterious visitor that demonstrates the degree to which Freeman was willing to take creative risks with her holiday writing.

We might think of these stories, then, as an unexpected stocking crammed with neglected and forgotten delights to savor on a snowy winter's morning. They deeply enrich our sense of Freeman as a writer while also reshaping our sense of the cultural history of Christmas in America and beyond. Brought together in one place, we can fully appreciate the way that these stories rightly sit at the center of her career, not on the mar-

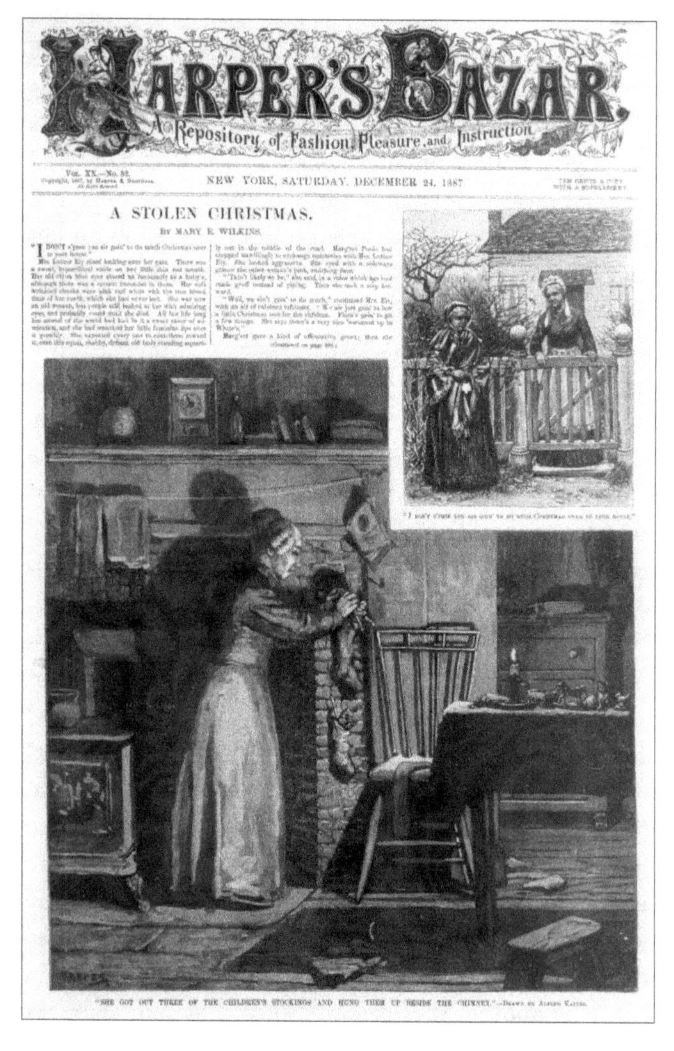

HARPER'S BAZAR.

A Repository of Fashion, Pleasure, and Instruction

Vol. XX.—No. 52.

NEW YORK, SATURDAY, DECEMBER 24, 1887.

A STOLEN CHRISTMAS.

BY MARY E. WILKINS.

"SHE GOT OUT THREE OF THE CHILDREN'S STOCKINGS AND HUNG THEM UP BESIDE THE CHIMNEY."—Drawn by Alfred Kappes.

"A Stolen Christmas," cover of *Harper's Bazar. Harper's Bazar,* December 24, 1887, 885.

gins—as exemplars of her art, not outliers—and serve as a true testament to her creativity and professionalism both. More than any other American writer—arguably, even more than Dickens—Freeman was a true stylist of the season who apparently found constant inspiration in Christmas as it affected the lives of her characters and readers, in ways that still ring true. She clearly delighted in the trappings of the holiday and understood its commercial significance, but she also took the season and its emotional ambiguities very seriously. As a whole, these stories serve as an extended, interconnected meditation on a time of year that still brings forth complicated feelings today; neglected for a century, they can seem remarkably timely in their concerns. Connie Willis—no stranger to a Christmas story herself and perhaps the closest heir to Freeman's sustained creative engagement with the holidays—concluded that "the Christmas-story writer has to walk a narrow tightrope between sentiment and skepticism, and most writers end up falling off into either cynicism or mawkish sappiness."[62] Freeman rarely slipped, which is why, for extraordinary numbers of readers, these stories were an essential part of the celebration of Christmas for decades, responding to and defining the development of the holiday as it took its modern form. I hope this collection means that they can be again. Rich in possibility, they offer comfort and companionship, warm humor, sweet sadness, difficult decisions, deep yearning, hard lessons, self-assertion and self-denial, subversion and mystery and the chance of transformation, even redemption. In short, they are Freeman's last Christmas gift to us as readers.

A NOTE ON THE TEXTS

All of the stories presented in this collection first appeared in magazines and newspapers. Some of them were later collected by Freeman in collections of her short stories; some haven't been republished since their first appearance in print. For this collection, I have used the original magazine versions of the stories: this is the form in which, as eager consumers purchased their seasonal reading material, they would have been most widely encountered. In a few rare instances, obvious proofing errors (*knew* for *new,* for example) have been silently corrected. The syndicated newspaper stories present more of a textual challenge. As they appeared in publications across the country (indeed, the globe), editors, copyeditors, and typesetters all introduced their own changes to Freeman's words—sometimes adding or eliding a comma, sometimes excising entire sentences or paragraphs in order to fill column space more efficiently. Inevitably, such a process also introduced proofing errors. Therefore, in the absence of a single text that can be considered definitive, I have consulted a number of versions of the stories, cross-referencing them against each other. I have then employed a maximalist approach to the stories presented here, including longer textual variants in the assumption that regional editors were more likely to cut than to add to Freeman's words, especially when corroborated by another newspaper edition. As such, each of the syndicated stories presented here should be considered a composite of a number of published versions scattered around the world across Christmases past.

NOTES

1. [Agnes Macdonell], "Mary E. Wilkins," *Bookman* (December 1891): 102.

2. Ibid.

3. Mary R. Reichardt, "Mary Wilkins Freeman: One Hundred Years of Criticism," in *Critical Essays on Mary Wilkins Freeman,* ed. Shirley Marchalonis (Boston: G. K. Hall & Co., 1991), 83.

4. Sylvia Townsend Warner, *The Music at Long Verney* (Washington, DC: Counterpoint, 2001), 151.

5. Shirley Marchalonis, "Introduction," in *Critical Essays on Mary Wilkins Freeman,* ed. Shirley Marchalonis (Boston: G. K. Hall & Co., 1991), 11.

6. William Dean Howells, "Editor's Study," *Harper's New Monthly Magazine,* September 1887, 640.

7. William Dean Howells, "Editor's Study," *Harper's New Monthly Magazine,* January 1887, 322.

8. William Dean Howells, "Editor's Study," *Harper's New Monthly Magazine,* February 1888, 479; William Dean Howells, "Editor's Study," *Harper's New Monthly Magazine,* September 1887, 640.

9. William Dean Howells, "Editor's Study," *Harper's New Monthly Magazine,* December 1889, 158.

10. Edward Foster, *Mary E. Wilkins Freeman* (New York: Hendricks House, 1956), 179, 166.

11. Mary R. Reichardt, ed., *The Uncollected Stories of Mary Wilkins Freeman* (Jackson: University Press of Mississippi, 1992), xiii.

12. Mary R. Reichardt, ed., *A Mary Wilkins Freeman Reader* (Lincoln: University of Nebraska Press, 1997), xiii.

13. Perry Westbrook, *Mary Wilkins Freeman* (Boston: Twayne Publishers, 1988), 129.

14. See, for example, Susan Koppelman, *"May Your Days Be Merry and Bright": Christmas Stories by Women* (New York: Mentor, 1991); Valerie Kinsey, "A Recovered Children's Christmas Story by Mary E. Wilkins Freeman: 'The White Witch,'" *American Literary Realism* 44:3 (2012):

267–70; Jana Tigchelaar, "The Neighborly Christmas: Gifts, Community, and Regionalism in the Christmas Stories of Sarah Orne Jewett and Mary Wilkins Freeman," *Legacy* 31:2 (2014): 236–57.

15. Charles Johanningsmeier, "The Current State of Freeman Bibliographical and Textual Studies," *American Transcendental Quarterly* 13:3 (1999): 178, 183.

16. Stephanie Palmer, "Prospects for the Study of Mary E. Wilkins Freeman," *Resources for American Literary Study* 42:2 (2020): 169.

17. Katharine Allyn See, "The Christmas Story in American Literature" (master's thesis, University of Louisville, 1943), 94.

18. Washington Irving, *The Sketch Book of Geoffrey Crayon, Gent., No. V: Christmas* (New York: C. S. Van Winkle, 1819).

19. "Mind among the Spindles" (review), *Broadway Journal,* January 4, 1845, 2.

20. Philip B. Eppard, "Mary E. Wilkins Freeman's First Published Story," *American Literary Realism* 45:3 (Spring 2013): 269.

21. "Muggy Junction," *London Times,* December 5, 1866, 5.

22. Quoted in Elizabeth Wallace, *Mark Twain and the Happy Island* (Chicago: A. C. McClurg & Co., 1913), 134. For more on the development of modern American Christmas celebrations across the nineteenth century, see Penne L. Restad, *Christmas in America: A History* (New York: Oxford University Press, 1995); Stephen Nissenbaum, *The Battle for Christmas* (New York: Vintage Books, 1997); Karal Ann Marling's *Merry Christmas! Celebrating America's Greatest Holiday* (Cambridge: Harvard University Press, 2000). For more on the history of America's surprising contentious literary relationship with the season, see Thomas Ruys Smith, *Christmas Past: An Anthology of Seasonal Stories from Nineteenth-Century America* (Baton Rouge: Louisiana State University Press, 2021).

23. Clifton S. Wady, "'Timely' Articles," *Writer,* November 1898, 162–63.

24. "Editor's Table," *Yale Literary Magazine,* January 1893, 167.

25. Anthony Trollope, *An Autobiography,* 2 vols. (Edinburgh: William Blackwood & Sons, 1883), 2:213–14.

26. Brent Kendrick ed., *The Infant Sphinx: The Collected Letters of Mary E. Wilkins Freeman* (Metuchen, NJ: Scarecrow Press, 1985), 77, 78–79, 104, 105, 165, 168.

27. Ibid., 195, 311, 335, 319.

28. Johanningsmeier, "Current State," 180.

29. "Harriet Ann's Christmas" isn't listed in any of the standard checklists of Freeman's writing. It doesn't appear in Philip Eppard and Mary Reichardt, "Checklist of Uncollected Short Fiction by Mary Wilkins Freeman," *American Literary Realism, 1870–1910* 23:1 (Fall 1990): 70–74; or in the bibliography of Freeman's work that Reichardt appends to *The Uncollected Stories of Mary Wilkins Freeman* (319–32). Nor does it feature in Johanningsmeier's correction to those listings ("Current State of Freeman Bibliographical and Textual Studies"). Perhaps most significantly, it isn't listed on Jeff Kaylin's invaluable website, wilkinsfreeman.info, the most complete online collection of Freeman's work.

30. Stephanie Palmer, *Transatlantic Footholds: Turn-of-the-Century American Women Writers and British Reviewers* (New York: Routledge, 2020), 72.

31. "Found in the Snow," *Northern Echo Christmas Budget,* December 1899, 21–22; "Found in the Snow," *Young Woman,* December 1899, 95–98; "Found in the Snow," *Buckingham Adver-*

tiser, December 29, 1900, 6; "Found in the Snow," *Biggleswade Chronicle,* December 21, 1900, 3; "Found in the Snow," *Totnes Weekly Times,* December 28, 1901, 7.

32. "Found in the Snow," *Saturday Night's Christmas* (Toronto), December 1899, 32–33; "Found in the Snow," *Kerryman,* December 25, 1909, 10.

33. "Santa Claus and Two Jack-Knives," *Cambridge Independent Press,* December 20, 1909, 3; "Santa Claus and Two Jack-Knives," *London Daily News,* December 24, 1906, 4.

34. Koppelman, "*May Your Days Be Merry and Bright,*" 62.

35. "Shall We Banish Santa Claus?" *Mother's Magazine,* December 1913, 31–32.

36. Mary E. Wilkins, *The Portion of Labor* (New York: Harper & Brothers, 1901), 127.

37. Mary E. Wilkins Freeman, "The Art of Christmas Giving," *Success,* December 1905, 830–31.

38. *Boston Daily Globe,* December 26, 1900, 4.

39. Kendrick, *Infant Sphinx,* 85, 86.

40. Ibid., 100.

41. "That Freeman-Wilkins Engagement," *Boston Daily Globe,* July 17, 1901, 7.

42. Kendrick, *Infant Sphinx,* 256, 312.

43. Ibid., 338, 396–97, 398, 431, 432.

44. Kate Gardner, "The Subversion of Genre in the Short Stories of Mary Wilkins Freeman," *New England Quarterly* 65:3 (1992): 447.

45. Alfred Bendixen, ed., *Haunted Women: The Best Supernatural Tales by American Women Writers* (New York: Frederick Ungar, 1985), 2.

46. Tigchelaar, "Neighborly Christmas," 248.

47. Leah Blatt Glasser, *In a Closet Hidden: The Life and Work of Mary E. Wilkins Freeman* (Amherst: University of Massachusetts Press, 1996), xvi.

48. William Dean Howells, "Editor's Study," *Harper's New Monthly Magazine,* December 1889, 155–59.

49. Julia R. Tutwiler, "Two New England Writers—In Relation to Their Art and to Each Other," in *Critical Essays on Mary Wilkins Freeman,* ed. Shirley Marchalonis (Boston: G. K. Hall & Co., 1991), 93.

50. Blanche Colton Williams, *Our Short Story Writers* (New York: Moffat, Yard & Co., 1920), 174.

51. Eliza Butler, "John Henry Twachtman and the Materiality of Snow," *American Art* 33:3 (Fall 2019): 75, 76.

52. George Philip LeBourdais, "Cryoscapes: Snow and Fantasies of Freezing in the Art of George Henry Durrie," in *Ecocriticism and the Anthropocene in Nineteenth-Century Art and Visual Culture,* ed. Maura Coughlin and Emily Gephart (New York: Routledge, 2019), 95, 99.

53. George William Curtis, "Christmas," *Harper's New Monthly Magazine,* December 1883, 3, 16.

54. Alexandra Urakova, *Dangerous Giving in Nineteenth-Century Literature* (New York: Palgrave Macmillan, 2022), 207.

55. Freeman, "Art of Christmas Giving," 830–31.

56. *Atlanta Sunny South,* December 10, 1904, 8.

57. Tigchelaar, "Neighborly Christmas," 237.

58. "The Christmas Tree," *Ladies' Home Journal,* December 1923, 178.

59. "Christmas Tree," *Marysville (OH) Evening Tribune,* December 20, 1923, 2.

60. "Story Matinees for Children," *Harrisburg (PA) Telegraph,* December 12, 1919, 10.

61. Frederic Taber Cooper, "What Are the Great Christmas Stories and Why," *New York Herald,* "Books and Magazines" section, December 3, 1922, 1–2.

62. Connie Willis, *Miracle and Other Christmas Stories* (New York: Bantam Books, 1999), 14.

FIRST CHRISTMASES

The Puritan Doll

from *Wide Awake,* January 1882, 35–36

OUR PURITAN FATHERS, stern and good,
  Had never a holiday;
Sober and earnest seemed life to them—
  They only stopped working to pray.
And the little Puritan maidens learned
  Their catechisms through;
And spun their stints, and wove themselves,
  Their garments of homely blue.
And they never made merry on Christmas Day—
  It would savor of Pope and Rome;
And never there was a Christmas-tree
  Set up in a Puritan home.
And Christmas Eve, in the chimney-place,
  There was never a stocking hung;
There never was woven a Christmas wreath,
  There was never a carol sung
Sweet little Ruth, with her flaxen hair
  All neatly braided and tied,
Was sitting one old December day
  At her pretty young mother's side.
She listened, speaking never a word,
  With her serious, thoughtful look,

To the Christmas story her mother read
  Out of the good old Book.
"I'll tell thee, Ruth!" her mother cried,
  Herself scarce more than a girl,
As she smoothed her little daughter's hair,
  Lest it straggle out into a curl,
"If thy stint be spun each day this week,
  And thou toil like the busy bee,
A Christmas present on Christmas Day
  I promise to give to thee."
And then she talked of those merry times
  She never could quite forget;
The Christmas cheer, the holly and yule—
  She was hardly a Puritan yet.
She talked of those dear old English days,
  With tears in her loving eyes,
And little Ruth heard like a Puritan child,
  With a quiet though glad surprise.
But nevertheless she thought of her gift,
  As much as would any of you,
And busily round, each day of the week,
  Her little spinning-wheel flew.
Tired little Ruth! but oh, she thought
  She was paid for it after all,
When her mother gave her on Christmas day
  A little Puritan doll.
'Twas made of a piece of a homespun sheet,
  Dressed in a homespun gown
Cut just like Ruth's, and a little cap
  With a stiff white muslin crown.
A primly folded muslin cape—
  I don't think one of you all
Would have been so bold as to dare to play
  With that dignified Puritan doll.
Dear little Ruth showed her delight
  In her queer little quiet way;
She did not say much, but she held her doll
  In her arms all Christmas day.

And when at twilight her mother read
  That Christmas story o'er,
Happy Ruth took the sweetness of it in
  As she never had done before.
And then (she always said "good-night"
  When the shadows began to fall)
She was so happy she went to sleep
  Still holding her Puritan doll.

Christmas for Once

Christian Union, December 18, 1890, 845; December 25, 1890, 883

I.

"Maria!"

"What say?"

"I want to know what that Tompkins boy is cartin' all them evergreen boughs past here for. This is the third time I've seen him go by with his wagon full, sence I've set here. There's the Tompkins boy, and another one, I guess it's the oldest Jones boy, with him."

"Oh, land! They're carryin' evergreen boughs down to trim the meetin'-house, of course! I call it all a piece of foolishness fer my part."

"Trim' the meetin'-house?"

"Why, pity sakes! Nancy, don't you know it's Christmas to-morrow!"

"Well, I declare, Maria, I had clean fergot it."

"I guess you wouldn't have fergot it, if you'd had it in your face an' eyes the way I have for the last two weeks. It ain't been nothin' but 'What shall I hang on the tree for Mother, an' what shall I hang on for Tommy and Sukey?' Hang on a cat's tail! I'm sick of the whole business. Cuttin' the woods down, an' luggin' 'em into the meetin'-house, an' wastin' money on a lot of gimcracks fer folks that would be a good deal better off without 'em. I know one thing—folks didn't do it once."

Maria Emmet stood at the kitchen table making biscuits for tea. She brought the rolling-pin down upon the dough with energetic thuds as she talked. Nancy Emmet, her sister, sat in the calico-covered rocking-chair by the window. She sat there all day, from morning until night. She was nearly helpless from rheumatism. Nancy was as small as a child. She had been very pretty when a young girl, and she was pretty still. Her tender little features were unaltered, and old age seemed to have cast only a film over her youthful bloom, which was as bright as ever behind it. She sat staring out of the window at the white, rigid road, with stiff maple boughs reaching over it. The wagon loaded with evergreens rolled slowly out of sight.

"Well, I dunno, Maria," said Nancy. "I s'pose they take consider'ble comfort doin' of it."

"Comfort? I should think folks was a parcel of fools."

"I can't remember that we ever did anything about keepin' Christmas, can you, Maria?"

"I ruther think I can't. I've had about all I could do, ever since I come into the world, to keep the Sabbath an' git time enough week days to earn bread and butter. I ain't had no time for extra kinks that ain't mentioned in the Ten Commandments."

"Well, I s'pose folks that has time an' money enough takes consider'ble comfort in it." Nancy drew a soft, sighing breath; her profile showed pale and delicately sharp against the window.

Maria cast a quick glance at her as she set the pan of biscuits in the stove oven. "I dunno whether they do or not," said she, severely; "an' if they do, it don't make it out there's any sense in it. They'd 'nough sight better spend their time an' money on something else."

"The Tompkins boy is comin' back," said Nancy.

"You ain't done nothin' but watch that Tompkins boy the whole afternoon."

Nancy said nothing in reply. She eyed the blue farm wagon, the red-cheeked, stout boy, and the clumping farm horse, soberly. The light was beginning to wane. The sky was very pale and clear. "Maria," said she, and a sudden flush overspread her face and neck.

"Well, what say?"

"It looks as if it would be real pleasant to-morrow."

"Well, what of it?"

"You don't s'pose that—I could—No, I don't s'pose I could, noways."

"Could what?"

"You—don't s'pose—I—could—go there, to-morrow?"

"Go where?"

"To—the meetin'-house. To—the Christmas tree."

Maria Emmett was wiping off the kitchen table. She turned and faced her sister, holding the cloth rigidly in her outstretched hand. She was some years younger than Nancy, but she seemed older. Her dominant manner gave her the superiority of age. She was a short, heavy woman. She stood squarely, and her broad, dark face fronted Nancy with a relentless scrutiny. “Now, Nancy Emmet,” said she, “are you crazy, or what?”

Nancy cowered. “I jest thought—I'd—kinder like to have Christmas fer once, Maria, jest fer the sake of sayin' I had.”

“Christmas fer once! Nancy Emmet, how do you s'pose you could get down to that meetin'-house, when it's much as ever you can do to crawl across the room? S'pose you think you can have a coach an' four to carry you, mebbe!”

“I—didn't—know—but what—Mr. Jones would—carry me down in his covered wagon,” returned Nancy, feebly.

“Covered wagon! I'd like to know how you would git in an' out of that covered wagon. You might jest as well set out to climb Bunker Hill monument.”

“Well—I don't s'pose I can, Maria.”

“I shouldn't thought you'd s'posed you could a minute, if you had any sense.”

“Well, I didn't really. Only, I couldn't help thinkin' I'd kinder like to keep Christmas fer once.”

“I should think you was old enough to have got beyond such notions. I should think you was jest out of tires and pantalettes,” said Maria, severely. She returned to the table, which she wiped punctiliously, then she laid it for tea.

When tea was ready, she took hold of the back of Nancy's chair and pushed her gently to the table. There was the plate of hot biscuits, a bowl of quince sauce, and a little plate of spice cake.

Nancy ate slowly, without speaking a word. Her sister kept looking curiously at her. “I'd like to know what ails you, Nancy Emmet,” said she. “You don't act as if you tasted them biscuit.”

“Yes, I do; they're real nice, Maria,” replied Nancy, arousing herself. But she soon returned to her meditations. Gradually her face seemed to alter, the color in her cheeks deepened, her eyes grew more alive, she was all of a strange, silent glow.

All the evening, Maria at intervals glanced at her uneasily. Nancy was usually given to much gentle chatter. Now her silence and her eager face were very strange.

"You don't feel any worse than common, do you?" asked Maria, when the two were preparing for bed.

"No, I feel uncommon well," returned Nancy, eagerly.

"Well, you ain't acted like yourself the whole evenin'."

"Why, yes, I have, ain't I, Maria?"

"No, you ain't hardly spoke a word sence supper time."

"I've been kinder thinkin', that's all," said Nancy. "Maria, do you s'pose that black alpaca dress of mine is much gone-by."

Maria, staring at her sister, turned quite pale. "Now, you ain't thinkin' about dyin', be you?" said she, in a sharp, shocked voice.

Nancy looked at her wonderingly. "No, I ain't, Maria. Why?"

"I couldn't think of nothin' else you'd want that alpaca dress for, when you ain't been out of the house for ten year. No, I dunno as it's much gone-by. I s'pose the basque is kinder long."

Maria Emmet could not go to sleep readily that night. She lay awake, and pondered over her sister's strange demeanor, and her questions about the dress. She was not nervous, nor given to odd fancies; but she felt much as if she had seen the old rose-bush out in the front yard rocked by some wind to which she herself was insensible. She was sure there was some mysterious excitement over Nancy, and she could think of nothing but a presentiment of her own death. Once she lighted the lamp, and looked at her sleeping sister anxiously. "She's sleepin' jest like a baby," she said to herself; "I ain't goin' to be such a fool another minute." Maria blew out the light and went to sleep herself.

The next morning, Nancy's manner was not in the least changed; she scarcely spoke, but her lips were compressed, and her eyes shone.

Maria did not question her again, but she watched her. She was a dress-maker, and went out to work nearly every day; but to-day she was at home, since it was Christmas.

Nancy seemed to grow at once quieter and more restless as the day wore on. After dinner, when the dishes were cleared away, and Maria had changed her dress, she spoke out suddenly:

"Maria," said she, "I think you'd most ought to carry home that dish Mis' Benton brought over them apples in; I know it's one she uses."

Maria hesitated. Nancy's eyes were full of anxiety. She held her breath, watching her. Maria looked out of the window; it was a beautiful day.

"Well, I dunno," said she, slowly. "I s'pose I might run over there now, as long as I've got a chance. I've got to go the other way to-morrow."

Nancy's eyes danced. "Seems to me I would," said she, meekly.

Maria got her bonnet and shawl, and went out with the dish under her arm. Nancy watched her out of sight, and still kept her eyes fixed on the road. "I s'pose he won't come now I've got a chance," she muttered.

II.

She watched, but nobody came in sight on the long stretch of white road. "Oh, dear me suz!" she sighed, "I'm dreadful afraid he won't come."

Maria had been gone about twenty minutes, when a tall boy came in sight, swinging awkwardly up the road. When he was opposite the house, Nancy pounded on the window. The boy stopped and stared. Nancy beckoned wildly. Then the boy turned hesitatingly in at the gate, came up the path, and opened the front door. "Come right in," Nancy called out.

The boy opened the kitchen door, and stumbled in clumsily. He looked at Nancy, and smiled with good-natured embarrassment.

"It's Eddie Jones, ain't it?" said Nancy.

"Yes, marm."

"Well, I want to know, ain't I seen you go by here with a good-sized sled?"

"Yes, marm."

"Well, what I want to know is, do you s'pose you could carry me down to the meetin'-house to-night on your sled? I can't git into a wagon, nohow, an' I'm dreadful light; 'twouldn't be nothin' to drag me."

The boy stood staring at her with his mouth open. His face was very red. "I'll ask mother," he stammered finally.

"I don't want you to say nothin' to your mother about it. 'Tain't likely she'll care. I jest want you to come over here about seven o'clock, with your sled, an' drag me down to the meetin'-house, an' take me home when it's time. You open that door, an' go into the outer room, an' bring me out a little wooden box you'll see on the table."

The boy obeyed. His thick snowy shoes clamped loudly as he went across the floor. He brought the little mahogany work-box to Nancy, who opened it eagerly and produced a jackknife. "There," said she, "here's a nice jackknife, that I'll give you, if you'll take me to the meetin'-house. It's got three blades, an' there's only a little teenty end of one of 'em broke."

The boy eyed the knife. "Ain't you goin' to?" asked Nancy.

"Yes, marm," replied the boy doubtfully.

"Well," said Nancy, "you carry this box back, an' put it where you found it. I'll keep the knife, an' give it to you when you've brought me back to-night."

The boy went back with the box. "Now," said Nancy, when he returned, "I want you to go into the bedroom, an' open the top drawer in the bureau, an' bring me out a white pasteboard box that's in the right-hand corner."

The boy clattered into the bedroom, and presently emerged with the box. "Now," said Nancy, "I want you to go into the other room again, an' get me a black dress that's a-hangin' in the chimney closet, an' a flat green box that's on the shelf."

The boy went. His honest, boyish face was fairly stupid with wonder.

The white box contained a white lace cap, the green one, some old artificial flowers. Nancy selected some old pink roses, which she fastened on the front of the cap; then she put it on.

"Does it look nice?" said she.

"Yes, marm," said the boy.

"I always used to wear pink flowers," said Nancy, "but I ain't been out anywheres for ten year."

She examined the alpaca dress carefully. "I guess that'll do," said she. "Now, I want you to carry that green box back to the parlor closet, an' then put this cap back in the bureau drawer, an' hang this dress up behind the bedroom door. I can never git into the parlor after it in creation."

After the boy had done these last commissions, she dismissed him. "You can go now," said she, "only be sure to be here by seven o'clock."

After he had gone, she reached to a little shelf between the windows for a bottle that stood there. It was half full of some liquid. She took out the stopper, and deliberately poured out all the liquid over her right ankle to the floor. A pungent odor of turpentine and ether arose. "It's dreadful wasteful," she muttered, "but I can't see no other way."

It was not long before Maria came home. She sniffed when she entered the door. "I hope that linament smells strong enough," said she.

"Oh, Maria, I've spilled it all over!"

"Spilled it! Why, there was most half a bottle full!"

"I know it. I'm dreadful afraid you'll have to go down to the store after supper, an' git some more. I don't s'pose I shall darse be without it in the house."

"Well, I must say I don't see how you managed to spill all that linament," said Maria, taking off her shawl.

"My hands ain't very stiddy, you know."

Maria went about getting tea. She was good-natured about the spilled liniment, although it involved a long, cold walk for herself. It seemed to her that Nancy was no longer as strange as she had been. She chattered as usual at supper. After the dishes were cleared away, Maria went to the store. It was about half-past six o'clock. "I may jest as well go and have it over with," said she, and set out with the bottle in her pocket.

How little, rheumatic Nancy Emmet ever in the space of a half-hour arrayed herself in that alpaca dress, and that white lace cap with its cluster of faded roses, she could not herself have told. She had not dressed herself entirely for years. Maria always helped her. But to-night she not only put on the black alpaca and the cap, but she hobbled around and looked in the kitchen glass afterward. She smiled at her face in the glass with an innocent delight. It was so long since she had been out in the world that she had almost forgotten, and the excitement of a young girl was in her heart.

The Jones boy came promptly at half-past seven, and his mother was with him. He had been too bewildered not to tell her. She wondered that Maria was not at home, but she helped Nancy tenderly on to the sled, and tucked a shawl over her feet. Then she walked beside her. She was a tall, portly woman. Nancy sat erect on her sled, holding firmly to the sides. She looked up at the sky; her hood was drawn so closely over her face that there was only a pale line of it visible. "It seems to me I never see the stars so bright," said she.

"They are bright," said Mrs. Jones. "You're sure you ain't cold? I'm afraid it's a dreadful risk."

"No, I ain't cold. I never see 'em so bright. I kinder felt as if I would like to keep Christmas for once."

Mrs. Jones grew uneasy as they went on. She began to have doubts as to whether Maria knew of this. Nancy had evaded all questions. She speculated as to whether she had done right. When they reached the church, and Nancy had been helped in and seated well in front near the tree, she whispered to some other women about it. "I do hope Maria will come pretty soon," said she. "I'm dreadful uneasy."

But Maria did not come for a half-hour, when the tree was being unloaded. She came hurriedly up the aisle, with her pale, stern face turning to either side. When she saw Nancy she stopped short and looked at her. "Come in an' set down, Maria," said Nancy in a loud whisper, and she moved along to make room. She was all elation. Her white cap was awry, her hair was softly tumbled, her cheeks were pink, and her eyes were as blue as a baby's. She had a lace bag of peppermints, that had been hung for her on the tree, in her lap.

Maria hesitated. The Sunday-school children were being called up to receive their presents; people were sitting in radiant quiet; she could not make a disturbance. She sat stiffly down beside Nancy, and her face flushed red.

Nancy pushed the bag of peppermints toward her. "Take a pep'mint," she whispered.

Maria pushed the bag away.

"I'm dreadful sorry," Nancy whispered. "I tipped the linament over on purpose. I did want to keep Christmas jest for once, Maria."

"I should think you hed kept it," Maria whispered back fiercely, "runnin' away like this! I've been 'most scared to death. You can smell that linament all over the meetin'-house. You'll get sick a-bed, that's what'll come of it."

"No, I won't, Maria; I wrapped up real warm. It seemed to me I couldn't stan' it if I didn't keep Christmas jest for once. Take a pep'mint—do, Maria." Maria sat sullenly immovable. Nancy looked at the glittering Christmas tree, then piteously at her sister. She thrust the peppermint bag into her lap again. "Do take a pep'mint, Maria."

Maria took a peppermint and put it in her mouth; her face relaxed. Nancy looked again at the Christmas tree; and of all the children there, the happiest was this old child who was having Christmas for once.

Serena Ann

Short Stories, January 1895, 106–14

FIFTY YEARS AGO Serena Ann lived in Braintree, and Christmas-keeping was not yet much the fashion in New England. Serena Ann was ten years old, and she had never seen a Christmas-tree, hung up her stocking, or had a Christmas present even.

Serena Ann's father was a farmer; she had a mother, and an Aunt Love, her mother's sister, who lived with them and was to be married in February, and a brother Ebenezer.

Ebenezer was two years older than Serena Ann, and went to the district school winters. Serena Ann herself went to school only in the summer. She was a delicate little girl, and the school-house was too far away for her to walk in cold weather. So she stayed at home, and her mother heard her spell every day, and she did sums on a piece of old slate, and was reading the Bible through, a chapter every morning. So her education was not neglected.

One night in the first week in December, Serena Ann was sitting beside the fire, with the piece of broken slate on her lap, trying to do a sum about ten greyhounds running a race, and how long it would take for one to catch up with the other, when Ebenezer came home from school. There was a light snow falling, and Ebenezer was powdered with it. He came in stamping his cowhide shoes and shaking himself like a dog. Aunt Love was sewing green velvet on her wedding pelisse, and Mrs. Bagley was paring apples for sauce. "Don't stamp so, Ebenezer," said she. "And don't shake the snow on my pelisse," cried Aunt Love. Aunt Love was very pretty, with smooth brown hair and pink cheeks.

"I've got to get the snow off," panted Ebenezer. "Oh, mother—!"

"You ought to get it off in the shed, then," said his mother.

"Oh, mother—!"

"And not shake it all over the clean floor and your aunt's pelisse."

"Oh, mother, Sammy Morse says he's going to hang up his stocking the night before Christmas!"

Then Serena Ann looked up from her piece of slate and her greyhounds.

"I don't want to hear any such nonsense," said Mrs. Bagley.

"He says his folks are going to put something in it for him."

"If they want to be so silly, they can."

"Mother, can't I hang up my stocking?"

"Yes," said his mother, "you can hang it up all you want to, but you won't get anything in it. You have all the presents your father can afford to give you, right along. Now go out in the shed and bring in an armful of that apple-tree wood for the fire."

And Ebenezer went out disconsolately.

Serena Ann pulled her mother's apron. "Mother, can't I hang up my stocking," she whispered.

"You can hang it up, but I shall tell you what I did Ebenezer. You won't get anything in it. I sha'n't treat one of you any better than I do the other."

"I never hung up my stocking since I was born," said Serena Ann, plaintively.

"Neither did I," said her mother. "I never thought of such a thing when I was a little girl. Now 'tend to your sum."

And Serena Ann attended to her sum; but the thought of Christmas seemed to gain upon her childish mind much faster than one greyhound upon the other. She could not quite give up the hope that possibly, if she did hang up her stocking, somebody might put something in it. If not her mother, Aunt Love, or her father might, or even Joshua Simmons, the young man whom Aunt Love was going to marry; he sometimes gave her a peppermint. And, after all, her mother was a pretty tender one, and she might relent. So Serena Ann hung up her stocking the night before Christmas.

It is quite possible if Mrs. Bagley had seen that poor little blue-yarn stocking hanging in the chimney-corner she might have slipped at least a bunch of raisins and a cinnamon-stick or two in it, and Aunt Love might have tucked in a bit of blue ribbon. But nobody saw it, for Serena Ann, with the want of calculation of her innocent heart, slipped out after everybody was in bed and hung it up.

At breakfast the next morning Serena Ann's mouth dropped pitifully at the corners, and she did not eat much.

"You are a silly girl to act so," said her mother. "You know what I told you."

"I s'pose Sammy Morse has got his stocking chuck full," said Ebenezer. He felt Serena Ann's injury to be his own.

"Go out in the shed and bring in some more of that apple-tree wood, if you've finished your breakfast," said his mother, and then she sent Serena Ann upstairs to make her bed.

As soon as the door closed Aunt Love turned to her sister. "Suppose Joshua and I take Serena Ann to Boston with us," said she.

Mrs. Bagley looked at her doubtfully. "I'm afraid she'll be in your way," she said.

"Oh, no, she won't, and it'll make up to her for not having anything in her stocking. I felt sorry for her. Serena Ann is a good little girl."

"Well, I felt sorry she took it so to heart," said Serena Ann's mother, "but it's a silly custom, and I don't know how to begin it. I suppose she would be tickled to death to go with you and Joshua. She never went to Boston but once. Ebenezer's been twice."

"She must come right down and get ready if she's going," said Aunt Love, "for Joshua will be here with the chaise."

And Serena Ann was called and told, to her joy and wonder, that she was to go to Boston with Aunt Love and Joshua Simmons.

"But you must be a good girl and not make any trouble," said her mother, "for your Aunt Love has a great deal to do. She is going to buy some of her furniture and her wedding bonnet and shoes, and she is very kind to take you."

And Serena Ann promised beamingly. She had never felt so happy in her life as she did that Christmas morning, when she set forth to visit Boston, tucked in between Aunt Love and Joshua Simmons in the chaise. It was very pleasant, but cold; there was a slight rime of snow on the ground, which shone like silver. Serena Ann wore her thick wadded coat, her lamb's-wool tippet, and her wadded brown silk hood with cherry strings. She was quite warm, and her face was so pink and radiant with bliss that Aunt Love and Joshua looked at her and smiled at each other above her head.

Serena Ann, moreover, had, tightly grasped in one red-mittened hand, her mother's silk purse, and it contained two ninepences, one of which she was to spend for herself and the other for a jackknife for Ebenezer. Her father had given them to her when she started. She made up her mind, as they jogged along over the frozen road, that she would spend her nine-pence for an apron for her mother, instead of anything for herself, because she could not go to Boston in a chaise.

When they reached the city they stopped at the Sign of the Lamb, where Joshua Simmons put up his team; then they all went shopping down Hanover Street, where the fashionable stores were at that time.

Serena Ann enjoyed buying Aunt Love's and Joshua Simmons's wedding furniture quite as much as they did. She thought there was never anything quite so handsome as their hair-cloth sofa, and mahogany card-table, and looking-glass, and she trudged after them to all the shops where they priced articles, and then back to the one where they found them cheapest and best, and never thought of being tired.

But she was glad at noon to go back to the Sign of the Lamb, and have some baked beans and a piece of pumpkin pie. They seemed to her far superior to the baked beans and pie at home.

After dinner Joshua Simmons left them. He had to go a little farther to see about his own wedding-suit, and Aunt Love meanwhile was to buy her wedding-bonnet and shoes, and Serena Ann make her purchases. Then they were to meet at the Sign of the Lamb, and go home.

Serena Ann went with her aunt from shop to shop, and watched her try on bonnets until she finally bought a beautiful one of green uncut velvet trimmed with white plumes and white lutestring ribbon. Then they started to buy the shoes, Aunt Love carrying the bonnet in a large green bandbox.

There was quite a crowd in Hanover Street that afternoon. A great many ladies were out shopping. Serena Ann could not walk beside her aunt very well, she was so jostled, so she fell behind. Now and then she took hold of the skirt of her aunt's blue delaine gown, so as not to lose her.

Nobody ever knew how it happened, but suddenly, after she had been pushed by the hurrying people, and had caught hold of the blue delaine gown, the lady who wore it looked around and she was not Aunt Love. She was very pretty, but her hair was black and fell in bunches of curls, instead of smooth braids over her red cheeks, and her eyes were black instead of blue. Moreover, she was very finely dressed, wearing a velvet pelisse and a rich fur tippet and bearing before her a great fur muff. The blue delaine gown was the only thing about this strange young lady that in the least resembled Aunt Love. She stood looking with great surprise at Serena Ann, who looked up at her quite pale with fright, still keeping fast hold of the blue delaine.

Finally the young lady laughed, and then her face, which had appeared rather haughty, looked very sweet. “What is the matter?” said she, “and why are you holding to my gown?”

“I—thought you were Aunt Love,” faltered Serena Ann, and the tears began to come.

“Were you holding to your aunt’s gown?”

“Yes, ma’am.”

The young lady laughed again. “My name is Miss Pamela Soley,” said she. “Take hold of my hand, and don’t cry, and we’ll go find your aunt.”

So Serena Ann curled her red-mittened hand timidly around the kid-gloved fingers of the young lady, and then went back down Hanover Street. They walked on both sides, they looked in every shop, but all in vain.

The truth was that poor Aunt Love had missed Serena Ann much sooner, and had started off on a wrong tack in search.

When she had discovered that her little niece was not behind her and looked around in dismay and lost the color out of her pretty pink cheeks, several sympathizing ladies had gathered around her, and one had been quite sure she had seen a little girl just like Serena Ann, in a lamb’s-wool tippet and brown silk hood, run down a side street a little way back. So Aunt Love went down the side street, looking and inquiring of everybody.

She almost cried as she went along, carrying her big green bandbox, looking in vain for Serena Ann. She did not know what to do, but finally it occurred to her that it was nearly the time set to meet Joshua Simmons at the Sign of the Lamb, and that in all probability some benevolent person would have taken Serena Ann with her. So Aunt Love hastened to the Sign of the Lamb, but it took her some time, for she had wandered quite a distance.

But Miss Pamela Soley was not wise enough to think that the best plan was to take Serena Ann to the Sign of the Lamb at once, since they could not find her Aunt Love on Hanover Street. She was quite a young lady, in spite of her stately manners, and had not had much experience in rescuing lost little girls. She stood still for some time in Hanover Street, holding Serena Ann’s hand, deliberating what to do. But finally a bright thought struck Miss Pamela Soley. “My brother Solomon is coming for me in our chaise to take me home to Jamaica Plain, where we live,” said she. “He is going to meet me at the corner just below here in about half an hour. We will make your purchases and then we will ask him what to do. My brother Solomon always knows what is best to do. He is older than I, and carried off many honors at Harvard College. Don't cry, Serena Ann. He'll be sure to find your aunt for you."

Serena Ann was somewhat comforted, for the young lady had a way at once sweet and commanding, and she went hand-in-hand with her and purchased a beautiful jackknife for Ebenezer with one ninepence, and a piece of white nainsook for her mother's apron with the other. Miss Pamela Soley herself made two purchases: a little rosewood workbox, with scissors and thimble and ivory bodkin, all complete, and a doll in a very handsome spangled dress like a princess. The last purchase rather surprised Serena Ann, for she had thought the young lady too old to play with dolls, but she eyed it admiringly. She had never had a doll herself, except one which Aunt Love made for her out of a corncob. She sighed when Miss Pamela Soley tucked the doll with the rosewood workbox out of sight in her great muff.

Mr. Solomon Soley was waiting in the chaise on the corner when his sister appeared with Serena Ann and told her story. He was a handsome young man, in a very fine mulberry-colored cloak.

"We must take her to the Sign of the Lamb at once," Mr. Solomon Soley said, decidedly, and Miss Pamela and Serena Ann got promptly into the chaise and they made haste to the Sign of the Lamb. However, just before they reached the tavern, Miss Pamela remembered an errand which her mother had begged her to do at Mr. Thomas Whitcomb's store, and had her brother leave her there, saying she would join them in a few minutes.

But when Mr. Solomon Soley inquired at the Sign of the Lamb, he found that Joshua Simmons and Aunt Love had driven away in their chaise some half an hour before, and the hostler, who had been told, did not remember that they had merely gone to look about the city a little for the missing child, and were then coming back to the tavern to see if she had in the meantime been brought there. However, another hostler remembered that the lady carried a large, green bandbox, and was crying.

"That was Aunt Love," said Serena Ann, and she began to cry too.

"Don't cry," said Mr. Solomon Soley. "You shall be taken home safely to-night."

Then he turned the chaise around and drove back to the store where his sister had stopped, and before Serena Ann fairly knew it, they were on the road to Braintree.

It had grown very cold, and the wind blew. Mr. Solomon got out a great, plaid camlet cloak from under the chaise seat, and put it on over his mulberry-colored one. Then presently, because Serena Ann began to shiver a little, tucked in between the two as she was, he threw an end of the camlet cloak around her, over her brown silk hood. She was quite warm under that, and also quite hidden from sight. Nobody meeting them would have dreamed that there was a little girl in the chaise.

In the meantime, Aunt Love and Joshua Simmons returned to the Sign of the Lamb, and the hostler, who had forgotten they were coming, told her that a gentleman in a chaise had been there with the little girl and said he was going to take her home to Braintree. "Guess you'll overtake 'em," said he. "Gentleman was alone in the chaise with the little girl, wore a mulberry-colored cloak."

Aunt Love fairly wept for joy. "Oh, Joshua, I am so thankful," she cried. "I never could have told Sarah I'd lost Serena Ann. And I haven't got my shoes, but I don't care. I'll get married in my old ones. Let's start right away, so we'll overtake them."

Joshua Simmons started up the horse, and the chaise rattled out of the tavern yard and down the road toward Braintree.

But their chapter of accidents was not quite finished, for as they were crossing Neponset Bridge, peering ahead to see if they could catch a glimpse of the other chaise, a gust of wind took off Joshua Simmons's hat and tossed it into the river. He had a cold in his head, too. Aunt Love pulled off her hood promptly. "Put this on," said she, "don't you say a word. If you don't you'll be laid up with influenza, and the wedding will have to be postponed, and that's a very bad sign."

"What'll you do?" asked Joshua Simmons, hesitatingly.

Aunt Love untied the green bandbox. "Put on this bonnet," said she. "It'll be so dark when we get home that the neighbors can't see it."

So Joshua put on the hood and Aunt Love the wedding-bonnet, and it happened that when they finally overtook Solomon Soley, who had not much the start, and whose horse had got a stone in his shoe once and made a delay, that the occupants of the two chaises looked hard at each other and saw nothing that they were looking for.

For Joshua Simmons, who was naturally somewhat ashamed of his woman's headgear, kept his face turned well away, and both Solomon Soley and his sister, Pamela, thought there were two ladies in the chaise, and not the aunt and the young man for whom they were looking.

As for Serena Ann, she was fast asleep under the camlet cloak and saw nobody, and her Aunt Love and Joshua never dreamed she was there. Moreover, they were looking for one gentleman in the chaise with her, and there was a young lady also. He wore a camlet cloak, too, instead of a mulberry cloak, as they had been told.

So the two chaises rattled on almost abreast for quite a stretch on the turnpike, but finally Solomon Soley's forged ahead a little, for his horse was fresher.

They reached Braintree, and when they were within a half a mile of the Bagley farmhouse, Joshua Simmons turned into another road, which was a little shorter cut. Aunt Love was impatient to see if Serena Ann had reached home. And so it happened, since Solomon Soley's horse was a little faster, that both chaises turned into the Bagley yard at the same time, and Serena Ann returned from her Christmas outing with something more exciting than a flourish of trumpets.

Serena Ann herself was so tired and sleepy that she could not fairly realize anything. It seemed to her like a dream: the chorus of surprise and delight, Mr. Solomon's and Miss Pamela's coming into the house and getting warm, and eating supper, and borrowing a foot-stove, before they started on their homeward journey, and everything. She scarcely even grasped in its full measure of delight the fact that Miss Pamela presented her with the rosewood workbox and the doll when she kissed her good-by, but Serena Ann had gotten one of the pleasantest memories of her life, and had her first Christmas-keeping.

Josiah's First Christmas

Collier's, December 11, 1909, 9–10

I THINK ONE OF the most pathetic Christmas stories which I have ever heard is that of poor young Josiah Adams's first Christmas, which dates back to the earlier days of New England. Josiah was the youngest of twelve children. When he was born, six of his brothers and sisters had married and set up homes of their own, but he was very much younger, a mere baby to those who still remained under the parental roof. He was at once the pet and butt of the others. He was quick-tempered, and that made him more of a temptation to his older brothers and sisters, who thought it great fun to provoke the little fellow into a fit of baby rage and then coax and cajole him out of it after their amusement of teasing.

It seems that Christmas had never been celebrated in the Adams family, and Josiah had arrived at the age of five years and had never heard of Santa Claus and his reindeer team, nor stocking-hanging, and suddenly one Christmas Eve the knowledge was gained. Josiah had been sent on an errand to a neighbor's, where there was a boy of his own age, and he came home full of excitement.

"Benny White is going to hang up his stocking on the oven door tonight," he announced, "and Santa Claus will come riding over the roof in a sleigh with reindeer and bells, and he will come down the chimney and fill Benny's stocking with presents."

Josiah's brother Caleb and his sister Sarah and his mother were in the room. Caleb and Sarah laughed, but Mrs. Adams frowned. She was a sober, overworked woman in a white cap, and she was spinning flax. She opened her mouth to speak, but Sarah clapped her hand over her mother's lips, and Sarah was her darling, the beauty and the sweetest-tempered of them all, although her love of fun often led her into pranks, which her mother feared were ungodly.

"I am going to hang up my stocking like Benny," announced Josiah, and Sarah cried: "So you shall, Josiah, and we will see what Santa Claus will bring you down the chimney!"

Caleb, who was next in age to Sarah and as full of mischief, echoed her. "Hang your stocking, Josiah," said he, then he doubled up with laughter, and little Josiah did not know what he was laughing at. His sister Sarah kept a very grave face, although her blue eyes were dancing.

So it happened that poor little Josiah hung up his stocking on the old-fashioned oven door when he went to bed, and Mrs. Adams, for the sake of her darling Sarah, was seemingly oblivious. She spun at her wheel with her back to the fireplace, but Mr. Ozias Adams, who was Josiah's father and a very severe man, noticed the stocking, and inquired concerning it.

"Why is Josiah's stocking there?" said he, and he glared at the little blue yarn stocking through his iron-rimmed spectacles.

Sarah was very quick, and she answered him with a toss of her pretty fair head. "Josiah left it when he went to bed, sir," said she, "and it would be in the way on the floor." Caleb coughed to conceal a chuckle, Mrs. Adams trembled as she whirred her wheel.

Mr. Adams nodded gravely, for the explanation seemed very plausible and simple, and the others, Cynthia, Abel, Jonas, and Abigail, paid no attention. They were not yet in the secret. But when the dignified Ozias Adams and his consort were retired for the night, an excited, giggling, whispering group gathered in the great kitchen, around poor little Josiah's stocking, hanging limp as to appearance, but in reality filled with the blooming fancies of childhood. At that very instant little Josiah was lying awake in his hard bed under the eaves, and it had begun to snow, and white stars drifted in upon his counterpane, and he was listening for the sleigh-bells and the fairy clatter of Santa Claus's reindeers' hoofs upon the roof. Finally Josiah became quite sure that he did hear them, but at that time his blue eyes were closed.

His brothers and sisters downstairs were busy for quite a time perpetrating what they meant only for an innocent joke, but it may have been a cruel one. They probably never suspected such a possibility. They were healthy, unimaginative boys and girls, and little Josiah, although of their own blood, was of a different make-up.

The next morning Josiah was downstairs pattering in his bare feet before even his thrifty parents were up and before the ashes had been raked away from the hearth fire. There hung the blue yarn stocking crammed to the brim, and the baby boy knew that he had really heard Santa Claus riding over the roof the night before. Here was proof positive.

Josiah, although the great kitchen was very cold, did not shiver in his homespun night-gown. His big blue eyes blazed, his round cheeks glowed with roses, his mouth widened deliciously with joy. He seized upon the stocking and pattered back to his own freezing little nest under the eaves, and then he explored. It was a tragedy of childhood, and one of the tragedies which might have been spared the child. So often the comedies of older people are the tragedies of babyhood, and should never be acted. Poor little Josiah Adams found in his stocking a most wonderful assortment of Christmas presents, collected from the odds and ends of the household stores. There were old nails, a broken back-comb of his sister Abigail's, a discarded front piece of his mother's, an old scratch wig which had belonged to his grandfather Adams, one little red slipper which had belonged to his married sister Dorcas, a knife which his brother Caleb had contributed, utterly destitute of blades, a faded knot of blue ribbon which Sarah had worn in her hair, and, crowning insult, done up carefully in the blue paper in which the sugar loaves of the day came wrapped, the little stick with which his father had chastised him when guilty of childish misdemeanors. That was the very last thing in the stocking, that poor parody of a Christmas stocking, which was never seen again by any of the Adams family for many years, not until Josiah's name, with appropriate texts and funereal verses, had been rudely carved on a rude stone, for the little boy departed this life at an early age. On that Christmas morning Josiah came downstairs with only one stocking on, and his mother's admonitions and his father's stern reproofs and chastising with another little stick were entirely ineffectual to make him reveal the whereabouts of the other with its sorry load of Christmas presents. Mr. Adams never knew about the presents; neither his wife nor children dared tell him, but he did know that Josiah was disobedient, and he commanded and chastised as he esteemed his duty until forced by the singular obstinacy of his little son to give it up.

Josiah seemed to forget all about his attempt at celebrating Christmas. He was sweet-tempered, although quick, and, while possessed of a strong will, not sulky. He seems to have been as happy as most children until he passed away at an early age, although he was never strong and always more sensitive than was good for him. The little stone had stood over his grave for two years before the Christmas Eve when Caleb came in with his arms full of wood for the hearth fire and a very sober face. One of his coat pockets was bulging. That was the winter when Mrs. Adams was laid up with the rheumatism. Mr. Adams had died the year after Josiah, and of the brothers and sisters there were only Caleb and Sarah at home. The others had married during the two years. After Caleb had heaped more wood on the fire and stacked up the rest on the hearth, he turned and looked at Sarah, who was knitting stockings. "What is that in your pocket and why do you look so sober, Caleb?" said she.

Caleb slowly drew from his pocket little Josiah's Christmas stocking. "Found it under the wood-pile," he stated laconically, but his face worked.

Sarah laid down her knitting. "So that was where he hid it," she said in a quivering voice.

Caleb nodded.

"It has been there all the time; poor little Josiah," said Sarah.

She began to weep. Caleb put the stocking away in a drawer of the highboy and stalked out of the room. Sarah wept softly lest her mother hear. She was alone in the great firelit room. A pot of rose geranium, all in flower, stood on a little table under a south window, and a delicate breath of perfume came in Sarah's face when she finally dried her eyes and looked up. Nobody would ever know how sorry she was about Josiah's Christmas stocking. It no longer seemed at all funny to her. She was older and had had trouble, and she understood better the heart of a child.

The tall clock ticked, the fire glowed and snapped, and the rose geranium in the window gave out its sweetness. Sarah began to wonder where Caleb was, for it was nearly supper-time. Suddenly she rose and stole softly across the room to the door of the bedroom where her mother lay. Sarah peeped in. Mrs. Adams was fast asleep. Then Sarah muffled herself quickly in hood and shawl, and ran softly across the room to the rose geranium; then she went out, closing the door softly. The room was still faintly scented with the blossoms, but the green plant stood robbed of its pink crown.

When Sarah reached the graveyard and little Josiah's headstone, she started at the sight of her brother Caleb. He had just finished planting a tiny perfect evergreen tree on the snowy mound. Sarah, without a word, placed her bunch of geraniums in the close-set greenness of the tree, which seemed suddenly to bloom. Then the brother and sister went home. Sarah looked up at a great planet burning out in the violet gloom of the sunset sky, and said in a voice which was sad, yet sweet with a timid hope: "How bright that star is."

"Real bright," assented Caleb. Then neither spoke again all the way home.

THE ART OF CHRISTMAS GIVING

The Pink Shawls

Harper's Monthly Magazine, December 1905, 138–47

THE TWO CROSBY SISTERS, Honora and Ellen, their niece Annette, their deceased brother's daughter, and her brother Franklin were all in the sitting-room the day before Christmas, at work on Christmas presents. Franklin was whittling paper-knives out of whitewood, and sniffling painfully and dejectedly the while. He was only ten, and out of school on account of a cold. He did not like to go to school, but it was snowing hard, and he was eager to be out-of-doors.

Honora was crocheting a shawl of pink wool, Annette was dressing a doll, and Ellen was covering a pincushion with blue silk. Later she intended sticking in pins in letters representing, "To Cora." Ellen was a conservative, and that which always had been seemed the best to her. Pincushions made in such wise had been a fashion of her departed youth. Honora crocheted with her lips set in a curious way which she always maintained when at work. Annette dressed the doll listlessly. She was a pretty girl, although to-day she looked somewhat wan. A young man, Harry Roel, who had been openly attentive to her, had lately deserted her for another girl. That very afternoon she had seen them pass in a sleigh. She had said nothing, but her aunt Honora had spoken.

"It seems to me folks must be in an awful strait to go sleigh-riding in such a storm as this," said she, with an odd mixture of sympathy for her niece and indignation at the young man.

Franklin considered it a good opening for a plea of his own. He spoke with a hoarse whine. "Can't I just go out and coast down Adkin's hill just twice if I tie my tippet over my ears?" he asked.

"I rather guess you can't," replied his aunt Honora.

"I'll wear my thick coat, and something under it."

"Don't you say another word. You keep on with your paper-knives."

Franklin applied his damp handkerchief to his nose, and the tears trickled down his rasped cheeks. He was a fair little boy, and cold made ravages in his appearance. "I'm sick of these old paper-knives," he muttered.

"No muttering," Honora said, sternly. "Christmas is the one time of the year when we ought to think of other people and not of ourselves. Just look at your aunt Ellen and your sister and me working. Maybe we don't feel any more like it than you do."

Annette, fitting in a fussy little sleeve to the doll's dress, gave a weary sigh. "That is so," she said. "If ever I hated to do anything, it was to dress a doll."

"But she knows how tickled little Minnie Green will be with it," said Honora; "and here is your aunt Ellen making a pincushion for Cora Abbot, and she woke up with a headache; and here I am crocheting a shawl to give away to a lady in Bilchester, when I really need one myself. Christmas isn't the time to think of yourself."

"Pink was always so becoming to you, too," said Ellen.

"It used to be," said Honora. In spite of herself she could not resist placing the fluff of pink wool under her chin and gazing at herself in the glass opposite. Honora was old and her hair was snow white, but she had the tints of youth in her fine skin, and the pink wool cast its roseate hues over her face and thick white locks.

"It's just as becoming as it ever was," said Ellen.

Honora could not avoid a conscious simper at the charming reflection of herself. She had always been covertly pleased to meet herself in the glass. "Well," said she, "I shall have to do without a pink shawl."

Ellen regarded her with a troubled expression. "Oh dear, sister," said she. "I only wish I had thought, for I could have got a pink shawl for you as well as the present I have.

"So could I," said Annette.

"Well," said Honora, in a resigned voice, "I know I shall like what you have for me. It is only that I have always wanted a pink shawl, and I have never seen the time when I felt that I could conscientiously get one for myself."

"You have made so many for other people, too," said Annette.

"Yes, I know I have," agreed Honora, "but it always seemed to me that they needed them more than I did. Here is poor Abby Judd. She has just barely enough money to live on, and she has the prayer-meeting at her house every week since the church burned down, and she has the sewing society at least once a month, and her house is always chilly, and she really needs a dressy shawl."

"You are always thinking of somebody else," said Annette, and the remark pleased Honora. Annette looked very much as Honora had done at her age. Her hair was a brilliant brown with red lights in it, and her complexion was really wonderful. Annette, as she worked, cast every now and then a glance out at the storm. It seemed to her that she constantly heard sleigh-bells ever since that sleigh with Harry Roel and the other girl had passed. "It's an awful storm," she said, with a half-sigh. This was the night of the week—Wednesday—when Harry Roel had been accustomed to call, and she had always made a wood fire in the stove in the best parlor. She would not need to do that to-night.

The next morning Franklin went about carrying the presents on his sled. He was better, and so wrapped up that he could scarcely walk. He had to carry some of the parcels to the post-office and the express-office, and some to houses in the village. He was usually quite a trustworthy errand-boy, but possibly this morning the quinine which he had taken for the grippe, or the grippe itself, confused his young mind. Instead of taking the pink shawl, which was enveloped daintily in pink tissue-paper tied with pink ribbons, then enclosed in a nice white box, to the express-office, he carried it to Harry Roel's house. Harry lived with his widowed mother, and the maid who came to the door and took the box could not read English, and she had no hesitation about receiving it.

"This is a Christmas present from my aunt Honora," said Franklin.

The Swedish girl smiled at the beaming eyes above the red tippet. Then she carried the package into the kitchen to her mistress, who was there superintending the pudding. Mrs. Roel was an impetuous soul, and had never gotten over her childish delight in presents. She did not look at the address, but cut the string with the first knife at hand. She unfolded the pink tissue-paper and shook out the shawl.

"Oh, what a pretty shawl!" she cried, "and it's just what I wanted, for I am going to have the sewing-circle next week, and I've got cold."

Then she spied the card attached to the shawl with pink ribbon, and read, "To Abby Judd, with loving wishes for Christmas and the New-year, from her old friend, Honora Crosby," and her face fell.

"Goodness! This isn't mine, after all," she said. "It's for Abby Judd in Bilchester. I used to know her. She and Honora Crosby were always intimate. Well, this must be done up again, and when Harry comes in he must take it down to the express-office."

It thus happened that poor Annette Crosby heard the jingle of sleigh-bells that morning, and she did not know that Harry was carrying the pink shawl which her aunt Honora had crocheted for Abby Judd to the express-office.

In due time Honora received a letter of thanks from Abby Judd, along with a pretty little pious book bound in white and gold. Honora looked very sharply at the book, then she laid it on the table with her other gifts.

"It is very pretty," said she, "and Abby was very kind to send it." There was an odd tone in her voice. Franklin and Ellen were in the room. After Franklin went out, Ellen examined the book closely, then she looked at her sister.

"It's one somebody gave her," she said. "I can see where the name was rubbed out."

"Well, I don't suppose she could afford to buy a new one," said Honora, generously. "She has an awful time to make both ends meet, and of course she had read it. All I hope is that the one who gave it to her won't see it."

"That is so," said Ellen. "I made out the name; didn't you?"

Honora nodded.

"It was Mrs. Addison Roel."

"Yes, Etta Roel was the name. She scratched it out, and I suppose she thought nobody would notice it."

"Well, Mrs. Addison Roel won't be very apt to come in here now," said Ellen.

"That is so," assented Honora.

Ellen lowered her voice. She nodded toward the kitchen, where Annette was making some chocolate creams to please Franklin. "Do you suppose she minds much?" she whispered.

"If she does, there won't nobody know it," said Honora.

She was quite right, nobody did know it. Time went on, and Harry Roel never came to see Annette, and it was reported that he was constant in his attentions to the other girl, that they were engaged, but Annette never lowered her crest. She dressed just as painstakingly and prettily as ever.

She went everywhere. She did not in the least avoid meeting her old lover and his new sweetheart. People said that she did not care. It was even rumored that Annette had dismissed him, and that he was paying attentions to Laura Ames out of spite. His mother heard of it and told him. She had just come home from the mission circle one afternoon in December; it was a year later than the first Christmas when she had received Honora's pink shawl by mistake.

"I heard something that made me mad this afternoon," she said to her son when they sat together at the tea-table. Mrs. Addison Roel was a very pretty woman, astonishingly young for her age, and when she was excited color flushed her cheeks and her eyes sparkled like a girl's. She was prettily dressed, too, in a lace-trimmed silk waist and a black satin skirt.

"What was it?" asked Harry.

"Well, I heard that Annette Crosby had jilted you, and that was the reason you were going with Laura."

Harry paled a little. He had inherited his mother's good looks, and even her childishness of expression. "Well, maybe it sounds better to have it go so," he said.

"I don't think it sounds any better for you," said his mother, hotly.

"It sounds better for Annette," said Harry, and suddenly his pale face flushed.

Mrs. Addison Roel looked sharply at him. "Goodness! You don't mean to say that you are thinking of Annette now?" she said.

Harry said nothing.

"Well, I'd stick to one thing two minutes," said his mother.

"Maybe I am not the only one to be accused of that," said Harry, gloomily.

"Harry Roel!" cried his mother. "Annette Crosby didn't—"

"Never mind what she did or didn't," Harry returned, and took his hat and went away, leaving his mother staring after him.

"He didn't half eat his supper," she thought; "and there was that chocolate cake he is so fond of, too." She wondered if Annette Crosby had really dismissed her son; she felt an active dislike toward her, aroused by the mere imagination of such a thing. "I wonder who she thinks she is?" she thought; and yet she positively disliked Laura Ames, and the anticipation of having to live with her had really caused her to lose some of her pretty youthful curves. She had always rather looked forward to living with Annette, who was exceedingly sweet-tempered and a good housekeeper, whereas the other girl was openly called a spitfire, if she was pretty, and she had the name of letting her mother do all the work. There was no servant in the Ames' house. However, the possibility of Annette's having treated Harry badly, served to partly reconcile her with the other girl. She resolved to ask Laura to tea Christmas day, and it so happened that Annette saw Harry drive past with her as she had the year before.

The Crosbys had their gifts all finished and despatched; it was four o'clock in the afternoon, and their little tables were spread with those which they had received. Honora had two which rather nonplussed her. Annette and Ellen each presented her with a pink crocheted shawl. When the gifts were displayed, and they saw that each had chosen the same thing for Honora, they at first looked sober, then they laughed, and Honora joined them.

"Well, I declare I've got pink shawls now if I never had any before," said she.

"It all happened because I went to that church fair when I was in Norcross," said Annette. She had been visiting the married friend for whose little girl she had dressed the doll the preceding Christmas. She had been a little out of health, and they had thought a change might benefit her. "I happened to see that shawl at the fair," said Annette, "and I knew it was just the shade Aunt Honora liked, so I bought it. I was going to crochet one, but I didn't feel quite up to it, and I thought this would do just as well."

"I didn't dream you were going to give her a pink shawl or I would have said something to you about it," said Ellen. "I had made up my mind to give her one, but you know I can't crochet, and I happened to see this one in the Woman's Exchange in Winchester last November when I went there shopping with Mrs. Green; so I got it. I've had it hidden away ever since. I wish they weren't both the same stitch."

"Never mind. I don't care anything about that," said Honora. "I always thought this was the prettiest stitch there was, and I am delighted with them. It is a great deal nicer to have two, because I shall feel that I can wear them all I want to. If I had only one, I dare say I should have kept it done up in a towel and hardly ever worn it."

"Well, there is something in that," agreed Ellen. She looked admiringly at her sister, who threw one of the shawls over her shoulder.

However, as she sat beside the window, a boy came to the door and left a package for her, and when it was opened her face changed. "I declare, if Mrs. John Eggleston hasn't sent me another pink shawl!" said Honora.

"And it is the same stitch," said Ellen.

Annette, in spite of her troubles, was young and had a sense of humor. She sank into a chair and doubled over with laughter. In a moment Honora and Ellen joined her.

Honora had a dainty little note enclosing a Christmas card, and she read it. "At all events, Mrs. Eggleston is honest," she said. "She tells me right out that she had this shawl sent her three years ago from a friend, and she had never worn it, and she sends it to me with Christmas greetings, because she heard me say once that I wished I had a pink shawl."

"Yes, she is honest," said Ellen. "Maria Eggleston always did speak right out."

"Well, I declare!" said Honora, looking at the shawl with an odd expression.

"You will have to wear pink shawls morning, noon, and night," said Annette.

It was not long after that when Franklin came home; he had been sent to the office for the night mail, and he brought several packages, evidently presents for the two aunts and the niece. Honora had two. One she opened at once.

"What a lovely doily!" said she. "Cora sent it to me."

"What is in your other package?" asked Annette.

Honora hesitated. She sat looking at the unopened package in her lap with an expression of chagrin, amusement, and distress. She had caught a glimpse of rose-color through one end of the parcel. It was not very carefully tied up.

"I declare, it looks like—" began Ellen.

"I do believe it is," said Annette, with a shriek of laughter.

Honora lifted the parcel. "It is light and soft," said she, in a resigned voice.

Then Annette caught sight of the pink color at the end. "It is, it is," she cried.

Honora opened the parcel and shook out another pink shawl.

"Thank the Lord, it is a different stitch," said Ellen, with a gasp.

"Ellen, you ought to be ashamed bringing the Lord into it," said Honora, reproachfully.

"Well, I can't help it. I do feel thankful, and I don't see any sin in being thankful for little things as well as big ones," said Ellen.

Then they all looked at the shawl and laughed. Franklin was a little bewildered. He did not quite understand what the laughter was about.

"Aunt Honora has got four pink shawls," explained Annette to him.

Then Franklin bent over with laughter. "Well, she's going to have another," said he. "Willy Bennet's mother is going to give Aunt Honora a pink shawl. I know, because Willy's got a cold and can't come to bring it over, and Mrs. Bennet wanted me to come over after supper and get it. She hadn't got it done up. Willy's mother said she heard Aunt Honora say last year that she wanted a pink shawl, and she made up her mind she should have one."

"I wonder if she made it herself?" said Annette.

"She couldn't have," said Ellen. "Mrs. Bennet doesn't know how to crochet, I know."

"I remember saying to Mrs. Bennet that I wanted a pink shawl," remarked Honora, still with that queer expression.

"Good land! Five pink shawls," said Ellen.

"Maybe you will have another," said Annette. "There is a letter you haven't opened, Aunt Honora."

"Thank the Lord, there can't be a pink shawl in that, anyhow," said Ellen.

Honora opened the letter. Then she laughed. "There is something about a pink shawl in it, anyhow," said she. "It's from Sarah Mills, and she was always honest, too. She says she has had a pink shawl sent her for a Christmas present, but she never wears pink, because it makes her look yellow; she doesn't say who sent it; so she is sending it to me by express."

"I begin to feel nervous," said Ellen.

"Yes, there is something awful about so many pink shawls," said Annette. Then she laughed again, her rather hysterical laugh. She was really very unhappy. She did not get over her unhappiness about Harry Roel, although she held her head high.

"Why don't you have a rummage sale and get rid of them?" said Franklin.

"Franklin Crosby, I am ashamed of you," said Honora; "a rummage sale of presents which were given me by my friends! You must remember that when anything is given you there is something sacred about it, because it is not only the thing itself, but the love and kindness that go with it from the giver, and it isn't anything to be treated lightly or to be made fun of. Everything I have ever had given me since I was a girl I have treasured up, and I wouldn't part with them for any money, even if they don't happen to be quite what I need. The need is not the main thing."

Franklin was looking hard at a book which he himself had just received. "Well, I suppose I'll have to treasure up this book," said he. "I had one just like it year before last. I don't want to read it, so I suppose I'll have to treasure it."

"Of course you will," said his aunt, severely, "and you must remember that you treasure up not only the book but your teacher's kind thought of you."

"Yes'm," said Franklin, meekly, with inward reservations. "She gave Willy Bennet a great box of candy," said he. "He's teacher's favorite."

"Nonsense! Miss Lowny is a good woman, and she hasn't any favorites," said his aunt Honora, "and the book cost probably more than the candy."

"No, it didn't," said Franklin, "for that candy is fifty cents a pound, and there were two pounds of it, and they are selling books just like this for twenty-nine cents at White and Adams's. I saw 'em in the window my own self yesterday."

"Franklin Crosby, aren't you ashamed of yourself?" cried his aunts and sister as one.

"I don't see why," returned Franklin, stoutly. He had very good reasoning powers for his age. "I don't see why kind thoughts and a dollar ain't more than kind thoughts and twenty-nine cents. So there!"

"Franklin, you can go out in the woodshed and bring in some wood and start up the fire in the kitchen stove. It is almost time for supper, and let me hear no more of such talk," said Honora, sternly.

However, she could not quite make up her mind to wear the dainty rose-colored things as often as she had planned. It happened that all six shawls were for the most of the time packed carefully away, each folded in a clean white towel, and that she only wore one, scented strongly with camphor, on a state occasion. When the next Christmas came, not one shawl was the worse for wear.

"I hope to goodness you won't get any more pink shawls this Christmas," said Ellen. The two sisters and Annette were as usual the day before Christmas engaged in finishing up some presents and packing others to be sent. Franklin had some Christmas duties which were much more acceptable to him than usual. He had developed an amazing ability for a boy in making candy, and the fragrant fumes of his concoctions filled the house.

Honora was crocheting, putting the last stitches to a head-tie for Abby Judd.

Ellen was finishing a centre-piece, and Annette was tying up parcels in dainty white paper with ribbons and writing cards with loving Christmas messages. Annette had grown distinctly wan and thin, although she was still pretty. She had heard that very morning that Harry Roel was to be married in the spring. The reflection of that seemed to be pricking her heart all the time while she was doing up the dainty parcels, but she forced herself to talk and laugh as usual. She was prettily dressed, too. She wore a pink cashmere house-dress which she had made herself, and which suited her wonderfully. Her aunt Honora had looked at her with a little surprise when, after the dinner dishes were cleared away, she had appeared in that gown and settled down to her afternoon work on the Christmas presents.

"Do you expect anybody?" she asked.

"No," replied Annette. "Why?"

"Why, you are so dressed up."

Annette laughed. Her thin, sweet face under her soft puffs of brown hair flushed. "Oh, I just took a notion to put this dress on," said she. She did not own the truth, that she wore the dress from a species of self-defiance. Harry Roel had always been accustomed to come Christmas eve, and she had considered that, if things were as they had been, she would have worn that pretty pink dress. Then she said to herself, "Well, I will wear the dress, anyhow." Therefore she had put it on.

She felt her aunts looking at each other with wonder and some suspicion, but she pretended not to notice it.

"I think you had better put on an apron, anyhow, with that dress," her aunt Honora said, finally.

Annette obediently got one of her aunt's aprons from the secretary drawer and tied it around her waist. It was of a sheer white material, and the pink of her gown showed faintly through it.

It was about four o'clock when a boy was seen racing past the windows. He ran so fast that he was not seen distinctly by any of them.

It was not two seconds before the flying figure again passed the window, and Franklin entered with a neat parcel.

"Here is something Gus Appleby brought for Aunt Honora," said he.

Honora took it, and the others gathered around.

"I wonder what it is and who sent it?" said Annette.

"Another pink shawl, perhaps," said Ellen. "Honora hasn't had one this year so far."

Honora opened the nice white parcel, and there was disclosed an inner parcel of white tissue-paper tied with pink ribbon. Through the tissue-paper a rosy gleam was evident.

"I declare, it *is* another pink shawl," said Annette.

Honora untied the dainty pink bow, unrolled the tissue-paper, and slowly shook out the pink shawl. She laughed a little, then she looked rather sober.

"Who sent this one?" said Ellen.

Honora took up a card which was tied to the shawl with a bit of narrow pink ribbon. "'Christmas greetings from Caroline Roel,'" she read. Annette turned pale.

"I shouldn't have thought she would have had the face!" gasped Ellen.

Annette said nothing. She turned again to the table where were the parcels which she was tying up, and she began working on them with her mouth shut tightly.

Meanwhile Honora was closely examining the pink shawl in a grim silence. She opened her mouth as if to speak, then she closed it again; then her desire to reveal something was too much for her. "Franklin, go out in the kitchen," said she, sharply. "I think that candy is catching on."

When the door had closed behind the boy she turned to her sister and her niece. "Do you want me to tell you something?" said she.

"For goodness' sake, what is it, Honora?" asked Ellen, and Annette turned a pale, inquiring face from her parcels.

"Well," said Honora, "I thought at first I wouldn't speak, but I guess I can't help it. This is the very identical shawl I sent to Abby Judd two years ago."

Ellen gasped. "Why, Honora, how do you know?"

"I know," replied Honora, conclusively.

"But how?"

"I know. I made a wrong stitch in the lower left-hand corner, and I have some of the wool left, too."

"I don't believe it."

Honora went majestically over to the secretary. She took out of the lowest drawer a neat little parcel labelled, "Pink wool left from Abby Judd's shawl." "Look," said she.

"Yes, it is the same shade," said Ellen. "Goodness!"

"But how on earth did Mrs. Roel get hold of it?" asked Ellen, in a bewildered fashion.

"I know," said Honora, shortly.

"How?"

"Abby Judd gave it to her for a Christmas present last year."

"My land!" exclaimed Ellen, gazing blankly at her sister.

"It's so," said Honora.

"Why, I can't believe it."

"I can't help it whether you believe it or not; it's so."

Just then there was a ring at the front door-bell, and a sudden hush pervaded the room.

"There's somebody at the door," whispered Ellen, agitatedly. She began gathering up scraps of ribbons and strings which littered the floor and thrusting them into the adjoining bedroom. Honora assisted. "This room looks as if it were going to ride out," said she, "but whoever it is has got to come in here. The parlor isn't warm enough." Annette hurriedly straightened the things on the table where she was working. Honora peeked out of the side window. "It's she," said she, in a whisper.

"Who?" whispered Ellen.

"Mrs. Roel."

Annette made a motion as if to run from the room, then she tied a little blue bow on a package resolutely.

Honora glanced at Annette. "I'll go to the door," said she, and just as she started the bell rang again. Presently she ushered in Mrs. Roel, who looked fluttered and embarrassed. She did not accept the offer of the best rocking-chair.

"No, thank you," said she. "I can't stop, but I felt as if I must come over." She stopped and hesitated, and her pretty, middle-aged face, looking forth from the folds of a blue worsted head-tie, flushed a deep pink. "I felt as if I must come and—explain," she said again. Then she again stopped and hesitated, and her face was blazing. She glanced at the pink shawl on Honora's table. "I don't know what you thought," she stammered, "and I—I—felt as if I had better come right over here and tell you the whole story. I felt as if maybe I wasn't quite straightforward, but I didn't want anybody else blamed, and I don't know now, but—well, I can't help it; I'm going to tell you." She addressed herself directly to Honora, and spoke rapidly. "Well," said she, "two years ago last Christmas your nephew brought that shawl to my house by mistake. I opened it before I saw the direction on the wrapper. When I saw it afterward I did it right up again, and my son carried it to the express-office and sent it where it was meant to go; and then the next Christmas Hannah Mills must have had it sent to her for a present from Abby Judd; at least, that's the way I reasoned it out; and this year—Hannah and I always exchange presents—she sent it to me. Hannah meant all right. She never wore pink; it always made her look yellow; and I don't believe either she or Abby Judd ever had this shawl on their backs.

It has been kept just as nice, and it's all scented with camphor. You can smell the camphor, though there was a real strong sachet in with it. I kept the sachet. Well, when I got it I knew it the very minute I set my eyes on it. I never saw such a shade of pink before, for one thing, and I always did carry colors in my eyes very well; and then there was another thing. I always notice every little thing, and I happened to notice it when I saw it first—a little tiny bit of white in the pink at the neck; you know how it will happen so sometimes. I suppose the dye don't take, and I knew it was the same shawl. And I'll own up I felt kind of mad at first. There I'd worked and made an afghan for Hannah, and she had sent me a shawl that somebody else had given her; and as for Abby Judd, I didn't think much of her giving it away, either. But my first thought was that I wouldn't tell on them, that I'd just see to it that you had your shawl back again. I thought maybe you wouldn't know it was your shawl. So I called in the Appleby boy and gave him five cents for bringing it over. And then I got to thinking it over, and I felt dreadful mean, and as if you wouldn't know what to make of it; and I began to think that Abby and Hannah meant all right, and Hannah always did look as yellow as saffron in pink, and I dare say Abby Judd does, too—she's something the same complexion—and I thought I'd come over and make a clean breast of the whole thing."

Annette, very pale, continued tying her parcels, but in spite of her pallor and the shock of having Harry's mother in the house her mouth twitched a little. Honora looked at the shawl, then at Mrs. Roel, with an inexplicable face; then she laughed.

"It's all right," said she, "but I wish you'd keep the shawl, Mrs. Roel."

"No; you keep it and wear it yourself."

Then Ellen laughed. "Land! I don't see how she's going to," said she, "not if she lives to be a hundred; she's got six more pink shawls she had given her last Christmas."

"Good land!" cried Mrs. Roel.

"Do take it and keep it," said Honora. "I know pink must be real becoming to you."

"Yes, it always was becoming," admitted Mrs. Roel. "It never made me look yellow, but—"

"You've got to take this shawl or I shall feel real hurt," said Honora. She tried to speak pleasantly, but her manner was a little stiff. She could not help thinking how Harry Roel had treated Annette.

"Well, to tell the truth," said Mrs. Roel, "when that shawl came two years ago, it did look so pretty, and I tried it on, and it was so becoming that I sent right away for some worsted and made myself one. I always loved to crochet. And I've kept it real nice, so it is just as good as new. But I thank you just as much."

"Of course, then, you don't want this," said Honora.

"I thank you just as much as if I took it," said Mrs. Roel. She was going out, with a remark about the weather to make her exit easy and graceful, when she stopped as if she had made a sudden resolution, and turned upon Annette. "Well," said she, "as long as I am here I may as well have it out, and I suppose your aunts know all about it. What made you treat my son so awful mean?"

Annette looked at her. She blushed first, then she looked ready to faint. "I don't know what you mean," she said.

"Yes, you do; you needn't pretend you don't."

"I don't," said Annette. Then she gave way. Her nerves were strained to the utmost. She sank upon a chair and began to weep.

Her aunt Honora came to her rescue. She looked fiercely at Mrs. Roel.

"When it comes to treating mean," said she, "there may be two ways of looking at it."

"Don't, Aunt Honora," sobbed Annette.

"Yes, I am going to have it out, now it is begun," said Honora. "When it comes to accusing you of treating Harry Roel mean, I am going to say something. I call it treating a girl pretty mean when a young man comes to see her as steady as your son came to see Annette, and then goes with another girl right before her face and eyes, without her giving him any reason."

"She did give him reason," declared Mrs. Roel. "She gave him a good deal of reason—reason enough for any young man if he had a mite of pride."

"I'd like to know what?" said Honora, and even Annette stared inquiringly over her handkerchief at Mrs. Roel.

"I call it reason enough," said Mrs. Roel, "when a young man who has been going with a girl the way my son Harry had been going with Annette sees her coming out of a store with another young man—"

"What young man?" interpolated Annette, curious in spite of herself.

"John Appleby. You needn't pretend you have forgotten."

"I don't know what you mean, and I have forgotten," Annette said, brokenly.

"Well, my son hasn't forgotten. He saw you coming out of Rogers and Gray's with John Appleby, and you had a little package, and when he asked you what it was you just laughed and wouldn't tell him, and made him think it was something John had bought for you—it was two weeks before Christmas—and there you were as good as engaged to my son."

Annette completely lowered her handkerchief. She looked brighter, although her eyes were still brimming with tears. "I do remember now," she said, "but I have never thought of it since."

"Well, my son has thought of it a good deal, I can tell you that."

"I never thought of it. I did it just to tease him."

"Some folks don't take to teasing easy," said Mrs. Roel. "My son is one who doesn't. He takes everything serious."

"The package was just pink worsted that Aunt Honora sent me for, to finish that pink shawl," said Annette, and in spite of herself she laughed.

"Well," said Honora, with acrimony, "your son consoled himself pretty quick. I don't see as he has much reason to find any fault."

"Who says he consoled himself?"

"Well, I should think he did, if he is going to marry that other girl in the spring."

"He isn't going to marry her. She's going to marry a man out West."

"So she's given him the mitten?" said Honora.

"No, she hasn't," returned Mrs. Roel, angrily. "My son doesn't take mittens. He was never in earnest in going with her, and she knew he wasn't, and he knew he wasn't. He knew all the time about that other man out West. He has felt used up over the whole thing," said she. "He didn't think that Annette could treat him so."

"I don't see that Annette has done anything so very much out of the way," said Honora. "It looks to me as if all the trouble was your son's having a faculty of bringing his foot down on a fly as if it were a sledgehammer on a rattlesnake. If a man can't take a little joke, why, he's got to take the consequences."

"Harry always took things just as they were said," returned his mother, but her face was much softer. She looked at Annette. "Are you going to be at home this evening?" said she.

Annette colored. "I am always at home," she replied, in a low voice.

Mrs. Roel turned again to Honora. "It's queer, but it does seem as if that shawl was at the root of a good deal," said she; "I hope you don't think I did anything out of the way coming to you about it."

"I think you did just right," said Honora.

That evening after supper Annette made up a fire in the parlor stove. Her face had changed wonderfully in a short time. She looked years younger. Irrepressible dimples showed in her pink cheeks. She fastened a little pink rosette in her brown hair. She was fairly glowing and blooming with youth and happiness. About eight o'clock the door-bell rang, and she went to the door. Then voices were heard in the hall, and the parlor door closed.

"It's he," said Honora.

"Yes, it is," said Ellen. "I am glad; the poor child has tried to make the best of it, but she's been real low in her mind, and she has lost flesh." Ellen was examining happily a handkerchief which she had just received in the mail from Hannah Mills. "It's real fine," said she. "If there's anything I do like, it's a real nice, fine pocket-handkerchief."

Franklin was eating one of his chocolate caramels, and enjoying intensely the sweet on his tongue.

Honora looked at the pink shawl which was lying in a rosy fluff on the table by her side. "It seems to me this room is kind of chilly," said she, "and I've a good mind to put that shawl on."

"I would," said Ellen.

"I guess I'll just wear it and get the good of it," said Honora.

"I would, so long as I had so many laid away," said Ellen.

Honora took the shawl and put it over her shoulders. Then she looked at her sister and began to speak, and hesitated.

"What is it?" asked Ellen.

"Will you promise me that you will never tell as long as you live if I tell you something, Ellen Crosby?" said Honora.

Ellen looked wonderingly at her. "Of course I won't tell," said she. "What is it, Honora?"

"Nothing, only I made every one of those pink shawls myself," said Honora.

"Honora Crosby!"

"Yes, I did. I know I am right. I can't quite see how some of them got back to me, but they did."

"Good land!"

"It's so. I don't suppose I shall ever know the true inside of it; but there's one thing sure—my friends did want to give me something I wanted for a Christmas present, if they only knew what it was, and that's worth more than anything else."

Ellen stared, then she laughed, but Honora in her pink shawl did not seem amused at all. There was the faintest murmur of voices from the parlor. Honora had never had any love-affair of her own, but as she listened to that low murmur of Annette and her lover, her face took on the expression which it might have worn had she been in Annette's place. And the pink shawl cast a rosy glow over her silvery hair of age all like the joy of the giver upon beholding the joy over the gift.

For the Love of One's Self

Harper's Monthly Magazine, January 1905, 303–16

AGAINST THE SOUTH wall of the shoe-factory stood a tall spruce-tree. One branch of it crossed like an arm Amanda Dearborn's window, in front of which she stood at work on her machine. At first, when she was learning her monotonous task, she scarcely noticed the branch of the tree; now that she had worked a year, she sometimes glanced up at no risk, and her glance of bitter patience fell upon the everlasting greenness of it. She got, in spite of herself and her attitude of spiritual revulsion against comfort, a slight amelioration in the hot midsummer days in the suggestion which the tree gave her of coolness and darkness and winter. In the winter itself the arm draped with changeless green did not suggest so much; still, she sometimes noticed it, and it was a relief to her weary eyes.

Nobody knew how the girl hated her work in the great factory, or how she hated life, yet endured it with a sort of contemptuous grimness. She had a highly strung nervous organization; everything in her surroundings jarred upon her,—the noise, the odors, the companionship. She was herself superior to those about her—that is, to the most of them, although she never realized it. All that she did realize was that she stood day after day at work, at a task which stretched her nerves and muscles to breaking-point, to maintain a life in a world which honestly appeared entirely unattractive to her. She was neither hysterical nor sentimental, but she was naturally pessimistic, and she naturally reasoned from analogy. She was, besides, clear-visioned, and her outlook on the future was not apt to be dazzled by hope. She saw herself exactly as she was, as she had been, and in all probability as she would be. She had not yet reached middle age, but she was no longer exactly young; in fact, she had never been exactly young as some of the girls around her were. She listened to their chatter as she might have listened to a language of youth which she herself had never spoken. She did not understand, and she had a sort of unconscious contempt for it, as she had for most of the girls themselves. She saw their innocent attempts to be beautiful—to be like those who had not to toil like themselves, to the quick wasting of youth and beauty,—and she in a way despised them for it.

Nothing would have induced her to arrange her abundant brown hair in a fluffy crest, as the girl who stood next her arranged hers. She wore her own hair brushed straight back, exposing her temples, which showed faint lines of care and weariness, but which had nevertheless something noble about them. Nothing would have induced her to muffle her throat in stocks; she had a plain turn-over collar, of the same material as her waist. She indulged in no eccentricities of belts and buttons. She was saving all that she was able from her hard earnings against an old age of inability to work, and want. And yet she might have been distinctly pretty had she cared to make herself so. As she was, she was homely with a hard, stern homeliness. She was stiff and straight and flat-chested; her long arms were becoming every day more and more bony from the strain upon them, but her rigid back of burden was never yielding.

Perhaps she came the nearest to happiness when she went to the savings-bank to make a tiny deposit. The ignoble greed of the miser had an attraction to a nature like hers, non-acquiescent with its conditions, yet with a contemptuous sense of its own helplessness, rather than with any leaning to rebellion. When a strike was talked about she held a position aloof, although her sympathies were entirely with the party who wished to strike. It was only that she realized the futility of fighting with weapons of straw. Had they been weapons of steel, she might have been the most dangerous of them all; but she saw too clearly the ultimate outcome of it all, just as she saw her own face in the looking-glass of her little room in the boarding-house. However, in that she did not see quite as clearly, since she saw only facts, and not possibilities. She saw only a dark, harsh, sternly set face, not one which was susceptible of other things, as in fact it was.

She had never thought much about her personal appearance, except with regard to its subservience to cleanliness and order and goodness. Her training was partly responsible for that. Her mother had been a very plain-visaged woman, and quite destitute of sentiment or romance. Marriage itself had been in her case a queer coincidence. She had married a widower older than herself, who had died when Amanda was a child; she could scarcely remember him. In his younger days he had held a petty rank in the civil war, and her mother, as long as she lived, had a small pension. It was that pension which had enabled Amanda and her mother to have a home. The house was heavily encumbered; Amanda's father, who had worked like herself in the factory for a living, had been obliged to lay off much on account of an old wound. He had not been able to leave even the house clear to his family. The pension money had paid the interest on the mortgage, the taxes, the repairs; and Amanda's mother took boarders—shopgirls—to eke out the remainder of their living.

After Amanda was old enough, and had graduated from the high school, in a cheap white dress, coming forward in her turn and reading gravely—for she had even as a young girl much self-poise—her stupid little essay, heavy with platitudes, she assisted her mother with the housework. It was necessary, for her mother was growing old; she was not very young when she married. However, she remained still of so much assistance that when she died Amanda realized the impossibility of going on with her work of keeping a boarding-house. They had barely made both ends meet as it had been. When the pension stopped, and the interest, taxes, and repairs were to be paid for out of the small sums received from the boarders, and she would also be obliged to hire help, she saw nothing ahead except bankruptcy. Therefore she sold at auction, with a resolute stifling of her heartache, most of the old household goods with which she had been familiar since her infancy, keeping only enough to furnish one room, and her mother's bed and table-linen and wedding-china, which she had obtained permission to store in the garret of the house after it had ceased to belong to her. After the mortgage was paid there was a small sum remaining, which she placed in the savings-bank. She took a certain comfort in thinking of that as a last resource in case of illness and inability to work. Her mother had been in the habit of saying often, "Everybody ought to have a little laid by in case they are took sick." Amanda had the same pessimistic habit of thought, though not of speech—for she had no intimate friend.

She boarded in a house where there were several other girls and one married couple who worked in the factory, but she had nothing to do with them. They resented it, and said that Amanda Dearborn was "stuck up," while she had no good reason for being so.

"What if her mother did take boarders, and kept her out of the shop as long as she lived?" said they; "she's there now, and she ain't no call to turn up her nose at them as is as good as she is."

However, they were wrong; Amanda did not feel above them; she simply realized nothing in common with them; and when she came home from work she preferred remaining alone in her own room, sewing or reading. She was fond of books of a certain kind,—simple tales which did not involve much psychological analysis. Overwork in a shoe-factory does not fit the mind for strenuous efforts, except in its own behalf. Amanda used all her reasoning powers upon her own situation in the world and life. Sometimes while she sat sewing of an evening her thoughts were anarchistic, almost blasphemous; then, as always, came the contemptuous realization of their futility. Sometimes, as she sat there, she realized with a subtle defiance and rebellion that she was not in a spiritual sense a good woman. She realized that she was a woman without patience, destined to a hard monotony of life, and non-acquiescent with it. And yet in reality her demands from life, could she have made them, were small enough. She did not ask so very much, only a house no better than she had been accustomed to have, away from the buzz of the machines and the pressure upon her sensitive soul of the most heterogeneous elements of humanity. She was entirely willing to work beyond her strength, but she wanted herself to herself, and she wanted her home.

Often she took a pencil and paper and calculated at what age, if she had in the mean time no illness or disaster to infringe upon her small resources, she might possibly be able to buy a little house and set up her home again. At such times the impulse of saving grew fairly fierce within her. She went without everything that she possibly could; she patched and darned, although she always looked neat. She had learned that of her mother as she might have learned a tenet of faith. There was never a spot on the black gown she wore in the shop. It smelled of leather, but it was tidy. She was a good worker. One day not long before Christmas the foreman came to her and told her that her wages were to be raised at the beginning of the year. She had been, in fact, considered hitherto as only learning the art of stitching shoes, and her wages had been only nominal. Amanda looked at the foreman as he gave her the information, and there was a curious expression in her serious eyes. In fact, she was not only considering the raise in her wages, but she was considering him, as a brown sparrow, a dusty plebeian among birds, might consider a bird of paradise. She looked upon him as a male of her species, of course, but with a certain wonder, and even intimidation, because of his superior brilliance.

Frank Ayres, the foreman, was in fact an unusually handsome young man. He came of a good family. He was distantly related to the senior member of the firm, and might even in time belong to it. In the mean time he had his own personal advantages, which were enormous. He was only a year younger than Amanda, but he looked almost young enough to be her son. Hair as soft and golden and curly as a child's tossed above his white forehead, which had a childlike roundness. His cheeks were rosy, his lips always smiling, and with it all he was not effeminate. There was rather about him the triumph of youth and joyousness, which seemed never-ending. He, although only a foreman in a shoe-factory, carried himself like a young prince. The girls all adored him, some covertly, some boldly. He appealed to them all in a double sense, as a lover and as a child,—and the man who appeals to women after that fashion is irresistible. However, he did not take advantage of his power. He smiled at all the girls, but particularized none.

Amanda had watched with furtive disdain the other girls pushing up the fluffs of their pompadours as he drew near, and seeing to it that their shirt-waists were fastened securely in the back, straightening themselves with that indescribable movement of the female of the day, which involves at once a throwing back of the shoulders, a lengthening of the waist, a hollowing of the chest, and a slight bend of the back. She had always continued at her dogged work, and paid no attention to him. However, to-day, when he approached her (it was the hour of closing, and the girls in the vicinity had quitted their machines), she was conscious of a different sentiment. Almost the same expression entered her grave brown eyes that might have entered those of the other girls as she looked up in the joyous, triumphant face of the man. All at once a feeling of tenderness seemed to contract her heart, but it was the feeling that she had sometimes experienced at seeing a beautiful child. It was compounded of admiration and an almost painful protectiveness. In reality the maternal instinct came first in her, and the young man consequently reached it first. She gazed at him with eyes in which was no coquetry, but a gentle tenderness which transformed her whole face. The young man himself started and gazed at her as if he had seen her for the first time. She appealed to a need in his nature, and that is the strongest appeal in the world. That night he remarked to his younger brother, who was a foreman in the packing-room, that the prettiest girl in the factory was Amanda Dearborn. The brother stared. The two were smoking in Frank's room in their boarding-house.

"What! That Dearborn girl?" he said. "You are crazy."

"She is the best-looking girl in the factory, and I am not sure that she is not the best-looking girl in town," repeated Frank, stanchly.

"Why, good Lord!" cried his brother, staring at him, "she is the homeliest of the lot. Hair strained tight back from her forehead, and she dresses like her own grandmother."

"I like it a good deal better than so many frills," replied Frank, "and I am dead tired of those topknots the girls wear nowadays, and I am dead tired of the way they look at a fellow."

"Nothing conceited about you," remarked his brother, dryly. Although younger than Frank, he looked older, and was of a heavy build. He had not much attention from the other sex—that is, not much gratuitous attention.

"It is just because I am not conceited that I am tired of it," said Frank. "I would rather a girl would look at me as if she would nurse me through a fever than as if I was a handsome man, and that is the way that Dearborn girl looked at me to-night when I told her her wages were raised. It is high time they were, too. She has been working under rate too long as it is."

As the two young men talked, the snow, or rather sleet, drove on the windows. It was a bitter night—so bitter that neither thought of going out. Amanda Dearborn also remained at home. There was a sociable in the church vestry, and she had thought a little of going, although it was not her usual custom. But when it began to storm she decided to remain where she was. Her room was cold. It was a northeast room, and when the wind was that way little heat came from the register. She sat in the dark beside her window, wrapped in an old shawl which had belonged to her mother, and which always seemed to her to partake of the old atmosphere of home, and she gazed out at the white slant of the frozen storm. The sleet seemed to drive past the windows like arrows. There was an electric light a little farther down the street, and that seemed a nucleus for the swarming crystals. Amanda sat there huddled in her shawl and thought.

All thoughts are produced primarily by suggestion, and so were hers. A little package which had been found on her bureau on her return from the shop produced hers. She knew what was in it before she opened it. It required little acuteness to know, because a week before Christmas she and her mother for years had received a similar package from a distant cousin in Maine, and it contained invariably the same thing. Amanda opened the package, and found, as always, an ironing-holder. This year it was made of pink calico bound with green, and the year before, if she remembered rightly, it had been made of green calico bound with pink. Back of that she could not remember. An enormous package of these holders was stored away up in the garret of her old home. Amanda, although she was pessimistic, had a sense of humor. When she regarded this last holder she laughed, albeit a little bitterly.

"What on earth does Cousin Jane Dearborn think I want of an ironing-holder now?" she said, quite aloud. Then she considered that soon, by the last mail that night or the first in the morning, would come another package, from Cousin Maria Edgerly, and that that package would contain as usual a knitted washcloth. She then reflected upon the speedy arrival of another package from still another cousin in the second degree, containing a hemstitched duster of cheesecloth. She and her mother in the old days had often smiled over these yearly tokens, and said to each other that if they ironed every week-day, and bathed every hour, and dusted betweenwhiles, they would have enough of these things to last for a lifetime. But her mother's smile had always ended with an expression of sympathetic understanding.

"Poor Maria," or "Poor Jane," or "Poor Liza," as the case might have been, the mother always remarked, "she wants to do something, and she ain't got any means and no faculty, and it's all she can do." Amanda's mother had had a curious tenderness for these twice and third removed cousins of hers, whom she had not seen for years, and Amanda took comfort in the reflection that she had never expressed the conviction uppermost in her mind on the receipt of these faithful tokens a week before Christmas. It had been a dozen times on her tongue's end to say, "She is just sending this so as to make sure she gets something from us," but she had never said it. Instead she had aided her mother in preparing the best return presents they could afford—presents which meant self-denial for themselves. She recalled how the very Christmas before her mother died they had sent Cousin Jane a pair of black kid gloves, although her mother's were shabby. "Poor mother, she did not need gloves very long after that, anyway," Amanda reflected; then she also reflected that, knowing what she was now earning, they kept up this absurd deluge of holders and washcloths and dusters, in the hope of a reward. They were to her understanding nothing more than so many silent requests for benefits. Suddenly she became filled with an ignoble anger because of it all.

"Why should I drudge all my life and go without, in order to send Christmas presents to these cousins of mother's whom I have not seen more than two or three times in my life, and who send me things which I don't want, like so many machines?" she asked. Suddenly she resolved that this year she would not. They should get nothing. She had planned to spend fifteen dollars—an enormous sum for her—upon these cousins. She had made up her mind, since she did not know what they needed, to send the money this year, five dollars to each cousin. Suddenly she resolved that she would not. She considered how much she herself needed a new gown—a really nice black gown,—how if she had gone to the sociable that night she had not one gown which was suitable. She reflected, not fairly realizing that she did so, that Frank Ayres might have been at the sociable, and, also without fairly knowing, she saw herself as she might have looked in her poor best dress, in those dancing blue eyes of his. She imagined also herself as she would look, in those same eyes in a dainty costume of black crêpe, similar to one which a girl had who worked in the same room with her. She imagined the fluffy sweep of the long skirt, the lace trimming.

"That fifteen dollars would just about buy the material for the dress," she said to herself. Fifteen dollars when she had paid her board, due the first of the month, was nearly all the ready money she had. She did not dream of drawing upon her little bank-account. Her increase in wages would not begin until the following Monday. She remembered that there was to be a New-year's festival at the church the week following Christmas, and how she might have the dress made and wear it to that.

Suddenly she thought further; her feminine imagination became sharpened. She thought of a rosette of black lace in her hair. "Why should I give all that money to those far-away cousins?" she asked of herself. "While mother was alive we gave to please her, but now—Why should I in return for all these holders and wash-cloths and dusters, which are absolutely valueless to me, go without things I really need?" She thought furthermore in the depths of her heart, even veiling her thought from her own consciousness, how her youth was fast passing, and she thought again how she would look, in Frank Ayres's eyes. She had an under-realization of what that new black dress might mean to her. After all, in spite of her steadfastness and even severity of character, she was only a woman, and a woman untaught except by her own nature and that of her mother. She thought of this girl and that girl whom she had known, who had had her love affair, and had married and become possessed of a happy home, and she wondered if, after all, she was so without the pale as she had always thought. She began to have dreams as she sat there staring out into the storm, of chance meetings with Frank Ayres, of what he might say and do, of what she might say and do. A warmth stole all over her from her fast-throbbing heart in spite of the cold. She trembled, she smiled involuntarily, and all seemed to hinge upon the new black dress and the lace rosette for her hair.

Suddenly she gave her head a resolute shake. "What a fool I am!" she whispered. She was distinctly angry with herself. She got up, lit her lamp, and looked in the glass. There had been a flush on her cheeks, but that and the smile had gone. Her face looked back at her from the glass, above her flat chest, and her uncompromising collar hostile to that which was the legitimate desire and need of her kind. She glowered at herself in the looking-glass. "What a fool I am!" she said again.

She took a little stationery-box from the shelf under her table, and got her pen and ink from the shelf. Then she proceeded to cut little slips of paper, and write on them, "For Cousin Jane, with a merry Christmas from Amanda," and so on. She did not own any visiting-cards. She proposed to put a slip with a five-dollar note in each envelope, and send to the three cousins by registered mail. But now the cold of her room struck her again. Her hands felt stiff with it.

"There isn't any hurry," she said to herself. "Mother never sent anything until the day before Christmas. She thought they liked to get their presents on Christmas day." Then, too, she began to wonder if, after all, it was best to send the money,—if the value of money in gifts would not please them better. She thought that she might buy a pair of blankets for Cousin Jane, who was the poorest of the lot, and a silk waist for Cousin Liza, who had not quite given up, in her remote corner of Maine, the vanities of life, and about whom there had been rumors of a matrimonial alliance with an elderly widower. She also thought that a chenille table-cloth might please Cousin Maria. She decided, on the whole, that she had better wait until the next day before she got the five-dollar notes ready to send, although she was not conscious of a faltering in her determination to send the presents. Therefore she put away her paper carefully—she was very orderly—and went to bed, and lay for a long time awake watching the storm drift and swirl past the window in the electric light.

Amanda probably caught cold that night, for cold air instead of heat came from her register, and the covers on her bed were not so very thick, being well-worn quilts which had belonged to her mother. She had taken a sort of comfort in using them instead of the coverings which the mistress of the boarding-house would have furnished. Sometimes at night she felt, as she nestled under the well-worn quilts, which were heavy rather than warm, as if she were still under the wing of home. Every bit of calico in these quilts had been connected in some way with her family. However, she caught cold that night, and the next day was so ill that she was obliged to stay away from the shop. She did not even feel equal to getting the presents ready for the cousins. She was, moreover, still undecided whether to buy some gifts or send the money, but she felt too ill even to put the money in the envelopes and make arrangements about registering. The next day she was no better, and it was the fourth day before she could drag herself out of bed and go to the factory. Frank Ayres came and spoke to her, after she had been at work an hour, and inquired if she had been sick, and she felt the blood rise to her steady forehead. A chuckle from the girl at her right after he had gone made her angry, not only with the girl, but with herself and the foreman. The imagination of anything particular in his attention had come to her, but not the belief in it. She simply felt that he was making her an object of ridicule by a notice which must in her case mean nothing.

When she got home that night she was so worn out that she was obliged to go directly to bed. She resolved that the next evening, since the stores were open in the evening during the holiday season, she would go out and look for gifts for her cousins. But the next evening—she had caught a little more cold during the day—she was even more unable to go out. Then she resolved that she would send the money, as she had planned to do in the first place. It was the day but one before Christmas at last, when she dragged herself home, and took out the three new five-dollar notes to put in the envelopes. She had not taken off her wraps, for she wanted to go to the post-office, which was only a block away, to post them and have them registered. Then all at once a revulsion seized her. She again thought of the new black dress which she needed. She thought of the pile of miserable holders and dusters and wash-cloths. She looked at the money.

"What a fool I am!" she said to herself,—"what a fool! Here I shall not have one Christmas present for myself,—not one *real* present, for these are not presents; these are only reminders to me to send the cousins something. Here I am, with no Christmas presents coming to me, going to give away money which I actually need!" Again she seemed to see the foreman's happy, handsome face before her. She remembered the display which the girls around her had made of their gifts that very day. Suddenly she made up her mind that this year she would give her Christmas present to herself. "There is nobody else in this whole world to give me a Christmas present," she thought, "but myself. I will give myself the present."

When she had made this resolve a singular sense of guilt, as if she had blasphemed, was over her, but with it came a certain defiance in which she took pleasure. She began planning how she would have the new black dress made. There was, moreover, all the time the oddest conviction, for which she could not account, of something unfamiliar about the room. It was as if some strange presence was there. Every now and then she looked about. She had her lamp lighted and was seated beside her table doing some mending, but she saw nothing for a long while. She told herself that the quinine which she had taken for her cold affected her nerves. Then all at once she gave a great start. She saw, what it seemed inconceivable that she had not seen before, a package on a little ancient stand, which had belonged to her maternal grandmother, and had always stood by the side of her mother's bed in her lifetime, and now stood beside her own.

She gazed a moment at the package, which was done up in glossy white paper and tied with a gold cord; then she rose, and went across the room, and took it up. She saw what it was—a two-pound box of candy. It was directed to Miss Amanda Dearborn. She carefully took off the glossy white wrapping-paper, and a beautiful box of gold paper decorated with bunches of holly and tied with green ribbon appeared. She opened it, and on the lace-paper covering the candy was a card—"Frank Ayres." Amanda turned pale; she actually felt her limbs tremble under her; but all the while she was assuring herself that there was a mistake, that the candy did not belong to her. She reflected that there was another girl in the factory, working in another room, of the same surname, although her Christian name was different—Maud. This other girl was very pretty—a beauty some considered her. "This was meant for her," she said to herself, and at the same moment a deep, although ungrudging, jealousy of the other girl seized her. Amanda had good reasoning powers. She admitted that it was quite right and proper that Frank Ayres should send a Christmas token to this other girl in preference to her. She admitted that it was entirely right that the girl should have it instead of her. She was a good girl, besides being pretty and having all the graces which Amanda lacked. She had not one doubt but the box was intended for this other girl, and the more so because she herself knew quite well a young woman who was employed in the store from whence the candy came. She told herself, and with much show of reason, that this young woman, in preparing the package to be sent, had, from knowing her so well, absently confused the two names.

She carefully laid back the folds of lace-paper and looked at the dainty bonbons and fruits glacés. Then she replaced the paper, and neatly folded up the box in the outer wrappings and tied it with the gilt cord, after which she laid it on another table where it would not come to harm, and stood for a moment regarding it. It was only a box of candy, a gift which a man could send to any young woman without in the least compromising himself; it was so slight a matter that taking it seriously would in any case have been absurd, but she thought how she would have felt had it been really intended for her, and if Frank Ayres had sent it. There was something about the very uselessness of the thing which gave it a charm to her. She was not even very fond of sweets, but she had never had a Christmas present except those which savored of the absolutely essential, and which somehow missed something in being so essential. Of course there had been the holders and wash-cloths and dusters, and when her mother was alive they had been accustomed to give each other things which they really needed. That had been all. Amanda, reflecting, could not remember that she had ever had in her life, not even when she was a child, such an expensive and utterly needless gift as that box of candy. "Such a large box!" she considered, looking at it, "and such a lovely box in itself, and such a waste of ribbon, and if Frank Ayres had sent it, too!"

She began to imagine so intensely what her state of mind would have been in that case that her whole face changed; the downward curves at the corners of her mouth disappeared, she actually laughed. For a second she was as happy as if the box had actually been hers. Then her face sobered, but a change of resolution had come to her with that instant's taste of happiness on her own account. The sweet had been in her heart and relieved it of selfishness because of the joy of possession. One need not covet if one has, and the imagination of having had served her as well as the actuality, accustomed as she was to having little. She wondered how she could for a second have thought of depriving those poor cousins, those women who had had so little of the joys of life, of the Christmas gifts which she and her mother had always bestowed upon them. Her mother's dear reproachful face seemed to look upon her. She imagined the three women going to the post-office—the single one had a mile to go—and finding nothing, and her own heart ached with the ache of theirs. She seemed to put herself completely in their places, to change personalities with them. She looked at her clock and found that she had time enough, and hurried on her coat and hat, took the box of candy, and set out. The candy-store, with its windows radiant with the most charming boxes of bonbons, with evergreens and holly, was first on her way. She entered, and waited patiently for a chance to speak to the young woman whom she knew and who had been an old schoolmate of hers. She had to wait a few minutes, for the shop was packed with customers. Finally she found her chance, and approached the counter with the box.

"Alice," she said, in a low voice, almost a whisper, "here is something which has been sent to me from here by mistake." She spoke in a low tone both because she was embarrassed and because she was afraid that she might make trouble for her friend.

But the young woman, who was fair and plump, with a slightly imperious air, although she had greeted her pleasantly, stared at her, then at the box. "Why, I did not sell this, Amanda," she said. "I don't know anything about it." Then she called to another girl. "Nellie," she said, "did you sell this box of candy?"

There was a moment's lull in the rush of customers. The other young woman leaned her elbows on the counter and stared with distinct superciliousness at Amanda in her plain garb. She had an amazing bow at her throat, and her blond locks nearly reached Amanda's face with their fluffy scoop. She examined the box with an odd haughtiness which nothing could exceed. She might have been a princess of the blood examining a crown jewel. This girl who worked in a shoe-factory seemed to her immeasurably below her. She felt a contempt for the girl at her side because she treated her so pleasantly.

"Yes, I sold that box to Mr. Ayres," said she. "Why?" She raised her eyes in interrogation rather than pronounced the why.

"It does not belong to me," said Amanda. "It belongs to Miss Maud Dearborn instead of me."

"I am certain Mr. Ayres said Amanda," replied the girl, icily.

But Amanda had also a spirit of her own. She straightened herself. She pushed the box firmly toward the girl. "The box does *not* belong to me," she said, sternly. "Will you be kind enough to erase the Amanda and write Maud instead and have it sent to its proper address?—Good night, Alice." Then she walked out of the candy-store like a queen. She distinctly heard the haughty young woman say that she guessed there must have been a mistake, although she was almost sure he had said Amanda, for she could not imagine what any man in his senses would want to send a box of candy to a cross, homely old thing like that for.

But Amanda did not mind; she was quite accustomed to her own estimate of herself, which was so far from complimentary that its confirmation did not sting her as it might have otherwise done. She went on to the other stores, and bought a beautiful pair of blankets with a blue border—which she had sent by express—for Cousin Jane, a table-cloth for Cousin Maria, and a silk waist for Cousin Liza. Then she returned home and enclosed her slips of paper with her name and Christmas greetings with the waist and the table-cloth, and got them ready for the mail. She also wrote a letter to Cousin Jane, which she sent the next morning, that it might reach her at the same time the blankets arrived. Then she went to bed and thought of the delight which the other girl would feel when she received the box of candy from Mr. Frank Ayres. She seemed to enter so intensely into her state of mind that the same happiness came to her. The suggestion precipitated a dream. She dreamed, when at last she fell asleep, that she was the other Dearborn girl—the one with the pretty face—and that the candy had come to her, and she wondered how she could ever have thought she was anybody else. Then she awoke and remembered herself, and it was time to get up, although not yet light; still the unreasoning happiness had not yet gone.

She went to the shop, and saw Maud Dearborn, looking unusually pretty, standing near the office door. She was evidently waiting for Frank Ayres to come out, and, in fact, he did at that moment. "Thank you so much for the lovely box of candy," Amanda heard Maud say, in her pretty voice; then she passed on to her own room and took her place at her machine. She wondered a little when after a while Mr. Ayres came up to her and said good morning and asked her if she was quite recovered. She answered him quietly and resumed work, and heard the girls near her chuckle as he went away; and again the feeling of anger and injury that they should make a mock of one like her came over her. She reflected how she had gone her own way, and never knowingly hurt any one, and the feeling of revolt against a hard providence was over her. She thought of Maud Dearborn, and how prettily she had thanked Mr. Ayres, and again she seemed to almost change places with her. A great gladness for the other girl who was more favored than she irradiated her very soul. Then she fell to thinking of the joy of the cousins when they would receive their gifts. Her face relaxed, the expression of severity disappeared. She fairly smiled as she bent over her arduous, purely mechanical task. For the first time she seemed to realize the soul in that, as in all work, or rather the power in all work, for spiritual results. "If I did not have this work," she thought, "I could not have given those presents. I could not have made those poor souls happy."

That night when she went home she reflected with delight that the next day was a holiday, and she would be free of the humming toil of her hive of work for one day at least. She went directly up-stairs to her own room to wash her face and hands and remove her wraps before supper. The minute she entered the room she had, as she had the night before, that sense of something strange, almost the sense of a presence. She looked involuntarily at the little stand beside her bed, and there was another package of candy, directed plainly to her. She opened it with trembling fingers, and there was Frank Ayres's card. Even then she did not dare to understand. The thought, foolish as it was, flashed through her mind that Mr. Ayres might be making presents to all the girls, that she was simply one of many. Even as she stood divided between joy and uncertainty she heard a quick step on the stairs, and there was a knock on the door. The maid employed by the boarding-house mistress gave her a note from the young woman whom she knew in the candy-store. It was this:

> "DEAR AMANDA,—Do, for goodness' sake, keep this box of candy. Mr. Ayres just bought it of me, and when I said Miss *Maud* Dearborn, he fairly snapped me up. I guess the other was for you fast enough. Guess you've made a mash.
>
> ALICE."

Even the rude slang of the note did not disturb the joy of conviction that came to the girl. She knew that the present, the sweet, useless, very likely meaningless present, was hers. She realized the absurdity of her suspicion that Mr. Ayres was presenting two-pound boxes of candy to all the girls in the factory. She laughed aloud. She opened the box, and folded back the lace-paper, and gazed admiringly at the sweets. She no more thought of eating them than if they had been pearls and diamonds. She gazed at them, and she again seemed to see the foreman's handsome, laughing face.

Suddenly she made a resolution. There was a Christmas tree in the church that evening and she would go. She had not taken off her wraps. She hurried down-stairs and into the busy, crowded street. She went to a store where a young woman whom she knew worked at the lace-counter.

"See here, Laura," she said, "I want to buy a lace collar. I want to go to the tree to-night, and my dress is too shabby to wear without something to smarten it up a bit. But I can't pay you till Saturday night."

"Lord! that's all right," replied the young woman. She gave a curious glance at Amanda's face, and began taking laces out of a box. She looked again. "How well you do look!" she said; "and I heard you were laid up with a cold, too."

"My cold is all gone," replied Amanda. She selected a lace collar which would cost a third of her week's wages.

"Well, you *are* going in steep," said the young woman.

"I would rather not have any lace than cheap lace," Amanda replied.

"Well, I guess you are right. It don't pay in the long run. That will look lovely over your black dress. I wish I could go to the tree, but I can't get out; my steady will be there, too. You are lucky to work in a shop, after all."

"Maybe I am," laughed Amanda, as she went away with her lace collar.

When she got home there was a loud hum of voices from the dining-room, and an odor of frying beefsteak and tea and hot biscuits. She tucked her lace collar in her coat pocket and went in and drank a cup of tea and ate a biscuit. Then she hurried up to her room and got out her best black dress and laid it on the bed. Then she smoothed her hair, and gazed at herself a moment in her glass. She loosened the soft brown locks around her face, and saw that she was transformed. There was a pink glow on her cheeks; the smiling curves of her lips were entrancing. She put on her dress and fastened the lace collar, which hung in graceful folds over the shoulders, with a little jet pin which had been her mother's. Then she looked again at herself. She looked a beauty, and she wondered if she saw aright. She looked away from the glass, then looked again, and the same beautiful face smiled triumphantly back at her. She was meeting herself for the first time, and not only admiration and joy but tenderness was in her heart. The woman who sees herself beloved for the first time sees something greater and fairer in herself than she has ever seen. Amanda glanced at the beautiful box on the stand—she had not replaced the wrapping-paper,—and the gold of the box, decorated with holly, gleamed dully. She had become quite sure that Mr. Ayres would not have sent it to her unless he had singled her out from the others; she had become sure that the first box had been meant for her. She laughed aloud when she thought of the other Dearborn girl; then she felt sorry—so careful had she always been of money—that he had been obliged to buy another box,—of the most expensive candy, too. Then she put the box in her bureau drawer and locked it. The thought had come to her that the maid might enter the room and take a piece, and that would seem like sacrilege.

Amanda put on her coat and hat and went to the Christmas tree. She was rather late, and the gifts were nearly distributed. She took a seat at the back of the vestry, which was fragrant with evergreen. She listened to the names which were called out, and saw those called go forward for their presents. Her name was not called, and she did not expect it to be. She had from a side glance a glimpse of Frank Ayres near her. After the presents were distributed, and people began moving about, she felt rather than saw him coming toward her. She was quite alone on the settee.

"Good evening, Miss Dearborn," he said, and she turned quite sedately—she had much self-control.

"Good evening," she replied. Then she thanked him for his present. He laughed gayly, and yet with a certain tenderness of meaning.

"I meant the box that Miss Maud Dearborn got for you," he said, "but somehow there was a mistake in sending it."

"It was sent to me," replied Amanda, in a low voice, "but I thought that you could not have meant it for me."

"Why not?" asked Frank Ayres, gazing at her with an admiration which she had never seen in his eyes before. He was in reality thinking to himself that, much as he had liked her, he had never known she was so pretty.

Amanda stole a glance at him. "Oh, because," she said.

"Because what?"

"Why, I thought she was a girl you or any man would be more likely to send a box of candy to," she said, simply, and a soft blush made her face as pink as a baby's.

"Nonsense!" said Frank Ayres. "You underrate yourself." Then he added, "But a man rather likes a girl to underrate herself."

When Amanda went home that night, Frank Ayres went with her. When they reached the door of her boarding-house they stopped, and there was a pause.

"You must miss your home dreadfully since your mother died," he said.

"Yes, I do," replied Amanda.

"I have missed mine a good deal, too," Frank Ayres said. There was another pause. "I have been thinking pretty hard about setting up another one before long," he said, in a low, almost timid voice.

Amanda said nothing.

"I saw last week that the house you used to own was for sale," said Frank Ayres.

"Yes, it is, I believe," replied Amanda, faintly.

"It is a good house, just the kind I like."

"Yes, it is a good house."

There was another pause. Frank Ayres's face had lost its gay, laughing expression; he looked sober, afraid, yet determined. "May I come and see you sometime?" he asked.

"I shall be very glad to have you," replied Amanda, in a whisper.

They shook hands then, and Amanda went into the house. When she was in her own room she took the pretty box out of the drawer and sat with it in her lap, thinking about Frank Ayres and her mother, and kept Christmas holy.

The Revolt of Sophia Lane

Harper's Monthly Magazine, December 1903, 20–34

THE LEVEL OF new snow in Sophia Lane's north yard was broken by horse's tracks and the marks of sleigh-runners. Sophia's second cousin, Mrs. Adoniram Cutting, her married daughter Abby Dodd, and unmarried daughter Eunice had driven over from Addison, and put up their horse and sleigh in Sophia's clean, unused barn.

When Sophia had heard the sleigh-bells she had peered eagerly out of the window of the sitting-room and dropped her sewing. "Here's Ellen and Abby and Eunice," she cried, "and they've brought you some wedding-presents. Flora Bell, you put the shawl over your head, and go out through the shed and open the barn. I'll tell them to drive right in."

With that the girl and the woman scuttled—Flora Bell through the house and shed to the barn which joined it; Sophia, to the front door of the house, which she pushed open with some difficulty on account of the banked snow. Then she called to the women in the sleigh, which had stopped at the entrance to the north yard: "Drive right in—drive right in. Flora has gone to open the barn doors. She'll be there by the time you get there."

Then Sophia ran through the house to the kitchen, set the teakettle forward, and measured some tea into the teapot. She moved with the greatest swiftness, as if the tea in so many seconds were a vital necessity. When the guests came in from the barn she greeted them breathlessly. "Go right into the sittin'-room," said she. "Flora, you take their things and put them on the bedroom bed. Set right down by the stove and get warm, and the tea'll be ready in a minute. The water's 'most boilin'. You must be 'most froze." The three women, who were shapeless bundles from their wraps, moved clumsily into the sitting-room as before a spanking breeze of will. Flora followed them; she moved more slowly than her aunt, who was a miracle of nervous speed. Sophia Lane never walked; she ran to all her duties and pleasures as if she were racing against time. She hastened the boiling of the teakettle—she poked the fire; she thrust light slivers of wood into the stove. When the water boiled she made the tea with a rush, and carried the tray with cups and saucers into the sitting-room with a perilous sidewise tilt and flirt. But nothing was spilled. It was very seldom that Sophia came to grief through her haste.

The three women had their wraps removed, and were sitting around the stove. The eldest, Mrs. Ellen Cutting—a stout woman with a handsome face reddened with cold,—spoke when Sophia entered.

"Land! If you haven't gone and made hot tea!" said she.

Sophia set the tray down with a jerk, and the cups hopped in their saucers. "Well, I guess you need some," said she, speaking as fast as she moved. "It's a bitter day; you must be froze."

"Yes, it is awful cold," assented Abby Dodd, the married daughter, "but I told mother and Eunice we'd got to come to-day, whether or no. I was bound we should get over here before the wedding."

"Look at Flora blush!" giggled Eunice, the youngest and the unmarried daughter.

Indeed, Flora Bell, who was not pretty, but tall and slender and graceful, was a deep pink all over her delicate face to the roots of her fair hair.

"You wait till your turn comes, Sis, and see what you'll do," said Abby Dodd, who resembled her mother, being fat and pink and white, with a dumpy, slightly round-shouldered figure in a pink flannel shirt-waist frilled with lace. All the newcomers were well dressed, the youngest daughter especially. They had a prosperous air, and they made Sophia's small and frugal sitting-room seem more contracted than usual. Both Sophia and her niece were dressed in garments which the visitors would characterize later among themselves, with a certain scorn tinctured with pity, as "fadged up." They were not shabby, they were not exactly poor, but they were painfully and futilely aspiring. "If only they would not trim quite so much," Eunice Cutting said later. But Sophia dearly loved trimming; and as for Flora, she loved whatever her aunt Sophia did. Sophia had adopted her when her parents died, when she was a baby, and had brought her up on a pittance a year. Flora was to be married to Herbert Bennet on the next day but one. She was hurrying her bridal preparations, and she was in a sort of delirium of triumph, of pride, of happiness and timidity. She was the centre of attention to-day. The visitors' eyes were all upon her with a half-kindly, half-humorous curiosity.

On the lounge at the side of the room opposite the stove were three packages, beautifully done up in white paper and tied with red and green ribbons. Sophia had spied them the moment she entered the room.

The guests comfortably sipped their tea.

"Is it sweet enough?" asked Sophia of Mrs. Cutting, thrusting the white sugar-bowl at her.

"Plenty," replied Mrs. Cutting. "This tea does go right to the spot. I did get chilled."

"I thought you would."

"Yes, and I don't like to, especially since it is just a year ago since I had pneumonia, but Abby thought we must come to-day, and I thought so myself. I thought we wanted to have one more look at Flora before she was a bride."

"Flora's got to go out now to try on her weddin'-dress the last time," said Sophia. "Miss Beals has been awful hurried at the last minute; she don't turn off work very fast, and the dress won't be done till to-night; but everything else is finished."

"I suppose you've had a lot of presents, Flora," said Abby Dodd.

"Quite a lot," replied Flora, blushing.

"Yes, she's had some real nice presents, and two or three that ain't quite so nice," said Sophia, "but I guess those can be changed."

Mrs. Cutting glanced at the packages on the sofa with an air of confidence and pride. "We have brought over some little things," said she. "Adoniram and I give one, and Abby and Eunice each one. I hope you'll like them, Flora."

Flora was very rosy; she smiled with a charming effect, as if she were timid before her own delight. "Thank you," she murmured. "I know they are lovely."

"Do go and open them, Flora," said Eunice. "See if you have any other presents like them."

"Yes, open them, Flora," said Mrs. Cutting, with pleasant patronage.

Flora made an eager little movement toward the presents, then she looked wistfully at her aunt Sophia.

Sophia was smiling with a little reserve. "Yes, go and open them, Flora," said she; "then bring out your other presents and show them."

Flora's drab skirt and purple ruffles swayed gracefully across the room; she gathered up the packages in her slender arms, and brought them over to the table between the windows, where her aunt sat. Flora began untying the red and green ribbons, while the visitors looked on with joyful and smiling importance. On one package was marked, "Flora, with all best wishes for her future happiness, from Mr. and Mrs. Adoniram Cutting."

"That is ours," said Mrs. Cutting.

Flora took off the white paper, and a nice white box was revealed. She removed the lid and took out a mass of crumpled tissue-paper. At last she drew forth the present. It was in three pieces. When she had set them on the table, she viewed them with admiration but bewilderment. She looked from one to the other, smiling vaguely.

Abby Dodd laughed. "Why, she doesn't know how to put them together!" said she. She went to the table and quickly adjusted the different parts of the present. "There!" said she, triumphantly.

"What a beautiful—teakettle!" said Flora, but still in a bewildered fashion.

Sophia was regarding it with an odd expression. "What is it?" she asked, shortly.

"Why, Sophia," cried Mrs. Cutting, "don't you know? It is an afternoon-tea kettle."

"What's that thing under it?" asked Sophia.

"Why, that's the alcohol-lamp. It swings on that little frame over the lamp and heats the water. I thought it would be so nice for her."

"It's beautiful," said Flora.

Sophia said nothing.

"It is real silver; it isn't plated," said Mrs. Cutting, in a slightly grieved tone.

"It is beautiful," Flora murmured again, but Sophia said nothing.

Flora began opening another package. It was quite bulky. It was marked, "Flora, with best wishes for a life of love and happiness, from Abby Dodd."

"Be careful," charged Abby Dodd. "It's glass."

Flora removed the paper gingerly. The present was rolled in tissue-paper.

"What beautiful dishes!" said she, but her voice was again slightly bewildered.

Sophia looked at the present with considerable interest. "What be the bowls for?" said she. "Oatmeal?"

The visitors all laughed.

"Oatmeal!" cried Abby. "Why, they are finger-bowls!"

"Finger-bowls?" repeated Sophia, with a plainly hostile air.

"Yes,—bowls to dip your fingers in after dinner," said Abby.

"What for?" asked Sophia.

"Why, to—to wash them."

"We wash our hands in the wash-basin in the kitchen with good hot water and soap," said Sophia.

"Oh, but these are not really to wash the hands in—just to dabble the fingers in," said Eunice, still giggling. "It's the style. You have them in little plates with doilies and pass them around after dinner."

"They are real pretty," said Flora.

Sophia said nothing.

"They are real cut glass," said Mrs. Cutting.

Flora turned to the third package, that was small and flat and exceedingly dainty. The red and green ribbon was tied in a charming bow with Eunice's visiting-card. On the back of the card was written, "Flora, with dearest love, and wishes for a life of happiness, from Eunice." Flora removed the ribbons and the white paper, and opened a flat, white box, disclosing six dainty squares of linen embroidered with violets.

"What lovely mats!" said she.

"They are finger-bowl doilies," said Eunice, radiantly.

"To set the bowls on?" said Flora.

"Yes; you use pretty plates, put a doily in each plate, and then the finger-bowl on the doily."

"They are lovely," said Flora.

Sophia said nothing.

Abby looked rather aggrievedly at Sophia. "Eunice and I thought Flora would like them as well as anything we could give her," said she.

"They are lovely," Flora said again.

"You haven't any like them, have you?" Abby asked, rather uneasily.

"No, she hasn't," answered Sophia, for her niece.

"We tried to think of some things that everybody else wouldn't give her," said Mrs. Cutting.

"Yes, you have," Sophia answered, dryly.

"They are all beautiful," said Flora, in a soft, anxiously deprecating voice, as she gathered up the presents. "I keep my presents in the parlor," she remarked further. "I guess I'll put these in there with the rest."

Presently she returned, bringing a large box; she set it down and returned for another. They were large suit-boxes. She placed them on the table, and the visitors gathered round.

"I've had beautiful presents," said Flora.

"Yes, she has had *some* pretty nice presents," assented Sophia. "Most of them are real nice."

Flora stood beside the table and lifted tenderly from the box one wedding-gift after another. She was full of shy pride. The visitors admired everything. When Flora had displayed the contents of the two boxes, she brought out a large picture in an ornate gilt frame, and finally wheeled through the door with difficulty a patent rocker upholstered with red crushed plush.

"That's from some of his folks," said Sophia. "I call it a handsome present."

"I'm going to have a table from his aunt Jane," remarked Flora.

"Sit down in that chair and see how easy it is," said Sophia, imperatively, to Mrs. Cutting, who obeyed meekly, although the crushed plush was so icy cold from its sojourn in the parlor that it seemed to embrace her with deadly arms and made her have visions of pneumonia.

"It's as easy a chair as I ever sat in," she said, rising hastily.

"Leave it out here and let her set in it while she is here," said Sophia; and Mrs. Cutting sank back into the chair, although she did ask for a little shawl for her shoulders.

Mrs. Cutting had always had a wholesome respect for her cousin Sophia Lane, although she had a certain feeling of superiority by reason of her wealth. Even while she looked about Sophia's poor little sitting-room and recalled her own fine parlors, she had a sense that Sophia was throned on such mental heights above mahogany and plush and tapestry that she could not touch her with a finger of petty scorn even if she wished.

After Flora had displayed her presents and carried them back to the parlor, she excused herself and went to the dressmaker's to try on her wedding-dress.

After Flora had gone out of the yard, looking abnormally stout with the gay plaid shawl over the coat and her head rolled in a thick, old, worsted hood of Sophia's, Mrs. Cutting opened on a subject about which she was exceedingly curious.

"I'm real sorry we can't have a glimpse of the wedding-dress," said she, ingratiatingly.

Sophia gave an odd sort of grunt in response. Sophia always gave utterance to that nondescript sound, which was neither assent nor dissent, but open to almost any interpretation, when she wished to evade a lie. She was in reality very glad that the wedding-dress was not on exhibition. She thought it much better that it should not be seen in its full glory until the wedding-day.

"Flora has got many good presents," said Sophia, "and few tomfool ones, thanks to me and what I did last Christmas."

"What do you mean, Sophia?" asked Mrs. Cutting.

"Didn't you hear what I did, Ellen Cutting?"

"No, I didn't hear a word about it."

"Well, I didn't know but somebody might have told. I wasn't a mite ashamed of it, and I ain't now. I'd do the same thing over again if it was necessary, but I guess it won't be; I guess they got a good lesson. I dare say they were kind of huffy at the time. I guess they got over it. They've all give Flora presents now, anyhow, except Angeline White, and I guess she will."

"Why, what did you do?" asked Abby Dodd, with round eyes of interest on Sophia.

"Why, I'd jest as soon tell you as not," replied Sophia. "I've got some cake in the oven. Jest let me take a peek at that first."

"Wedding-cake?" asked Eunice, as Sophia ran out of the room.

"Land, no!" she called back. "That was made six weeks ago. Weddin'-cake wouldn't be worth anything baked now."

"Eunice, didn't you know better than that?" cried her mother.

"It's white cake," Sophia's explanatory voice came from the kitchen, whence sweet odors floated into the room. The oven door opened and shut with an exceedingly swift click like a pistol-shot.

"I should think she'd make the cake fall, slamming the oven door like that," murmured Abby Dodd.

"So should I; but it won't," assented her mother. "I never knew Sophia to fail with her cake."

Sophia flew back into the sitting-room and plumped into her chair; she had, indeed, risen with such impetus and been so quick that the chair had not ceased rocking since she left it. "It's done," said she; "I took it out. I'll let it stand in the pan and steam a while before I do anything more with it. Now I'll tell you what I did about Flora's Christmas presents last year if you want me to. I'd jest as soon as not. If I hadn't done what I did, there wouldn't have been any weddin' this winter, I can tell you that."

"You don't say so!" cried Mrs. Cutting, and the others stared.

"No, there wouldn't. You know, Herbert and Flora have been goin' together three years this December. Well, they'd have been goin' together three years more, and I don't know but they'd been goin' together till doomsday, if I hadn't taken matters into my own hand. I ain't never been married myself, and maybe folks think I ain't any right to my opinion, but I've always said I didn't approve of young folks goin' together so long unless they get married. When they're married, and any little thing comes up that one or the other don't think quite so nice, why, they put up with it, and make the best of it, and kind of belittle that and make more of the things that they do like. But when they ain't married it's different. I don't care how much they think of each other, something may come up to make him or her kind of wonder if t'other is good enough to marry, after all. Well, nothin' of that kind has happened with Flora and Herbert Bennet, and I ain't sayin' there has. They went together them three years, and, far as I can see, they think each other is better than in the beginnin'. Well, as I was sayin', it seemed to me that those two had ought to get married before long if they were ever goin' to, but I must confess I didn't see how they were any nearer it than when they started keepin' company."

"Herbert has been pretty handicapped," remarked Mrs. Cutting.

"Handicapped? Well, I rather guess he has! He was young when his father died, and when his mother had that dreadful sickness and had to go to the hospital, he couldn't keep up the taxes, and the interest on the mortgage got behindhand; the house was mortgaged when his father died, and it had to go; he's had to hire ever since. They're comin' here to live; you knew that, I s'pose?"

"Sophia, you don't mean his mother is coming here to live?"

"Why not? I'm mighty glad the poor woman's goin' to have a good home in her old age. She's a good woman as ever was, just as mild-spoken, and smart too. I'm tickled to death to think she's comin', and so's Flora. Flora sets her eyes by his mother."

"Well, you know your own business, but I must say I think it's a considerable undertaking."

"Well, I don't. I'd like to know what you'd have her do. Herbert can't afford to support two establishments, no more than he earns, and he ain't goin' to turn his mother out to earn her bread an' butter at her time of life, I rather guess. No; she's comin' here, and she's goin' to have the south chamber; she's goin' to furnish it. I never see a happier woman; and as for Herbert—well, he has had a hard time, and now things begin to look brighter; but I declare, about a year ago, as far as I could see, it didn't look as if he and Flora ever could get married. One evenin' the poor fellow came here, and he talked real plain; he said he felt as if he'd ought to. He said he'd been comin' here a long time, and he'd begun to think that he and Flora might keep on that way until they were gray, so far as he could help it. There he was, he said, workin' in Edgcomb's store at seven dollars a week, and had his mother to keep, and he couldn't see any prospect of anything better. He said maybe if he wasn't goin' with Flora she might get somebody else. 'It ain't fair to Flora,' said he. And with that he heaves a great sigh, and the first thing I knew, right before me, Flora she was in his lap, huggin' him, and cryin', and sayin' she'd never leave him for any man on the face of the earth, and she didn't ask anything any better than to wait. They'd both wait and be patient and trust in God, and she was jest as happy as she could be, and she wouldn't change places with the Queen. First thing I knew I was cryin' too; I couldn't help it; and Herbert, poor fellow, he fetched a big sob himself, and I didn't think none the worse of him for it. 'Seems as if I must be sort of lackin' somehow, to make such a failure of things,' says he, kind of broken like.

"'You ain't lackin',' says Flora, real fierce like. 'It ain't you that's to blame. Fate's against you and always has been.'

"'Now you look round before you blame the Lord,' says I at that—for when folks say fate they always mean the Lord. 'Mebbe it ain't the Lord,' says I; 'mebbe it's folks. Wouldn't your uncle Hiram give you a lift, Herbert?'

"'Uncle Hiram!' says he; but not a bit scornful—real good-natured.

"'Why? I don't see why not,' says I. 'He always gives nice Christmas presents to you and your mother, don't he?'

"'Yes,' says he. 'He gives Christmas presents.'

"'Real nice ones?'

"'Yes,' said poor Herbert, kind of chucklin', but real good-natured. 'Last Christmas Uncle Hiram gave mother a silver card-case, and me a silver ash-receiver.'

"'But you don't smoke?' says I.

"'No,' says he, 'and mother hasn't got any visitin'-cards.'

"'I suppose he didn't know, along of not livin' in the same place,' says I.

"'No,' says he. 'They were real handsome things—solid; must have cost a lot of money.'

"'What would you do if you could get a little money, Herbert?' says I.

"Bless you! he knew quick enough. Didn't have to study over it a minute.

"'I'd buy that piece of land next your house here,' says he, 'and I'd keep cows and start a milk route. There's need of one here,' says he, 'and it's just what I've always thought I'd like to do; but it takes money,' he finishes up, with another of them heart-breakin' sighs of his, 'an' I ain't got a cent.'

"'Something will happen so you can have the milk route,' says Flora, and she kisses him right before me, and I was glad she did. I never approved of young folks bein' silly, but this was different. When a man feels as bad as Herbert Bennet did that day, if the woman that's goin' to marry him can comfort him any, she'd ought to.

"'Yes,' says I, 'something will surely happen. You jest keep your grit up, Herbert.'

"'How you women do stand by me!' says Herbert, and his voice broke again, and I was pretty near cryin'.

"'Well, we're goin' to stand by you jest as long as you are as good as you be now,' says I. 'The tide 'll turn before long.'

"I hadn't any more than got the words out of my mouth before the express drove up to the door, and there were three Christmas presents for Flora, early as it was, three days before Christmas. Christmas presents so long beforehand always make me a little suspicious, as if mebbe folks wanted other folks to be sure they were goin' to have something. Flora she'd always made real handsome presents to every one of them three that sent those that day. One was Herbert's aunt Harriet Morse, one was Cousin Jane Adkins over to Gorham, and the other was Mis' Crocker, she that was Emma Ladd; she's a second cousin of Flora's father's. Well, them three presents came, and we undid them. Then we looked at 'em. 'Great Jehosophat!' says I. Herbert he grinned, then he said something I didn't hear, and Flora she looked as if she didn't know whether to laugh or cry. There Flora she didn't have any money to put into presents, of course, but you know what beautiful fancy-work she does, and there she'd been workin' ever since the Christmas before, and she made a beautiful centrepiece and a bureau scarf and a lace handkerchief for those three women, and there they had sent her a sort of a dewdab to wear in her hair! Pretty enough, looked as if it cost considerable—a pink rose with spangles, and a feather shootin' out of it; but Lord! if Flora had come out in that thing anywhere she'd go in Brookville, she'd scared the natives. It was all right where Herbert's aunt Harriet lived. Ayres is a city, but in this town, 'way from a railroad—goodness!

"Well, there was that; and Cousin Jane Adkins had sent her a Japanese silk shawl, all over embroidery, as handsome as a picture; but there was poor Flora wantin' some cotton cloth for her weddin' fix, and not a cent to buy a thing with. My sheets and pillow-cases and table-linen that I had from poor mother was about worn out, and Flora was wonderin' how she'd ever get any. But there Jane had sent that shawl, that cost nobody knew how much, when she knew Flora wanted the other things,—because I'd told her. But Mis' Crocker's was the worst of all. She's a widow with a lot of money, and she's put on a good many airs. I dun'no' as you know her. No, I thought you didn't. Well, she does feel terrible airy. She sent poor Flora a set of chessmen, all red and white ivory, beautifully carved, and a table to keep 'em on. I must say I was so green I didn't know what they were when I first saw 'em. Flora knew; she'd seen some somewhere she'd been.

"'For the land sake! what's them little dolls and horses for?' says I. 'It looks like Noah's ark without the ark.'

"'It's a set of chess and a table,' said Flora, and she looked ready to cry, poor child. She thought, when she got that great package, that she really had got something she wanted that time, sure.

"'Chess?' says I.

"'A game,' says Flora.

"'A game?' says I.

"'To play,' says she.

"'Do you know how to play it, Flora?' says I.

"'No,' says she.

"'Does Herbert?'

"'No.'

"'Well,' says I, and I spoke right out, 'of all the things to give anybody that needs things!'

"Flora was readin' the note that came with it. Jane Crocker said in the note that in givin' her Christmas present this year she was havin' a little eye on the future—and she underlined the future. She was twittin' Flora a little about her waitin' so long, and I knew it. Jane Crocker is a good woman enough, but she's got claws. She said she had an eye on the *underlined* future, and she said a chess set and a table were so stylish in a parlor. She didn't say a word about playin'.

"'Does she play that game?' says I to Flora.

"'I don't know,' says Flora. She didn't; I found out afterward. She didn't know a single blessed thing about the game.

"Well, I looked at that present of poor Flora's, and I felt as if I should give up. 'How much do you s'pose that thing cost?' says I. Then I saw she had left the tag on. I looked. I didn't care a mite. I don't know where she got it. Wherever it was, she got cheated, if I know anything about it. There Jane Crocker had paid forty dollars for that thing.

"'Why didn't she give forty dollars for a Noah's ark and done with it?' says I. 'I'd jest as soon have one. Go and put it in the parlor,' says I.

"And poor Flora and Herbert lugged it into the parlor. She was almost cryin'.

"Well, the things kept comin' that Christmas. We both had a good many presents, and it did seem as if they were worse than they had ever been before. They had always been pretty bad. I don't care if I do say it."

There was a faint defiance in Sophia's voice. Mrs. Cutting and her daughters glanced imperceptibly at one another. A faint red showed on Mrs. Cutting's cheeks.

"Yes," repeated Sophia, firmly, "they always had been pretty bad. We had tried to be grateful, but it was the truth. There were so many things Flora and I wanted, and it did seem sometimes as if everybody that gave us Christmas presents sat up a week of Sundays tryin' to think of something to give us that we didn't want. There was Lizzie Starkwether; she gave us bed-shoes. She gave us bed-shoes the winter before, and the winter before that, but that didn't make a mite of difference. She kept right on givin' 'em, red and black bed-shoes. There she knits beautiful mittens and wristers, and we both wanted mittens or wristers; but no, we got bed-shoes. Flora and me never wear bed-shoes, and, what's more, I'd told Lizzie Starkwether so. I had a chance to do it when I thought I wouldn't hurt her feelin's. But that didn't make any difference; the bed-shoes come right along. I must say I was mad when I saw them that last time. 'I must say I don't call this a present; I call it a kick,' says I, and I'm ashamed to say I gave them bed-shoes a fling. There poor Flora had been sittin' up nights makin' a white apron trimmed with knit lace for Lizzie, because she knew she wanted one.

"Well, so it went; everything that come was a little more something we didn't want, especially Flora's; and she didn't say anything, but tried to look as if she was tickled to death; and she sent off the nice, pretty things she'd worked so hard to make, and every single one of them things, if I do say it, had been studied over an hour to every minute the ones she got had. Flora always tried not to give so much what she likes as what the one she's givin' to likes; and when I saw what she was gettin' back I got madder an' madder. I s'pose I wasn't showin' a Christian spirit, and Flora said so. She said she didn't give presents to get their worth back, and if they liked what she gave, that was worth more than anything. I could have felt that way if they'd been mine, but I couldn't when they were Flora's, and when the poor child had so little, and couldn't get married on account of it, too. Christmas mornin' came Herbert's rich uncle Hiram's present. It came while we were eatin' breakfast, about eight o'clock. We were rather late that mornin'. Well, the expressman drove into the yard, and he left a nice little package, and I saw the Leviston express mark on it, and I says to Flora, 'This must come from Herbert's uncle Hiram, and I shouldn't wonder if you had got something real nice.'

"Well, we undid it, and if there wasn't another silver card-case, the same style as Herbert's mother had given her the Christmas before. Well, Flora has got some visitin'-cards, but the idea of her carryin' a silver card-case like that when she went callin'! Why, she wouldn't have had anything else that come up to that card-case! Flora didn't say much, but I could see her lips quiver. She jest put it away, and pretty soon Herbert run in—he was out with the delivery-wagon from the store, and he stopped a second. He didn't stay long,—he was too conscientious about his employer's time,—but he stayed long enough to tell about his and his mother's Christmas presents from his uncle Hiram, and what do you think they had that time? Why, Herbert had a silver cigarette-case, and he never smokin' at all, and his mother had a cut-glass wine-set.

"Well, I didn't say much, but I was makin' up my mind. I was makin' it up slow, but I was makin' it up firm. Some more presents came that afternoon, and not a thing Flora wanted, except some ironin' holders from Cousin Ann Drake, and me a gingham apron from her. Yes, Flora did have another present she wanted, and that was a handkerchief come through the mail from the school-teacher that used to board here—a real nice, fine one. But the rest—well, there was a sofa-pillow painted with wild roses on boltin'-cloth, and there every sofa we'd got to lay down on in the house was this lounge here. We'd never had a sofa in the parlor, and Minerva Saunders—she sent it—knew it; and I'd like to know how much we could use a painted white boltin'-cloth pillow here? Minerva was rich, too, and I knew the pillow cost enough. And Mis' George Harris, she that was Minnie Beals—she was Flora's own cousin, you know,—what did she send but a brass fire-set—poker and tongs and things—,and here we ain't got an open fireplace in the house, and she knew it. But Minnie never did have much sense; I never laid it up against her. She meant well, and she's sent Flora some beautiful napkins and table-cloths; I told her that was what she wanted for a weddin'-present. Well, as I was sayin', I was makin' up my mind slow but firm, and by afternoon it was made up. Says I to Flora: 'I wish you'd go over to Mr. Martin's and ask him if I can have his horse and sleigh this afternoon. Tell him I'll pay him.' He never takes any pay, but I always offer. Flora said: 'Why, Aunt Sophia, you ain't goin' out this afternoon! It looks as if it would snow every minute.'

"'Yes, I be,' says I.

"Well, Flora went over and asked, and Mr. Martin said I was welcome to the horse and sleigh—he's always real accommodatin'—and he hitched up himself and brought it over about one o'clock. I thought I'd start early, because it did threaten snow. I got Flora out of the way—sent her down to the store to get some sugar; we were goin' to make cake when I got home, and we were all out of powdered sugar. When that sleigh come I jest bundled all them presents—except the apron and holders and the two or three other things that was presents, because the folks that give 'em had studied up what Flora wanted, and give to her instead of themselves—an' I stowed them all in that sleigh, under the seat and on it, and covered them up with the robe.

"Then I wrapped up real warm, because it was bitter cold—seemed almost too cold to snow,—and I put a hot soapstone in the sleigh, and I gathered up the reins, an' I slapped 'em over the old horse's back, and I set out.

"I thought I'd go to Jane Crocker's first,—I wanted to get rid of that chess-table; it took up so much room in the sleigh I hadn't any place to put my feet, and the robe kept slippin' off it. So I drove right there. Jane was to home; the girl came to the door, and I went into the parlor. I hadn't been to call on Jane for some time, and she'd got a number of new things I hadn't seen, and the first thing I saw was a chess-table and all them little red and white Noah's-ark things, jest like the one she sent us. When Jane come in, dressed in black silk stiff enough to stand alone—though she wa'n't goin' anywheres and it looked like snow—I jest stood right up. I'd brought in the table and the box of little jiggers, and I goes right to the point. I had to. I had to drive six miles to Ayres before I got through, and there it was spittin' snow already.

"'Good-afternoon, Jane,' says I. 'I've brought back your presents.'

"Jane she kind of gasped, and she turned pale. She has a good deal of color; she's a pretty woman; well, it jest slumped right out of her cheeks. 'Mercy! Sophia,' says she, 'what do you mean?'

"'Jest what I say, Jane,' says I. 'You've sent Flora some playthings that cost forty dollars—you left the tags on, so we know,—and they ain't anything she has any use for. She don't know how to play chess, and neither does Herbert; and if they did know, they wouldn't neither of 'em have any time, unless it was Sundays, and then it would be wicked.'

"'Oh, Lord! Sophia,' says she, kind of chokin', 'I don't know how to play myself, but I've got one for an ornament, and I thought Flora—'

"'Flora will have to do without forty-dollar ornaments, if ever she gets money enough to get married at all,' says I, 'and I don't think a Noah's ark set on a table marked up in squares is much of an ornament, anyhow.'

"I didn't say any more. I jest marched out and left the presents. But Jane she came runnin' after me. 'Sophia,' says she—and she spoke as if she was sort of scared. She never had much spunk, for all she looks so up an' comin'—'Sophia,' says she, 'I thought she'd like it. I thought—'

"'No, you didn't, Jane Crocker,' says I. 'You jest thought what you'd like to give, and not what she'd like to have.'

"'What would she like to have?' says she, and she was 'most cryin'. 'I'll get her anything she wants, if you'll jest tell me, Sophia.'

"'I ain't goin' to tell you, Jane,' says I, but I spoke softer, for I saw that she meant well, after all,—'I ain't goin' to tell you. You jest put yourself in her place; you make believe you was a poor young girl goin' to get married, and you think over what little the poor child has got now and what she has to set alongside *new* things, and you kind of study it out for yourself,' says I. And then I jest said good-by, though she kept callin' after me, and I run out and climbed in the sleigh and tucked myself in and drove off.

"The very next day Jane Crocker sent Flora a beautiful new carpet for the front chamber, and a rug to go with it. She knew Flora was goin' to have the front chamber fixed up when she got married; she'd heard me say so; and the carpet was all worn out.

"Well, I kept right on. I carried back Cousin Abby Adkins's white silk shawl, and she acted awful mad; but she thought better of it as I was goin' out to the sleigh, and she called after me to know what Flora wanted, and I told her jest what I had Jane Crocker. And I carried back Minerva Saunders's boltin'-cloth sofa-pillow, and she was more astonished than anything else—she was real good-natured. You know how easy she is. She jest laughed after she'd got over bein' astonished. 'Why,' says she, 'I don't know but it *is* kind of silly, now I come to think of it. I declare I clean forgot you didn't have a sofa in the parlor. When I've been in there I've been so took up seein' you and Flora, Sophia, that I never took any account at all of the furniture.'

"So I went away from there feelin' real good, and the next day but one there come a nice hair-cloth sofa for Flora to put in the parlor.

"Then I took back Minnie Harris's fire-set, and she acted kind of dazed. 'Why, don't you think it's handsome?' says she. You know she's a young thing, younger than Flora. She's always called me Aunt Sophia, too. 'Why, Aunt Sophia,' says she, 'didn't Flora think it was handsome?'

"'Handsome enough, child,' says I, and I couldn't help laughin' myself, she looked like sech a baby,—'handsome enough, but what did you think Flora was goin' to do with a poker and tongs to poke a fire, when there ain't any fire to poke?'

"Then Minnie she sort of giggled. 'Why, sure enough, Aunt Sophia,' says she. 'I never thought of that.'

"'Where did you think she would put them?' says I. 'On the parlor mantel-shelf for ornaments?'

"Then Minnie she laughed sort of hysterical. 'Give 'em right here, Aunt Sophia,' says she.

"The next day she sent a clock—that wasn't much account, though it was real pretty; it won't go long at a time,—but it looks nice on the parlor shelf, and it was so much better than the poker and tongs that I didn't say anything. It takes sense to give a present, and Minnie Harris never had a mite, though she's a pretty little thing.

"Then I took home Lizzie Starkwether's bed-shoes, and she took it the worst of all.

"'Don't they fit?' says she.

"'Fit well 'nough,' says I. 'We don't want 'em.'

"'I'd like to know why not,' says she.

"'Because you've given us a pair every Christmas for three years,' says I, 'and I've told you we never wear bed-shoes; and even if we did wear 'em,' says I, 'we couldn't have worn out the others to save our lives. When we go to bed, we go to sleep,' says I. 'We don't travel round to wear out shoes. We've got two pairs apiece laid away,' says I, 'and I think you'd better give these to somebody that wants 'em—mebbe somebody that you've been givin' mittens to for three years, that don't wear mittens.'

"Well, she was hoppin', but she got over it, too; and I guess she did some thinkin', for in a week came the prettiest mittens for each of us I ever laid eyes on, and Minerva herself came over and called, and thanked Flora for her apron as sweet as pie.

"Well, I went to all the others in town, and then I started for Ayres, and carried back the dewdab to Herbert's aunt Harriet Morse. I hated to do that, for I didn't know her very well; but I went, and she was real nice. She made me drink a cup of tea and eat a slice of her cake, and she thanked me for comin'. She said she didn't know what young girls liked, and she had an idea that they cared more about something to dress up in than anything else, even if they didn't have a great deal to do with, and she had ought to have known better than to send such a silly thing. She spoke real kind about Herbert, and hoped he could get married before long; and the next day she sent Flora a pair of beautiful blankets, and now she's given Flora all her bed linen and towels for a weddin'-present. I heated up my soapstone in her kitchen oven and started for home. It was almost dark, and snowin' quite hard, and she said she hated to have me go, but I said I didn't mind. I was goin' to stop at Herbert's uncle Hiram's on my way home. You know he lives in Leviston, half-way from Ayres.

"When I got there it was snowin' hard, comin' real thick.

"I drew up at the front gate and hitched the horse, and waded through the snow to the front door and rung the bell; and Uncle Hiram's housekeeper came to the door. She is a sort of cousin of his—a widow woman from Ayres. I don't know as you know who she is. She's a dreadful lackada'sical woman, kind of pretty, long-faced and slopin'-shouldered, and she speaks kind of slow and sweet. I asked if Mr. Hiram Snell was in, and she said she guessed so, and asked me in, and showed me into the sittin'-room, which was furnished rich; but it was awful dirty and needed dustin'. I guess she ain't much of a housekeeper. Uncle Hiram was in the sittin'-room, smokin' a pipe and readin'. You know Hiram Snell. He's kind of gruff-spoken, but he ain't bad-meanin'. It's more because he's kind of blunderin' about little things, like most men; ain't got a small enough grip to fit 'em. Well, he stood up when I come in. He knew me by sight, and I said who I was—that I was aunt to Flora Bell that his nephew Herbert Bennet was goin' to marry; and he asked me to sit down, but I said I couldn't because I had to drive a matter of three miles to get home, and it was snowin' so hard. Then I out with that little fool card-case, and I said I'd brought it back.

"'What's the matter? Ain't it good enough?' says he, real short. He's got real shaggy eyebrows, an' I tell you his eyes looked fierce under 'em.

"'Too good,' says I. 'Flora she ain't got anything good enough to go with it. This card-case can't be carried by a woman unless she has a handsome silk dress, and fine white kid gloves, and a sealskin sacque, and a hat with an ostrich feather,' says I.

"'Do you want me to give her all those things to go with the card-case?' says he, kind of sarcastic.

"'If you did, they'd come back quicker than you could say Jack Robinson,' says I, for I was gettin' mad myself.

"But all of a sudden he burst right out laughin'. 'Well,' says he, 'you've got horse-sense, an' that's more than I can say of most women.' Then he takes the card-case and he looks hard at it. 'Why, Mrs. Pendergrass said she'd be sure to like it!' says he. 'Said she'd got one for Herbert's mother last year. Mrs. Pendergrass buys all my Christmas presents for me. I don't make many.'

"'I shouldn't think you'd better if you can't get more sensible ones to send,' says I. I knew I was saucy, but he was kind of smilin', and I laughed when I said it, though I meant it all the same.

"'Why, weren't Herbert's all right?' says he.

"'Right?' says I. 'Do you know what he had last year?'

"'No, I don't,' says he.

"'Well, last year you sent him a silver ash-tray, and his mother a card-case, and this year he had a silver cigarette-case, and his mother a cut-glass wine-set.'

"'Well?'

"'Nothin', only Herbert never smokes, and his mother hasn't got any visitin'-cards, and she don't have much wine, I guess.'

"Hiram Snell laughed again. 'Well, I left it all to Mrs. Pendergrass,' says he. 'I never thought she had brains to spare, but then I never thought it took brains to buy Christmas presents.'

"'It does,' says I,—'brains and consider'ble love for the folks you are buyin' for.'

"'Christmas is tomfoolery, anyhow,' says he.

"'That's as you look at it,' says I.

"He stood eyin' me sort of gruff, and yet as if he were sort of tickled at the same time. 'Well,' says he, finally, 'you've brought this fool thing back. Now what shall I give your niece instead?'

"'I don't go round beggin' for presents,' says I.

"'How the devil am I going to get anything that she'll like any better if I don't know?' says he. 'And Mrs. Pendergrass can't help me out any. You've got to say something.'

"'I sha'n't,' says I, real set. 'You ain't no call to give my niece anything, anyway; you ain't no call to give her anything she wants, and you certainly ain't no call to give her anything she don't want.'

"'You don't believe in keepin' presents you don't want?'

"'No,' says I, 'I don't—and thankin' folks for 'em as if you liked 'em. It's hypocrisy.'

"He kind of grunted, and laughed again.

"'It don't make any odds about Flora,' says I; 'and as for your nephew and your sister, you know about them and what they want as well as I do, or you'd ought to. I ain't goin' to tell you.'

"'So Maria hasn't got any cards, and Herbert don't smoke,' says he, and he grinned as if it was awful funny.

"Well, I thought it was time for me to be goin', and jest then Mrs. Pendergrass came in with a lighted lamp. It had darkened all of a sudden, and I could hear the sleet on the window, and there I had three miles to drive.

"So I started, and Hiram Snell he followed me to the door. He seemed sort of anxious about my goin' out in the storm, and come out himself through all the snow, and unhitched my horse and held him till I got nicely tucked in the sleigh. Then jest as I gathered up the reins, he says, speakin' up loud against the wind, "'When is Herbert and your niece goin' to get married?'

"'When Herbert gets enough money to buy a piece of land and some stock and start a milk route,' says I. Then off I goes."

Sophia paused for a climax. Her guests were listening, breathless.

"Well, what did he give Herbert?" asked Mrs. Cutting.

"He gave him three thousand dollars to buy that land and some cows and put up a barn," said Sophia, and her audience drew a long, simultaneous breath.

"That was great," said Eunice.

"And he's made Flora a wedding-present of five shares in the Ayres street-railroad stock, so she should have a little spendin'-money," said Sophia.

"I call him a pretty generous man," said Abby Dodd.

"Generous enough," said Sophia Lane, "only he didn't know how to steer his generosity."

The guests rose; they were looking somewhat uncomfortable and embarrassed. Sophia went into the bedroom to get their wraps, letting a breath of ice into the sitting-room. While she was gone the guests conferred hastily with one another.

When she returned, Mrs. Cutting faced her, not unamiably, but confusedly. "Now look here, Sophia Lane," said she, "I want you to speak right out. You needn't hesitate. We all want the truth. Is—anything the matter with our presents we brought to-day?"

"Use your own jedgment," replied Sophia Lane.

"Where are those presents we brought?" asked Mrs. Cutting. She and her daughters all looked sober and doubtful, but not precisely angry.

"They are in the parlor," replied Sophia.

"Suppose you get them," said Mrs. Cutting.

When Sophia returned with the alcohol-lamp and afternoon-tea kettle, the finger-bowls and the doilies, the guests had on their wraps. Abby Dodd and Eunice at once went about tying up the presents. Mrs. Cutting looked on. Sophia got her little shawl and hood. She was going out to the barn to assist her guests in getting their horse out.

"Has Flora got any dishes?" asked Mrs. Cutting, thoughtfully.

"No, she hasn't got anything but her mother's china tea-set," replied Sophia. "She hasn't got any good dishes for common use."

"No dinner-set?"

"No; mine are about used up, and I've been careful with 'em too."

Mrs. Cutting considered a minute longer. "Has she got some good tumblers?" she asked.

"No, she hasn't. We haven't any too many tumblers in the house."

"How is she off for napkins?" asked Eunice, tying up her doilies.

"She ain't any too well off. She's had a dozen give her, and that's all."

The guests, laden with the slighted wedding-gifts, followed Sophia through the house, the kitchen, and the clean, cold wood-shed to the barn. Sophia slid back the heavy doors.

"Well, good-by, Sophia," said Mrs. Cutting. "We've had a nice time, and we've enjoyed seeing Flora's presents."

"Yes, so have I," said Eunice.

"I think she's fared real well," said Abby.

"Yes, she has," said Sophia.

"We shall be over in good season," said Eunice.

"Yes, we shall," assented Abby.

Sophia untied the horse, which had been fastened to a ring beside the door; still the guests did not move to get into the sleigh. A curious air of constraint was over them. Sophia also looked constrained and troubled. Her poor faithful face peering from the folds of her gray wool hood was defiant and firm, but still anxious. She looked at Mrs. Cutting, and the two women's eyes met; there was a certain wistfulness in Sophia's.

"I think a good deal of Flora," said she, and there was a hint of apology in her tone.

Simultaneously the three women moved upon Sophia, their faces cleared; lovely expressions of sympathy and kindly understanding appeared upon them.

"Good-by, Sophia," said Mrs. Cutting, and kissed her.

"Good-by, Cousin Sophia," said the daughters, and they also kissed her.

When they drove out of the snowy yard, three smiling faces turned back for a last greeting to Sophia. She slid together the heavy barn doors. She was smiling happily, though there were tears in her eyes.

"Everybody in this world means to be pretty good to other folks," she muttered to herself, "and when they ain't, it ain't always their fault; sometimes it's other folks'."

The Gift of Love

Woman's Home Companion, December 1906, 21–22, 73

"I SORT OF hate to leave you alone, Caroline," said Julia.

Caroline, fair and delicate, with a middle-aged fairness and delicacy as fine in their way as those of youth, looked up at her sister with her faint, gentle smile. She never smiled broadly, and almost never laughed. She was one of those women in whom extreme tenderness and sentiment exclude the sense of the ridiculous. There is always in humor at least a faint suggestion of cruelty, and a laugh and a jeer are nearly related. Caroline Willis had never in her whole life seen anything ridiculous in other people, she was so tenderly inclined toward all. She had always, for instance, been disposed to weep rather than laugh when she had seen anyone fall down.

"I don't mind in the least being left alone," she said to her sister.

"You don't seem to mind much of anything," returned Julia, and her tone was inexplicably cross.

"I haven't much to complain of with all you do for me," replied Caroline, "I should be very wicked to complain."

"I don't see as you have either," said Julia, and again her tone was cross. "Here you have a good home and everything you need, and if I do say it as shouldn't, I have always looked out for you more as if I had been your mother than your sister."

"Yes, you always have," said Caroline lovingly. She was sitting in a soft-cushioned rocking-chair beside a window, on the sill of which stood a row of blooming plants, mostly geraniums. The earthen pots which held the plants were carefully covered with green crêpe paper. Caroline had some embroidery work in her hands. She was embroidering a wreath of violets on a centerpiece of white linen for a Christmas present.

"Still," said Julia, "I sort of hate to leave you alone when you have such a cold."

"I think my cold is much better," said Caroline, "and it isn't as if you were going far, or were to be away long."

"I know it," assented Julia, "and I don't honestly see how I can get out of it, that's a fact."

"Of course you can't."

"Here I've been one of the head ones about getting up the tree, and this afternoon, when there is so much to be done, to back out wouldn't seem just right."

"Of course you must go," said Caroline, "and I don't mind a bit. I shall sit here and work on my centerpiece until you get back."

"Mind, you don't stir out of this warm room."

"No, I won't, Julia."

"Don't you dare step foot out in the kitchen to get supper. I shall be back by half-past five at the very latest, and there isn't much to do to get supper to-night anyway. I thought we would have some cream toast. I can toast the bread in here."

"Yes, you can."

"Mind, you don't stir."

"No, I won't; honest, Julia."

Julia was a short, stout woman with a firm, florid face. She had been called pretty in her youth, and was considered good-looking now, although by some the character showing in her face was esteemed too imperative. She tied on her bonnet before the old-fashioned looking-glass which hung between the sitting-room windows, repeated yet again her instructions to her sister, and went out. Caroline watched her trudging down the snowy road, then she took another stitch on her embroidery with a gentle sigh, not so much of sadness as of acquiescence.

When Julia entered the church vestry redolent with the spicy fragrance of evergreens and fir balsam, one girl whispered to another, "Oh, dear! here comes Miss Julia Willis, and now the bossing begins."

"She can't boss *me* very much," returned the other girl, who had a face of Julia's own type; "I don't have much to say to her, nor she to me. She knows I don't like her. I have never forgiven her for what she did about my brother, though it all happened when I was nothing but a child, and I can hardly remember it."

"I suppose she *did* break off the match between your brother John and her sister Caroline," said the other girl.

"Break it off! I should say she did, and poor John went away to California, and father died without seeing him again, and poor mother has never got over it. Sometimes I think it will shorten her life. I know it shortened father's."

"Does your brother write home?"

"Oh, yes, he writes every week as regular as clockwork. He has done splendidly out there, and he does everything for mother and me. He sends us lots of money and other things, but that doesn't make up to poor mother for losing her only son. I know she dwells on it, and thinks she will die without seeing him, the way father did." The girl took up a sprig of evergreen and tied it to another with a vicious jerk. Her brown eyes cast a sidelong glance of dislike at Julia Willis. "Just hear the way she bosses!" she said. "She thinks she owns this whole church; she always did. There's no sense in putting up that evergreen the way she is telling them to. It looked twice as pretty the way it was before, and she has made them pull it all down."

"That's so," said the other girl.

Julia's rather low, but hard voice of command seemed to fill the whole vestry. Two boys on a step-ladder were anxiously altering the arrangement of some garlands over the arch which surmounted the platform on which the Christmas-tree was to stand. Julia was in her element. There was about her something fairly splendid and dominant, on a small scale. The little tuft of velvet roses and the loop of velvet ribbon on her bonnet were as erect as a bird's crest. "People have to be right on the spot to be sure things are done the way they ought to be," she remarked in a triumphant voice to a woman beside her. The woman was a sort of disciple of hers. Julia had a following of weaker feminine souls in the village, who seemed to base their very ideas upon hers.

"I never saw anything like the way they were putting it up," said Julia. "I guess it's lucky I came. But I really didn't know how I was going to. I didn't like to leave Caroline."

"How is Caroline?" asked the other woman, who was tall and slender, and had a way of inclining toward the person whom she was addressing.

"I think she is a little better, but she has a pretty hard cold, and I am always afraid of pneumonia. I don't think Caroline's lungs are any too strong," replied Julia.

"Have you had a doctor?"

"Doctor? no! I always use a medicine which mother used to make out of herbs and rum and molasses. Then I put lard and ginger on her chest at night. I don't think much of doctors!" Julia sniffed in a way she had when she said "doctors." It expressed infinite contempt. The other woman sniffed also, although more mildly. "I guess you are about right," said she.

The two young girls, who were covertly watching them, noticed the sniffs. "See them turn up their noses!" said one. "Mrs. Watson is just about as bad as Miss Willis."

"Yes, she is. But I do think Miss Caroline Willis is lovely. I don't wonder your brother fell in love with her."

"He set his life by her."

"Well, I don't wonder."

"She's just as sweet as she can be; and her whole life and my brother's have been ruined just by that woman's selfishness. I declare! sometimes when I look at Miss Julia Willis and think what she has done I feel fairly wicked. The idea of spoiling two lives, to say nothing of poor mother's and father's, for the sake of one!"

"Miss Julia wasn't in love with your brother?"

"In love with him? No! She was never in love with anyone but herself. She just didn't want Caroline to get married and go off and leave her. I guess it wouldn't have hurt her to live alone. I guess nobody would have molested her." The girl gave a fairly malevolent glance at Julia.

"Your brother must have fairly worshiped her sister," the other girl observed with a sentimental sigh.

In the meantime while Julia was superintending—"bossing," as the irreverent young girls called it—the Christmas decorations in the church vestry, Caroline continued to sit by herself at the window embroidering. She was in a faintly pretty room. There were pieces of fine old mahogany, but the paper and carpet were faded, and so were the handworked roses on the chairs and footstools. On the table between the windows stood a lamp hung about with prisms which caught the afternoon sunlight and sent rainbows wavering over the dull elegance of the room. Beside the lamp books were carefully arranged—old autograph albums and volumes of poetry. Just before Caroline was one book bound in red and gold upon which she occasionally cast a glance. The "brother John," of whom the young girls had talked had given it to her. It was the one gift that she had kept. There had been others—a pearl spray, a rosewood work-box, a shell comb and various other pretty things, but she had returned all these gifts when she was bidden to do so by Julia. But somehow Julia had overlooked the book; Julia did not read much. Caroline was quite aware, when she dusted that red and gold book every day, that Julia had forgotten whence it came. She felt guilty, but she could not give it up. Besides, now, it was too late. It would be ridiculous to send that book of a by-gone age of sentiment, entitled "The Gift of Love" and filled with a compilation of sentimental tales and poems, with some fine steel engravings, to its donor in California. Very probably he too had forgotten all about the poor little book. That reflection used always to sting Caroline, but she bore the sting gently as she bore everything.

Caroline was still very pretty.

That afternoon as she sat embroidering she wore a violet-colored gown of soft wool, and her blue eyes took on the color of the gown. Her blonde hair was very thick and glossy. She had always taken great care of her hair. Julia did not know why she brushed it so faithfully every night and morning, but it was because John Leavitt, the old lover of her youth, had admired it. She could hear his young ardent voice after all these years—"There isn't a girl in the whole village with such beautiful hair as yours, Caroline." She still arranged it in the way which he had liked, although it was long out of fashion. However, it suited her thin, delicate face; the loose, soft knot of hair at the back, and the two soft curls on each side shading her faintly pink cheeks. Julia wore her own hair in a hard aggressive pompadour. Although not in the least vain, she had a keen eye to the race, and was not to be left behind in any respect if she knew it. "I should think you would do up your hair like other folks, Caroline," she told her sister sometimes. "You would look ten years younger."

"I like it better this way," Caroline would reply, meekly.

"Well, have your own way, you always *were* set," Julia would answer; "but it does seem to me that with such hair as yours anybody would rather keep up to the times. Your hair is a good deal nicer than mine, but the way you do it up nobody would think so." Julia's hair was an iron gray, and so thin that she was obliged to wear a rat under her firm pompadour.

Caroline had a little girlish trick of putting up one slender white hand to see if her knot of hair was secure and her curls were properly adjusted. She had just done so, although she was alone, and had resumed her needle when somebody passed the window. She looked and saw a man, a stranger. Her heart gave a little leap. She thought of a tramp, but to her swift glimpse the man did not look like a tramp. Then there came a ring at the door. Caroline was all alone in the house. There was no maid. Caroline was very timid. It occurred to her to hide, not to answer the ring at all. Then she reflected that the man had probably seen her, and visions of doors or windows being forced flashed across her mind. She had a fertile imagination for ill.

The bell rang a second time, and Caroline laid her work on the table, rose, shook out her violet skirts carefully and went to the door. She had to traverse the length of an icy entry, and her sister's parting injunction came to her mind. "But I didn't have time to get a shawl," she said to herself. She further reflected that the man was probably a book-agent, and Julia need never know anything about it. Caroline, through concealing her sorrows, had acquired the habit of harmless concealments in other directions. She was moreover afraid of Julia, and the mere anticipation of a chiding from her was enough to make her ill. She unlocked the front door, feeling as she did so that she ran a frightful risk, but when it was open, so firmly had the conviction of the book-agent seized upon her, that she said directly, "We don't care to buy any books to-day, thank you."

But the man laughed. "Books?" said he, "I haven't any books. Don't you remember me, Caroline?" Then Caroline looked up in the man's face, and her own grew white. It was an awful experience that had come to her. Her old lover had in reality returned, and she had not known his face at once. It looked strange to her. The boy who took his mad flight westward because of his rejected love, had a smooth pink and white face like a girl, he was slim. This man was portly and wore a thick, gray beard. His face above his beard was as pale as Caroline's.

"You don't mean to say that you have forgotten me, Caroline?" he asked.

Caroline continued to stare at him, and suddenly a wonderful inner light seemed to possess her. She saw what had been through what was. She saw the boy in the man. She had the vision of an angel for that which was beneath all externals. She saw John Leavitt in the spirit, as he really was; the true man in him, who had held her in his heart all his life. Her face flushed pink, then paled again, and John caught her in his arms. "For the Lord's sake, let us go in the house, or we'll have all the neighbors at the windows," he said with that laugh of his which she remembered so well, and which was still the laugh of a boy, and they passed through the long lane of freezing entry to the warm sitting-room. "I knew I would find you alone, dear," he said as they went. "I knew *she*" (he placed an emphasis both of humor and indignation on the she) "had gone to the vestry."

He sat down and gathered Caroline in his arms, and she hid her face on his shoulder. He stroked her hair fondly. "Just the same beautiful hair," said he, "and only think how gray I have grown."

Caroline said nothing. She was faint and dizzy with it all.

"Poor little girl," John said, leaning his head down close to hers. "I suppose I was a brute to come in so suddenly and surprise you so, but mother said *she* was gone, and I couldn't resist the temptation. Oh, Caroline! God alone knows how afraid I was I should come back and find you married to some other man! I don't dare think of what I might have done."

A quiver of delight came over Caroline. Just as she had recognized the true spiritual self in John Leavitt in spite of the external changes the years had brought about, he recognized the true spiritual self which endured despite her faded cheeks. She was in fact just the same young girl whom John Leavitt had held in his arms so many years before. Each saw the other, as it were, in a looking-glass of true love. "I was afraid you were married," she whispered after a while.

"Did you think I ever could marry anybody except you?" he asked in return, "did you?"

"I didn't know."

"Yes, you did know. You knew I never could even *think* of any other woman as my wife except you."

And it directly seemed to Caroline that he was right. That she did know that he never could. An ineffable bliss took possession of her. The weight of years had rolled from her heart, and the rebound made it lighter than it had ever been in her distant youth. She had never been so happy. She was on a very pinnacle of happiness.

"When did you come?" she whispered.

"I got home about half an hour ago. Then I came right over here." Then after a pause, "Caroline—"

"What, John?"

"This time, I am not going to take no for an answer. This time, sister or no sister, you must listen to me."

"It would kill Julia," said Caroline, and she seemed to slip from her height of happiness. "It would kill her, John."

"Let it kill her then," said John, with his mouth set. "I have had just about all of this I propose to stand."

"She is my sister," said Caroline.

"I don't care if she is," said John. "This time you must listen to me instead of her. We will live right here in the village. I have sold out where I was. You can see her often, but I rather think it wouldn't do for us all to try to live together."

"I can't leave Julia all alone after all these years," sobbed Caroline.

"Now, don't cry, dear. I didn't think Julia was afraid of anything, but if she is, I will hire a girl to stay here with her. I have come home with a lot of money, Caroline, though God knows the money is nothing compared with the hope of having you with me at last. I am going to build a new house, just the way you like it. But I will hire a good girl to stay with Julia if she is timid."

"Oh, it isn't that," sobbed Caroline. "I don't know as she is so very timid, but—"

"But what, my own dear?"

"Oh, John, how can I leave my only sister, the only sister I've got, all alone?"

"She won't be alone if she has a girl, dear."

"Yes, she will in one way. She will be all alone as far as her very own are concerned. Oh, John, I don't believe Julia would ever get married and go off and leave me."

"Did she ever have a chance, tell me that?" asked John brutally.

"Of course she has had chances, every woman has," replied Caroline, fibbing for the sake of her sister.

"He must have been a pretty brave man, then," returned John simply, "braver than I am. I confess it would take more courage than I've got to marry Julia, and I haven't been called behindhand in bravery where I've been either."

"I can't go and leave her alone after all these years, when she's been so good to me. You don't know how good she has been to me, John, and I haven't been very well, and a deal of care."

"Poor dear," said John. "Well, I am going to take care of you now. You'll be well enough when you are happy. Confess, you haven't been any too happy, Caroline."

"I couldn't help thinking of what might have been," admitted Caroline, and she hid her flushed face against John's rough coat.

"Couldn't help it? Good Lord, I should think not!" said John. "Hasn't that been at the bottom of my heart through thick and thin? No matter what I have been doing—and I have hustled, I tell you that, dear—that thought has never for one minute left me. I have never had you one minute out of mind, and here you are after all these years, just the same little girl."

"Oh, no, John."

"Yes, you are I tell you. Don't you suppose I've got eyes and can see?" John held off Caroline's blushing face, and looked at it with the most loyal devotion in the world; that devotion of him who loves through years of change and absence, and it was actually for him as if he saw the same little girl-face which he had left. "I didn't expect to find you looking this way," he said. "I had made up my mind to find you changed, and to love you just the same, but you are not changed at all."

"Oh, yes, John."

"No, you are not, I tell you." He fondled with reverent, tender fingers one of the soft curls that shaded her face. "I didn't know but you would have one of those great bumps on top of your head that girls wear nowadays," said he, "but it is all just the same. You have had sense enough to stick to a pretty way of doing up your hair, no matter how other girls did theirs."

"I remembered you liked it this way," said Caroline.

"Of course you did. Caroline, I have a beautiful ring for you at home. I didn't bring it. I didn't quite dare to. I said to myself, maybe when she sees me she won't think so much of me as she used to. I know I have grown stout and gray."

"You are a great deal better looking than when you were a boy," said Caroline; then she added inconsistently, "you look just the same to me as you always did," for at that moment, the gray hairs on her faithful lover's head actually appeared gilded, and his stoutness became the graceful litheness of youth.

"Nonsense!" said John Leavitt, "I have changed, but if I don't seem changed to you, your eyes are the only looking-glass I care about in the world. I wonder what kind of a house you would like."

Then Caroline again remembered Julia. "Oh, John, I can't leave my sister," she sobbed faintly.

"Nonsense, you've got to. We have had our lives spoiled long enough."

"I can't."

"You must!"

Suddenly Caroline slipped from John's knees in an absolute frenzy of terror. Her face was pale. If there had been a wild lion on her track, she could not have looked more frightened. "Oh," she whispered, "she's coming, now."

"Nonsense, she can't be through her work of bossing the Christmas-tree."

"Yes, she said she shouldn't stay late, because she didn't want to leave me alone, and it's after five. That's Julia crossing the street!"

John Leavitt folded his arms across his broad chest coolly. "Let her come," said he.

"Oh, John, I can't, I can't!"

"You can't what, dear?"

"She is crossing the street. I can't have her come in and find you sitting here. I can't!"

"It might as well come first as last, dear."

"It can never come. I can't leave her, and—and—I can't have her come in and find you sitting here. I—I haven't strength enough to stand it, John."

It was quite true that Caroline did not look as if she had much strength. She was white and stood trembling before John, a piteous little figure under the tyranny and terror of a lifetime. John looked at her half amusedly, half pityingly. "Well, what do you want me to do, dear?" he asked. "I can't get out now without Julia's spotting me, that is out of the question. Come Caroline, you are not afraid of Julia with me here to take care of you? What on earth can she do to you?"

"I am—afraid."

"Well, what shall I do?"

Caroline looked around her wildly. By some freak of village architecture, the long, icy cold pantry opened, as in many other houses, out of the sitting-room instead of the kitchen. Caroline looked at the pantry door. "Oh John, go into the pantry," she begged, "go, go!"

John rose, laughing, and made one stride across the room into the pantry. He was just in time, for at that moment Julia entered, muffled in her warm winter coat and fur cape. "It feels like snow out," she said. That was what she said first. Then she sniffed. "Seems to me I smell something dreadful queer," she said.

"Maybe it's the geraniums," faltered Caroline.

"Geraniums! Those geraniums don't have any smell at all. Caroline Willis! what is the matter with you? Don't you feel so well?"

"I feel a good deal better; I do, honest, Julia."

"You look just as white as a sheet. You don't look nearly as well as when I went away. Are you sure you haven't got a pain in your lungs?"

"I can breathe real deep down. I do feel better, Julia."

"Well, you don't look nearly so well." Julia began removing her outer wraps, still with anxious eyes on her sister, and she sniffed again. "Queer, what is it I smell?" said she.

"Maybe it's something from outside."

"Outside with the windows shut down tight? I should think you were crazy!"

Caroline, who was not as a rule at all subtle, was seized with an inspiration. "I can smell the fir balsam on your clothes," said she, "real strong."

That diverted Julia for the time from the odor of tobacco from the clothes of John Leavitt that had permeated the room. "Well, I suppose you do," said she; "you notice it almost before you open the vestry door. It seems as if it was stronger than usual this year."

"Maybe the fir balsam is sweeter some years than others," remarked Caroline, following up her advantage.

"Maybe it is," said Julia, taking off her wraps, and going with them into the entry. "It's queer" she said, returning "but I can smell that same smell out in the entry. The baker-boy didn't come here by the front door, the way I've told him not to, did he Caroline?"

"No."

"I wouldn't have had you go out in that entry for anything, let alone his impudence in coming to the front door; it's as cold as the north pole out there." Julia looked at the clock. "Mercy! it's half-past five," said she, "I must get supper."

Caroline trembled. Julia looked sharply at her. "I don't care what you say," she declared, "you look about ready to drop."

"I am all right," Caroline replied faintly.

"You don't look all right. Well, maybe you'll feel better after you've had a good hot cup of tea."

Caroline reflected quickly that the tea was out in the kitchen closet, and not in the long pantry where John Leavitt was concealed.

"I guess I'll make some cream toast, too," said Julia, and Caroline reflected that the bread jar was in the kitchen closet.

"Yes, I guess I would relish some cream toast," said she. But her heart sank when Julia said she would have some peach preserve with the toast, because the preserves were kept in the sitting-room pantry.

"Somehow I don't feel a mite like peach preserves," said she faintly.

"Well, we'll have pear then," said Julia in a magisterial voice, and Caroline's heart sank again, because the pear preserve was also in the sitting-room pantry.

"I don't care myself if we don't have *any* preserves," said she in a feeble voice.

"Well, I am going to have some, whether or no," said Julia. "I wouldn't give a cent for cream toast without preserves, and I guess you'll eat some when it's set before you. It'll be good for your cold. I am going to have some apple pie, too. I'll warm it while I'm toasting the bread. I guess I'll go out now, and see to getting the bread cut."

The apple pie also was in the sitting-room pantry. Caroline felt as if she were going to faint, but she knew that she must not. She held on to herself with a resolute will until Julia returned from the kitchen. "I guess I may as well get that apple pie in the oven now," said she, "it may be frozen," and she made toward the pantry door. Then Caroline grew fairly desperate. She did something for which she never fairly forgave herself. She resorted to deception; at least it was almost deception, to say the least, and she had never in her whole life been deceptive. Just as Julia put out her hand toward the latch of the pantry door, she began to cough. It was easy enough, for she had in fact a hard cold, a bronchial cold. She had been restraining her cough all day, now she bent over and coughed, and coughed. It was almost as if she had the croup. Julia took a step away from the pantry door and stood regarding her with an odd expression; something between anxiety and severity. She was evidently worried almost to death, but there was a certain anger withal that her sister should cough so.

"There is no use talking any longer," said she. "I've doctored you all I know how, and now I'm going to call somebody else in. If you have pneumonia, I don't mean to have myself to blame. I don't think much of Doctor Edgham; never did, but I'm going to call him in anyhow. You haven't coughed since you had your cold the way you are coughing now."

Julia made a stride toward the entry where she had deposited her wraps. Caroline continued to cough. Indeed it was quite true that now she could not stop. Julia thrust her arms into the sleeves of her coat. "I'd cough down to the cellar while I was about it, if I were you," said she, and again her voice was full of the utmost love and anxiety, and yet with a certain anger. She tied the strings of her bonnet with a jerk.

"I hate to have you go," Caroline managed to wheeze out, and that was hypocritical, and later on she prayed to be forgiven. Then she continued to cough while Julia went out of the door, closing it after her with a bang. Immediately after the door closed the pantry door opened and John Leavitt appeared. He looked anxious, for he had not altogether understood Caroline's maneuvers.

Caroline could not stop coughing immediately, but she cast a reassuring glance at John. "It's—not—so bad—as it sounds," she gasped out presently. "But if—Julia hadn't gone—she, she—would have gone into the—pantry and—found—you." "Oh," said John, but he still regarded Caroline with loving concern.

She managed to stop coughing. "I know I was wicked," she said, "but I let the cough—come, when I suppose I might, if I had tried hard, have—stopped it, for I couldn't have Julia go in the pantry, and find you."

John regarded her a moment, then he grinned. "Well," he said, "I don't know what Julia would have done if she had come into the pantry and found me, that's a fact."

"You had better go now, I guess," Caroline said anxiously. "It isn't far to the doctor's, and she may be right back."

"Well, I am coming again, and she has got to make up her mind to it," said John.

Caroline began to weep again. "Oh dear," she said, half strangled between her sobs and her cough. "I never can leave her, I never can. You don't know how good she has been to me, you don't John."

"She hasn't been any better to you than I would have been if I had been given the chance," said John.

"I can't leave her."

"Do you mean to say that you really will give me up again on account of your sister?" asked John sternly.

"I've got to; I can't help it. Oh, John!"

John stood looking at Caroline for a moment. "You can't care very much for me after all, then," he said.

"Oh, John!"

"You can't. Well, then if you won't leave her, you won't. I am not going down on my knees to any woman, especially after all these years, and, and—the lonely life I've led. Good-by Caroline."

John Leavitt went out without another word. Caroline looked dully out of the window, and saw him going down the road. She felt benumbed. She felt too benumbed even to bemoan herself over her hard fate. It seemed, after John had gone out of sight, almost incredible that he had been there at all. After a while she saw the doctor's buggy come in sight. He was bringing Julia back with him. When he came in she answered his questions mechanically. She watched him prepare some medicines for her, still with the same numbness. When the doctor went, Julia followed him into the entry, and she heard the dull murmur of their voices without the slightest curiosity. When Julia reëntered the room she had an air of forced jocularity. She went about briskly getting supper. "The doctor says your cold is all on the bronchial tubes," said she cheerfully. "He says you will be all right in a few days."

Caroline was too sunken in concealed misery that John had been there and had gone away again forever to attempt any reply. She sat still, looking at the frozen landscape fast disappearing in the night. "After a while it will be over for me, just as this day will be over for the world," thought she, "and then it will not matter whether it has been a winter or a summer day."

Julia kept glancing at her as she set the table. Since Caroline had been ill with a cold, they had eaten in the sitting-room, because it was warmer. "What is the matter with you, you don't act half alive?" said she.

"Nothing," replied Caroline gently.

Julia went to the secretary, and opened the top drawer. Then she came with a little box in her hand to Caroline. "Here," said she, "I meant to have hung this on the tree for you, but now you can't go, you may as well have it now."

"Thank you, sister," said Caroline. She tried to look pleased as she opened the little box. It held a little pin set with pearls.

"I thought you would like it; you didn't have a real nice pin," Julia said, and there was a wistful accent in her voice.

"I do like it, and it is lovely, Julia," said Caroline.

Caroline remembered a brooch; one of John Leavitt's returned presents. That had been a cluster of pearl grapes with gold leaves, on onyx, and even this gift which Julia had planned for her pleasure hurt her.

After supper, Julia carried away the dishes, and put everything in order; then she brought her wraps in from the hall. Caroline looked at her with a dull surprise. "Now, Caroline," said Julia, "I am going out again. I've got to, but I am not going far, and I shall not be long. I will lock the front door, and take the key. You won't be afraid?"

"No," replied Caroline meekly, "I won't be afraid, Julia."

Julia stood looking at her after she had on her wraps. Her strong face worked strangely under the crest of velvet roses. "I am going to bring your Christmas present, Caroline," said she.

"Why you have given it to me."

"This is another," said Julia, and her voice had never been more imperious. Then she went out.

Caroline, left alone, continued to sit in her rocking-chair. After a while tears commenced to roll slowly down her delicate cheeks. She did not weep convulsively. She was conscious of no anger or rebellion against fate or her sister, who had been in a way her fate, but she was realizing the sharp pain in her heart; it had been benumbed at first.

Julia was not gone long. It was scarcely half an hour before Caroline heard the key turn in the lock of the front door. She wiped her eyes, and straightened herself.

Then Julia came in with John Leavitt. He stalked behind Julia, beaming, but his face was working with emotion, which he tried to restrain. Julia was very pale. She looked at her sister as she had never looked before.

"I heard from the doctor that he had come," she said simply, "and I made up my mind that after supper I would go over and see him. The doctor said he wasn't married. I didn't know but he might be, and I didn't know but he might have changed his mind about you, and I didn't want to fling my sister at any man's head. But I saw the minute he looked at me that he hadn't changed. I don't see why he should have. You are just as good looking as you ever were. He has told me how he has been here, and hid in the pantry. You must have been scared to death of me, both of you, like a couple of children," Julia laughed. "The doctor said it was more your mind than your cold that was to be worried about. I won't stand between you any longer. He's a good man, and I hope you'll be happy. He's your Christmas present I told you about."

Caroline began to weep. She ran toward her sister, then she altered her course, and made for the secretary. "Oh, I forgot," she sobbed out wildly, for she was fairly hysterical—"I forgot your Christmas present, Julia." She pulled open a drawer, and produced a neat white parcel. "It's—it's a scarf I embroidered for your bureau," she sobbed. She thrust the parcel into Julia's hand, and flung her arms around her neck. "Oh, Julia, you came first, and—I won't leave you unless you are sure you don't mind," whispered Caroline, her cheek against Julia's.

But Julia put her away firmly. "Nobody with Christian feelings should rebel at anything that comes in the course of nature," said she. "I did wrong, and I ain't afraid to say so. But you are young yet, and you will have a good many happy years before you. And I sha'n't live alone. I am going to send for Cousin Maria Fisher to come and live with me. She's as poor as Job's off ox, and I know as well as I want to that she doesn't have half enough to eat, and she lives alone, and she was always afraid of her own shadow. I am going to write her to come, and she'll have a good home with me as long as she lives. Don't you worry about me. I ain't a child, and when I fairly sense what is right I hope I've spunk enough to do it. Take your Christmas present!"

Caroline, being pushed by Julia toward John, stood before him. Both were smiling and flushing. John pulled a little box out of his pocket, and spoke abruptly to Julia. "Here's a little present for you," he said in a nervous voice.

Julia took the box. "Thank you, John," said she.

"It is a little pearl breast-pin. I meant it for Caroline, if she would take it," said John, "but you take it now, and I'll buy her another."

"No, let her keep this," said Julia.

"Julia, if you don't take it, I can't bear it," sobbed Caroline.

"Well, thank you very much, John," said Julia. Then she gave a look at Caroline. Caroline's face had met with a wonderful change. She looked as beautiful as she had ever looked in her youth. A lovely color flamed in her cheeks, her blue eyes gleamed. Julia laughed outright as she looked at her. "Well, I must say I never saw anybody get over a cold so quick in my life," said she.

Her voice was full of loving sarcasm. She went out of the room, and upstairs to her own. Then she sat down beside the window and thought. Her room was warmed by a register in the floor from the room below in which the lovers sat. She could hear a faint murmur of voices, but no distinct words, until she heard Caroline say quite distinctly, "That book? Yes, don't you remember the book called 'The Gift of Love' that you gave me? That was the only one of your presents that I kept. I don't think poor Julia ever knew. I was always afraid I was not doing right in not telling her."

Then Julia heard no more. She recalled the red and gold book that had lain on the table so many years. "Yes, I do remember now, he gave her that book," she mused.

She folded the shawl which she had put on more closely around her, for the room was rather chilly, and looked out at the Christmas moonlight on the Christmas snow. At first it seemed to her that she had fallen from an immense height into such loneliness and desolation as she had never known. Then suddenly an enormous delight and peace was over her.

She realized that instead of falling she had climbed, had flown even. She seemed to see quite distinctly that red and gold book called "The Gift of Love," and it became symbolic. She held in her heart what she had never held in any Christmas of her life before—the Gift of unselfish Love.

Friend of My Heart

Good Housekeeping Magazine, December 1913, 733–40

FRIEND of my heart, tho' many years
We journey thro' this vale of tears;
Tho' eyes grow dim, and white thy hair,
Forever to me young and fair:
To thee this little book I give,
And if you love me, pray receive,
And let the giver be to thee
What thou hast always been to me:
Friend of my heart, for weal or woe,
For time and for eternity.

With a fine pen and in her very best hand, Catherine Dexter had copied the verse of faulty rhythm and rhyme from a yellow old manuscript, which had belonged to her Aunt Catherine, long since dead, considered by her intimates a poetess. Then Catherine, her face still grave and her kind eyes still intent, had sent the verse in an album to Elvira Meredith for a Christmas present, for she considered that Elvira was indeed the friend of her heart. And Elvira had sent in return a sweet little note of thanks, written on gilt-edged paper, and a beautifully embroidered black silk apron.

That afternoon the two ladies had thanked each other in person, and now Elvira was at Catherine's house, and they were making little lace candy-bags for the Sunday-school Christmas-tree the next day. It was the time before the Civil War, when Sunday-school Christmas-trees were at their prime. Both Elvira and Catherine had Sunday-school classes.

"We might just as well admit that we are not girls any longer," Elvira declared, as she reached for another piece of lace.

"Women cannot remain girls forever," replied Catherine, who had a goodly supply of philosophy, and a disposition to accept the inevitable gracefully.

But Elvira was different. She had been a great beauty. She had smiled at and scorned many lovers. She had played the harp and sung. She had possessed all the accomplishments of her day. Now they seemed to pale. She was in a way still a beauty, but a beauty whose charms had been in the world so long that they had become as an unconsidered rose. Elvira herself no longer took pleasure in regarding her face in her looking-glass. She was dainty about her dress from force of habit; but in her heart of hearts it did not seem to her to matter. Nothing of that sort had mattered very much since Lucius Converse had gone away after her last rejection of his suit.

Elvira had not intended the rejection to be final. In those days of her youth, she had been unable to consider any adverse decision with regard to love of herself final. Then it had seemed to her that, once love, it must be always love. Then she had believed in the enduring power of that face in the looking-glass. How many times her thoughts had run in this groove! Until they had worn it so deep they could no longer climb over the sides of it, she now realized. And they would soon give up trying to climb over, she told herself, as she sewed bag after bag. It was because she was growing old. She shook her head hopelessly. There were young girls out in the kitchen, making molasses candy and stringing popcorn for the Christmas-tree, and their happy laughter and chatter made Elvira sadder still.

"I, for one, shall be glad when Christmas is over," she said to Catherine. "I feel too old for Christmas. I feel left out. Hear those young things in the kitchen, talking and laughing! Addie Emerson is telling Faith Wheeler how Tommy Keene took her sleigh-riding. You and I never go sleigh-riding nowadays, Catherine."

"Jonas can take us, any time you wish," said Catherine.

"Thank you," replied Elvira. "Going sleigh-riding behind your hired man, driving your fat old black horse, is not the kind of sleigh-riding I mean. I mean flying over the hard, white snow on a moonlight night, with the horse shying at the shadows and the bells ringing like mad and—a young man driving—with one hand." Elvira laughed a little in spite of herself.

Catherine colored. Then she also laughed. "Elvira Meredith, I am ashamed of you!"

"Well, I am not quite old enough or sour enough not to laugh and be ashamed of myself when I say a foolish thing," said Elvira, "but I do feel sad this Christmas. I realize that I have lost, and by my own fault, so many of the great gifts of life. I wonder whether by another Christmas my hair will not be gray, and I obliged to wear a cap and front-piece?"

Catherine laughed again. "Elvira," said she, "I cannot see a single gray hair."

"There are a few, and I shall look a fright in a cap. I tried on mother's the other day. However, that will not matter." Elvira meant that Lucius Converse would not see her in a cap, and that was a comfort.

"I don't think things of that sort really do matter," said Catherine in her philosophical way, "and I do not think you need to worry about the cap for a good many years, anyway."

"Of course that is unworthy," admitted Elvira, "but you must know, Catherine, that my life is—well—not exactly what I expected, not quite calculated to make me very happy."

Catherine glanced about, and in her face was a covert sense of satisfaction, and of self-accusation before the satisfaction. Catherine had the best house in the village. The room in which she was seated was handsomely furnished. There was a Brussels carpet, there were a haircloth sofa and chairs, and the south windows were filled with blooming oleander-trees. Beyond was a glimpse on one side of a fairly glorious "best" parlor, with red silk-damask sweeps of curtains; on the other, of a dining-room with a Chippendale sideboard, laden with glass and old silver. The house was warm from a hot-air furnace, the only one in the village. "I realize that I have more to make me satisfied with my lot than you have, dear," said Catherine, and her eyes were apologetic.

"Oh, I am glad you have such nice things," said Elvira. "I don't mind that. Of course it is hard, having so very little—we have to manage so carefully. But poor mother is so trying nowadays that I can hardly bear it, although I do try. Henrietta does not seem to mind. She has a better disposition than I have, I suppose." Henrietta was Elvira's older sister.

"Henrietta has never expected so much of life, therefore she is naturally not so disappointed at not having it," remarked Catherine.

"I fear that does not excuse me," said Elvira, "but I will own that this is the saddest Christmas I ever knew—and these foolish little lace candy-bags are driving me crazy!"

Catherine laughed. They were sewing the bags with colored wool, and Elvira's had knotted under her nervous taper fingers. "Here, don't break that wool," cried Catherine. "Give it to me; I will get the knot out!"

Elvira thanked her when she took it back. "What have you for your Sunday-school class?" said she.

Catherine hesitated. "Little coral pins."

"Oh," exclaimed Elvira, "the girls will be delighted. I have nothing for mine except some little books—not very interesting, I fear."

"Girls always like books."

"I don't know. When I was a girl, I would have much preferred a coral pin. I do hope my Sunday-school class and my friends will not give me any more worsted things this year. I had so many last year that I can never use them up if I live to be a hundred; and they are dreadful things for moths. I am not able to give much, but I have tried to give what people would not be miserable over. Oh, the girls are coming! It is time to go home. The days are short now. Well, the candy-bags are done: this is the last."

The young girls flocked in and took formal leave of Elvira and Catherine, whom they considered very old. Elvira, watching them scurry down the path between the box-borders, sighed. She was pinning her shawl. Catherine was also pinning hers. It was after sunset, and Catherine always walked home with Elvira if she remained late. Elvira was a timid soul, and Catherine had never known what fear was.

Elvira lived in the next house, but the road was lonely, skirting a wide field. Elvira's house, the old Meredith homestead, showed in the moonlight a curious vagueness of outline, like a sketch done with a soft pencil. It was out of repair. Its shingles flapped like the very rags of a home. Its sills were rotten; the doors and windows sagged. The interior showed a stately shabbiness.

When Elvira entered, she realized the contrast between her home and her friend's. It was chilly. There was also a not altogether disagreeable, but musty odor, like the breath of the old house. That night when Elvira went up-stairs to her own room the cold was so intense that a rigid chill held her like the arms of a skeleton. There was no heat in the room. Elvira seldom afforded a fire on the hearth. She hurried to bed, and lay there long awake and shivering, with the moonlight lying in a broad blue shaft across the floor.

She could see from the bed a light in Catherine's dining-room; and she wondered why she was up so late, for it was after ten, which was considered very late in Abbotsville.

Catherine, when she had returned, had been accosted by her old servant-woman. "I found some jars of that peach preserve beginning to spoil," said she, "and I didn't dare to leave it, for all it's so cold. So I have been scalding it up. I didn't find it out till I went to the store-room to get the jelly for supper; then I noticed the peach looked sort of queer." Maria wished Catherine to taste of the preserve to make sure that it was right; and Catherine, who was fond of sweets, sat down at the dining-table with a saucer of peaches before her, and began to eat. "It is very nice," said she.

Maria, who was privileged, sat in a chair in the corner, beaming. "I'm glad," she replied proudly. "I know you set store by peach. I'm glad I happened to notice it." Maria was a tall woman, with a thin skin roughened by frequent scrubbing with soap and water, with gray-blonde hair, and a sharp nose terminating unexpectedly in a knob, upward turned. "Mr. Lucius Converse is in town," she added.

Catherine started and paled slightly. "Who told you, Maria?"

"Nobody told me. I saw him go by when I was in the butcher's shop," she replied, with pleased importance.

Catherine took another spoonful of peach preserve. Her hand was quite steady, but she could hear her heart beat.

"He hasn't changed one mite, except he's raised a beard, and mebbe he's a little bit heftier," said Maria.

"Hasn't he?"

"He was dressed real handsome, too. He wore a greatcoat and a silk hat, and he carried a cane."

Catherine took another spoonful of peach preserve.

"The butcher said he was stopping at the tavern," continued Maria; "said he'd spoke to him—just as pleasant as he used to be. Mr. Lucius Converse always was real pleasant spoken."

"Yes, he was," assented Catherine. She took another spoonful of peach preserve, and the sweet, smiling face of a young man of long ago seemed just before her. How Lucius had smiled, had smiled at everybody, at her, Catherine, as well as at Elvira! Perhaps Lucius Converse had smiled too often and too impartially, had said pleasant things too often and impartially. It was quite probable, indeed, that Lucius had smiled as pleasantly at the butcher as he had smiled at Catherine. But in her heart the smile had remained, like a rose pressed in a book of memory. Catherine could look at it, but she seldom did. She was entirely too sensible; moreover, she had not known that Lucius had not married. She did not know, that evening, until Maria spoke again.

"The butcher says he ain't never married," said Maria presently.

"Hasn't he?"

"No, he ain't. Mebbe he's come back to get Miss Elvira."

"Perhaps he has," assented Catherine. However, she remembered one evening when she was a girl, when Lucius had escorted her home from evening meeting. It was true that Elvira was visiting in Boston at the time; but on that evening, walking along the sidewalk upon which the hard-packed snow glistened under the moonlight, making it like a track of blue and crystal, Lucius had, if ever a woman could tell when she was made love to, made love to her, to Catherine.

Even now Catherine, bringing her hard common sense to bear upon the sweet old memory, told herself that it was entirely true: Lucius had made love to her. He had said things which could have only one meaning. He had looked at her with eyes which expressed devotion. He had not asked her to marry him, but Catherine, when she entered her house door, was convinced that he loved her, and not Elvira, as she had thought. She dreamed of wedding Lucius.

Then Elvira had returned, and appeared at meeting in a green-shot silk and a hat trimmed with roses, tied under her chin with white lutestring ribbons. And Lucius had never taken his eyes from that face of delicate, drooping loveliness. That evening he had walked home with Catherine and Elvira, had dismissed Catherine not ungently with a good night at her own gate, and had walked on with Elvira.

Catherine had sat on her front porch that evening and watched Elvira's house. It had remained dark nearly an hour. Then a window had gleamed out with light, and soon she heard a quick step. She had hurried into her own house and closed the door; but through a side light of the door she had seen Lucius falter and hesitate, as if he had a half-mind to enter. Then he had gone on, and the next day Elvira had come over and told her of his going West, and her rejection of his offer of marriage.

Now, after all these years, hearing that Lucius Converse had returned to Abbotsville and was still unmarried, Catherine wondered why he had come back. He had a married sister living in Boston; but there was nobody, apparently, to bring him back to the little village. Catherine was a shrewd woman, and she had come to estimate Lucius rather shrewdly, to understand him. He was a successful lawyer, and had made a considerable fortune. He had flitted from pillar to post in his wooing of women; but when the time arrived for him to settle for life, he would inevitably choose an harbor which he considered safe.

Catherine said to herself: "Lucius has come back here for a wife. He wants a wife and a home. He knows that neither Elvira nor I have married. Which of us does he wish to marry?" She considered Elvira's beautiful face. She considered her own—not unattractive—and her disposition, which was of a steadier, serener type than Elvira's and might appeal to an older man wishing for a peaceful and well-ordered household. She did not consider her superior financial state as an asset. Lucius had money enough of his own, and he had never been a fortune-hunter. Catherine, finishing her peach preserve, decided that she did not know which of them he wanted, Elvira or herself.

The next day was Christmas. Catherine heard early in the morning that Lucius had gone to Boston to spend the day with his sister. She said nothing about him to Elvira. She thought that Elvira also might have heard; but she decided that she had not, when they were working together in the church vestry over the tree. Elvira would have betrayed it, had she known. The nervous, high-strung creature could not hold a secret; it rasped her soul until she had rid herself of it. A woman of no mystery, except the inevitable mystery of every individual; one always knew, however one might disapprove, that there was nothing hidden in her for further disapprobation.

That day Elvira displayed all her weaknesses. It was Christmas. She was sad, almost pettish, because she missed for herself what would have made the day really Christmas. The lines between her blue eyes were strongly marked; her sweet mouth drooped at the corners. In the evening, when they were all assembled for the Christmas-tree, she did not look as pretty as usual.

Catherine regarded her uneasily. She had not told her about Lucius, because she feared to make her more nervous. Now she had a guilty feeling that if he should come to the tree he would not see Elvira at her best. Her hair was drawn back too tightly, her smile was forced. Her dress, even, was not as tasteful as usual. Elvira, although she had little money, managed her dress very well; but that evening her old black silk was shiny across the back, and gave her a bent appearance. Moreover, black never suited her.

When her name was called, she went to the tree to receive her gifts, and returned with the same set smile.

The low-ceilinged vestry was aromatic with the odor of evergreen. The tree twinkled with lights, and its boughs were bravely festooned with strung popcorn. From all the settees looked eager faces, of youth, middle-age, and even age. There was an effect, to the imaginative, as of hands outstretched for the bounty of love itself. The children, although hampered by the uncouth fashions of their day—the girls with hoops, and starched pantalettes showing under crude-colored woolen gowns, with their childish locks pulled back from their candid brows; the boys in absurd jackets and trousers made by unskilled hands—were still beautiful with the unrivaled beauty and radiance of youth, which, having as yet had nothing, expects the whole earth.

Poor Elvira was as an introverted high-light of melancholy upon the festive picture. When people talked to her, she replied politely. Elvira was a lady, born and bred, but her face never once changed. She opened none of her packages while she was in the vestry.

Catherine walked home with her, along that track of snow gleaming with blue and crystal under the moon, waved over with lovely shadows from the trees bowing gracefully before the north wind. At first they were of a numerous company, which gradually dispersed, some entering home-doors, some turning into by-streets; and when they reached Catherine's gate, the two were quite alone. Then Elvira spoke, and her speech was at once tragic, absurd, pitiful. She railed, she raged, she gestured. Always she was graceful; never once did she lose the sweet undertone from her voice. Poor Elvira had an essentially sweet nature, but her highly-strung nerves quivered into discords under the strain of her life. Suddenly she tore the wrapping from a package. "An old blue head-tie!" said she, and gave the thing a fling.

Catherine stared, aghast. "Elvira, are you crazy?"

"No," said Elvira, in her strained, sweet voice, "I am not crazy. I am keeping from being crazy." She tugged at the cord of another package. "*Another* blue head-tie!" said she, and flung it.

"Why, Elvira!"

"Don't mind me, Catherine. I *must* do it." Elvira opened the next package. "A great green and white pin-cushion," said she. She gave that a toss, and it rolled like a ball.

"Why, Elvira!"

"I must, Catherine! Here is another pin-cushion, a red and white one." Elvira tossed that, and kicked it with her slender, pointed foot. "Here is another, and another! Just as I thought—all my Sunday school class has given me pin-cushions. I must have ten!" One after another, the pin-cushions dropped on the hard snow and were propelled by Elvira's lady-feet.

"Why, Elvira!"

"Catherine, they *knew* I did not want these things! They *knew,* and they did not care! We have things we do not want because nobody cares. It is awful; I am wicked, but it *is* awful!" Suddenly Elvira wept. She sobbed aloud like a child. The two were before Elvira's gate. "Somehow, this Christmas," Elvira lamented, "I have lost all courage, and all these worsted things seem to just make my heart break. I seem to look ahead and see nothing but worsted things that I don't want, on all my Christmas-trees, the rest of my life."

"You are not well, Elvira," said Catherine. "How much have you eaten today?"

Elvira hesitated. "We had a very good roast of pork," said she, with a show of defiance.

"You did not have chicken?"

"We none of us care so very much for chicken," Elvira said, but Catherine knew the truth: that her friend could afford nothing except the roast of pork, and that Elvira had never liked pork.

"They talked about having an oyster-supper tonight in the vestry, and I did not know they had changed their plans," said Catherine.

"Yes, they did talk about an oyster-supper," returned Elvira, in a hungry voice, "and they had cake and coffee. The cake was very nice."

Catherine knew that Elvira never ate cake. She gave her friend's arm a little pull. "Come home with me," she whispered. "There are oysters enough for a nice stew."

Then Elvira spoke lamentably. She never quite lost her dignity, her innate ladyhood; but she spoke as her friend had never dreamed she could speak. She revealed depths of her nature hitherto unsuspected. "It is not oyster-stews I want," said she, "neither do I want a lot of worsted things. I want the gifts of life that matter!"

"I don't think you ought to mind not being married quite so much," said Catherine calmly. She spoke with reason. At that time, spinsterhood was not usually voluntary.

Elvira turned upon her fiercely. "You think that is all? You know, and I know, that marriage is the crown of life for a woman, whether she owns to it or not; but women can live without crowns. It isn't alone being not married! It is everything else. I shall never, during all my life, have anything more than I have now. I have to give up my dreams, and I suppose I love my dreams more than I would the reality. I have to give up a real home. Sometimes I feel as if mother fairly hated me, because—with my face—I have this sort of life. Henrietta is more contented than I *can* be, although she has no more than I have. I know she is a better woman, but I am the way I was made, and I can't get outside of myself to make myself over. Of course, I know it is all my own fault that my life is not different, but that makes it harder. Catherine, I know you despise me, and I despise myself, but somehow, tonight, I have to tell what is in my heart. Somehow all those worsted things are the last straws. I can see nothing ahead of me but pin-cushions and tidies and head-ties, paving the road to my grave: all things I don't want." Elvira flourished another small parcel. "Here is another!" she cried. She tore the package open. "Nothing was lacking except a worsted lamp-mat," said she, "and now I have that!" She flung the fluffy thing down. Some beads on it sparkled tinily in the moonlight. She trampled on it.

Again it seemed monstrous to Catherine, who had never so lost control of herself. "Why, Elvira!" she said.

"Yes, I know how I seem. But perhaps I may be better for telling you, for speaking out just once. Ever since father died and mother got so nervous, Henrietta and I have just lived along like beads on a string, afraid to move lest we wear our string out. Henrietta has never realized that she was a bead on a string, but I have, and it is awful. Now I will go in, and mother will hear me. No matter how softly I move, she always hears me. She will scold me, and Henrietta will not say anything, and I shall go to bed and not be able to sleep, and—Christmas day will be over." Elvira flung her beshawled arms around her friend and kissed her cool cheek with hot lips. "God bless you, Catherine," she said; "I know I am wicked, but tonight I had to be wicked in order to be good."

"Well, go in now and be good," returned Catherine, with a soft, soothing laugh.

Elvira fled into the house.

Catherine turned and went her way. She did not fairly understand her friend, but she had strong convictions with regard to the oyster-stew, also reluctant convictions with regard to Lucius Converse. Catherine had a suspicion that he was at the root of it all: that Elvira had never forgotten him. She was surer because Elvira never mentioned his name. If Elvira, as frank as she was, was silent, her silence shouted.

Then Catherine met Lucius Converse—a big, blond-bearded man.

"Hullo, Catherine," he said, as if they had met but yesterday.

"Is it you, Lucius," said Catherine, and she also spoke as if they had met but yesterday.

The man looked down at the woman, and his face was tender. "As far as I can see, and the moon makes it as bright as day, you look exactly the same," said he.

"You look the same, only you have raised a beard."

"Yes, I raised a beard right after I went away. I weigh more than I used to."

"So do I."

"Well, I can't tell about that, you are so wrapped up in that shawl thing. What are all those bundles you are carrying? Let me take some of them."

"No, they are not heavy, and I am almost home. They are Christmas presents. I have been to the Sunday-school Christmas-tree in the vestry."

"I meant to get home for that. I thought I would see my old friends there, but I missed my train at the Junction, and the station was closed, and I have been three solid hours on the road, and I am cold and half-starved; but I thought I would look up somebody tonight, anyhow, as long as it is Christmas. Why are you headed this way? The church isn't back there."

"I went home with Elvira. You remember Elvira?"

"Of course I do, and you, too. I was going to make a call—" Lucius Converse hesitated. Suddenly he became not entirely sure whether he had been about to call on Catherine or Elvira. Catherine's face looked very good, even dear, to him, uplifted, with the moonlight flooding down upon it. She wore a white wool hood, and her calm face was framed softly in pale folds.

Catherine was thinking very swiftly, she who seldom thought swiftly, "If he goes to Elvira's now, he will get no supper, and the house will be cold." It also flashed through her mind that Elvira was not looking as pretty as usual. "You had better call on me first, Lucius," said Catherine, "and I will make you a hot oyster-stew. Then it will not be too late. You can still call on Elvira."

"A hot oyster-stew sounds good to me," replied Lucius happily. "Exactly what I want."

"And coffee?"

"That, too."

They entered the warm house. "This is comfortable," said the man. It seemed like home to him. Listening to Catherine stepping about in the kitchen, from which presently issued savory odors, he became almost convinced that he had intended to call at this house whose door he had passed. He was not essentially romantic, nor in the fullest sense a lover. He had returned to Abbotsville with the express purpose of seeking a helpmate. He knew that Elvira was still unmarried, and he could bring up the image of her lovely face quite distinctly to his memory. Still he knew, and also with interest, that Catherine was still unmarried. Now here was Catherine, in some respects more attractive than in her early youth; and more than herself was what she personified—the warm shelter and peace of Home.

And he leaned back in the haircloth rocker, and felt distinctly disinclined to make another call that night.

Meantime Catherine, preparing his supper, reflected and decided. She knew what she knew. She could have Lucius Converse for a husband if she chose. She knew that she was fond of him, and that he would be as fond of her, as the years passed, as of any woman. She had also a sudden illumination, this unimaginative, unromantic woman: she realized what the best of a marriage might be—the comradeship, the homemaking, possible only for the opposite sexes. She understood perfectly what she had to accept, or to resign. She loved Lucius with the best love that a good woman past her youth could give a man. She did not think of him as vacillating and swayed this way and that by the wills of women. She judged him correctly: he was of the type which, seemingly swayed by others, is swayed in reality only by themselves, never losing an osierlike foothold in their own interests. At the same time, no man would make a better and kinder husband. He was essentially a good man. This home-hunt, which the woman divined, proved it to her. It spelled more goodness than merely a wife-hunt. Catherine loved Lucius, but she loved him after the manner of a queen dignified before her own needs, and capable of foregoing them.

She had only one doubt: would Elvira make Lucius a good wife? Her whole faith clamored, "Yes." Elvira would probably be better for the man than she. Elvira loved him, and her dependence would arouse his strength. "The women who need men to take care of them are the women who make men able to take care of them," Catherine, forced into epigram by the strenuousness of the situation, told herself. Then she made her choice.

When Lucius was seated in the dining-room, with the steaming oyster-stew and the coffee, Catherine was flying across the field between her house and Elvira's. Catherine pounded on a side door, and Elvira came running.

"Hurry, and put on your blue silk," gasped Catherine. "I will put some more wood on the fire. Hurry! Lucius Converse is coming over to see you! He is eating an oyster-stew at my house. I ran over to tell you. Hurry!"

Elvira paled. Then a wonderful flush spread over her face and neck. She smiled a heavenly smile of a soul abashed by happiness undeserved, coming in the midst of complaints and ingratitude.

Her old mother had followed her to the door, her nightcap askew, grizzled locks flying around her face of a shrew. Now she smiled, and her smile was also wonderful before unexpected blessing. She called out to her daughter Henrietta, who occupied a room on the ground floor, "Elvira's old beau is coming to see her!" And the scolding old voice gave a chord of love and repentance and amazing gratitude.

Henrietta looked out of her bedroom door at Catherine, stirring the hearth fire into a blaze, at Elvira, fumbling with her hair. Henrietta's large, patient face, surmounting the frill of her nightgown, had a charming expression. She held forth a mass of shimmering blue. "Here is your blue silk, Elvira. It was in the closet here," she said. "Put it on out there where it is warm. If you go into a cold room to dress, you will get chilled. Here is a brush, too. Don't strain your hair too tight from your face!"

Elvira took the blue silk and ran to the old gilded pier-glass. The room, although shabby, was still stately, full of lovely effects of faded rose and lilac from ancient damask curtains and chair-coverings. The glass reflected, beside Elvira's face, the high-leaping flames of orange and violet on the cleanly-swept hearth.

Catherine hurried home.

Lucius had finished his oyster-stew. He gazed at Catherine with eyes ready to see in her face the fulfilment of his dreams and his longing.

But Catherine, seeing, would not see. She brought out pound-cake, and poured another cup of coffee. Then she said: "After you have eaten your cake and finished the coffee, you had better go, for it is really late. Elvira has not yet retired. There is a light in the parlor."

Lucius looked at her. He obviously hesitated.

Catherine held his overcoat ready. When he had finished his coffee, she touched his shoulder. "You must go," she said firmly, "or Elvira will retire for the night; and as for me—I must attend to making some ginger-tea for Maria. I have heard her cough since I came in."

Lucius looked longingly at her. He stammered. Catherine did not flinch. She held his coat. He shrugged into it, and went.

After the man was seated in the old parlor of the other house, with the other woman, beautiful as he had never known her, clad in shimmering blue, with her soft curls drooping over her crimson cheeks, with a dawn-surprise of happiness in her blue eyes, with the sweetest smile, as of a soothed infant, on her lips, Catherine stood gazing out of a window across the moonlit field. She spoke aloud. A great loneliness was over her, and she wished to hear a human voice, even her own. "Elvira has got the Christmas present she wants," said she. There was in her voice the utmost womanly sweetness, and yet a high courage, as of one who leads herself to battle. A peace and happiness so intense that it seemed fairly celestial came over her. She could not understand why she was so happy. She did not even dream of the truth: that the gift of the Lord, the true Christmas gift, is, for some of his children—the more blessed and the nearer Him—self-renunciation. She did not know that, by giving, she had received a fuller measure than she had given.

Then, smiling blissfully, all alone there in the moonlight, softly she repeated to herself the beginning of the stanza she had written in Elvira's album: "Friend of my heart—." And that friend of her heart seemed standing before her, radiant, and blessing her.

The Christmas Sing in Our Village

Ladies' Home Journal, December 1897, 11

THE SINGING-SCHOOL is, of course, a regular institution in our village during the winter months, but the one of special interest is held on Christmas Eve. That is called, to distinguish it from the others, "The Christmas Sing." On that night only the psalms and fugues appropriate to the occasion are sung, and the town hall is trimmed with holly and evergreen.

The Sing begins at eight o'clock and is always preceded by a turkey supper. The supper is in the tavern, as it used to be called—now we say "hotel"—still it is the tavern, and always will be the same old house where the stages drew up before the railroad was built.

The turkey supper is at six o'clock, and full two hours are required to dispose of the good things and speechify, then the people cross the road to the town hall, where the Sing is held. It is a great occasion in our village, and the women give as much care to their costumes as if they were going to a ball. The dressmaker is hard worked for weeks before the Sing. Everybody who can afford it has a new dress, and those who cannot, have their old ones made over. The women all try to keep their costumes secret until the night of the Sing, and the dressmaker is bound over by the most solemn promises not to reveal anything. The Christmas Sing is often most brilliant and surprising to our humble tastes in the matter of dress, and was especially so last year. The Sing of last year was also noteworthy in another respect: there were three betrothals and a runaway marriage that night.

• • •

It was ideal weather for Christmas Eve and our Sing: very cold and clear, a full moon, and a beautiful, hard level of snow for sleighing. At six o'clock everybody was assembled at the tavern: past and present members of the singing-school—even old man Veazie, who is over ninety—were there. There were also some guests—fine singers—from out of town.

The turkey supper was excellent, and so were the speeches. One of the best was made by Mr. Cassius C. Dowell from East Langham, a village about eight miles from ours. He is a very fine tenor singer and quite a celebrity. He sings in the church choir in Langham, and is in great demand to sing at funerals. He is not very young, but fine looking and a great favorite with the ladies. He has a gentle, deferential way of looking at them which is considered very attractive. Lottie Green sat next him at the supper-table, and he looked at her, and made sure that she had plenty of white meat and gravy. Mr. Lucius Downey was on the other side of Lottie, but she paid no attention to him. Had it not been for Lurinda Snell, who was next on his right, he might have felt slighted. She looked very well, too, in a fine new silk dress, plum color with velvet trimming. Lurinda was quite pretty in her youth, and sometimes dress and excitement seem to revive something of her old beauty. Her cheeks were pink and her eyes bright; her hair, which is still abundant, was most beautifully crimped.

Lottie Green, also, looked very pretty. She had not been able to afford a new dress, but she had made over her old blue cloth one and put in silk sleeves, and it was as good and quite as pretty as when it was new.

• • •

Probably Maria Rice had the finest new dress of any of the girls. Everybody stared at Maria when she entered with a great rustle of silk and rattle of starched petticoats. The dress was of pink silk, and—a most startling innovation in our village—the waist was cut square and quite low. Maria has a beautiful neck, and she wore a great bunch of pink roses on one shoulder. She had elbow sleeves, too, and drew off her long gloves with a very fine air when she sat down to table. The other girls were half admiring, half scandalized. No such costume as that had ever been worn to our singing school before. Poor Zepheretta Stockwell, in a black silk which might have been worn appropriately by her grandmother, was entirely eclipsed by Maria in more senses than one. Jim Paine sat between the two girls at supper. Maria's pink skirts spread over his knee, her pretty face was tilted up in his and her tongue was wagging every minute. Once I saw Jim try to speak to Zepheretta, but Maria was too quick for him.

When supper was over the people all assembled in the town hall without delay. The hall was finely decorated—green wreaths hung in all the windows, and the portrait of the gentleman who gave the town house to the village fifty years ago, 'Squire Ebenezer Adams, was draped with an American flag. It is a life-size portrait, and hangs on the right of the stage. Our old singing master and choir leader, Mr. Orlando Sage, stood on the stage, and conducted the school, as usual. The piano was on his right. The south district teacher, Miss Elmira Crane, played that. There was old Mr. Joseph Nelson, with his bass viol, which he used to play in the church choir, and Thomas Farr and Charlie Morse, with their violins.

• • •

The school was arranged in the usual manner, in the four divisions of sopranos, tenors, bassos and altos. At eight o'clock Mr. Sage raised his baton, and the music began.

Everybody stood up, and sang their best and loudest, with, perhaps, one exception. The result was quite magnificent, unless you happened to stand close to certain singers, and did not sing loud enough yourself to drown them out.

We went on with the fine old fugues, and it was grand, had it not been for the weakness in the sopranos. At length, Mr. Orlando Sage stood directly in front of the sopranos, waving his baton frantically, raising himself up on his toes, and jerking his head as if in such ways he would stimulate them to greater volume of voice. Mr. Sage is a nervous little man. Finally, with an imperious switch of his baton, and a stamp of his foot, he brought the whole school to a dead stop.

"Miss Stockwell," he said, "why don't you sing?"

Everybody stared at Zepheretta. She turned white, then red, and replied meekly that she was singing.

"No, you are not singing," returned Mr. Sage. "I was riding past your father's yesterday, and I heard you singing. You have a voice. Why don't you sing?"

Mr. Sage brandished his baton, as if he would like to hit her with it, and poor Zepheretta looked almost frightened to death. "Why don't you sing?" sternly demanded Mr. Sage again. "You never sing in this school as you can sing."

* * *

Zepheretta looked as if she were going to cry. She opened her mouth, as if to speak, but did not. Then, suddenly, Lurinda Snell, who sat on her right, spoke for her. "I can tell you why, if you want to know, Mr. Sage," she said; "I haven't told a soul before, but much as three years ago I heard Maria Rice tell Zepheretta not to sing so loud, she drowned her all out, and Zepheretta hasn't sung so loud since."

When Lurinda stopped, with a defiant nod of her head, you could have heard a pin drop. Maria Rice, on the other side of Zepheretta, was blushing as pink as her dress. Then Mr. Sage brought his baton down. "Sing!" he shouted, and we all began again—"When shepherds watch their flocks by night."

Zepheretta did let out her voice a little more then, and we were all amazed; nobody had dreamed she could sing so well. Still it was quite evident that she held her voice back somewhat on her high notes, on account of Maria's feelings, though Maria would not sing at all during the rest of the evening. I think she was glad when the Sing was over, though everybody else had enjoyed it.

* * *

It was ten o'clock when we closed, after singing "When marshaled on the nightly plain," and all the young men who had come with teams hastened out to get them. Many a young woman who had come to the Sing with her father or brother went home in the sleigh of some gallant swain who was waiting for her when she emerged from the town hall. All the girls in coming down the steps ran a sort of gauntlet of love and jealousy between double lines of waiting beaus, beyond whom the restive horses pranced with frequent flurries of bells.

Then Maria Rice, to the great delight of the vindictive of her sex and the amused pity of others, was seen, after manifestly hurrying and lingering, and peering with eagerly furtive eyes toward Jim Paine, to gather up her pink silk skirts and go forlornly down the road with Lydia Wheelock, who lived her way. It was rumored that she wept all the way home, in spite of Lydia's attempts to comfort her, but nobody ever knew. She was not far on the road before Jim Paine and Zepheretta passed her in Jim's sleigh, drawn by his fast black horse.

Everybody was astonished to see Jim step out from the waiting file, accost Zepheretta, and lead her to his sleigh as if she had been a princess, and probably Zepheretta was the most astonished of all.

Mr. Cassius C. Dowell, who had driven over from Langham, took Lottie Green home, and Mr. Lucius Downey escorted Lurinda Snell. He had brought a lantern, though it was bright moonlight—he is fond of carrying one because his eyes are poor. The lantern light shone full on Lurinda's face as she went proudly past on his arm, and she looked like a young girl.

• • •

The next day we heard that all three couples were going to be married, and that another very young couple, who had driven down the road at such a furious rate that everybody had hastened out of the way, and there had been narrow escapes from collisions, were married. They had driven ten miles to Dover for that purpose, nobody ever knew why. The parents on either side would have given free consent to the match, but they drove to Dover that Christmas Eve as if a whole regiment of furious relatives were savagely charging at their backs.

However, that marriage has been happy so far, and the others also. Jim and Zepheretta are a devoted pair; Lurinda Snell makes a good wife for Lucius Downey, and does not talk as bitterly about her neighbors as was her unpleasant custom of doing formerly. Cassius C. Dowell seems very happy with Lottie, so the neighbors all say, and Lydia Wheelock, now that she has not Lottie and her children to look after and provide for, has bought herself a new parlor carpet and a bonnet.

Take it altogether that Sing seemed to our village to bring much happiness, set, as it were, to sweet Christmas music.

CHRISTMAS TREES, STOCKINGS, AND SANTA'S LITTLE HELPERS

The Balsam Fir

Harper's Bazar, December 1901, 715–21

MARTHA ELDER HAD lived alone for years on Amesboro road, a mile from the nearest neighbor, three miles from the village. She lived in the low cottage which her grandfather had built. It was painted white, and there was a green trellis over the front door shaded by a beautiful rose-vine. Martha had very little money, but somehow she always managed to keep her house in good order, though she had never had any blinds. It had always been the dream of Martha's life to have blinds; her mild blue eyes were very sensitive to the glare of strong sunlight, and the house faced west. Sometimes of a summer afternoon Martha waxed fairly rebellious because of her lack of green blinds to soften the ardent glare. She had green curtains, but they flapped in the wind and made her nervous, and she could not have them drawn.

Blinds were not the only things which aroused in Martha Elder a no less strong, though unexpressed, spirit of rebellion against the smallness of her dole of the good things of life. Nobody had ever heard this tall, fair, gentle woman utter one word of complaint. She spoke and moved with mild grace. The sweetest acquiescence seemed evident in her every attitude of body and tone of voice. People said that Martha Elder was an old maid, that she was all alone in the world, that she had a hard time to get along and keep out of the poor-house, that it was as much as ever she had enough to wear or even to eat, but that she was perfectly contented and happy. But people did not know; she had her closets of passionate solitude to which they did not penetrate. When her sister Adeline, ten years after her father's death, had married the man who everybody had thought would marry Martha, she had made a pretty wedding for her, and people had said Martha did not care, after all; that she was cut out for an old maid; that she did not want to marry. Nobody knew, not her sister, not even the man himself, who had really given her reason to blame him, how she felt. She was encased in an armor of womanly pride as impenetrable as a coat of mail; it was proof against everything except the arrows of agony of her own secret longings.

Martha had been a very pretty girl, much prettier than her younger sister Adeline; it was strange that she had not been preferred; it was strange that she had not had suitors in plenty; but there may have been something about the very fineness of her femininity and its perfection which made it repellent. Adeline with her coarse bloom, and loud laugh, and ready stare, had always had admirers by the score, while Martha, who was really exquisite, used to go to bed and lie awake listening to the murmur of voices under the green trellis of the front door, until the man who married her sister came. Then for a brief space his affections did verge toward Martha; he said various things to her in a voice whose cadences ever after made her music of life; he looked at her with an expression which became photographed, as by some law of love instead of light, on her heart. Then Adeline, exuberant with passion, incredulous that he could turn to her sister instead of herself, won him away by her strong pull upon the earthy part of him. Martha had not dreamed of contesting the matter, of making a fight for the man whom she loved. She yielded at once with her pride so exquisite that it seemed like meekness.

When Adeline went away, she settled down at once into her solitary old-maiden estate, although she was still comparatively young. She had her little ancestral house, her small vegetable garden, a tiny wood-lot from which she hired enough wood cut to supply her needs, and a very small sum of money in the bank, enough to pay her taxes and insurance, and not much besides. She had a few hens, and lived mostly on eggs and vegetables; as for her clothes, she never wore them out; she moved about softly and carefully, and never frayed the hems of her gowns, nor rubbed her elbows; and as for soil, no mortal had ever seen a speck of grime upon Martha Elder or her raiment. She seemed to pick her spotless way through life like a white dove. There was a story that Martha once wore a white dress all one summer, keeping it immaculate without washing, and it seemed quite possible.

When she walked abroad she held her dress skirt at an unvarying height of modest neatness revealing snowy starched petticoats and delicate ankles in white stockings. She might have been painted as a type of elderly maiden of peace and pure serenity by an artist who could see only externals. But it was very different with her from what people thought. Nobody dreamed of the fierce tension of her nerves as she sat at her window sewing through the long summer afternoons, drawing her monotonous thread in and out of dainty seams; nobody dreamed what revolt that little cottage roof, when it was covered with wintry snows, sometimes sheltered. When Martha's sister came home with her husband and beautiful first baby to visit her, her smiling calm of welcome was inimitable.

"Martha never did say much," Adeline told her husband, when they were in their room at night. "She didn't exclaim even over the baby." As she spoke she looked gloatingly at his rosy curves as he lay asleep. "Martha's an old maid if there ever was one," she added.

"It's queer, for she's pretty," said her husband.

"I don't call her pretty," said Adeline; "not a mite of color." She glanced at her high bloom and tossing black mane of hair in the mirror.

"Yes, that's so," agreed Adeline's husband. Still, sometimes he used to look at Martha with the old expression, unconsciously, even before his wife, but Martha never recognized it for the same. When he had married her sister he had established between himself and her such a veil of principle that her eyes ever after could never catch the true meaning of him. Yet nobody knew how glad she was when this little family outside her pale of life had gone, and she could settle back unmolested into her own tracks, which were apparently those of peace, but in reality like those of a caged panther. There was a strip of carpet worn threadbare in the sitting-room by Martha's pacing up and down. At last she had to take out that breadth and place it next the wall, and replace it.

People wondered why, with all Martha's sweetness and serenity, she had not professed religion and united with the church. When the minister came to talk with her about it he was non-plussed. She said with an innocent readiness which abashed him that she believed in the Christian religion, and trusted that she loved God; then it was as if she folded wings of concealment over her maiden character, and he could see no more.

It was at last another woman to whom she unbosomed herself, and she was a safe confidante; no safer could have been chosen. She was a far-removed cousin, and stone-deaf from scarlet fever when she was a baby.

She was a woman older than Martha, and had come to make her a visit. She lived with a married sister, to whom she was a burden, and who was glad to be rid of her for a few weeks. She could not hear one word that was spoken to her; she could only distinguish language uncertainly from the motion of the lips. She was absolutely penniless, except for a little which she earned by knitting cotton lace. To this woman Martha laid bare her soul the day before Christmas, as the two sat by the western windows, one knitting, the other darning a pair of white stockings.

"To-morrow's Christmas," said the deaf woman, suddenly, in her strange unmodulated voice. She had a flat pale face, with smooth loops of blond hair around the temples.

Martha said, "It ain't much Christmas to me."

"What?" returned the deaf woman.

"It ain't much Christmas to me," repeated Martha. She did not raise her voice in the least, and she moved her lips very little. Speech never disturbed the sweet serenity of her mouth. The deaf woman did not catch a word, but she was always sensitive about asking over for the second time. She knitted and acted as if she understood.

"No, it ain't much Christmas to me, and it never has been," said Martha. "I 'ain't never felt as if I had had any Christmas, for my part. I don't know where it has come in if I have. I never had a Christmas present in my whole life, unless I count in that purple crocheted shawl that Adeline gave me, that somebody gave her, and she couldn't wear, because it wasn't becomin'. I never thought much of it myself. Purple never suited me, either. That was the only Christmas present I ever had. That came a week after Christmas, ten year ago, and I suppose I might count that in. I kept it laid away, and the moths got into it."

"What?" said the deaf woman.

"The moths got into it," said Martha.

The deaf woman nodded wisely and knitted.

"Christmas!" said Martha, with a scorn at once pathetic and bitter—"talk about Christmas! What is Christmas to a woman all alone in the world as I am? If you want to see the loneliest thing in all creation, look at a woman all alone in the world. Adeline is twenty-five miles away, and she's got her family. I'm all alone. I might as well be at the north pole. What's Christmas to a woman without children, or any other women to think about, livin' with her? If I had any money to give it might be different. I might find folks to give to; other folks's children; but I 'ain't got any money. I've got nothing. I can't give any Christmas presents myself, and I can't have any. Lord! talk about Christmas to me! I can't help if I am wicked. I'm sick and tired of livin'. I have been for some time." Just then a farmer's team loaded with evergreens surmounted with merry boys went by, and she pointed tragically; and the deaf woman's eyes followed her pointing finger, and suddenly her great smiling face changed. "There they go with Christmas-trees for other women," said Martha; "for women who have got what I haven't. I never had a Christmas-tree. I never had a Christmas. The Lord never gave me one. I want one Christmas before I die. I've got a right to it. I want one Christmas-tree and one Christmas." Her voice rose to daring impetus; the deaf woman looked at her curiously.

"What?" said she.

"I want one Christmas," said Martha. Still the deaf woman did not hear, but suddenly the calm of her face broke up, she began to weep. It was as if she understood the other's mood by some subtler faculty than that of hearing. "Christmas is a pretty sad day to me," said she, "ever since poor mother died. I always realize more than any other time how alone I be, and how my room would be better than my company, and I don't ever have any presents. And I can't give any. I give all my knittin' money to Jane for my board, and that ain't near enough. Oh, Lord! it's a hard world!"

"I want one Christmas, and one Christmas-tree," said Martha, in a singular tone, almost as if she were demanding it of some unseen power.

"What?" said the deaf woman.

"I want one Christmas, and one Christmas-tree," repeated Martha.

The deaf woman nodded and knitted, after wiping her eyes. Her face was still quivering with repressed emotion.

Martha rose. "Well, there's no use talkin'," said she, in a hard voice; "folks can take what they get in this world, not what they want, I s'pose." Her face softened a little as she looked at the deaf woman. "I guess I'll make some toast for supper; there's enough milk," said she.

"What?" said the deaf woman.

Martha put her lips close to her ear, and shouted, "I guess I'll make some toast for supper." The deaf woman caught the word toast, and smiled happily, with a sniff of retreating grief; she was very fond of toast. "Jane 'most never has it," said she. As she sat there beside the window, she presently smelled the odor of toast coming in from the kitchen; then it began to snow. The snow fell in great damp blobs, coating all the trees thickly. When Martha entered the sitting-room to get a dish from the china-closet the deaf woman pointed, and said it was snowing.

"Yes, I see it is," replied Martha. "Well, it can snow, for all me. I 'ain't got any Christmas-tree to go to to-night."

As she spoke, both she and the deaf woman, looking out of the window, noted the splendid fir-balsam opposite, and at the same time a man with an axe, preparing to cut it down.

"Why, that man's goin' to cut down that tree! Ain't it on your land?" cried the deaf woman.

Martha shrieked and ran out of the house, bareheaded in the dense fall of snow. She caught hold of the man's arm, and he turned and looked at her with a sort of stolid surprise fast strengthening into obstinacy. "What you cuttin' down this tree for?" asked Martha.

The man muttered that he had been sent for one for Lawyer Ede.

"Well, you can't have mine," said Martha. "This ain't Lawyer Ede's land. His is on the other side of the fence. There are trees plenty good enough over there. You let mine be."

The man's arm which held the axe twitched. Suddenly Martha snatched it away by such an unexpected motion that he yielded. Then she was mistress of the situation. She stood before the tree, brandishing it. "If you dare to come one step nearer my tree, I'll kill you," said she. The man paled. He was a stolid farmer unused to women like her, or, rather, unused to such developments in women like her. "Give me that axe," he said.

"I'll give you that axe if you promise to cut down one of Lawyer Ede's trees, and let mine be!"

"All right," assented the man, sulkily.

"You go over the wall, then, and I'll hand you the axe."

The man, with a shuffling of reluctant yielding approached the wall and climbed over. Then Martha yielded up the axe. Then she stationed herself in front of her tree, to make sure that it was not harmed. The snow fell thick and fast on her uncovered head, but she did not mind. She remembered how once the man who had married her sister had said something to her beside this tree, when it was young like herself. She remembered long summer afternoons of her youth looking out upon it. Her old dreams and hopes of youth seemed still abiding beneath it, greeting her like old friends. She felt that she would have been killed herself, rather than have the tree harmed. The soothing fragrance of it came in her face. She felt suddenly as if the tree were alive. A great protecting tenderness for it came over her. She began to hear axe strokes on the other side of the wall. Then the deaf woman came to the door of the house, and stood there staring at her through the damp veil of snow. "You'll get your death out there, Marthy," she called out.

"No, I won't," replied Martha, knowing as she spoke that she was not heard.

"What be you stayin' out there for?" called the deaf woman in an alarmed voice. Martha made no reply.

Presently the woman came out through the snow; she paused before she reached her; it was quite evident what she feared even before she spoke. "Be you crazy?" asked she.

"I'm going to see to it that John Page don't cut down this tree," replied Martha. "I know how set the Pages are." The deaf woman stared helplessly at her, not hearing a word.

Then John Page came to the wall. "Look at here," he called out. "I ain't goin' to tech your tree. I thought it was on Ede's land. I'm cuttin' down another."

"You mind you don't," responded Martha, and she hardly knew her voice. When John Page went home that night he told his wife that he'd "never known that Martha Elder was such an up and comin' woman. Deliver me from dealin' with old maids," said he; "they're worse than barbed wire."

The snow continued until midnight, then the rain set in, then it cleared and froze. When the sun rose next morning everything was coated with ice. The fir-balsam was transfigured, wonderful. Every little twig glittered as with the glitter of precious stones, the branches spread low in rainbow radiances. Martha and the deaf woman stood at the sitting-room window looking out at it. Martha's face changed as she looked. She put her face close to the other woman's ear and shouted: "Look here, Abby, you ain't any too happy with Jane; you stay here with me this winter. I'm lonesome, and we'll get along somehow." The deaf woman heard her, and a great light came into her flat countenance.

"Stay with you?"

Martha nodded.

"I earn enough to pay for the flour and sugar," said she, eagerly, "and you've got vegetables in the cellar, and I don't want another thing to eat, and I'll do all the work if you'll let me, Marthy."

"I'll be glad to have you stay," said Martha, with the eagerness of one who grasps at a treasure.

"Do you mean you want me to stay?" asked the deaf woman, wistfully, still fearing that she had not heard aright. Martha nodded.

"I'll go out in the kitchen and make some of them biscuit I used to make for breakfast," said the deaf woman. "God bless you, Marthy!"

Martha stood staring at the glorified fir-balsam. All at once it seemed to her that she saw herself as she was in her youth, under it. Old possessions filled her soul with rapture, and the conviction of her inalienable birthright of the happiness of life was upon her. She also seemed to see all the joys which she had possessed or longed for in the radius of its radiance; its boughs seemed overladen with fulfilment and promise, and a truth came to her for the great Christmas present of her life. She became sure that whatever happiness God gives He never retakes, and, moreover, that He holds ready the food for all longing, that one cannot exist without the other.

"Whatever I've ever had that I loved, I've got," said Martha Elder, "and whatever I've wanted, I'm goin' to have." Then she turned around and went out in the kitchen to help about breakfast, and the dazzle of the Christmas tree was so great in her eyes that she was almost blinded to all the sordid conditions of her daily life.

About Hannah Stone

Everybody's Magazine, January 1901, 25–33

IT HAPPENED TEN years ago, the first Christmas we ever had a tree in our Sunday-school. It isn't so very much to tell, only it is curious how a man or woman may live almost a whole lifetime in one place, and people think they know them root and branch, then all of a sudden something happens that sort of tops off and rounds up the whole, as it were, and people find out that they are beyond and above what they'd always thought.

Folks had always thought they knew Hannah Stone pretty well. I'm sure I thought I did, and so did sister Caroline. Caroline and I often used to talk about Hannah, and it wasn't any too complimentary what we said. Caroline and I, through our never being married and always living together, had come to say exactly what was in our minds to each other. It didn't amount to much more than thinking with us, but everybody else talked just as we did, right out. Everybody said that Hannah Stone was a strange woman. In the first place she lived all alone on the finest farm in the county, in a dreadful lonesome spot, too, almost on the top of Crook Neck Mountain. It is called Crook Neck because it has a queer long slope to the southward, then a great bulge, for all the world like a crook-neck squash. Hannah lived well up the long southern slope, all alone, except for the dummy man that her father had taken, when he was a boy, from the almshouse. The dummy, according to all accounts, wasn't much more than a machine; but he was a good machine.

They do say that dummy can turn off more work than three men that can talk and hear. Maybe it is because he doesn't have his mind taken from his work so much. Sister Caroline often says that if we had all the time we waste in talking, and hearing other people, we could do a good deal more work in the world. But when it comes to that, Hannah Stone doesn't talk much more than the dummy man, and she works. I suppose there isn't a man in the village can begin to do a bigger day's work than Hannah. She goes right out in the field and works, ploughing and planting, wood-chopping, too. Many's the time I've seen Hannah Stone driving her ox-sled through the village with a load of wood, and she'd pitch it off just like a man, too. One winter she brought a load to Caroline and me, and I felt dreadful queer to see another woman pitching off wood at our back door, and so did Caroline.

I said to Caroline that it didn't seem right and according to the fitness of things, and she said she felt so too. It was a bitter cold day, and the wind was coming in blasts enough to take your head off round the corner of our house. Hannah had on mittens and a Bay State shawl, with the ends crossed in front and tied behind, and a worsted hood, but her face was blue. Finally I couldn't stand it another minute. I wrapped up real warm, and I went out. Caroline had a cold, and couldn't, anyhow. I went round to the tail of that ox-sled, and I began dragging off the wood. It was all I could do—I never was a strong build. Then Hannah stopped and came round to me. "What be you doin', Kate?" said she. Hannah and I used to go to school together, and had always been Hannah and Kate to each other.

I spoke up real sharp. "If a woman as well off as you are, with a man to help her, is going to haul wood such a day as this, I ain't going to sit in a warm room and look out of the window and see it," said I. Then I dragged off another great stick. Hannah she didn't say anything, but she just took hold of my arm, and walked me up to the house, and I hadn't any more strength against her than a baby. "Now you go right in," said she, then, and her lips were so stiff with the cold that she could hardly speak. I had to go, but I was angry enough, and I just called back at her that she ought to be ashamed of herself; that it was a disgrace to the whole town to have a woman working like that such a day; and that she needn't ever bring any more wood to Caroline and me, anyhow.

Hannah didn't say a word back; she just kept on unloading her team, with Caroline and me looking on, and scolding her out the window. Then she drove her oxen out of the yard. She looked as shapeless as a Hindoo idol standing up in front of the sled. The fringe of her Bay State shawl blew in the wind, but Hannah Stone didn't look as if any mortal wind could move her if she didn't want to go.

Caroline and I heard afterward that the dummy man was down with rheumatism, and we had written to Hannah that we were dreadful hard off for wood, and we felt kind of conscience-stricken.

Hannah had the name of being very well off. People said that she had a great deal in the savings-bank, besides her farm, and she was called very hard at a bargain. Nobody could overreach her, and, maybe in consequence, it was said that she overreached other people. Caroline and I never really believed that, but she was so exactly just that it did use to seem rather mean to us. For instance, Caroline and I were out driving one day and stopped at Hannah's to buy some peas, and she had to measure them out in a pail, because the dummy man was out peddling with the peck measure, and she came way down from her farm that night because she had given us about a gill too many. I can see her now as she stood at our door with her arm crooked around her peck measure. "I found out I give you a gill extra, and as long as I knew you wasn't going to boil them till to-morrow, I came for them," said she, and she didn't act as if she was doing a thing out of the way. Caroline and I looked at each other, then I went and measured out those peas, and gave them to Hannah.

Hannah was always doing things like that; the village rang with them. Sometimes, though, it worked the other way around. I know for a fact about Hannah's driving down in a blinding snow-storm because Alexander Dean had given her two cents too much for a load of wood. Alexander Dean is a church-member now, but he used to be a very profane man, and sometimes his old habit takes him unawares. They said he swore at Hannah awfully when he went to the door, and saw her pulling that two cents from her mitten. I *can't* repeat just what he said, but he asked what in—— made her come down in that howling storm with that—— two cents; and Hannah said that she was afraid that something might happen to her, and he would lose it. They did say that Alexander Dean was so mad that he flung the two cents into a snowbank, but I don't know about that.

There are a great many stories of unsuccessful attempts to overreach Hannah Stone. Once Deacon Alvin Gay sold her a cow, and when she sent the dummy man for her, the deacon sent the wrong cow, not worth more'n a quarter of the one Hannah had bought. Hannah had paid a good round sum for the cow, too. Alvin Gay has always had the name of doing things like that, if he is a deacon, so people were inclined to believe it, though he declared it wasn't so, and Hannah had overreached him, instead of him her. Anyway, it was late Saturday night when the dummy man took that wrong cow home. They said he made all sorts of signs that it wasn't right, but the deacon he made believe that he didn't understand. Well, bright and early the next morning, on the Sabbath Day, Hannah came, dressed in her meeting dress and bonnet, walking down from her farm, leading the cow. She led her up to the deacon's front door—the deacon lives next to the meeting-house—and she knocked, and the deacon's wife, who is a real mild-spoken woman, came to the door. She didn't know what it all meant, and she looked sort of scared-like at Hannah standing there with the cow. "Good-morning," said she.

"I want to see the deacon," said Hannah.

Then the deacon's wife called him, and he came with his face all red with the soap and water scrubbing he had given it, and with struggling into his Sunday collar, and trying to hide that he was in a twitter. "Why, good-mornin', Miss Stone," said he, just as if he was going to speak in meeting, kind of pleasant, but solemn. Hannah told me all about it afterward, when I had come to know her better.

Hannah didn't waste any ceremony. She always went straight to the point. "Where is the cow I bought?" said she.

"Why, ain't that the cow you bought?" said the deacon.

"No, it ain't," said she.

Then the deacon kind of cleared his throat. It was queer, but he hated to tell a downright lie, though he would always overreach in a bargain, if what folks say is true. "Why, you talked about buying that cow, didn't you?" said he. "You looked at that cow."

"I looked at her, and I looked away again," said Hannah. "I wouldn't take her as a gift. You know this ain't the cow I bought, Deacon Gay; she's something the same color, but you know she ain't the one, and you don't dare to say she is. Now I want the cow I bought."

Then the deacon got desperate, and he *did* lie. "That is the cow you bought," said he.

"It ain't," said she.

"Yes, it is," said he, "and what is more, it's all the cow you'll get. A bargain is a bargain."

"Do you mean to say that you, a deacon of the church, are goin' to try to palm off this old cow on me for that fine young Jersey I bought?" said Hannah.

"This is the cow you bought," declared the deacon. "This is the cow I understood you wanted, and the one your dummy man came for. I wouldn't have let that Jersey go, anyhow."

Hannah didn't say any more; she had talked a good deal for her, as it was. She just gathered up her best black silk, and she sat down on the deacon's front door-step. She was still holding the rope with the cow at the other end of it.

The deacon looked at her. "I suppose you know it's the Sabbath Day?" said he finally.

"I ain't lost my reckonin'," said Hannah.

"And it don't look becomin' for a woman to be leadin' around cows when it's most time for the bell to ring for meetin'," said the deacon.

Hannah didn't say anything. The cow begun to eat the top of Mrs. Gay's peony bush, which was all in full blow.

"What be you goin' to do?" said the deacon finally, kind of feeble like.

"I'm going to set here till you give me that cow I bought," said Hannah.

"Why, don't you know that the folks will be comin' to meetin' in a minute? And this is next door to the meetin'-house, and you settin' here with this cow," said the deacon.

Hannah said nothing.

The deacon gave a kind of grunt and went into the house. The cow went on eating the peony.

Pretty soon a team drove up to the meeting-house, and the deacon came out again. He looked after the team kind of wild, then he looked at the cow. "I dunno but pinies are bad for cows to eat," said he.

"Well, it is nothin' to me, it ain't my cow," said Hannah.

"Of course it's your cow."

"No, it ain't, it's your cow. If you don't want her to eat pinies, you can take her and put her in the barn, and give me my cow that I bought and paid for."

Well, the upshot of it all was, Deacon Gay was so scared at the idea of Hannah sitting there when folks were going to meeting, and his wife came out and cried a little and whispered to him, too, that he gave in. He got fairly desperate. He promised solemn that Hannah should have the Jersey, and he promised, too, in the presence of his wife and the hired girl. Hannah had them both out for witnesses. Then the deacon led off the old cow to the barn, and Hannah rose up, and shook her black silk dress, and went to meeting. That story got all over town, and though it didn't reflect to the credit of the deacon, for some reason or other it did not seem to prepossess people in favor of Hannah. Sister Caroline and I, in talking it over one afternoon, agreed that sometimes it seemed as if people, especially men folks, liked women better that they *could* take in.

Hannah, besides the reputation of being very sharp at a bargain, had also the name of being very close in money matters. It was said that she never gave a cent to anybody. So when it was decided to have a Christmas tree in the Sunday-school, nobody thought that Hannah would do anything toward it. I was on the committee to solicit presents for the tree, and so was Caroline, and we both of us thought that we wouldn't ask Hannah to give anything. "It's no use going way up there," said Caroline; "I know she won't give a cent." I thought so, too. However, when the time came, and I was starting out one afternoon, I thought to myself, "Well, I will ask Hannah Stone, whether or no. It can't do any harm, and if she's ever called to account for not giving, she won't have for an excuse that she wasn't asked. It won't be my fault." So I climbed up the slope of Crook Neck Mountain to Hannah's house. It was quite a climb on such a cold day, with the wind in my face all the way. When I got there I looked around, and I thought to myself that it did look prosperous, and as if Hannah could afford to give if she wanted to. Everything was spick and span; not a picket loose on the fences, nor a stone off the walls. There was a great flock of hens and another of turkeys in front of the barn, and the dummy man was feeding them. The barn-door was open, and I could see the long row of tails of Hannah's heard of Jersey cows. I went round to the side door, and knocked, and Hannah came. She had on her Bay State shawl and hood.

"Why, good-afternoon, Kate; come in," said she.

"Are you going out?" said I; "because I won't hinder you if you are."

"Oh, I'm only goin' to help David milk," said she.

Then I spoke right out the way I always do when I see anybody treated unjustly, whether it's by other folks or themselves. "You don't mean to say that you are going out to milk on such a cold day as this, when you've got that great strapping man to help!" said I.

"Don't you know?" asked Hannah, and I saw the tears in her eyes.

"Know what?" said I.

"I'm afraid he's got the consumption, the first stages," said Hannah.

"How do you know?"

"He coughs," said she; "besides the doctor as good as says so. He says his lungs are weak, and he's got to be very careful."

"Well, of course, I didn't know that," said I.

"He's been in the family ever since I can remember, and poor father thought a lot of him, and he's been as faithful and good as he could be, and he all the time livin', as it were, behind prison-bars, and never gettin' the comfort out of life that other folks do," said Hannah, and she wiped her eyes with the back of her mitten.

"Why, I'm real sorry he's so poorly," said I, and I felt sort of ashamed of myself. I asked Hannah if he had tried molasses and butter and vinegar boiled together till it was thick, and she said he had, and it hadn't done a mite of good, and now he was taking cod-liver oil. I just stepped inside, so I shouldn't cold the house, and asked Hannah if she wanted to do something for the Christmas tree, and to my surprise she jumped at it. "Of course I will," said she. "When do you want it?"

"Why, any time before Christmas," said I. "Would you rather give money or presents?"

"I would rather give presents," said she. "If I have it ready the day before Christmas it will be time enough, won't it?"

"Plenty, if you have it down to the meeting-house by three o'clock," said I.

"Well, I will," said she, and I couldn't help staring at her. Her eyes shone, and she looked as bright and full of interest as a girl.

That night when I got home and told Caroline that Hannah Stone was going to give something to the Christmas tree, she just leaned back and laughed till she cried. "I guess she'll give some last year's potatoes," said she.

I confess I begun to think that Hannah would not give much when that happened about young Thomas Green. Young Thomas is our minister Thomas Green's son, and we always call him young Thomas to distinguish him from his father, though he is through college long ago, and settled in a parish of his own. At that time he was just in college, and had come home for the holidays, and he went with some other boys to get the Christmas tree. Hannah had a piece of woodland covered with a fine growth of young hemlocks, and the boys went straight there and cut one. They never asked permission. I don't suppose it entered their heads that any human being would grudge one of all those hemlocks for a Christmas tree. But they didn't know Hannah Stone. They were getting down the mountain slope in great style with the tree on the ox-sled, all the boys laughing and hurrahing, when out came Hannah to her gate.

"Where did you get that tree?" said she.

Billy Snow, who was driving—they were his father's oxen—shouted to them to stop, and young Thomas spoke up sort of bewildered.

"We got it in the woods just above here," said he, pulling off his cap.

"Them is my woods," said Hannah.

Then young Thomas and the other boys looked at one another.

"I don't let folks have my trees for nothin' unless I set out to give them," said Hannah.

"But this is for the Christmas tree down to the church," said young Thomas, as red as a beet.

"That don't make no difference," said Hannah.

"How much do you want for this tree?" said young Thomas.

"Two dollars," said Hannah.

Well, the boys clubbed together and paid it, then they started up the oxen and came home pretty mad, and in an hour the story was all over the village. After that Caroline and I didn't have as much stock in Hannah's doing for the Christmas tree, but, as I said when I begun, nobody can tell about anybody else till things get through happening to bring them out; and as they never do get through happening, it follows that nobody ever does know, though they may make a sudden jump ahead in knowledge, as we did with Hannah Stone.

Caroline and I worked very hard getting up that Christmas tree. We went to Boston once to buy things, but we bought mostly in Rye, the big town six miles from our village. Several times when we were coming home from Rye, we met Hannah all wrapped up in her sleigh, with a lot of bundles. Once she stopped and spoke to us, and asked how we were getting on with the Christmas tree, and then I spoke right out; I couldn't help it. "We are getting on very well, and no thanks to you, Hannah Stone," said I.

"What do you mean, Kate?" said Hannah.

"I mean," said I, "that if I had known what a mean woman you would grow up to be, a woman mean enough to grudge one tree out of a whole grove for Christmas, and make those poor boys pay for it, I would never have sat next to you when we went to school if I'd been whipped for refusing to; that's what I mean," said I.

Hannah she never said one word back, and I slapped the reins over our horse and we went on. Caroline said she didn't know but I was most too harsh to speak so to Hannah, but I said it was no more than she deserved.

Well, the day before Christmas came, and Caroline and I had been hard at work in the meeting-house ever since eight o'clock in the morning, and had just run home at three o'clock in the afternoon to get a cup of tea and a mouthful to eat.

All of a sudden Caroline, who was facing the window, cried out: "My sakes, just look!" said she. "Just look, Kate!"

Then I looked, and Caroline and I both jumped up and ran to the window, and there she was! There was Hannah Stone standing on her ox-team, driving, and there was the dummy man, all wrapped up in a buffalo coat which Hannah had bought for him on account of his consumption, holding on to a tree all set up in a butter firkin. And the tree was a splendid hemlock, as straight and evenly pointed as if a special gardener had tended it on purpose, and it was loaded down with presents. We could see the dolls dancing, and the oranges bobbing, and bright-covered books, and paper parcels of all kinds and shapes.

Caroline looked at me, and she was as white as a sheet. "Hannah Stone has brought a whole Christmas tree," said she, and she gasped, and I had to get her a glass of water, though I was pretty near as bad myself.

"You don't suppose she's crazy, do you?" said Caroline, sort of faint-like. "I never heard of any crazy folks among the Stones, did you?"

"No, I never did," said I.

All of a sudden Caroline broke down and begun to cry.

"What are you crying for?" said I.

"She won't have a single present herself," said Caroline. "Oh, dear!"

"She shall, too," said I. Then I went upstairs and I got out a real handsome hemstitched apron that I had never worn, and Caroline she found a real pretty box and put a new handkerchief—a real fine one—in it, and then we went over to the meeting-house, and I declare if all the women weren't studying what they could give to Hannah.

When that great Christmas tree had been carried into the meeting-house, the women there most had hysterics.

That evening we found out that Hannah had given everybody in the Sunday-school and every member of the church a present, and some of them were pretty substantial.

I went up to Hannah after the presents were all distributed, with my album in my hand. Caroline was behind me with her box of paper, and she was almost crying. "I want to thank you, and I want to ask you to forgive me for speaking to you the way I did about the Christmas tree the other day," said I.

Hannah looked at me with a curious kind of dignity, like one standing up for her principles, though she was smiling. "Givin' is givin', and sellin' is sellin'," said she.

She gazed down at her load of presents. She had, I guess, as many as a dozen white aprons, and more handkerchiefs, and a blue worsted fascinator, and a pretty tidy, and I don't know what all. "I never had a Christmas present before in my life," said she.

Then she looked up at me and her eyes were full of tears, and I could see the little-girl look in her face, as I remembered her at school, very strong, and I begun to think that maybe we had both been learning the same lessons in life in different ways.

General: A Christmas Story

New-York Tribune Illustrated Supplement, December 22, 1901, 13

EUGENE WAS NAMED after his youngest uncle, on his mother's side, but everybody called him "General." First it had been "Genie," but as his masterly character developed, it became "General." When the neighbors saw him coming, usually at the head of a small troop of his brothers and sisters and friends, they said: "There's General Newman." As a rule, they finished with an indulgent chuckle, for General was a favorite. Everybody agreed that he was a good boy and very smart. He did an errand as if he were a peer of the realm and, with infinite condescension, he pocketed his penny in payment, as if it were a gratuity. But he did errands willingly and well, and while he made others obey he never disobeyed himself. "For all he's so up and comin' he minds me better than any of them," his mother often remarked.

General was the eldest of five children, three girls and two boys. His father was dead: his mother, Mrs. Abby Newman, supported the family by working a small farm. She kept one hired man, and worked herself like a slave. With great economy and toil she managed to keep her family in comfort, and she was determined that the children should have good educations. General was large and strong for his age, and many of the neighbors thought that she was foolish not to put him to work, but she was resolute. "He's goin' to know something," she declared, "and he helps a good deal out of school."

General, ever since he was ten, had risen in the mornings at 5 o'clock, assisted the hired man with the barn chores, drawn the water and made the kitchen fire. All the Newman children were trained to work, and they accomplished a good deal before they set off for school—washed, brushed and tidy.

The new teacher came in the fall when Eugene was nearly fourteen. She was a pretty girl, her name Aurelia May, and she had many new ideas. Among others was the Christmas tree. There had never been a Christmas tree in № 5 school, which was located on the outskirts of the village, among the scattered farming part of the population. There had been a Christmas tree in the Sunday school, but never one in the day school.

When Miss Aurelia May announced that this year there would be a tree on Christmas eve (the Sunday school tree was to be on Christmas night), there was much excitement, not only among the students, but their parents. The mothers met in each other's sitting rooms and kitchens and talked a good deal. Some of them declared that a tree in the Sunday school was enough, and all they could manage. "It took all the butter money I had saved last year for Christmas," declared one woman, and the others echoed her.

Finally, however, the pretty school teacher carried the day. "I declare I hated to say anything, she was so set on it," said Mrs. John Sargent. The teacher boarded at Mrs. John Sargent's, and little Lottie Sargent adored her.

But there was one woman who never abandoned her position, and she was General's mother. Mrs. Newman had said at first, she had told the neighbors and the teacher so, and she had told her children so, that she could and would do nothing about the Christmas tree. "If it had been an apple year I might have managed it, but it ain't an apple year and I haven't got enough money for another Christmas tree unless I run in debt or mortgage the place," she said. "I can manage to give you children some useful things, that you really need, and I'd have to get anyway, on the Sunday school tree, but as for doing anything about the day school, I can't do it, and I don't want to hear another word about it. I have enough to contend with without being teased to do something I can't do."

The younger children pouted, and little Sallie and Henry openly sobbed, but General only looked thoughtful.

"May I use my bank money?" he asked, finally.

"You can't have more than 50 cents, for you opened your bank last Fourth of July," the mother answered.

"Can I have what is in it?"

"Yes, if you want to," she replied grudgingly. "You ought to use the money, however, to buy shoes, but you can have it."

General's face cleared. "All right," he said, "guess I can do something."

His second sister, Addie, pulled his sleeve, when his mother's back was turned. "What be you goin' to do?" she whispered.

"You jest wait an' see," replied her brother mysteriously.

"You goin' to get presents for all of us?"

"I reckon so."

"For Tommy Jones, and Lottie, and Maria Dodd, and Willie Lapham, and"—

"Guess so."

"What?"

"You jest wait."

General was as important and secretive during the three weeks before Christmas as any commander before a strategic move upon the enemy. His brothers and sisters watched, but they could discover nothing. General was known to make several visits to the store, but they could find out nothing that he purchased except paper and string. They found rolls of nice white paper and brown paper and various colored balls of cord in his little hair trunk, which had belonged to his grandfather and in which he kept his treasures. "It's to tie up the presents," they said to one another, and their expectations grew.

Gradually it became noised about the school that General Newman was going to give splendid presents to a lot of children, and his popularity was on the increase. He had so much deference that his head might have been turned if he had not been a pretty stanch, honest little boy.

General worked hard helping the teacher, and, what was more, he made the others work—not a boy dared shirk when General's eyes were upon him. Even the teacher began to marvel at his power over his mates. "I declare I believe that boy can make the others mind better than I can," she said to Mrs. Sargent, with whom she boarded.

"He's an awful smart boy," agreed Mrs. Sargent.

On Christmas Eve the students and their big brothers and sisters and their parents assembled in the schoolhouse. Even Mrs. Abby Newman was there, in her old best black silk. The children had been so happy about it all that she had not the heart to stay away. Then, too, she had much pride in her eldest son and curiosity as to what he was going to do. She was conscious of a great faith in him. "He's an awful smart boy," she told herself.

Indeed, that evening sitting at his desk in the evergreen trimmed schoolroom, the General looked handsomer and smarter than ever. His fair hair curled aggressively on top, his blue eyes were brilliant, there was not a shade of doubt or anxiety in his face. He looked confident of all that Christmas or life might bring him. Mrs. Newman felt herself fairly glowing with pride as she gazed at him.

The beautiful lighted tree stood on the platform, and a young man named Abner Whittemore—he was said to admire the teacher—was dressed in a buffalo coat, to personate Santa Claus, and distributed the presents.

The names of the Newman children were called over and over—Miss Ruth Newman, Miss Sallie D. Newman, Master Henry Perkins Newman, Miss Addie Newman, Master Eugene Newman. Names also of a large number of the scholars who were particular friends of theirs were frequently repeated. They all marched away from the tree with jubilant faces. However, the faces changed when they came to examine their treasures more closely. They were very neat little packages tied up in fresh papers, with bright colored cords. They looked like boxes of various shapes and sizes. The students who had these boxes regarded them with expressions of mingled wonder and dismay. Not one was untied. Gradually the news of something was written, or rather printed, on the tops of the packages spread around. "Have you seen those funny presents General Newman has been giving?" everybody asked of everybody else. This was printed on the packages very plainly:

> Don't you open this till next Fourth of July. If you do, look out.
>
> E. NEWMAN.

Mrs. Abby Newman stood apart, talking to the minister's wife and the teacher, and knew nothing about the warning notes until little Sallie came crying to her with her unopened present and begged that she wouldn't let Genie scold her if she took the string off.

Then Mrs. Newman examined the package and the inscription with amazement. "They're all just like that," sobbed Sallie, "and they can't open them till the Fourth of July, he says."

"I'm going to see what all this foolishness means!" declared Mrs. Abby Newman.

When General looked up and saw his mother's face his heart sank.

The other boys, looking on, saw him quail before the small, weary looking woman. “Eugene Newman, what does all this mean?” she demanded. The room was quite still. The crowd about them became noiselessly augmented. Everybody came tiptoeing up. The children stood gaping with eyes of innocent wonder and curiosity.

“Eugene!” said Mrs. Newman.

The boy choked and gasped.

“Eugene, tell me this minute what is in those packages!”

The general hung his head; his candid forehead was red to the roots of his curly hair. Then suddenly he faced his mother, and them all, with his honest, confident look. He had done nothing to be ashamed of.

“What is in them?” asked his mother.

“Nothin’ but wood,” replied General Newman.

“Wood?” echoed the others.

“Yes, it’s nothin’ but wood in all of ’em,” proclaimed General, clearly.

“Eugene Newman!” gasped his mother. Her face was blazing with mortification. Was this her wonderful, smart boy? She realized how desirable it would be to sink through the floor away from all these curious eyes.

Then suddenly the boy came to the rescue.

“There’s somethin’ on the wood,” he admitted, with reluctance, yet as one who must clear his honor from imputation.

“What?” cried his mother, eagerly.

“My note,” replied General, and he held his head high.

“Your note?” his mother gasped, feebly.

“Yes, ma’am.”

His mother made a clutch at one of the packages, which a little boy near her held, and tore off the wrapping, and there was a nice little block of wood, and thereon printed, after the form in the arithmetic:

> For value received I promise to pay to Willy Lapham on order, six months and ten days from date, one good top.
>
> “EUGENE NEWMAN.”

Then Mrs. John Sargent caught her Lottie’s package, and opened it, and there was the same thing, only in that Eugene Newman promised to pay Lottie Sargent one doll with light hair, and others were opened and they were the same with a difference. Poor Eugene in all of them had given, for lack of presents, his promissory note.

"I'd like to know where you expected to get the money?" his mother inquired, sharply.

"Uncle Eugene said he was going to make me a present of $10 the Fourth when I was fourteen years old, and I'm goin' to give every one of 'em," he replied, sturdily.

Then a faint cheer went up and some of the women wiped their eyes.

Mrs. Abby Newman began to feel that perhaps she had no need to be ashamed of her boy after all.

General Newman had so many presents on the Sunday school tree the next evening that he was nearly overcome. He could not believe his eyes when he saw the jackknives, the tops, the sled and the books. Every one of the friends to whom he had presented his promissory note had been furnished with a present to hang on the tree for him, but he never dreamed why.

Jimmy Scarecrow's Christmas

The Children's Book of Christmas Stories, edited by Asa Don Dickinson and Ada M. Skinner (New York: Doubleday & Company, 1913), 103–12

JIMMY SCARECROW LED a sad life in the winter. Jimmy's greatest grief was his lack of occupation. He liked to be useful, and in winter he was absolutely of no use at all.

He wondered how many such miserable winters he would have to endure. He was a young Scarecrow, and this was his first one. He was strongly made, and although his wooden joints creaked a little when the wind blew he did not grow in the least rickety. Every morning, when the wintry sun peered like a hard yellow eye across the dry corn-stubble, Jimmy felt sad, but at Christmas time his heart nearly broke.

On Christmas Eve Santa Claus came in his sledge heaped high with presents, urging his team of reindeer across the field. He was on his way to the farmhouse where Betsey lived with her Aunt Hannah.

Betsey was a very good little girl with very smooth yellow curls, and she had a great many presents. Santa Claus had a large wax doll-baby for her on his arm, tucked up against the fur collar of his coat. He was afraid to trust it in the pack, lest it get broken.

When poor Jimmy Scarecrow saw Santa Claus his heart gave a great leap. "Santa Claus! Here I am!" he cried out, but Santa Claus did not hear him.

"Santa Claus, please give me a little present. I was good all summer and kept the crows out of the corn," pleaded the poor Scarecrow in his choking voice, but Santa Claus passed by with a merry halloo and a great clamour of bells.

Then Jimmy Scarecrow stood in the corn-stubble and shook with sobs until his joints creaked. "I am of no use in the world, and everybody has forgotten me," he moaned. But he was mistaken.

The next morning Betsey sat at the window holding her Christmas doll-baby, and she looked out at Jimmy Scarecrow standing alone in the field amidst the corn-stubble.

"Aunt Hannah?" said she. Aunt Hannah was making a crazy patchwork quilt, and she frowned hard at a triangular piece of red silk and circular piece of pink, wondering how to fit them together. "Well?" said she.

"Did Santa Claus bring the Scarecrow any Christmas present?"

"No, of course he didn't."

"Why not?"

"Because he's a Scarecrow. Don't ask silly questions."

"I wouldn't like to be treated so, if I was a Scarecrow," said Betsey, but her Aunt Hannah did not hear her. She was busy cutting a triangular snip out of the round piece of pink silk so the piece of red silk could be feather-stitched into it.

It was snowing hard out of doors, and the north wind blew. The Scare-crow's poor old coat got whiter and whiter with snow. Sometimes he almost vanished in the thick white storm. Aunt Hannah worked until the middle of the afternoon on her crazy quilt. Then she got up and spread it out over the sofa with an air of pride.

"There," said she, "that's done, and that makes the eighth. I've got one for every bed in the house, and I've given four away. I'd give this away if I knew of anybody that wanted it."

Aunt Hannah put on her hood and shawl, and drew some blue yarn stockings on over her shoes, and set out through the snow to carry a slice of plum-pudding to her sister Susan, who lived down the road. Half an hour after Aunt Hannah had gone Betsey put her little red plaid shawl over her head, and ran across the field to Jimmy Scarecrow. She carried her new doll-baby smuggled up under her shawl.

"Wish you Merry Christmas!" she said to Jimmy Scarecrow.

"Wish you the same," said Jimmy, but his voice was choked with sobs, and was also muffled, for his old hat had slipped down to his chin. Betsey looked pitifully at the old hat fringed with icicles, like frozen tears, and the old snow-laden coat. "I've brought you a Christmas present," said she, and with that she tucked her doll-baby inside Jimmy Scarecrow's coat, sticking its tiny feet into a pocket.

"Thank you," said Jimmy Scarecrow faintly.

"You're welcome," said she. "Keep her under your overcoat, so the snow won't wet her, and she won't catch cold, she's delicate."

"Yes, I will," said Jimmy Scarecrow, and he tried hard to bring one of his stiff, outstretched arms around to clasp the doll-baby.

"Don't you feel cold in that old summer coat?" asked Betsey.

"If I had a little exercise, I should be warm," he replied. But he shivered, and the wind whistled through his rags.

"You wait a minute," said Betsey, and was off across the field.

Jimmy Scarecrow stood in the corn-stubble, with the doll-baby under his coat, and waited, and soon Betsey was back again with Aunt Hannah's crazy quilt trailing in the snow behind her.

"Here," said she, "here is something to keep you warm," and she folded the crazy quilt around the Scarecrow and pinned it.

"Aunt Hannah wants to give it away if anybody wants it," she explained. "She's got so many crazy quilts in the house now she doesn't know what to do with them. Good-bye—be sure you keep the doll-baby covered up." And with that she ran across the field, and left Jimmy Scarecrow alone with the crazy quilt and the doll-baby.

The bright flash of colours under Jimmy's hat-brim dazzled his eyes, and he felt a little alarmed. "I hope this quilt is harmless if it *is* crazy," he said. But the quilt was warm, and he dismissed his fears. Soon the doll-baby whimpered, but he creaked his joints a little, and that amused it, and he heard it cooing inside his coat.

Jimmy Scarecrow had never felt so happy in his life as he did for an hour or so. But after that the snow began to turn to rain, and the crazy quilt was soaked through and through: and not only that, but his coat and the poor doll-baby. It cried pitifully for a while, and then it was still, and he was afraid it was dead.

It grew very dark, and the rain fell in sheets, the snow melted, and Jimmy Scarecrow stood halfway up his old boots in water. He was saying to himself that the saddest hour of his life had come, when suddenly he again heard Santa Claus' sleigh-bells and his merry voice talking to his reindeer. It was after midnight, Christmas was over, and Santa was hastening home to the North Pole.

"Santa Claus! dear Santa Claus!" cried Jimmy Scarecrow with a great sob, and that time Santa Claus heard him and drew rein.

"Who's there?" he shouted out of the darkness.

"It's only me," replied the Scarecrow.

"Who's me?" shouted Santa Claus.

"Jimmy Scarecrow!"

Santa got out of his sledge and waded up. "Have you been standing here ever since corn was ripe?" he asked pityingly, and Jimmy replied that he had.

"What's that over your shoulders?" Santa Claus continued, holding up his lantern.

"It's a crazy quilt."

"And what are you holding under your coat?"

"The doll-baby that Betsey gave me, and I'm afraid it's dead," poor Jimmy Scarecrow sobbed.

"Nonsense!" cried Santa Claus. "Let me see it!" And with that he pulled the doll-baby out from under the Scarecrow's coat, and patted its back, and shook it a little, and it began to cry, and then to crow. "It's all right," said Santa Claus. "This is the doll-baby I gave Betsey, and it is not at all delicate. It went through the measles, and the chicken-pox, and the mumps, and the whooping-cough, before it left the North Pole. Now get into the sledge, Jimmy Scarecrow, and bring the doll-baby and the crazy quilt. I have never had any quilts that weren't in their right minds at the North Pole, but maybe I can cure this one. Get in!" Santa chirruped to his reindeer, and they drew the sledge up close in a beautiful curve.

"Get in, Jimmy Scarecrow, and come with me to the North Pole!" he cried.

"Please, how long shall I stay?" asked Jimmy Scarecrow.

"Why, you are going to live with me," replied Santa Claus. "I've been looking for a person like you for a long time."

"Are there any crows to scare away at the North Pole? I want to be useful," Jimmy Scarecrow said, anxiously.

"No," answered Santa Claus, "but I don't want you to scare away crows. I want you to scare away Arctic Explorers. I can keep you in work for a thousand years, and scaring away Arctic Explorers from the North Pole is much more important than scaring away crows from corn. Why, if they found the Pole, there wouldn't be a piece an inch long left in a week's time, and the earth would cave in like an apple without a core! They would whittle it all to pieces, and carry it away in their pockets for souvenirs. Come along; I am in a hurry."

"I will go on two conditions," said Jimmy. "First, I want to make a present to Aunt Hannah and Betsey, next Christmas."

"You shall make them any present you choose. What else?"

"I want some way provided to scare the crows out of the corn next summer, while I am away," said Jimmy.

"That is easily managed," said Santa Claus. "Just wait a minute."

Santa took his stylographic pen out of his pocket, went with his lantern close to one of the fence-posts, and wrote these words upon it:

NOTICE TO CROWS

Whichever crow shall hereafter hop, fly, or flop into this field during the absence of Jimmy Scarecrow, and therefrom purloin, steal, or abstract corn, shall be instantly, in a twinkling and a trice, turned snow-white, and be ever after a disgrace, a by-word and a reproach to his whole race.

PER ORDER OF SANTA CLAUS.

"The corn will be safe now," said Santa Claus, "get in." Jimmy got into the sledge and they flew away over the fields, out of sight, with merry halloos and a great clamour of bells.

The next morning there was much surprise at the farmhouse, when Aunt Hannah and Betsey looked out of the window and the Scarecrow was not in the field holding out his stiff arms over the corn stubble. Betsey had told Aunt Hannah she had given away the crazy quilt and the doll-baby, but had been scolded very little.

"You must not give away anything of yours again without asking permission," said Aunt Hannah. "And you have no right to give anything of mine, even if you know I don't want it. Now both my pretty quilt and your beautiful doll-baby are spoiled."

That was all Aunt Hannah had said. She thought she would send John after the quilt and the doll-baby next morning as soon as it was light.

But Jimmy Scarecrow was gone, and the crazy quilt and the doll-baby with him. John, the servant-man, searched everywhere, but not a trace of them could he find. "They must have all blown away, mum," he said to Aunt Hannah.

"We shall have to have another scarecrow next summer," said she.

But the next summer there was no need of a scarecrow, for not a crow came past the fence-post on which Santa Claus had written his notice to crows. The cornfield was never so beautiful, and not a single grain was stolen by a crow, and everybody wondered at it, for they could not read the crow-language in which Santa had written.

"It is a great mystery to me why the crows don't come into our cornfield, when there is no scarecrow," said Aunt Hannah.

But she had a still greater mystery to solve when Christmas came round again. Then she and Betsey had each a strange present. They found them in the sitting-room on Christmas morning. Aunt Hannah's present was her old crazy quilt, remodelled, with every piece cut square and true, and matched exactly to its neighbour.

"Why, it's my old crazy quilt, but it isn't crazy now!" cried Aunt Hannah, and her very spectacles seemed to glisten with amazement.

Betsey's present was her doll-baby of the Christmas before; but the doll was a year older. She had grown an inch, and could walk and say, "mamma," and "how do?" She was changed a good deal, but Betsey knew her at once. "It's my doll-baby!" she cried, and snatched her up and kissed her.

But neither Aunt Hannah nor Betsey ever knew that the quilt and the doll were Jimmy Scarecrow's Christmas presents to them.

The Usurper

Washington Post, December 18, 1904, fifth part, 2, 6;
Baltimore Sun, December 18, 1904, 13

A WEEK BEFORE Christmas there was a meeting held in the schoolhouse of District № 2 to arrange for a tree on Christmas Eve. There were present the teacher, Miss Alice May, the three committeemen and the wife of one of them, who never trusted her husband to make a decision without her assistance, and the minister. The minister had been especially requested to be present, as the arrangements were considered to partake of a religious nature. The minister was a very young and very timid man and this was his first parish. He had the inclination to be a diplomat, without the requisite genius. He wished to please everybody and be on all sides, and had not the mental agility necessary to accomplish it. Consequently he sat in a place of honor, an arm chair on the platform beside the teacher, and he looked miserable. There was for the first time what the people considered quite a serious question involved in connection with the Christmas tree. There was always a Christmas tree and there had always been a Santa Claus. Mr. Elias Jones's buffalo coat had served for a garment from time immemorial, and there was a Santa Claus mask with long white beard, and a white wig, which was one of the perquisites of № 2. Now for the first time the question had arisen as to whether it was right to have a Santa Claus at all. The three committeemen, Mrs. Fisher, the wife of the eldest committeeman, the teacher, and the minister were considering the matter.

The teacher considered the matter wholly from the point of view of the scholars. "They will be so disappointed if there is no Santa Claus," said she. Miss Alice May, although not so very young, was very pretty, and was called an excellent teacher. She was said to have good government, and yet she made herself loved by the pupils. № 2 was considered very lucky to have her for a teacher. It was thought fortunate for the village that she had not married Frank Osborne, to whom she had been engaged five years before. In fact, her wedding outfit had been all ready, when a difference arose between them; nobody ever knew exactly what it had been. Miss May wore to-night one of the gowns which had belonged to her wedding outfit. It was a brown cashmere, with exceedingly pretty pink trimming, and it was very becoming. Mrs. Joseph Fisher, looking at her, remembered that it had been one of the teacher's intended wedding gowns, and she thought privately that she could not have cared very much or she could not wear it with such a smiling face. She was to have been married at Christmas time, too. She thought that it must bring it all back to her, and yet her cheeks were as pink as roses, and she was smiling as if she had never had a care in the world. For some reason Mrs. Joseph Fisher, who had never been, although she had kept it to herself, entirely satisfied with her own husband, felt exasperated. "It seems to me it isn't the question whether the scholars are disappointed or not," said she sharply. She was a sharp faced little woman, and her husband was large and lumbering and apt to hesitate in his speech. Everybody said that Joseph Fisher would never have been elected school committeeman if it had not been for his wife; that she told him what to say every time or he would never dare to open his mouth. Mrs. Fisher spoke with a sibilant hiss and she worked her face a good deal when speaking. "It seems to me that is not the question at all," she said again.

Then there was heard a confused rumble of masculine bass at her side equivalent to what was not a question at all. "It seems to me that all we ought to look at is whether it is right," said Mrs. Joseph Fisher, and she spoke with an air of stern virtue. Mr. Joseph Fisher at her right was heard to give vent to an incoherent rumble of assent, and the other two committeemen bowed their heads solemnly. Then the minister spoke. He realized that it was incumbent upon him, although he shrank from voicing his opinion.

"The question is, it seems to me," he said, addressing Miss Alice May diffidently—the pink trimming on her dress seemed to put him very much at a loss, since he fixed his eyes upon it, and his young cheeks assumed a similar color—"It seems to me," said he, "that the question is whether the children will be deceived by making use, as has heretofore been done, of a Santa Claus in the Christmas exercises. The question seems to me to be one of deception."

"No," said Miss Alice May, soberly, "I don't really think any of them will be deceived for a moment. The Santa Claus is to be George Osborne, and he will tell every scholar in the school before Christmas. I don't think any of them can possibly be deceived."

"You do not think," said the minister, "there is any danger that any one of them can for a moment think—the—the person distributing the gifts is—a heathen deity?"

"No, I don't," replied Miss Alice May.

Mrs. Henry Fisher had three children in № 2. "I know my children are too bright to think George Osborne is a heathen deity," said she, with a sniff, "but it seems to me that ain't exactly the question."

"If you will allow me, Mrs. Fisher," said the minister, and his young face was a bright scarlet, "to inquire what you really consider the question."

"The question is," said Mrs. Henry Fisher, "whether children in this school are going to be fools enough to think for a minute that anybody but their own folks give them their presents. I know my children won't, but I don't know about the others. The question is whether it is deception."
"Deception!" rumbled Mr. Joseph Fisher, at her right, and he blushed as furiously as the minister. "I think I can answer for it that none of them will," said Miss Alice May. "They are very bright children, and they will know that George Osborne, dressed up in the wig and mask and the buffalo coat, is Santa Claus, and they will know that he didn't bring their presents from—from—the North Pole." Miss Alice May was conscious of a little doubt as to where too credulous children might be supposed to think their gifts came from.

But the minister helped her out. "In other words," said he, "they will not, in your opinion, be in the slightest danger of ascribing their Christmas gifts to any supernatural agency."

"No, they will not," replied Miss Alice May, "and they will be very much disappointed not to have a Santa Claus, as they always have had. It is just a part of the fun, like the tree and the evergreens."

"I know my children are too bright to think for one minute that the mittens and balls and sleds that they are going to have came from the North Pole," said Mrs. Fisher.

The meeting ended with the decision to have the Santa Claus distribute the presents as usual, with the understanding that all the children were to be told plainly that it was George Osborne who was concealed in the buffalo coat and wig and beard, and not Santa Claus. Miss Alice May was relieved at the decision. In her own heart she had considered the meeting to discuss the matter rather in the light of an effort to make a mountain out of a molehill. "No danger the children won't know who is Santa Claus," said Mrs. Henry Fisher to her as they were going home. "Catch him keeping it to himself. The Osbornes ain't built that way. Anything that sets them up a little they ain't going to keep dark about. They ain't the kind to hide their candles under bushels; never was."

Mrs. Fisher thought that she might have an assent from the teacher, since it had been rumored that her engagement with Frank Osborne had been broken off, for the reason that he wanted to have a great church wedding and she wanted to save the money for housekeeping, but Miss Alice May said nothing at all. She pulled her fur boa closely around her throat, and said that it was a bitter night, as it certainly was. She boarded with the Fishers, and they had about a mile to drive in a sleigh. They sat there on a seat—the two women were small—and Mr. Joseph Fisher drove and never spoke a word the whole way.

After she reached home the teacher sat up until midnight in her room, where she had a little wood stove, and worked on Christmas presents. She did not feel very happy. She never did at Christmastime, although she had a pride about keeping her cheeks pink and her mouth smiling. Somehow, when Christmas drew near she always thought a good deal about what might have been, and how she, instead of teaching school for a living and boarding with the Fishers, whom she in the depths of her heart did not much care for, might have had a home of her own, with Frank Osborne for the head of it. George looked very much like his older brother, and somehow the sight of the boy's face always made her heart ache with loneliness. They had quarrelled about nothing at all, as it seemed to her now, and Frank, who was very impulsive, had taken the next train for the West, and that was the last of him so far as she was concerned. She knew he was not married, for if he had been his mother, who had always felt resentful toward her, first, because she had come between her and her son in the matter of affection, and, secondly, and inconsistently, because she had quarrelled with him and been responsible for his exile, would have found some means to tell her of it. However, married or not, she thought that she must be by this time quite out of his mind or he would have written to her. She resolved that, however badly she felt, nobody should know it by her looks or her manner. She would have been capable of rouge if the pink on her cheeks had not endured. She always made a great deal of Christmas, purposely that people might not know how sad she really was. She made a great many presents and was greatly interested in the school Christmas tree.

To-night she was finishing a pair of red mittens for one of the scholars, and as she crocheted she thought about the Santa Claus question. She made up her mind that the next day she would make a little speech to the scholars and tell them how Santa Claus was merely a pretty story invented to please the children, and how there was really no Santa Claus, but George Osborne was to make believe he was, with Mr. Elias Jones' buffalo coat and the white wig and beard, and that all the presents came from their friends and relatives. She said to herself that she thought it was all rather foolish, and she did not believe that there was any real need of such an explanation, but she supposed she must make it. Accordingly, the next day she did as she had planned. She rapped with her ruler on her desk to command attention, and then she made her little speech. Some of the scholars grinned openly, and George Osborne's face, which was so like his brother's, colored a vivid red at being thus made the center of attention. After school, when she was on her way home, with a number of the children, as usual, clinging to her hands and trailing in her rear, little Malvina Eddy, who was perhaps the youngest scholar in school, looked up at her with a shrewd little face. Malvina lisped, and the other scholars laughed at her for it, but she did not mind. Malvina, even at the age of six, had a soul impervious to ridicule. "Teasher," she said. "What is it, dear?" asked Miss May. "I wouldn't never have thought George Osborne wath Thanta Clauth, honeth, teasher." "I wouldn't neither," said little Charley Saunderson, who was kicking the snow up as he walked behind. "Them stories is for kids." "Those," said Miss May, severely, "and kids is slang, Charley."

"I don't care, I wouldn't," said Charley.

"Me neither," said pretty little Maudie Gleason at her side.

"I either, dear," said Miss May patiently.

"George Osborne, he tells everybody he's going to be Santa Claus," said Martha White, one of the older girls, marching soberly in the rear, with her books dangling in a strap. Martha was one of the best scholars in school, and always took her books home. "George Osborne, he can never keep anything to himself," she added with a tincture of contempt. She was at the age when a girl despises a boy as much as a boy does a girl. There is a period when the two sexes are at the antipodes as regards each other.

The period is transitory, but it exists. Martha White despised George Osborne as much as he despised her, and that was saying considerable. She ranked higher than he in the arithmetic class, and he could draw a much better map in colored crayons on the blackboard than she. Martha White told Minnie Jones that she thought George Osborne made a perfect fool of himself dressed up in her father's buffalo coat and the white beard and wig, which were the school properties, anyway, and Minnie Jones said she thought so, too. "I'd a heap rather hang my stocking myself," said Martha White, "but it pleases teacher, and she's real good to go to so much trouble, so I ain't going to say a word."

"I ain't," said Minnie Jones. She was a year older than Martha and not as good a scholar, but she privately thought that her father's old buffalo coat was to be rather honored by George Osborne wearing it.

Meanwhile, Miss Alice May knew nothing about all this. She worked very hard the week before Christmas, sitting up until midnight to finish Christmas gifts, for she made one for each of her scholars, and since her means were limited, she had to make up for richness of quality by her own handiwork. She crocheted mittens and made aprons until she was nearly worn out, and all the time her heart was aching over the memory of that other Christmas, five years ago, when she was finishing her pretty dresses and expecting to be married to Frank Osborne, and all the time she was going about smiling and working as if she had never had a care in her life.

However, the night before Christmas Eve she gave way for a few minutes. She had remained after school to complete some preparations, and all at once it seemed to her that she could not bear it all another minute. She just sank down in her worn chair and let her head fall on her desk and sobbed and sobbed as if her heart would break. She was all alone in the schoolroom, and she let her long restrained grief get completely the better of her. She even talked and moaned to herself. "Oh, Frank, Frank," she gasped, "how can I bear it, how can I? Another Christmas, another!"

She did not see or hear George Osborne enter the door, stare and listen a moment, then retreat precipitately. Then George Osborne went home immediately and told his mother.

"Brother Frank needn't worry, I guess," said George Osborne with an odd triumph. "I guess teacher feels enough sight worse than he does. You'd ought to have heard teacher, mother. If I was him I'd get another girl enough sight better lookin' than teacher, an' send her photograph home, so she could see it."

"She was crying, was she?" said Mrs. Osborne.

"Cryin', well, I guess you'd a thought so, mother, and sayin' 'Frank' over and over."

Mrs. Osborne's face softened a little. "Well, go and wash your hands," she said; "supper is about ready."

Miss Alice May passed the house rapidly while the Osbornes were eating supper, and Mrs. Osborne glanced at her, still with that softened look on her face. Alice wore her veil pulled well down over her face, so that nobody should remark her reddened eyes, and when she reached home she called to Mrs. Fisher that she did not want any supper that night and went straight up to her room. When Mrs. Fisher, who had a curious mind, came up to see why she did not want any supper she was bending over her wash basin washing her face with such assiduity that nobody could possibly discover that she had been weeping. She told Mrs. Fisher her head ached and she thought she was a little bilious, and it would be just as well for her not to eat anything. "You are working yourself to death over the Christmas tree," said Mrs. Fisher. "I shall be glad when it is over. I am almost worn out myself trying to finish that table cover for my sister."

She further asked if Alice were sure that she had not at least better have a cup of hot tea, but Alice, still with her face over the wash basin, assured her that she did not want anything.

When Mrs. Fisher had gone the teacher sat down again to her red mittens. She was on the last pair, and she was thankful. The next day she was busy all day trimming the tree and hanging on the presents. Mrs. Fisher helped her, and also Christine Munroe, who was the daughter of one of the committeemen. Once Mrs. Fisher whispered to Christine, when the teacher was in another part of the room, "I never saw such a sight of presents as she has got," indicating the teacher with a movement of her angular elbow.

"I suppose every scholar has given her something," replied Christine, who was a pretty girl and all aglow with thc joy of Christmas.

"There's things I've hung on that tree that didn't look as if they had ever come from any of the scholars in this school," replied Mrs. Fisher mysteriously. "It seems to me as if that tree was about covered with presents marked for her."

"Oh, I guess they are all from the scholars," said Christine. "They must be. She hasn't anybody outside to give them to her that I know of. She hasn't any relatives except that old aunt in Boston, and it's about all she can do to get along herself, I know, for I have heard Miss May say so."

"Maybe she's had some money left her," said Mrs. Fisher. "I know I've hung things on that tree that none of the scholars in this school ever got for her. There's been two little boxes done up in white paper, tied with silver cord."

"Candy?"

"Too small for candy."

The teacher wore to the Christmas tree still another of the pretty dresses she had made for her bridal outfit. They were all somewhat out of fashion, but fashions were slow in reaching this little inland village, and nobody thought of that. They looked at teacher in her red silk dress, and Mrs. Fisher whispered to a woman beside her: "I don't see how she could wear that dress if she had any feelings at all. That is the dress she was going to wear to receive her wedding callers in."

"I suppose she didn't have money to buy new ones, maybe," said the other woman, who was a charitable soul, and she was quite right. Alice had not felt that she could buy more dresses and put her poor bridal attire aside, for she had spent a goodly part of her savings upon it. Nobody knew how her heart ached under the red silk. She looked very pretty. The gown had quite a train and fluttered after her as she walked. She wore a sprig of holly in her hair, and she certainly did not look as if anything troubled her. She stood under the shade, or, rather, the light—for it was trimmed with candles—of the Christmas tree, and made a pretty little address to the scholars. Then the young minister, who had been asked to do so in order to allay a lingering doubt on the part of some as to the legitimacy of the tree at all, delivered a short, carefully prepared speech, in which he assured the impatient children that Santa Claus had in reality never existed, that it was only for the amusement of children that he had ever been personated, and that one of their schoolmates was now to take his part, but not one of them must for a moment think that the person who was about to distribute their presents, which their parents and friends had so carefully prepared for them, was anything supernatural. Then he solemnly seated himself in a seat of honor beside the teacher and the committee, and directly down from the loft of the schoolhouse on a little ladder clambered a figure in Mr. Elias Jones' buffalo coat and the mask with the white wig and beard.

It all began very well. The children's names were called and they went up and received their gifts. George Osborne spoke in an unusually firm voice, and Mrs. Fisher whispered to the woman beside her that he was terribly set up at being Santa Claus, and she wouldn't let a boy of hers holler so. But suddenly Miss Alice May's name was called and, as was the custom, Santa Claus brought the gift to her, instead of obliging her to go forward and receive it. Miss Alice May opened the dainty little white box innocently enough. She thought it contained some little offering from one of her pupils. She fairly gasped when a sapphire brooch, set in diamonds, blazed in her eyes from its white satin cushion. Several were looking over her shoulders, Mrs. Fisher among them. "For the land sakes!" gasped Mrs. Fisher.

"It must be imitation!" said another woman. "It beats all how they make imitation things nowadays. That looks as if it cost $25, and I don't suppose it cost over 25 cents." Alice had turned quite pale, regarding the beautiful jewel. She knew quite well that it had cost more than 25 cents and was not imitation. But she said quite calmly, "Yes, they do make wonderful imitations of jewelry," and closed the box. Then her name was called again, and this time it was a cotton handkerchief, trimmed with lace, from one of the scholars; then again, and a gift book was brought to her, then a box of home-made candy. Then the scholars' presents were distributed again, and it was some time before her name was called for a sachet from Maude Gleason. Nearly every scholar in the school gave something to the teacher, and her lap became filled with packages. The little box containing the brooch was underneath them all.

It was not until another suspiciously wrapped box had been brought to her, and she, opening it under the fire of wondering eyes, which would have been too wondering to endure had she not opened it at all, as she felt tempted to do, contained a beautiful little chatelaine watch, set with diamonds. This time Alice gave a great start, for she had seen that watch before, and she felt so faint that Mrs. Fisher's "Land sakes!" hardly reached her ears. But attention was all at once diverted from her by a great commotion among the scholars. Martha White had turned around and spied George Osborne sitting behind a post which had been put up to strengthen the ceiling at the end of the room. Martha's blank stare was infectious. All the other scholars turned around and looked. There was George Osborne, sitting at the back of the schoolroom, and they had just been told by the minister that he was impersonating Santa Claus. Several of the more nervous and imaginative children turned as pale as the teacher. They believed in Santa Claus in spite of the minister. How could they help it? George Osborne was to be Santa Claus, and there was George Osborne at the back of the room, and somebody was distributing the presents. Maudie Gleason's name was called next, to receive her red mittens, which the teacher had made for her, and she was afraid to go forward to the mysterious Santa Claus. She began to cry, when Martha White pushed her. Finally Martha herself, who had no belief in the supernatural, went forward and got the mittens. "He ain't Santa Claus any more'n you be," she said to Maudie, when she returned. "Take your mittens. I don't know who he is, but he ain't Santa Claus. There ain't no Santa Claus, and teacher made them mittens. You can't fool me."

It was very timidly and apprehensively, however, that many of the children went forward when their names were called. They would look at George Osborne, who had promised not to be seen and who was looking exceedingly red-faced and guilty at having broken his word, then they would go forward, aided by encouraging pushes from the bolder ones, who simply thought that some one else had been selected to serve as Santa Claus in George Osborne's place.

But the teacher sat pale and trembling, with her lap full of presents. Mrs. Fisher had turned around and seen with her sharp black eyes George Osborne at the back of the room. "Who is Santa Claus, if he ain't him?" she whispered in the teacher's ear. Mrs. Fisher might have gone to school with advantage as far as her English was concerned.

The teacher shook her head. Mrs. Fisher looked keenly at Santa Claus, who continued calling off the names of the bewildered children. "He speaks a good deal like George Osborne," said she. "I wonder—" She gave a furtive glance that would have done credit to a detective at the teacher, then she stopped.

"Wonder if they've heard anything lately from Frank Osborne," she whispered after a little to a woman near her.

The woman stared at her.

Mrs. Fisher nodded.

"You don't s'pos—" said the woman, with a glance at the pile of presents in the teacher's lap.

Mrs. Fisher nodded again. "I've seen a watch amazin' like that before," said she. "She never wore it after the engagement was broke off."

"Goodness sakes!" said the woman.

Santa Claus continued to call off the names until the tree was stripped. Then he made a lightning dash up the ladder and drew it after him into the loft.

There was a scream from the whole school and the guests.

"I declare," said Minnie Jones' mother, who was a nervous woman, "it's enough to make the shivers go down your back. Who was it?"

Then the teacher collected herself. She placed her presents on the desk, which had been moved into a corner, and mounted the platform beside the tree. She still looked pale, but she spoke in a firm voice. “Silence,” said she. “Some one else was selected to take George Osborne’s place as Santa Claus. There is no occasion for such a commotion.”

Mrs. Osborne came to her aid. “George has got such a cold he can hardly speak a loud word,” said she.

“George Osborne was unable to call out the names on account of his cold,” said the teacher. “You will now keep your places, and refreshments will be served.”

Refreshments consisted of cake and ice cream. Everybody ate, although many a glance was cast toward the loft. “Seems as if he, whoever he is, ought to come down and have some,” Martha White whispered in Minnie Jones’ ear.

“That’s so.”

“Wonder who it is.”

George Osborne’s eyes were upon Martha as she spoke, and he looked scornfully triumphant. He had come nearer the stove on account of his cold, and was eating ice cream and cake. “Who was it, George?” another boy asked, nudging him.

“Ask your grandmother,” replied George, politely.

“Bet you know.”

“Well, if I do, I know ’nough to keep it to myself.”

“It must be awful cold up there,” remarked the other boy, glancing with rather awed eyes toward the loft.

“Ain’t he got that buffalo coat on?”

When at last the festivities were over Mr. Fisher, the committeeman, was going to wait for the teacher as usual to take her home in his sleigh with himself and his wife, but his wife nudged him violently, then pushed him. “Come along,” said she. “Let her be.” “But how is she goin’ to git home, Lizy?” asked Mr. Fisher, anxiously. “It’s awful cold out, and it’s most a mile, and it’s late.”

“Let her be.”

“Do you mean for her to walk with the children? They don’t mind runnin’ along.”

“Let her be.”

“But, Lizy, if she ain’t comin’ with us the children may just as well ride. One of them can set betwixt us and the others can hang onto the runners.”

"Let 'em come, then."

"But how is the teacher goin' to git home, Lizy?"

"Let her be, I tell you."

Martha White and Minnie Jones lived very near the schoolhouse, and while Martha was not superstitious she was curious. "I'm bound I'll find out who he is," she whispered to Minnie. It so happened that when all the others were gone and the teacher was left alone, and Santa Claus let the ladder down from the loft and climbed down, Martha White and Minnie Jones, and Minnie's little brother Eddy, and a number of other boys, were peeping through a window. Then suddenly little Eddy Jones, who was a nervous child and very imaginative, shrieked and ran wildly after his parents, walking with creaking footsteps the long stretch of snowy, moonlit road ahead. "Oh, father, oh, mother!" cried little Eddy Jones in a panic of terror. "Santa Claus is huggin' teacher, he is, he is!"

The two elder Joneses said to each other in interrogative and confirmative tones, "Frank Osborne has come home?" "Yes, I heard so on the way to the tree, when I stopped in the store to order the sugar." Then Mrs. Jones turned to the little boy, "Hush, child," said she. "It's only George Osborne's big brother. He was Santa Claus instead of George, because George had a cold."

Meantime, in spite of the minister and the committeemen, and the scruples of the community as to the deception, there was in some degree truth in the myth of Santa Claus, for that night, at least in the school house of District № 2, Love, which is the patron saint of the whole earth, had come to the poor little schoolteacher, who thought he had passed her by for her whole life.

Santa Claus and Two Jack-Knives

Atlanta Sunny South, December 21, 1901, 6;
Indianapolis Journal, December 22, 1901, 7;
Galveston Daily News, December 22, 1901, 22

THE DESIRE OF possession is a curious thing. None can tell what an ignoble object even in a great mind may serve as a nucleus for its pearl of price. Tommy Barlow had not, presumably, a mind of unusual greatness, being only an ordinary village boy. Still, he might have had as great an ambition of possession as a George Washington, but all his desires were concentrated upon a jack-knife.

When the school teacher, stepping forward from behind her desk to the front of the platform that she might be heard to better advantage, held forth upon noble aims in life, and the duty of constant striving towards the distant heights, and wound up with a ringing quotation from "Excelsior," Tommy Barlow thought of a jack-knife, a jack-knife with four blades. So also did Zelotes, commonly called Loty, Dickinson, only his ambition was more circumscribed. He did not specify so clearly and determinately the number of blades. He would have been contented with less than four, so long as he had the jack-knife. Loty Dickinson and Tommy Barlow were close and inseparable friends, and shared wishes and aspirations, though Tommy was generally the leader, having a stronger imagination. Loty, in the state of his family finances, could scarcely, left to himself, have imagined even the possible possession of a new jack-knife—of any jack-knife at all, except the slender chance of his elder brother's with one broken blade.

When the elder brother grew old enough to go to work and earn a knife for himself, his old one might possibly fall to him; but it was a long wait, for the brother was only three years older than Loty, who was ten. As for Tommy Barlow, his chances were a little better, or he considered them so. Tommy had a rich uncle, his great-uncle, who was an old bachelor, and there was always a belief in the family that this uncle, after whom Tommy had been named, might some day do something for him. He never had, even to the extent of a silver spoon for his name, as Tommy's mother often remarked; but the belief always remained. Tommy's parents' imagination in that direction took the form of an education and a start in business; Tommy's took the form of a four-bladed jack-knife.

"Mebbe my Great Uncle Thomas will give me a jack-knife some day," he said to Loty Dickinson. "He's rich as mud, you know."

"Wish I had an uncle," returned Loty, kicking his heels against the rail of the fence.

The two boys sat on the top rail of the fence of the corner lot, where they would naturally have sat to whittle, if they had owned the jack-knives.

"Well, I'll let you use my knife if you're careful," said Tommy, generously.

"Hour to a time?" inquired Loty, eagerly.

"Mebbe."

At the right of Tommy, removed to a distance which indicated to a nicety the deference due a large boy from a small one, sat little Fanny Chase. His name was Francis, but he was so small and timid, and pink and white, that the boys had nicknamed him "Fanny." Even Tommy and Loty called him Fanny, though they had been fierce in his defence against a petty persecution when he first came to school. The Chases were under a sort of ban in the village. They were poor and shiftless, and had been so for generations, and there had been an occasional outbreak of actual crime. They were under a standing conviction of poverty and laziness, with a standing suspicion of something worse. There was always a large family of Chases, for they multiplied like the sprawling burdock weeds around their old shackly house, and a swarm of children, puny and dull for the most part, with their diseased hereditary tendencies strengthening with their growth, infested the schools. Fanny was the youngest, and the best of them, the school teacher said. There was something about Fanny's little pink-and-white face, his blue eyes full of fear, yet with a lingering confidence in one's kind intent toward him, his slight, puny little figure shrinking against the wall, falling to the rear of a pushing crowd, which appealed to a woman, but the boys had been merciless when Fanny Chase first appeared at school. It was one morning in September, the teacher had not arrived, and Tommy and Loty were late. When they reached the school yard this little new boy, pale and wild-eyed and dumb, cowering with utter defeat and helplessness, was the center of a crowd of little yelling, hooting, taunting savages. They were good-natured in a way; not one of them would have harmed the child; but the delight of the human boy in the torment of that which can be tormented, had awoke within them and made them drunk and mad with it.

Then it was that Tommy arose. Very probably, had he been on the scene from the first, he might himself have led the tormentors. Coming late he had an outside point of view, and the enormity of the failings of his kind were clearly evident to him.

"They are plaguin' that poor little chap," he cried to Loty, "an' it's a mean shame. He's awful little, an' he's scared 'most to death, an' now he's beginnin' to cry. Come on, Loty."

With that Tommy, with Loty, who loved a row, at heel, dashed into the crowd and carried the day by the suddenness and unexpectedness of the assault. Two boys, one of them bigger than either Tommy or Loty, were laid prostrate, and sat on, and pommelled, amid hoarse shouts of "Lemme up! Lemme up, I say, will ye?" while the intimidated crowd half-circled at a distance, and little Fanny Chase was nowhere until he reappeared, bringing a fence rail much longer than himself to Tommy with the wise idea that it could be used effectually for further chastisement of the enemy. Then there was a roar of mirth, and the teacher's blue-ribboned hat was seen above the green bushes in the road, and in a second the noise had subsided, the prostrate boys were up, dusting their jackets and muttering, and Tommy and Loty were walking off with their triumph of victory concealed under a mien of general peacefulness. But from that day both of them, and Tommy especially, had a most devoted and loyal follower in little Fanny Chase, though he followed them at a respectful distance. He never presumed. He always kept a space indicative of respect and deference, and the wide difference between their age and wisdom and his youth and ignorance between them, as he did now. He heard every word the two said with adoring interest, but he said nothing. Fanny never spoke to his two chiefs unless they first spoke to him. When they jumped down from the fence, where they would have sat to whittle if they had owned jack-knives, he jumped down also, and followed them down the road. The two older boys scuffled their bare feet as they went along, and so did Fanny. The three disappeared in a great cloud of dust.

That was in August, too early to think of Christmas, but two months later, Tommy, not Loty—he had too little hope—began to talk about the possibility of attaining the jack-knife as a Christmas present.

"'S'pose my Great-uncle Thomas should give me that knife for a Christmas present," he said to Loty.

"Never did give you anything, did he?" said Loty, who was at times a little envious of the ownership of this rich great-uncle.

"Well, no, he never has yet," admitted Tommy, "but, then, he might."

"Well, I ain't got any rich uncles," said Loty, "and I don't see any chance of me gittin' any knife, 'less I find one."

"Mebbe you will," said Tommy. "Folks do lose jack-knives, and it stands to reason that somebody has got to find 'em."

"Well, if we knew who lost it I'd have to give it back, I s'pose. Mother'd make me," growled Loty, who was pessimistic that day.

"Mebbe you wouldn't know who lost it," suggested Tommy, hopefully.

"It would be jest my luck to see him drop it," said Loty, "and I ain't goin' round hunting for jack-knives."

This time Tommy and Loty were on their way to school, with little Fanny Chase trotting after them. It was a cold day in late October, and Fanny had just put on shoes for the first time that season. They were his brother's old ones, the soles of one flapped, and he walked with difficulty. When they reached the schoolhouse, some girls standing in the door began to laugh, and Tommy turned to see what the matter was. He could not attack girls for making sport of his protege, but he looked at them fiercely. When he saw Fanny's clapping shoe, he seized him by the shoulders and ordered him to hold up his foot.

"Lemme see that shoe, kid," said he. "Loty, bring us a stone, will ye?"

Loty fetched the stone and assisted Fanny to stand on one foot while Tommy hammered away industriously at the sole of the shoe.

"It ain't any use," said he, finally. "The nails are all gone. There ain't any way but to cut off that sole up to where it's loose, and the bell's ringin'. Now is the time when a feller had ought to have a jack-knife. Seems to me a jack-knife is more necessary than some other things."

"That's so," said Loty.

"I told mother I'd rather have that knife than a new cap, and I'd make my old one do this winter," said Tommy. "And she said mebbe it would, but she didn't get the knife; said we needed the money to buy flour. I don't care much for bread, never did. 'Nough sight rather have cookies. Now, look at that, will ye? There, this kid has got to go into the school room with that sole clapping the floor every step and all the fellers laughin' and makin' him cry, poor little chap, just because we haven't got any jack-knives."

"That's so," said Loty.

The bell was ringing toward the finish. Suddenly Tommy made a motion of decision.

"Off with that shoe, youngster," he ordered; and while the wondering half-whimpering little fellow obeyed, Tommy pulled off his own shoe and extended it to the other.

"Here, get into that quick," said he.

"What you going to do yourself?" inquired Loty, astonished.

"I'm going barefoot," said Tommy stoutly. "Guess it won't hurt me any; my feet are about as tough as leather, anyhow. Give me that shoe, youngster. I'm goin' to get father to fix this to-night—reckon he can."

So Tommy went barefoot into the schoolroom with his pockets bulging with shoes, and when the teacher investigated and found the broken one he said never a word in explanation, but he had established a stronger bond, if that were possible, between his little follower and himself.

There was a week's vacation at Christmas time. Christmas came on a Thursday, and the vacation began on the Monday before. Tommy hung his stocking on Wednesday night. He knew he was too big a boy, and he felt mortified that he did so, and made up his mind never to speak of it even to Loty; but he had a hope, though his mother had told him that it was a vain one. "You can hang up your stocking, if you want to," said she, "but you know well enough you can't have any Christmas present in it. Your father got all behindhand with his sickness last year, and we've got to be careful of every penny if we don't want to mortgage the place. I'm sorry, and so is your father; we'd both of us give anything if we could buy you a jack-knife or anything you'd set your heart on; but we can't, and you must be a good boy and make the best of it."

"I don't expect you and father to buy me a jack-knife," said Tommy, "but I thought mebbe Uncle Thomas—"

"Your Uncle Thomas has never given a Christmas present in his life," said Mrs. Barlow; "and he's just given $5,000 to the town towards a library. He believes in giving big things that show; he isn't going to come down to anything small as jack-knives, so don't you get your hopes up, child."

A long struggle, not with poverty, but with scantiness, had made the woman bitter, and deprivation had caused her to value unduly that of which she was deprived. That night, after Tommy had gone to bed, her heart failed her at the sight of his much-mended stocking hanging limply from the mantel-shelf. "See, the poor child has hung his stocking, and I haven't got a thing to put in it!" she said to Mr. Barlow. "I told him I hadn't; but he wanted to hang it. He always has a forlorn hope that your Uncle Thomas is going to give him a jack-knife."

"Catch him giving anything, except big things that pay him well in praise and credit," said Tommy's father. He looked angrily and sadly at the dangling stocking. "Seems to me Tommy is too old to hang his stocking," said he, impatiently.

"Oh, he isn't very old, John—only ten," said his mother. "Poor little fellow, how he has wanted a four-bladed jack-knife."

"Well, he'll have to go without," said his father; "I never had one. I'm a poor man, and Tommy is the son of a poor man, and most likely he will be one himself. He's got to make up his mind that he can't have things, and make the best of it."

"If we can leave this place clear, Tommy will have something, and we ain't so poor after all, John; we have all we need. Folks can get along without four-bladed jack-knives, and not be poor, seems to me. I'm going to make some molasses candy and put it in his stocking, and cover his ball new—that will be better than nothing," said Tommy's mother.

Tommy's father said nothing, but he came home from the store that evening with a big orange and a little paper parcel. "Here's an orange to put in the stocking," said he, "and I met his school teacher and she gave me this for him. Said she had hoped she could have a tree at the school this year; but she wasn't able to, and so she'd send this by me."

"Wonder what it is," said Mrs. Barlow. "If it was only a knife, wouldn't he be tickled!"

But it was a little instructive book instead of a knife. "It's a pretty little book," said Tommy's mother, "and it looks real improving and interesting. It seems to be about Africa, and I should think he might be interested to read about Africa. I suppose it is a wonderful country, but I wish it had been a jack-knife. Who's that at the door at this time of night? Do ask who it is before you open the door, John."

"It's somebody to ask the way, I guess," said Mr. Barlow. "I heard a team stop out here."

"Well, do ask who it is before you open the door," charged Mrs. Barlow. She was very timid, and she ran upstairs to Tommy's room while her husband went to the door. She listened and heard a man's voice, and her husband ask some one in. Finally, when she heard the front door shut, she went to the head of the stairs, and called to know who it was. "It was Uncle Thomas; he was driving past, and he wanted to know if I had the deed of this house handy," said Mr. Barlow.

"What for?" asked Mrs. Barlow, going downstairs. "He ain't goin' to overreach you anyway, is he?"

"No, don't you be scared; it was only about the boundary lines; he's going to buy that piece of land south of the field; it's all right—just the way he thought it was."

"Well," said Mrs. Barlow, "I do wish your Uncle Thomas had brought a jack-knife for poor Tommy."

"Well, he didn't," replied Mr. Barlow. "Catch him; but I've thought of something else to put in the stocking—that Spanish silver dollar that belonged to father."

"Well, maybe he'll like it," said Mrs. Barlow, doubtfully; "but I don't know just what he can do with it."

"He can look at it," said Mr. Barlow, taking the great Spanish dollar out of the desk drawer and putting it on top of the stocking. It had been one of the wonders of his own childhood, and he thought his son must prize it.

So it happened that Tommy Barlow, when he crept out in the pale dawn of Christmas morning to the cold sitting room to inspect his stocking, found quite a full one. His heart gave a great leap of delight as he caught sight of the bulging stocking. He took it down and crept back upstairs, and took it into bed. He hardly dared open it; he felt it first—it certainly did seem as if there was something which felt like a knife.

Then he began pulling out the parcels with his trembling fingers and opening them one by one. He found the dollar, orange, the candy, the ball, and the school-teacher's little book, whose title he did not even look at; then he came to the last parcel, and it was—a jack-knife with four blades.

Tommy looked at it; he was fairly pale. It was the first real joy of possession of his whole life, and he would never, if he lived to be a man, and become as rich as Croesus, have a greater. He opened the blades one after another; he tried one a little on the bedpost. He found it very sharp; there never was such a knife.

But when he dressed himself and went downstairs to show his mother she turned so pale he thought she was going to faint away. "Why, Tommy Green Barlow," said she, "where did you get that knife?"

"Why, it was in my stocking, mother," replied Tommy, staring at her in bewilderment.

"No, it wasn't in your stocking. It couldn't have been in your stocking. Where is your father? John, come here; see this!"

When Mr. Barlow looked at the knife he turned to Tommy more sternly than he had ever done in his life. "Where did you get this, sir?" said he. When Tommy's father called him "sir," it was serious.

Tommy began to cry. His joy over his new knife seemed of short duration. "It—it was in my stocking, father," said he.

"No, it was not in your stocking. Your mother and I know it was not in your stocking. We know just what was in your stocking. Where did you get this knife, sir?"

"It was in—my—stocking," repeated Tommy amid his sobs.

Tommy's father and mother looked at each other. They did not know what to think. Tommy had always been a truthful boy, and yet here was the knife, and here was this story which they knew, or thought they knew, to be a downright falsehood. Tommy's father was a very decided man, and when it came to a question like this he was resolved not to give Tommy the benefit of the doubt. "Give me that knife, sir," said he, "and you go straight back upstairs till I tell you to come down."

When the sound of Tommy's sobs had died away, and they heard his chamber door shut, Mr. Barlow turned to his wife.

"I can't believe it," said he.

"Neither can I," said she.

"A downright lie like that," said Mr. Barlow.

"And where did he get the knife? Oh, John," she cried, "it looks as if— Oh, John, our Tommy never stole!"

"I don't believe he did," said Mr. Barlow, "but everything is against him. Here he's been wanting a jack-knife all this time, and he got up first this morning."

"He'd have done that, anyway," said Mrs. Barlow, suddenly. She looked at her husband. "John, you don't suppose your Uncle Thomas put that knife in that stocking, do you?" she cried.

"Oh, he couldn't," replied Mr. Barlow, but he looked reflective.

"Now, John Barlow, I ain't so sure. You know Tommy is a pretty boy, and you know old bachelors sometimes take fancies, and you know he's eccentric. Did you leave him alone in the room?"

"Well, yes, I did," admitted Mr. Barlow. "He was alone quite a spell, while I was in the bedroom getting the deed out of the box under the bed."

"Uncle Thomas put that knife in that stocking," said Mrs. Barlow, conclusively. Then she went to the door, and called: "Tommy, Tommy, it's all right. Mother's found out all about it. Come right down and get your breakfast. Poor little boy!" she said. She was half weeping over the cruel injustice with which they had treated Tommy. "Right after breakfast he must get dressed up and go and thank his Uncle Thomas," said she.

And so Tommy did, going down the street spick and span, in his little Sunday suit, with his hair very smooth and his rosy cheeks shining with soap and water, and the precious knife in his pocket. But he came home rueful. "He says he didn't give it to me," he whimpered out; "he says he ain't got money to throw away on jack-knives, and he acted real mad."

"Then where did you get that jack-knife, Tommy Barlow?" said his mother, and his father echoed her, in a sterner voice than he had used before.

But Tommy refused to tell, and upstairs to his chamber he went again, sobbing all the way. "I'd rather not have had—a jack-knife," he wailed out, and he snatched the knife out of his pocket and flung it on the floor hard, then he dived head foremost into his bed, and sobbed until he fell asleep.

In the evening of Christmas Day came still further developments. Loty Dickinson appeared with his father and mother, each holding a hand and dragging him reluctant and bewildered as before some tribunal of justice. Loty had a jack-knife which had been found in his stocking in the same mysterious fashion, and they had come to see if Tommy knew anything about it.

"We hate to think our dear little boy would do such a dreadful wicked thing as to steal," said his mother, tearfully, "and then tell lies to keep from being punished; but we can't account for it. Your Tommy didn't give it to him, did he?"

"Tommy didn't have any money to buy jack-knives," said Mrs. Barlow; "and he's got one we can't account for, too. He's upstairs in his chamber. We sent him up there because he wouldn't tell."

An audible sniff came from Loty at that. He had red curly hair which stood out fiercely, and his face was red and rasped and wild. "You stop crying, sir," said his father. Then Loty burst out in a loud, irrepressible wail.

They called Tommy downstairs, and the two little boys were together subjected to a cross-examination from their parents, but all to no purpose. Not one word beyond the simple reiteration that they did not know where the knives had come from, could be forced from either of them.

"I declare," Mrs. Barlow said to Mr. Barlow, when the Dickinsons had gone, "it most makes me believe in Santa Claus!"

"Nonsense!" said Mr. Barlow.

"Well, I'd rather believe in Santa Claus than to think that my dear precious Tommy could steal," said Mrs. Barlow, with a sob. She was getting fairly childish and hysterical.

"We haven't heard the last of it yet," prophesied Mr. Barlow, gloomily.

And it transpired that Mr. Barlow was right, for the next day came Mr. Ezra Tubbs, the storekeeper, who had heard of the mysterious jack-knives, and asked to see Tommy's. He looked at it, he opened the blades, he put on his glasses, and took it to the window, and squinted at it first with one eye, then the other, first on one side, then the other, while Mr. and Mrs. Barlow looked on trembling, and Tommy glared from the position which he had been bidden to take, with fear and despair.

"H'm! I thought so," said Mr. Ezra Tubbs at last.

"Oh, don't tell me it is—don't!" cried Mrs. Barlow.

"Yes, it is," said Mr. Ezra Tubbs, solemnly.

Then Mrs. Barlow flew to Tommy and caught him in her arms and held him and looked fiercely over his head at Mr. Tubbs. "You shan't touch him, you shall not," she said. "His father can pay you. We'll mortgage this place; we'll do anything. You shan't touch him."

"Gracious! I ain't goin' to touch him," said Mr. Ezra Tubbs, with a sort of angry stateliness. "What do you suppose I am goin' to do with a child like that? He is a badly trained child, and he'll fetch up on the gallows most likely, but I ain't goin' to set the law on him. All I want is either the price of that jack-knife, or that jack-knife. He ain't whittled no one with it, has he?"

"No, he ain't," said Mr. Barlow, "Here's the knife, and I'd rather have cut off my right hand with it than have this happen, and that's all I can say; and he won't fetch up on the gallows if not sparing the rod can save him!"

So it happened that Tommy Barlow felt the rod that he might be saved from the gallows, and so did Loty Dickinson, at whose house a similar scene with Mr. Ezra Tubbs had been enacted. Take it all together, it was the saddest Christmas which Tommy Barlow and Loty Dickinson had ever known.

It was two days after Christmas that Tommy and Loty, coming home from the long hill where they had been trying to solace themselves with a little coasting, met little Fanny Chase. He caught hold of Tommy's jacket-sleeve and stood looking palely up at him, his face twitching.

"Say," he whispered, "I—stole 'em."

"Jack-knives?" cried Tommy and Loty together.

Fanny nodded, swallowing hard.

"How—how—" gasped Tommy, "did you get 'em into the stockings?"

"Yes," gasped Loty. "How? Oh, my!"

"Winders," replied Fanny, faintly. Then he twitched loose and ran, while a long wail floated back from the depths of the poor little heart which had sinned for love.

Tommy and Loty looked at each other. "Say," said Tommy, then he stooped, but Loty nodded as if he had said something more.

"He'll have an awful time; get licked as bad as we was," said Tommy.

"Mebbe they'll put him in jail 'cause he's one of those Chases," said Loty.

Then the two boys looked at each other.

"It's no use," said Tommy, "we can't tell on him."

"No, we can't," said Loty.

And they did not. For a week to come the two experienced all the woes of scorn and contempt, and more. People began to say that they should not be allowed to go to school; that they would remove their own children rather than have them brought in contact with such youthful depravity. Then there came a night when the school committee, headed by the chairman, who was Uncle Thomas Barlow, who was resolved to be pitiless for the sake of justice, even when the culprit bore his own name, appeared at Tommy's father's. The three committeemen sat in an awful row in the Barlow sitting room and Tommy stood before them. His heart beat loud in his ears, his hands and feet were like ice. He did not know what could be coming, but he was resolved never to tell on little Fanny, come what would.

Uncle Thomas began to talk and Tommy listened without comprehending more than it was something awful and that the words fell on his ears like blows. He heard his mother sob.

Then there was a knock on the door. Mr. Barlow tiptoed solemnly to open it, as if it were a funeral, and in came Fanny Chase and his mother. She was a small, nervous woman, and she was quivering all over like a wire spring. She made nothing of interrupting Uncle Thomas.

"The Chases be poor and low down," said she: "but they don't lie nor steal not if I know it, without somethin' is done about it, and they don't let other folks suffer for what they did. My boy here was the one that stole them jack-knives to give to them boys, 'cause they took his part agin' the other boys in school, and he's just come and told me about it, and asked me if I wouldn't come here and tell the selectmen, so Tommy and Loty shouldn't git dismissed from school. An' here he is, an' now I'll take him home an' punish him."

Then Uncle Thomas Barlow did something unexpected. He caught hold of little Fanny, who was cowering before them all so pale that he looked as if he would fall, and he sat him on his magisterial knee.

"You are not going to punish this boy, madam," said he, "until we have sifted this case to the bottom."

Then, between them all, they got at the curious, unbelievable, pathetic truth, that poor little Fanny had stolen the knives for the sake of his love and gratitude to his two champions, and how he had told, and Tommy and Loty had gone on bearing blame and ignominy to shield him.

"I declare," said Uncle Thomas Barlow, to the committeeman nearest his own age, who was a crony of his, as they were going home after the call was ended, "I don't know but every one of those little fellows ought to be given a sound whipping, but I know one thing—that boy of John's a smart fellow, yes he is, holding his tongue rather than have the little one blamed. He ought to have been pummeled for making his father and mother all that trouble, he ought. But he's a smart fellow, and so is the Dickinson boy, though I guess Thomas is the leading spirit. And I know one thing, those boys are going to have those jack-knives, and that little Chase boy isn't going to be let to grow up like the rest of the Chases if I can help it."

Christmas Jenny

Harper's Bazar, December 22, 1888, 872–74

THE DAY BEFORE there had been a rain and a thaw, then in the night the wind had suddenly blown from the north, and it had grown cold. In the morning it was very clear and cold, and there was the hard glitter of ice over everything. The snow-crust had a thin coat of ice, and all the open fields shone and flashed. The tree boughs and trunks, and all the little twigs, were enamelled with ice. The roads were glare and slippery with it, and so were the door-yards. In old Jonas Carey's yard the path that sloped from the door to the well was like a frozen brook.

Quite early in the morning old Jonas Carey came out with a pail, and went down the path to the well. He went slowly and laboriously, shuffling his feet, so he should not fall. He was tall and gaunt, and one side of his body seemed to slant toward the other, he settled so much more heavily upon one foot. He was somewhat stiff and lame from rheumatism.

He reached the well in safety, hung the pail, and began pumping. He pumped with extreme slowness and steadiness; a certain expression of stolid solemnity which his face wore never changed.

When he had filled his pail he took it carefully from the pump spout, and started back to the house, shuffling as before. He was two thirds of the way to the door, when he came to an extremely slippery place. Just there some roots from a little cherry-tree crossed the path, and the ice made a dangerous little pitch over them.

Old Jonas lost his footing, and sat down suddenly; the water was all spilled. The house door flew open, and an old woman appeared.

"Oh, Jonas, air you hurt?" she cried, blinking wildly and terrifiedly in the brilliant light.

The old man never said a word. He sat still and looked straight before him solemnly. "Oh, Jonas, you 'ain't broke any bones, hev you?" The old woman gathered up her skirts and began to edge off the door-step, with trembling knees. Then the old man raised his voice—"Stay where you be," he said, imperatively. "Go back into the house!"

He began to raise himself, one joint at a time, and the old woman went back into the house, and looked out of the window at him.

When old Jonas finally stood upon his feet it seemed as if he had actually constructed himself, so piecemeal his rising had been. He went back to the pump, hung the pail under the spout, and filled it. Then he started on the return with more caution than before. When he reached the dangerous place his feet flew up again, he sat down, and the water was spilled.

The old woman appeared in the door; her dim blue eyes were quite round, her delicate chin was dropped. "Oh, Jonas!"

"Go back!" cried the old man, with an imperative jerk of his head toward her, and she retreated. This time he arose more quickly, and made quite a lively shuffle back to the pump.

But when his pail was filled and he again started on the return, his caution was redoubled. He seemed to scarcely move at all. When he approached the dangerous spot his progress was hardly more perceptible than a scaly leaf-slug's. Repose almost lapped over motion. The old woman in the window watched breathlessly.

The slippery place was almost passed, the shuffle quickened a little—the old man sat down again, and the tin pail struck the ice with a clatter.

The old woman appeared. "Oh, Jonas!"

Jonas did not look at her; he sat perfectly motionless. "Jonas, air you hurt? Do speak to me for massy sake!" Jonas did not stir.

Then the old woman let herself carefully off the step. She squatted down upon the icy path, and hitched along to Jonas. She caught hold of his arm—"Jonas, you don't feel as if any of your bones were broke, do you?" Her voice was almost sobbing, her small frame was all of a tremble.

"Go back!" said Jonas. That was all he would say. The old woman's tearful entreaties did not move him in the least. Finally she hitched herself back to the house, and took up her station in the window. Once in a while she rapped on the pane, and beckoned piteously.

But old Jonas Carey sat still. His solemn face was inscrutable. Over his head stretched the icy cherry branches, full of the flicker and dazzle of diamonds. A woodpecker flew into the tree and began tapping at the trunk, but the ice-enamel was so hard that he could not get any food. Old Jonas sat so still that he did not mind him. A jay flew on the fence within a few feet of him; a sparrow pecked at some weeds piercing the snow-crust beside the door. Over in the east arose the mountain, covered with frosty foliage full of silver and blue and diamond lights. The air was stinging. Old Jonas paid no attention to anything. He sat there.

The old woman ran to the door again. "Oh, Jonas, you'll freeze, settin' there!" she pleaded. "Can't you git up? Your bones ain't broke, air they?" Jonas was silent.

"Oh, Jonas, there's Christmas Jenny comin' down the road—what do you s'pose she'll think?"

Old Jonas Carey was unmoved, but his old wife eagerly watched the woman coming down the road. The woman looked oddly at a distance: like a broad green moving bush; she was dragging something green after her too. When she came nearer one could see that she was laden with evergreen wreaths; her arms were strung with them, long sprays of ground-pine were wound around her shoulders, she carried a basket trailing with them, and holding also many little bouquets of bright-colored everlasting flowers. She dragged a sled, with a small hemlock-tree bound upon it. She came along sturdily over the slippery road. When she reached the Carey gate she stopped and looked over at Jonas. "Is he hurt?" she sung out to the old woman.

"I dunno—he's fell down three times."

Jenny came through the gate, and proceeded straight to Jonas. She left her sled in the road. She stooped, brought her basket on a level with Jonas's head, and gave him a little push with it. "What's the matter with ye?" Jonas did not wink. "Your bones ain't broke, are they?"

Jenny stood looking at him for a moment. She wore a black hood, her large face was weather-beaten, deeply tanned, and reddened. Her features were strong, but heavily cut. She made one think of those sylvan faces with features composed of bark-wrinkles and knot-holes, that one can fancy looking out of the trunks of trees. She was not an aged woman, but her hair was iron gray, and crinkled as closely as gray moss.

Finally she turned toward the house. "I'm comin' in a minute," she said to Jonas's wife, and trod confidently up the icy steps.

"Don't you slip," said the old woman, tremulously.

"I ain't afraid of slippin'." When they were in the house she turned around on Mrs. Carey, "Don't you fuss, he ain't hurt."

"No, I don't s'pose he is. It's jest one of his tantrums. But I dunno what I am goin' to do. Oh, dear me suz, I dunno what I am goin' to do with him sometimes!"

"Leave him alone—let him set there."

"Oh, he's tipped all that water over, an' I'm afeard he'll—freeze down. Oh dear!"

"Let him freeze! Don't you fuss, Betsey."

"I was jest goin' to git breakfast. Mis' Gill she sent us in two sassage-cakes. I was goin' to fry 'em, an' I jest asked him to go out an' draw a pail of water, so's to fill up the tea-kittle. Oh dear!"

Jenny set her basket in a chair, strode peremptorily out of the house, picked up the tin pail which lay on its side near Jonas, filled it at the well, and returned. She wholly ignored the old man. When she entered the door his eyes relaxed their solemn stare at vacancy, and darted a swift glance after her.

"Now fill up the kittle, an' fry the sassages," she said to Mrs. Carey.

"Oh, I'm afeard he won't git up, an' they'll be cold! Sometimes his tantrums last a consider'ble while. You see he sot down three times, an' he's awful mad."

"I don't see who he thinks he's spitin'."

"I dunno, 'less it's Providence."

"I reckon Providence don't care much where he sets."

"Oh, Jenny, I'm dreadful afeard he'll freeze down."

"No, he won't. Put on the sassages."

Jonas's wife went about getting out the frying-pan, crooning over her complaint all the time. "He's dreadful fond of sassages," she said, when the odor of the frying sausages became apparent in the room.

"He'll smell 'em an' come in," remarked Jenny, dryly. "He knows there ain't but two cakes, an' he'll be afeard you'll give me one of 'em."

She was right. Before long the two women, taking sly peeps from the window, saw old Jonas lumberingly getting up. "Don't say nothin' to him about it when he comes in," whispered Jenny.

When the old man clumped into the kitchen, neither of the women paid any attention to him. His wife turned the sausages, and Jenny was gathering up her wreaths. Jonas let himself down into a chair, and looked at them uneasily. Jenny laid down her wreaths. “Goin’ to stay to breakfast?” said the old man.

“Well, I dunno,” replied Jenny. “Them sassages do smell temptin’.”

All Jonas’s solemnity had vanished, he looked foolish and distressed.

“Do take off your hood, Jenny,” urged Betsey. “I ain’t very fond of sassages myself, an’ I’d jest as liv’s you’d have my cake as not.”

Jenny laughed broadly and good-naturedly, and began gathering up her wreaths again. “Lor’, I don’t want your sassage-cake,” said she. “I’ve had my breakfast. I’m goin’ down to the village to sell my wreaths.”

Jonas’s face lit up. “Pleasant day, ain’t it?” he remarked, affably.

Jenny grew sober. “I don’t think it’s a very pleasant day; guess you wouldn’t if you was a woodpecker or a blue-jay,” she replied.

Jonas looked at her with stupid inquiry.

“They can’t git no breakfast,” said Jenny. “They can’t git through the ice on the trees. They’ll starve if there ain’t a thaw pretty soon. I’ve got to buy ’em somethin’ down to the store. I’m goin’ to feed a few of ’em. I ain’t goin’ to see ’em dyin’ in my door-yard if I can help it. I’ve given ’em all I could spare from my own birds this mornin’.”

“It’s too bad, ain’t it?”

“I think it’s too bad. I was goin’ to buy me a new caliker dress if this freeze hadn’t come, but I can’t now. What it would cost will save a good many lives. Well, I’ve got to hurry along if I’m goin’ to git back to-day.”

Jenny, surrounded with her trailing masses of green, had to edge herself through the narrow doorway. She went straight to the village and peddled her wares from house to house. She had her regular customers. Every year, the week before Christmas, she came down from the mountain with her evergreens. She was popularly supposed to earn quite a sum of money in that way. In the summer she sold vegetables, but the green Christmas traffic was regarded as her legitimate business—it had given her her name among the villagers. However, the fantastic name may have arisen from the popular conception of Jenny’s character. She also was considered somewhat fantastic, although there was no doubt of her sanity. In her early youth she had had an unfortunate love affair that was supposed to have tinctured her whole life with an alien element. “Love-cracked,” people called her.

“Christmas Jenny’s kind of love-cracked,” they said. She was Christmas Jenny in midsummer, when she came down the mountain laden with green peas and string-beans and summer squashes.

She owned a little house and a few acres of cleared land on the mountain, and in one way or another she picked up a living from it.

It was noon to-day before she had sold all her evergreens and started up the mountain road for home. She had laid in a small stock of provisions, and she carried them in the basket which had held the little bunches of life-everlasting and amaranth flowers and dried grasses.

The road wound along the base of the mountain. She had to follow it about a mile, then she struck into a cart-path which led up to the clearing where her house was.

After she passed Jonas Carey's there were no houses and no people, but she met many living things that she knew. A little field-mouse scratching warily from cover to cover, lest his enemies should spy him, had appreciative notice from Jenny Wrayne. She turned her head at the call of a jay, and she caught a glimmer of blue through the dazzling white boughs. She saw with sympathetic eyes a woodpecker drumming on the ice-bound trunk of a tree. Now and then she scattered, with regretful sparseness, some seeds and crumbs from her parcels.

At the point where she left the road for the cart-path there was a gap in the woods, and a clear view of the village below. She stopped and looked back at it. It was quite a large village; over it hung a spraying net-work of frosty branches; the smoke arose straight up from the chimneys. Down in the village street a girl and a young man were walking, talking about her, but she did not know that.

The girl was the minister's daughter. She had just become engaged to the young man, and was walking with him in broad daylight with a kind of shamefaced pride. Whenever they met anybody she blushed, and at the same time held up her head proudly, and swung one arm with an airy motion. She chattered glibly and quite loudly to cover her embarrassment.

"Yes," she said, in a sweet, crisp voice, "Christmas Jenny has just been to the house, and we've bought some wreaths. We're going to hang them in all the front windows. Mother didn't know as we ought to buy them of her, there's so much talk, but I don't believe a word of it, for my part."

"What talk?" asked the young man. He held himself very stiff and straight, and never turned his head when he shot swift smiling glances at the girl's pink face.

"Why, don't you know? It's town-talk. They say she's got a lot of birds and rabbits and things shut up in cages, and half starves them; and then that little deaf and dumb boy, you know—they say she treats him dreadfully. They're going to look into it. Father and Deacon Little are going up there this week."

"Are they?" said the young man. He was listening to the girl's voice with a sort of rapturous attention, but he had little idea as to what she was saying. As they walked, they faced the mountain.

It was only the next day when the minister and Deacon Little made the visit. They started up a flock of sparrows that were feeding by Jenny's door; but the birds did not fly very far, they settled into a tree and watched. Jenny's house was hardly more than a weather-beaten hut, but there was a grape-vine trained over one end, and the front yard was tidy. Just before the house stood a tall pine-tree. At the rear, and on the right stretched the remains of Jenny's last summer's garden, full of plough ridges and glistening corn stubble.

Jenny was not at home. The minister knocked and got no response. Finally he lifted the latch, and the two men walked in. The room seemed gloomy after the brilliant light outside; they could not see anything at first, but they could hear a loud and demonstrative squeaking and chirping and twittering that their entrance appeared to excite.

At length a small pink and white face cleared out of the gloom in the chimney-corner. It surveyed the visitors with no fear nor surprise, but seemingly with an innocent amiability.

"That's the little deaf and dumb boy," said the minister, in a subdued voice. The minister was an old man, narrow-shouldered, and clad in long-waisted and crinkly black. Deacon Little reared himself in his sinewy leanness until his head nearly touched the low ceiling. His face was sallow and severely corrugated, but the features were handsome.

Both stood staring remorselessly at the little deaf and dumb boy, who looked up in their faces with an expression of delicate wonder and amusement. The little boy was dressed like a girl, in a long blue gingham pinafore. He sat in the midst of a heap of evergreens, which he had been twining into wreaths; his pretty, soft, fair hair was damp, and lay in a very flat and smooth scallop over his full white forehead.

"He looks as if he was well cared for," said Deacon Little. Both men spoke in hushed tones—it was hard for them to realize that the boy could not hear, the more so because every time their lips moved his smile deepened. He was not in the least afraid.

They moved around the room half guiltily, and surveyed everything. It was unlike any apartment that they had ever entered. It had a curious sylvan air; there were heaps of evergreens here and there, and some small green trees leaned in one corner. All around the room—hung on the walls, standing on rude shelves—were little rough cages and hutches, from which the twittering and chirping sounded. They contained forlorn little birds and rabbits and field-mice. The birds had rough feathers and small, dejected heads, one rabbit had an injured leg, one field-mouse seemed nearly dead. The men eyed them sharply. The minister drew a sigh; the deacon's handsome face looked harder. But they did not say what they thought, on account of the little deaf and dumb boy, whose pleasant blue eyes never left their faces. When they had made the circuit of the room, and stood again by the fireplace, he suddenly set up a cry. It was wild and inarticulate, still not wholly dissonant, and it seemed to have a meaning of its own. It united with the cries of the little caged wild creatures, and it was all like a soft clamor of eloquent appeal to the two visitors, but they could not understand it.

They stood solemn and perplexed by the fireplace. "Had we better wait till she comes?" asked the minister.

"I don't know," said Deacon Little.

Back of them arose the tall mantel-shelf. On it were a clock and a candlestick, and regularly laid bunches of brilliant dried flowers, all ready for Jenny to put in her basket and sell.

Suddenly there was a quick scrape on the crusty snow outside, the door flew open, and Jonas Carey's wife came in. She had her shawl over her head, and she was panting for breath.

She stood before the two men, and a sudden crust of shy formality seemed to form over her. "Good-arternoon," she said, in response to their salutations.

She looked at them for a moment, and tightened her shawl-pin; then the restraint left her. "I knowed you was here," she cried, in her weak, vehement voice; "I knowed it. I've heerd the talk. I knowed somebody was goin' to come up here an' spy her out. I was in Mis' Gregg's the other day, an' her husband came home; he'd been down to the store, an' he said they were talkin' 'bout Jenny, an' sayin' she didn't treat Willy and the birds well, an' the town was goin' to look into it. I knowed you was comin' up here when I seed you go by. I told Jonas so. An' I knowed she wa'n't to home, an' there wa'n't nothin' here that could speak, an' I told Jonas I was comin'. I couldn't stan' it nohow.

"It's dreadful slippery. I had to go on my hands an' knees in some places, an' I've sot down twice, but I don't keer. I ain't goin' to have you comin' up here to spy on Jenny, an' nobody to home that's got any tongue to speak fer her."

Mrs. Carey stood before them like a ruffled and defiant bird that was frighting herself as well as them with her temerity. She palpitated all over, but there was a fierce look in her dim blue eyes.

The minister began a deprecating murmur which the deacon drowned. "You can speak for her all you want to, Mrs. Carey," said he. "We 'ain't got any objections to hearin' it. An' we didn't know but what she was home. Do you know what she does with these birds and things?"

"Does with 'em? Well, I'll tell you what she does with 'em. She picks 'em up in the woods when they're starvin' an' freezin' an' half dead, an' she brings 'em in here, an' takes care of 'em an' feeds 'em till they git well, an' then she lets 'em go again. That's what she does. You see that rabbit there? Well, he's been in a trap. Somebody wanted to kill the poor little cretur. You see that robin? Somebody fired a gun at him an' broke his wing.

"That's what she does. I dunno but it 'mounts to jest about as much as sendin' money to missionaries. I dunno but what bein' a missionary to robins an' starvin' chippies an' little deaf an' dumb children is jest as good as some other kinds, an' that's what she is.

"I ain't afeard to speak; I'm goin' to tell the whole story. I dunno what folks mean by talkin' about her the way they do. There, she took that little dumbie out of the poor-house. Nobody else wanted him. He don't look as if he was abused very bad, far's I can see. She keeps him jest as nice an' neat as she can, an' he an' the birds has enough to eat, if she don't herself.

"I guess I know 'bout it. Here she is goin' without a new caliker dress, so's to git somethin' for them birds that can't git at the trees, 'cause there's so much ice on 'em.

"You can't tell me nothin'. When Jonas has one of his tantrums she can git him out of it quicker'n anybody I ever see. She ain't goin' to be talked about, and spied upon, if I can help it. They tell about her bein' love-cracked. Hm, I dunno what they call love-cracked. I know that Anderson fellar went off an' married another girl, when Jenny jest as much expected to have him as could be. He ought to ha' been strung up. But I know one thing—if she did git kind of twisted out of the reg'lar road of lovin', she's in another one, that's full of little dumbies an' starvin' chippies an' lame rabbits, an' she ain't love-cracked no more'n other folks."

Mrs. Carey, carried away by affection and indignation, almost spoke in poetry. Her small face glowed pink, her blue eyes were full of fire, she waved her arms under her shawl. The little meek old woman was a veritable enthusiast.

The two men looked at each other. The deacon's handsome face was as severe and grave as ever, but he waited for the minister to speak. When the minister did speak it was apologetically. He was a gentle old man, and the deacon was his mouth-piece in matters of parish discipline. If he failed him he betrayed how feeble and kindly a pipe was his own. He told Mrs. Carey that he did not doubt everything was as it should be; he apologized for their presence; he praised Christmas Jenny. Then he and the deacon retreated. They were thankful to leave that small vociferous old woman, who seemed to be pulling herself up by her enthusiasm until she reached the air over their heads, and became so abnormal that she was frightful. Indeed everything out of the broad common track was a horror to these men and to many of their village fellows. Strange shadows that their eyes could not pierce lay upon such, and they were suspicious. The popular sentiment against Jenny Wrayne was originally the outcome of this characteristic, which was a remnant of the old New England witchcraft superstition. More than anything else, Jenny's eccentricity, her possibly uncanny deviation from the ordinary ways of life, had brought this inquiry upon her. In actual meaning, although not even in self-acknowledgment, it was a witch-hunt that went up the mountain road that December afternoon.

They hardly spoke on the way. Once the minister turned to the deacon. "I rather think there's no occasion for interference," he said, hesitatingly.

"I guess there ain't any need of it," answered the deacon.

The deacon spoke again when they had nearly reached his own house. "I guess I'll send her up a little somethin' Christmas," said he. Deacon Little was a rich man.

"Maybe it would be a good idea," returned the minister. "I'll see what I can do."

Christmas was one week from that day. On Christmas morning old Jonas Carey and his wife, dressed in their best clothes, started up the mountain road to Jenny Wrayne's. Old Jonas wore his great-coat, and had his wife's cashmere scarf wound twice around his neck. Mrs. Carey wore her long shawl and her best bonnet. They walked along quite easily. The ice was all gone now; there had been a light fall of snow the day before, but it was not shoe-deep. The snow was covered with the little tracks of Jenny's friends, the birds and the field-mice and the rabbits, in pretty zigzag lines.

Jonas Carey and his wife walked along comfortably until they reached the cart-path, then the old man's shoestring became loose, and he tripped over it. He stooped and tied it laboriously; then he went on. Pretty soon he stopped again. His wife looked back. "What's the matter?" said she.

"Shoestring untied," replied old Jonas, in a half inarticulate grunt.

"Don't you want me to tie it, Jonas?"

Jonas said nothing more; he tied viciously.

They were in sight of Jenny's house when he stopped again, and sat down on the stone wall beside the path. "Oh, Jonas, what is the matter?"

Jonas made no reply. His wife went up to him, and saw that the shoestring was loose again. "Oh, Jonas, do let me tie it; I'd just as soon as not. Sha'n't I, Jonas?"

Jonas sat there in the midst of the snowy blackberry vines, and looked straight ahead with a stony stare.

His wife began to cry. "Oh, Jonas," she pleaded, "don't you have a tantrum to-day. Sha'n't I tie it? I'll tie it real strong. Oh, Jonas!"

The old woman fluttered around the old man in his great-coat on the wall, like a distressed bird around her mate. Jenny Wrayne opened her door and looked out, then she came down the path. "What's the matter?" she asked.

"Oh, Jenny, I dunno what *to* do. He's got another—tantrum!"

"Has he fell down?"

"No; that ain't it. His shoestring's come untied three times, an' he don't like it, an' he's sot down on the wall. I dunno but he'll set there all day. Oh, dear me suz, when we'd got most to your house, an' I was jest thinkin' we'd come 'long real comfort'ble! I want to tie it fer him, but he won't let me, an' I don't darse to when he sets there like that. Oh, Jonas, jest let me tie it, won't you? I'll tie it real nice an' strong, so it won't undo again."

Jenny caught hold of her arm. "Come right into the house," said she, in a hearty voice. She quite turned her back upon the figure on the wall.

"Oh, Jenny, I can't go in an' leave him a-settin' there. I shouldn't wonder if he sot there all day. You don't know nothin' about it. Sometimes I have to stan' an' argue with him for hours afore he'll stir."

"Come right in. The turkey's most done, an' we'll set right down as soon as 'tis. It's 'bout the fattest turkey I ever see. I dunno where Deacon Little could ha' got it. The plum-puddin's all done, an' the vegetables is 'most ready to take up. Come right in, an' we'll have dinner in less than half an hour."

After the two women had entered the house the figure on the wall cast an uneasy glance at it without turning his head. He sniffed a little.

It was quite true that he could smell the roasting turkey, and the turnip and onions, out there.

In the house, Mrs. Carey laid aside her bonnet and shawl, and put them on the bed in Jenny's little bedroom. A Christmas present, a new calico dress, which Jenny had received the night before, lay on the bed also. Jenny showed it with pride. "It's that chocolate color I've always liked," said she. "I don't see what put it into their heads."

"It's real handsome," said Mrs. Carey. She had not told Jenny about her visitors; but she was not used to keeping a secret, and her possession of one gave a curious expression to her face. However, Jenny did not notice it. She hurried about preparing dinner. The stove was covered with steaming pots; the turkey in the oven could be heard sizzling. The little deaf and dumb boy sat in his chimney-corner, and took long sniffs. He watched Jenny, and regarded the stove in a rapture, or he examined some treasures that he held in his lap. There were picture-books and cards and boxes of candy and oranges. He held them all tightly gathered into his pinafore. The little caged wild things twittered sweetly, and pecked at their food. Jenny laid the table with the best table-cloth and her mother's flowered china. The mountain farmers, of whom Jenny sprang, had had their little decencies and comforts, and there were china and a linen table-cloth for a Christmas dinner, poor as the house was.

Mrs. Carey kept peering uneasily out of the window at her husband on the stone wall.

"If you want him to come in you'll keep away from the window," said Jenny; and the old woman settled into a chair near the stove.

Very soon the door opened, and Jonas came in. Jenny was bending over the potato kettle, and she did not look around. "You can put his great-coat on the bed, if you've a mind to, Mrs. Carey," said she.

Jonas got out of his coat, and sat down with sober dignity: he had tied his shoestring very neatly and firmly. After a while he looked over at the little deaf and dumb boy, who was smiling at him, and he smiled back again.

The Careys staid until evening. Jenny set her candle in the window to light them down the cart-path. Down in the village the minister's daughter and her betrothed were out walking to the church, where there was a Christmas tree. It was quite dark. She clung closely to his arm, and once in a while her pink cheek brushed his sleeve. The stars were out, many of them, and more were coming. One seemed suddenly to flash out on the dark side of the mountain.

"There's Christmas Jenny's candle," said the girl. And it was Christmas Jenny's candle, but it was also something more. Like all common things, it had, and was, its own poem, and that was—a Christmas star.

STOLEN CHRISTMASES, UNINVITED GUESTS

Found in the Snow

San Francisco Call, December 17, 1899, 16;
Young Woman, December 1899, 95–98;
Saturday Night's Christmas (Toronto), December 1899, 32–33

TOMMY AND LORENY had been to the store to do some errands and were on their way back to the almshouse where they lived. The light was getting low, and the western sky was red. The two went in file down the country road. There had been a heavy fall of snow the day before, and it was not yet trodden down; there was only a narrow foot-track between the drifts. Loreny kept ahead. She was three years older than her brother Tommy, and quite a tall girl. Her thin, wiry figure skipped over the snow as lightly as a sparrow. She wore an old brown cotton dress, a dim plaid shawl and a faded worsted hood, and her arms were full of brown-paper bundles. Tommy tugged a molasses jug in one hand and a kerosene can in the other. He was short and sturdy, with a handsome little red face. He wore an old coat of Mr. Palmer's, the almshouse keeper, which had been cut down for him, but the skirts still trailed in the snow.

The two went on silently; the bare branches overhead glistened redly in the setting sun. It was very still and cold. Suddenly Loreny stopped short and Tommy made a sudden halt at her heels.

"What's that?" she cried, in an excited voice.

Tommy set down the molasses jug and peered around her shoulder. A brown-paper package lay in the road before them.

"What do you s'pose it is?" asked Loreny.

"Pick it up," returned Tommy.

Loreny eyed it a minute, then she laid her own bundles down carefully on the snow, picked it up, and unrolled it.

"Oh!" she cried.

Tommy said nothing, but his mouth opened and his eyes grew big.

Loreny held a doll with a beautiful wax face and real flaxen hair. She looked at it, and the tears came into her eyes.

"What you goin' to do with it?" gasped Tommy.

"I dunno," answered Loreny, slowly. She looked anxiously at her brother. "Somebody dropped her," said she, "but I dunno who. Mrs. Palmer won't let me keep her."

Tommy stared at his sister, then at the doll.

"Mrs. Palmer won't let me keep her," Loreny repeated, and her lips quivered. Suddenly she wrapped her old shawl carefully around the doll, which was not dressed, and snuggled her close to her with a defiant air.

"What you goin' to do?" inquired Tommy.

"I'm agoin' to carry her home. Mrs. Palmer, she won't see her under my shawl."

"She'll whip you when she finds it out."

"I don't care if she does," returned Loreny, holding the doll closer. She picked up the other parcels and went on. Tommy took up the molasses jug and followed.

They had gone only a few steps when Loreny stopped again. "There's something else," she said, in an awed whisper.

Tommy set the jug down.

"You pick it up," said Loreny. Tommy set down the kerosene can also, and brushed past his sister. He picked up the parcel, which was a nice white one.

"Undo it," said Loreny, trembling.

Tommy's clumsy fingers tugged at the pink string. It was two pounds of Christmas candy. They looked at the beautiful red and white twists and were speechless. Then Loreny spoke in a quick, frightened way.

"You tie that right up again, Tommy Wood," said she. "Don't you eat a mite of it; it don't belong to us."

Tommy, with a last wistful gaze at the candy, tied it up. Then he looked at his sister. "Shall I lay it down again?" he asked.

Loreny hesitated. "I dunno, hardly. Somebody might step on it after dark."

"I can put it in my pocket," said Tommy, eagerly.

Tommy stowed away the candy in one of the pockets of Mr. Palmer's great-coat.

"Mind you don't eat a mite of it," charged Loreny sharply.

"No, I won't," promised Tommy, gathering up the jug and can.

They went on, then suddenly Loreny stopped again.

"Tommy Wood," she gasped, "there's another!"

Tommy set down the jug and can and sprang forward.

"Where?"

"There!"

It was a large, flat package. Tommy opened it breathlessly. There were books in that—story-books with handsome covers, and one beautiful picture-book. Tommy turned the leaves and Loreny looked over his shoulder.

"Ain't they handsome?" she sighed.

"What shall I do with them?" asked Tommy, breathing hard.

"I dunno, unless you can put them in your pocket. It won't do to leave them laying under foot."

Tommy tied up the books carefully, and they just slipped into a pocket of Mr. Palmer's great-coat. Then he took up the jug and can, and he and Loreny went on.

In a minute Loreny stopped again. "I'm scart 'most to pieces," said she. "There's another!" She and Tommy looked at each other. Loreny was quite pale. "I s'pose you had better pick it up," she said faintly.

Tommy picked up the parcel, and his hands shook when he unrolled it.

"Oh!" he cried.

It was a beautiful little concertina. He pulled it out gently, and there was a soft musical wheeze.

"Don't! Somebody will hear," cried Loreny. "Put it up, quick!"

A stubborn expression came over Tommy's face. "You've got the doll," said he; "I'm going to have this."

"Put it up, quick!"

"Can't I have it?"

"Mrs. Palmer won't let us have any of 'em when she sees 'em."

Tommy stowed the concertina into a pocket of Mr. Palmer's coat with a resolute air. "I can hide this jest as well as you can that doll," said he.

Tommy picked up the molasses jug and the kerosene can again; but this time he did not set them down again until he had reached the almshouse. He and Loreny looked sharply, but there were no more mysterious packages strewn along the road.

The almshouse was simply a large, white farmhouse on a hill. There were not many paupers in Green River; in fact there were only five—three old women and two old men, besides Tommy and Loreny.

The children went up the hill on which the almshouse stood. The north wind blew in their faces, and they were glad to get into the great warm kitchen where the five old people sat around the fire and Mrs. Palmer was preparing supper. Mr. Palmer was splitting kindling wood out in the shed; they could hear the ax strokes.

"Take off your coat, Tommy, and go out and bring in some of the kindlings. And you, Loreny, take off your hood and shawl and set the table," said Mrs. Palmer.

Mrs. Palmer was a thin little woman and she looked tired. Her voice had a fretful ring. People said that she worked too hard. He husband was not as energetic as she and most of the work came upon her.

It was fortunate that Tommy and Loreny were expected to leave their out-of-door garments in the passage. They shut the kitchen door and clattered upstairs in wild haste. Mrs. Palmer called after them, but they kept on. Tommy flew into his chamber and laid the concertina under his pillow, and the candy and books behind the door, while Loreny tucked the precious doll between the sheets of her own little cotbed. When they went downstairs Mrs. Palmer did not question them, she was too busy. There was a mild excitement through the almshouse that night. The next day was Christmas, and there was to be a great dinner. Mrs. Deacon Alden's rich sister, a widow lady, who was visiting her, had sent in two large turkeys, two chickens, and a quantity of raisins. The old men and women talked it over and chuckled delightedly. The fragrance of tea spread through the warm kitchen. Loreny set the table and Tommy brought in baskets of kindling. They, too, shared in the anticipation of the great dinner, but they had other things on their minds. They were full of guilty delight and tenderness over their treasures upstairs, and terror lest Mrs. Palmer should go up and find them.

After Loreny had washed the dishes, then she and Tommy pared apples and picked over raisins.

"Mind you don't eat more than you pick, now," charged Mrs. Palmer. She was too worn out to consider what a few raisins on Christmas Eve might mean to a little girl and boy.

However, Tommy and Loreny did not think much about raisins, they were too anxious to get upstairs. The old people went to bed early, but the children were up until 9 o'clock. There were a great many apples to be pared and pounds of raisins to be picked over.

At 9 o'clock they hurried up to their chambers; each had a little candle in a tin candlestick. Loreny's room was opposite Tommy's. She was just taking the doll out of the bed, when she heard a sweet wheeze from the concertina. She flew across the entry: "Tommy Wood," she whispered, "you stop this minute! She'll be up here."

Tommy himself looked frightened. "I won't do it again," said he; "I couldn't help it."

Finally, Tommy went to sleep with the concertina in his arms and Loreny with the doll. Once in the night she awoke suddenly, for she heard the concertina. She listened in a panic, but she did not hear it again, and went to sleep.

The next morning there was a sort of feeble merriment about the almshouse. There were no Christmas presents, but the dinner, that meant a great deal. Mrs. Palmer even smiled wearily as she stirred the plum pudding. Tommy and Lorena were kept very busy all the morning, but after the grand dinner, when they had eaten the roast turkey and chicken and plum pudding and all the paupers had feasted, they had a little time to themselves.

Loreny stole upstairs to her own room. She got a pink calico apron in which her heart delighted out of her bureau-drawer, and she dressed the doll in it. It was a cold Christmas and the window was thick with frost, but she stayed there with the doll all the afternoon. She got her best blue hair-ribbon and tied the pink apron round the doll's waist. She kissed its pretty face. "Ain't going to let you freeze in this cold weather, dear child," she whispered.

As for Tommy, he was out in the snowy pasture behind the almshouse, sitting on a rock which pierced a drift, playing his concertina in the freezing December wind. He actually picked out a little tune which he had heard in Sunday-school, and he was in a rapture. He did not feel the cold, but he was so numb that he could scarcely walk when he stowed away the concertina in the coat pocket and returned to the almshouse.

When he had hidden away his treasure he went down to the kitchen, where Loreny had just gone. She was warming her little blue hands over the stove.

"Serves you right for staying up there in the cold so long," said Mrs. Palmer.

Presently Mr. Palmer came in, stamping his snowy feet. He had been down to the village, and had some news.

"Deacon Alden's hired man lost a heap of things out of his cart yesterday afternoon," said he. "Spilt them out of the back. The horse was kind of frisky, and he never knew it till he got home. Then he went right back, but the things were gone. Somebody had picked 'em up."

"It's just as bad as stealing," said Mrs. Palmer, severely; "just as bad."

Loreny turned white. Tommy sat with his eyes downcast. As soon as she could, Loreny pulled him out into the entry. "Tommy Wood," she whispered, "we've got to carry 'em back. It's stealing."

"When can we?"

"To-night. We must go down the back stairs real still, after they think we've gone to bed."

It was half-past 9 o'clock when two small, dark figures ran down the almshouse hill. One was Tommy, with his coat pockets bulging, the other was Loreny, hugging the doll, which was still wrapped in her pink apron.

It was a mile to Deacon Alden's house. It was bitter cold, the full moon was up, and the snow creaked under foot. They ran most of the way. When they reached Deacon Alden's house they stood hesitating at the gate.

"You go in," said Loreny, giving Tommy a little push.

"No, you," he whispered.

Loreny marched up to the door and rang the bell. Mrs. Deacon Alden opened the door and stood looking amazedly at them.

Loreny spoke: "We found these things in the road yesterday," said she. She held out the doll and Tommy began removing the concertina from his pocket.

"Well, I never!" exclaimed Mrs. Deacon Alden. "Louisa, do come here this minute! No, you come in, you Tommy and Loreny; you are freezing out there."

Tommy and Loreny were bewildered. They had to think it all over for a long time afterward in order to understand exactly what had happened. They were pulled gently into the warm sitting room, where there was a lamp with a pink shade and green plants at the window, and Mrs. Deacon Alden's sister, soft-voiced, gentle and sweet-faced, in a beautiful black silk, was telling them that all those presents—the doll, the concertina, the books and the candy—were meant for them, and had been lost out of the sleigh, and that they could carry them home.

Presently they were sitting by the fire, eating frosted cake and drinking chocolate. Then there was a jingle of bells outside, and they were driven back to the almshouse, tucked warmly under fur robes, and had a Christmas sleigh-ride.

Mrs. Deacon Alden went with them to explain matters to Mrs. Palmer, and her sister whispered to her just before they started: "I mean to take them, Sarah. I am going to see about it to-morrow."

But Tommy and Loreny did not know what that meant until afterward. That night it was enough for Loreny to go to sleep with her own beautiful doll in her arms, and for Tommy to sit up in bed fearlessly and play softly on his concertina his little Sunday-school tune, which happened to be the tune of a Christmas hymn.

The Last Gift

Harper's Monthly Magazine, February 1903, 439–46

ROBINSON CARNES PILGRIMMED along the country road between Sanderson and Elmville. He wore a shabby clerical suit, and he carried a rusty black bag which might have contained sermons. It did actually hold one sermon, a favorite which he had delivered many times in many pulpits, and in which he felt a certain covert pride of authorship.

The bag contained, besides the sermon, two old shirts with frayed cuffs, three collars, one pocket-handkerchief, a Bible, and a few ancient toilet articles. These were all his worldly goods, except the clothes he wore, and a matter of forty-odd cents in his old wallet. Robinson Carnes subsisted after a curious parasitical fashion. He travelled about the country with his rusty black bag, journeying from place to place—no matter what place, so long as it held an evangelical church. Straight to the parson of this church he went, stated his name and calling, produced certain vouchers in proof of the same, and inquired if he knew of any opening for a clergyman out of employment, if he had heard of any country pulpit in which an itinerant preacher might find humble harbor. He never obtained any permanent situation; he sometimes supplied a pulpit for a day, or officiated at a funeral or wedding, but that was all. But he never failed to receive hospitality, some sufficient meals, and lodging for one night at least in the parsonage guest-chamber.

Although Carnes's living was so precarious, he looked neither forlorn nor hungry. He had, in fact, had at noon an excellent dinner of roast beef at the home of the Presbyterian minister in Sanderson. It was the day before Christmas, and a certain subtle stir of festive significance was in the very air. Every now and then a wagon laden with young hemlocks, and trailing with greens, passed him. The road was strewn with evergreen sprigs and stray branches, with an occasional jewel-like sprinkle of holly berries. Often he heard a silvery burst of laughter and chatter, and boys and girls appeared from a skirting wood with their arms laden with green vines and branches. He also met country carriages whose occupants had their laps heaped with parcels of Christmas presents. These last gave the tramp preacher a feeling of melancholy so intense that it amounted to pain. It was to him like the sight of a tavern to a drunkard when his pockets are empty and his thirst is great. It touched Robinson Carnes in his tenderest point. He had fallen a victim in early youth to a singular species of spiritual dissipation. Possessed by nature of a most unselfish love for his kind, and an involuntary generosity, this tendency, laudable in itself, had become in time like a flower run wild until it was a weed. His love of giving amounted to a pure and innocent but unruly passion. It had at one time assumed such proportions that it barely escaped being recognized as actual mania. As it was, people, even those who had benefited by his reckless generosity, spoke of him as a mild idiot.

There had been a day of plenty with him, for he had fallen joint heir to a large and reasonably profitable New England farm and a small sum in bank. The other heir was his younger brother. His brother had just married. Robinson told him to live on the farm and give him a small percentage of the profits yearly. When the crops failed through bad weather and mismanagement, he said easily, without the slightest sense of self-sacrifice, that the brother need not pay him the percentage that year. The brother did not pay it, as a matter of course, the next year, and in fact never did. In three years the brother's wife was ailing and the family increasing, and he was in debt for the taxes. Robinson paid them all, and he continued paying them as long as his money in the bank lasted. He wished his brother to keep his share intact, on account of his family. Then he gave from his poor salary to everything and everybody. Then he was in debt for his board. He rented a small room, and lived, it was said, on oatmeal porridge until the debt was paid.

Robinson Carnes had a fierce honesty. When he was in debt, he felt, for the first time in his life, disgraced, and like hiding his head. He often reflected with the greatest shame upon that period of his life when he had an impulse to go out of his way to avoid the woman whom he owed. He felt nothing like it now, although to some his present mode of existence might savor of beggary. He considered that in some fashion he generally rendered an equivalent for the hospitality which kept the breath of life in him. Sometimes the minister who entertained him was ailing, and he preached the sermon in his black bag in his stead. Sometimes he did some copying for him; often he had toiled to good purpose at his wood-pile or in his garden; he had even assisted the minister's wife with her carpet-beating in her spring cleaning. He had now nothing to be ashamed of, but he felt his very memory burn with shame when he remembered that time of debt. That had been the end of his career as a regularly settled minister. People might have forgiven the debt, but they could not forgive nor overlook the fact that while in such dire straits he had given away the only decent coat which he owned to wear in the pulpit, and also that he had given away to a needy family, swarming with half-fed children, the cakes and pies with which some female members of his parish had presented him to alleviate his oatmeal diet. That last had in reality decided the matter. He was requested to resign.

So Robinson Carnes resigned his pastorate and had never been successful in obtaining another. He went out of the village on foot. He had given away every dollar of the last instalment of his meagre salary to a woman in sore straits. He had given away his trunk years ago to a young man about to be married and settle in the West. He regretted leaving his sermons behind because of the lack of a trunk. He stored them in a barrel in the garret of one of the deacon's houses. He stowed away what he could of his poor little possessions in his black bag, feeling thankful that no one had seemed to need that also. Since he had given away his best coat, he had only his old one, which was very shabby. When he shook hands with his half-hearted friends at parting, he was careful not to raise his right arm too high, lest he reveal a sad rip in the under-arm seam. Since, he had had several coats bestowed upon him by his clerical friends, when an old one was on the verge of total disruption, but the new coat was always at variance as to its right under-arm seams. Robinson Carnes had thereby acquired such an exceedingly cautious habit of extending his right arm as to give rise to frequent inquiries whether he had put his shoulder out of joint, or had rheumatism. Now the ripped seam was concealed by an old but very respectable and warm overcoat which the Presbyterian minister in Sanderson had bestowed upon him, and which he had requited by an interpretation of the original Greek of one of the gospels, which aided the minister materially in the composition of his Christmas sermons. Carnes was an excellent Hebrew and Greek scholar, and his entertainer was rusty and had never been very proficient. Robinson had been in the theological seminary with this man, and had often come to his aid when there. Robinson had also set up the Christmas tree for the Sunday-school in the church vestry. He was exceedingly skilful with his hands. The Christmas tree had awakened in him the old passion, and his face saddened as he looked at the inviting spread of branches.

"I wish I had something to hang on the tree for your children and the Sunday-school," he said, wistfully, to the minister; and the other man, who knew his history, received his speech in meaning silence. But when Carnes repeated his remark, being anxious that his poor little gift of a Christmas wish, which was all that he had to offer, might at least be accepted, the other replied coldly that one's first duty was to one's self, and unjustified giving was pauperizing to the giver and the recipient.

Then poor Robinson Carnes, abashed, for he understood the purport of the speech, bade the minister good-by meekly, and went his way. When he saw the other Christmas tree on the road to Elmville, his wistful sadness became intensified. He felt the full bitterness of having absolutely nothing to give, of having even a kindly wish scorned when the wish was his last coin. He felt utterly bankrupt as to benefits towards his fellow-creatures, that sorest bankruptcy for him who can understand it.

Carnes had just watched a wagon loaded with Christmas greens pass slowly out of sight around a bend in the road, when he came unexpectedly upon a forlorn company. They were so forlorn, and so unusual in the heart of a prosperous State, that he could hardly believe his eyes at first. They seemed impossible. There were six of them in all: a man, two women—one young and one old—and three children: one a baby two years old, the others five and eight. The man stood bolt-upright, staring straight ahead with blank eyes; the women were seated on the low stone wall which bordered the road. The younger, the mother, held the five-year-old child; the older, evidently the grandmother, held the youngest; the eldest—all were girls—sat apart, huddled upon herself, her small back hooped, hugging herself with her thin arms in an effort to keep warm. As Carnes drew near, she looked at him, and an impulse of flight was evident in her eyes. The younger of the two women surveyed him with a sort of apathy which partook of anger. The youngest child, in the old woman's lap, was wailing aloud. The grandmother did not try to hush it. Her face, full of a dumb appeal to and questioning of something which Carnes felt dimly was beyond him, gazed over the small head in a soiled white hood which beat wrathfully against her withered bosom. The woman wore an old shawl which was warm; she kept a corner well wrapped about the crying child. The younger woman was very thinly clad. Her hat had a pathetic last summer's rose in it. Now and then a long rigor of chill passed over her; at such times her meagre body seemed to elongate, her arms held the little girl on her lap like two clamps. The man, standing still, with face turned toward the sky over the distant horizon line, gave a glance at Carnes with eyes which bore no curiosity or interest, but were simply indifferent. He looked away again, and Carnes felt that he was forgotten, while his shadow and the man's still intermingled.

Then Carnes broke the silence. He stepped in front of the man. "See here, friend," he said, "what's the matter?"

The man looked at him perforce. He was past words. He had come to that pass where speech as a means of expression seemed superfluous. His look said as much to his questioner. "You ask me what is the matter?" the look said. "Are you *blind?*" But the question in the man's dull eyes was not resentful. He was not one in whom misery arouses resentment against others or Providence. Fate seemed to have paralyzed him, as the clutch of a carnivorous animal is said to paralyze a victim.

"What is it?" Carnes inquired again. "What is the matter?"

Still the man did not answer, but the younger of the two women did. She spoke with great force, but her lips were stiff, and apparently not a muscle of her face moved. "I'll tell you what the matter is," said she. "He's good for nothing. He's a no-account man. He ain't fit to take care of a family. That's what's the matter." Then the other woman bore her testimony, which was horrible from its intensity and its triviality. It was the tragedy of a pin-prick in a meagre soul.

"He's left my hair-cloth sofy an' my feather-bed," said she, in a high, shrill plaint.

Then the forlorn male, badgered betwixt the two females of his species, who were, as it often happens with birds, of a finer, fiercer sort than he, broke silence with a feeble note of expostulation. "Now, don't, mother," said he. "You shall hev that sofy and that feather-bed again."

The younger woman rose, setting the little girl on the frozen ground so hard that she began to cry. "Have 'em back? How is she goin' to have 'em back?" she demanded. "There's the hair-cloth sofy she earned and set her eyes by, and there's the feather-bed she's always slept on, left over there in Sanderson, stored away in a dirty old barn. How's she goin' to ever get 'em again? What's the poor old woman goin' to sit on an' sleep on?"

"We'll go back an' git 'em," muttered the man. "Don't, Emmy."

"Yes, I will! I'll tell the truth, and I don't care who knows it. You're a no-account man. How are we goin' to git 'em back, I'd like to know? You hain't a cent and you can't get work. If I was a man, I'd git work if it killed me. How is your mother goin' to git that sofy and feather-bed again as long as she lives? And that ain't all—there's all my nice furniture that I worked and earned before I was married; you didn't earn none of it except jest that one bedstead and bureau that you bought. I earned all the other things workin' in the shop myself, and there they all be stored in that dirty old barn to be eaten up by rats and covered with dust."

"We will get 'em back. Don't, Emmy."

"How'll we get 'em back? You're a good-for-nothin' man. You ain't fit to support a family."

"He's left my sofy an' feather-bed," reiterated the old woman.

The man looked helplessly from one to the other; then he cast a glance at Carnes—that look full of agony and appeal which one man gives another in such a crisis when he is set upon by those whom he cannot fight.

Carnes, when he met his fellow-man's piteous look, felt at once an impulse of partisanship. He stepped close to him and laid a hand on the thin shoulder in the thin coat. "See here, friend," he said, "tell me all about it." The compassion in Carnes's voice was a power in itself; he had, moreover, a great deal of the clergyman evident, as well in his manner as in the cut of his clothes.

The man hesitated a moment, then he began, and the story of his woes flowed like a stream. It was a simple story enough. The man was evidently one of those who work well and faithfully while in harness, like a horse. Taken out, he was naked and helpless and ashamed, without spirit enough to leave his old hitching-posts and beaten roads of life, and gallop in new pastures unbridled. He became a poor nondescript, not knowing what he knew. The man, whose name was William Jarvis, had worked in a shoe factory ever since he was a boy. He had been an industrious and skilled workman, but had met with many vicissitudes. He had left a poor position for an exceedingly lucrative one in a large factory in Sanderson, and had moved there with his family. Then the factory had been closed through the bankruptcy of the owner. Since then he had had a hard time. He had left his family in Sanderson in their little rented house, and he had been about the country seeking in vain for employment. Then he had returned, to find that the old factory was to be reopened in a month's time, and then he could have a job, but every cent of his money was gone, and he was in debt. Not only Jarvis's money was gone, but his credit. The tradesmen had learned to be wary about trusting the shifting factory population.

The rent was due on the house; Jarvis paid that, and was literally penniless. He packed his humble furniture, and stored it in a neighbor's barn, on condition that it should be taken for storage if he did not claim it within a year.

Then he and his family set forth. It was the hopeless, senseless sort of exodus which might have been expected of people like these, who deal only with the present, being incapacitated, like some insects, from any but a limited vision in one direction. Carnes received a confused impression, from a confused statement of the man, that they had a hope of being able to reach a town in the northern part of the State, where the wife had some distant relatives, and the others of this poor clan might possibly come to their rescue. They had had a hope of friendly lifts in northward-journeying wagons. But there had been no lifts, and they had advanced only about five miles towards their forlorn Mecca on the day before Christmas. The children were unable to walk farther, and the parents were unable to carry them. The grandmother, too, was at the end of her strength. The weather was very cold, and snow threatened. They were none too warmly clad. They had only the small luggage which they could carry—an old valise, and a bundle tied up in an old shawl. The middle child had an old doll that had lost one arm, her blond wig, and an eye, but was going on her travels in her best, faded pink muslin dress and a bit of blue sash. The child stood sobbing wearily, but she still held fast to the doll. The eldest girl eyed her with tender solicitude. She had outgrown dolls. She got a dingy little handkerchief from her pocket and folded it cornerwise for a shawl; then she got down from the wall and pinned it closely around the doll. "There," she said, "that is better." After that the children themselves felt warmer.

Carnes saw everything—the people, the doll, their poor little possessions,—and an agony of pity, which from the nature of the man and its futility became actual torture, seized him. He looked at the other man who had confided in him, at the women who now seemed to watch him with a lingering hope of assistance. He opened his mouth to speak, but he said nothing. What could he say?

Then the man, William Jarvis, added something to this poor story. Two weeks before he had slipped on the ice and injured his shoulder; he had strained it with moving, and it was causing him much distress. Indeed, his face, which was strained with pain as well as misery, bore witness to the truth of that.

The wife had eyed her husband with growing concentration during this last. When he had finished, her face brightened with tenderness; she made a sudden move forward and threw her arms around him, and began to weep in a sort of rage of pity and love and remorse. "Poor Willy! poor Willy!" she sobbed. "Here we've been abusin' you when you've worked like a dog with your shoulder 'most killin' you. You've always done the best you could. I don't care who says you haven't. I'd like to hear anybody say you haven't. I guess they wouldn't darse say it twice to me." She turned on the old woman with unreasoning fury. "Hold your tongue about your old hair-cloth sofy an' your feather-bed, grandma!" said she. "Ain't he your own son? I guess you won't die if you lose your old hair-cloth sofy an' your feather-bed! The stuffin's all comin' out of your old sofy, anyhow! You ought to be ashamed of yourself, grandma! Ain't he your own son?"

"I guess he was my son afore he was your husband," returned the old woman, with spirit. "I ain't pesterin' of him any more'n you be, Emmy Jarvis." With that she began to weep shrilly like a child, leaning her face against the head of the crying child in her lap. The little girl with the doll set up a fresh pipe of woe; the doll slipped to the ground. The elder sister got down from the stone wall and gathered it up and fondled it. "You've dropped poor Angelina and hurt her, Nannie," said she, reproachfully.

"Poor Willy!" again sobbed his wife, "you've been treated like a dog by them you had a right to expect something better of, an' I don't care if I do say so."

Again the man's eyes, overlooking his wife's head, sought the other man's for an understanding of this peculiar masculine distress.

Carnes returned the look with such utter comprehension and perfect compassion as would have lifted the other's burden for all time could it have taken practical form. In reality, Carnes, at this juncture, suffered more than the man. Here was a whole family penniless, suffering. Here was a man with the impulse of a thousand Samaritans to bring succor, but positively helpless to lift a finger towards any alleviation of their misery. It became evident to him in a flash what the outside view of the situation would be: that the only course for a man of ordinary sense and reason was to return to Sanderson and notify the authorities of this suicidal venture; that it was his duty for the sake of the helpless children to have them cared for by force, if there was no other way. But still, this course he could not bring himself to follow. It seemed an infringement upon all the poor souls had left in the world—their individual freedom. He could not do it, and yet what else was there to do? He thought of his forty cents, his only available asset against this heavy arrear of pity and generosity, with fury. At that moment the philanthropist without resources, the Samaritan without his flask of oil, was fairly dangerous to himself from this terrible blocking of almost abnormal impulses for good. It seemed to him that he must die or go mad if he could not do something for these people. He cast about his eyes, like a drowning man, and he saw in a field on the left, quite a distance away, a small house; only its chimneys were visible above a gentle slope. A thought struck him. "Wait a moment," he ordered, and leaped the stone wall and ran across the field, crunching the frozen herbage until his footsteps echoed loudly. The forlorn family watched him. It was only a short time before he returned. He caught up the second little girl from the ground. "Come," cried Carnes in an excited voice. "Come. Nobody lives in that house over there! I can get in! There is a shed with hay in it! There's a fireplace! There's plenty of wood to pick up in the grove behind it! Come!"

His tone was wild with elation. Here was something which could be done. It was small, but something. The others were moved by his enthusiasm. Their faces lightened. The father caught the youngest child from the grandmother; the mother took the eldest by the hand. They all started, the old grandmother outracing them with a quick, short-stepped toddle like a child. "See your mother go," said the wife, and she fairly laughed. In fact, the old woman was almost at her last gasp, and it was an extreme effort of nature, a final spurt of nerve and will.

The house was a substantial cottage, in fair repair. The door at the back was unlocked. Carnes threw it open and ushered in the people as if they had been his guests. A frightful chill struck them as they entered. It was much colder than outside, with a concentration of chill which overwhelmed like an actual presence of wintry death. The children, all except the eldest girl, who hugged the doll tightly, and whispered to her not to mind, it would be warm pretty soon, began to cry again. This was a new deprivation added to the old. They had expected something from the stranger, and he had betrayed them. The grandmother leaned exhausted against the wall; her lips moved, but nothing could be heard. The wife caught up the youngest crying child and shook her.

"Be still, will you?" she said, in a furious voice. "We've got enough to put up with without your bawling." Then she kissed and fondled it, and her own tears dropped fast on its wet face.

But not one whit of Carnes's enthusiasm abated. He beckoned the man, who sprang to his bidding. They brought wood from the grove behind the house. Carnes built a fire on the old hearth, and he found some old boxes in the little barn. He rigged up some seats with boards, and barrels for backs; he spread hay on the boards for cushions. The warmth and light of the fire filled the room. All of a sudden it was furnished and inhabited. Their faces began to relax and lighten. The awful blue tints of cold gave place to soft rose and white. The children began to laugh.

"What did I tell you?" the eldest girl asked the doll, and she danced it before the ruddy glow. The wife bade her husband sit with his lame shoulder next the fire. The youngest child climbed into her grandmother's lap again, and sat with her thumb in her mouth surveying the fire. She was hungry, but she sucked her own thumb, and she was warm. The old woman nodded peacefully. She had taken off her bonnet, and her white head gleamed with a rosy tint in the firelight.

Carnes was radiant for a few minutes. He stood surveying the transformation he had wrought. "Well, now, this is better," he said, and he laughed like a child. Then suddenly his face fell again. This was not a solution of the problem. He had simply stated it. There was no food, there was no permanent shelter. Then the second little girl, who was the most delicate and nervous of them all, began to cry again. "I want somefin to eat," she wailed. Her father, who had been watching them with as much delight as Carnes, also experienced a revulsion. Again he looked at Carnes.

"Yes," said the wife in a bitter tone, "here is a fire and a roof over us, but we may get turned out any minute, if anybody sees the smoke comin' out of the chimney; and there's nothin' to eat."

The eldest little girl's lip quivered. She hugged the doll more closely.

"Don't cry, and you shall have a piece of cake pretty soon," she whispered. The man continued to look at Carnes, who suddenly stood straight and threw up his head with a resolute look. "I'm going, but I will come back very soon," said he, "and then we'll have supper. Don't worry. Put enough wood on the fire to keep warm." Then he went out.

He hurried across the field to the road under the lowering quiet of the gray sky. His resolve was stanch, but his heart failed him. Again the agony of balked compassion was over him. He looked ahead over the reach of frozen highway without a traveller in sight, he looked up at the awful winter sky threatening with storm, and he was in a mood of blasphemy. There was that misery, there was he with the willingness to relieve, and—forty cents. It was a time when money reached a value beyond itself, when it represented the treasure of heaven. This poor forty cents would buy bread, at least, and a little milk. It would keep them alive a few hours, but that was only a part of the difficulty solved. The cold was intense, and they were not adequately protected against it. There were an old woman and three children. He was only giving them the most ephemeral aid, and what would come next?

Carnes, standing there in the road all alone, mechanically thrust his hand in his pocket for the feel of his forty cents; but instead of putting his hand in his own coat-pocket, he thrust it in the pocket of the overcoat which the minister in Sanderson had given him. He pulled out, instead of his own poor old wallet, a prosperous portly one of black seal-skin. He did not at first realize what it meant. He stood staring vacuously. Then he knew. The minister in Sanderson had left his own wallet in the overcoat pocket. The coat was one which he had been wearing until his new one had come from the tailor's the day before.

Carnes stood gazing at this pocket-book; then he slowly, with shaking fingers, opened it. There were papers, which he saw at a glance were valuable, and there was a large roll of bills. Carnes began counting them slowly. He sat down on the stone wall the while. His legs trembled so that he could scarcely stand. There was over two hundred dollars in bills in the wallet. Carnes sat awhile regarding the bills. A strange expression was coming over his gentle, scholarly, somewhat weak face—an expression evil and unworthy in its original meaning, but, as it were, glorified by the motive which actuated it. The man's face became full of a most angelic greed of money. He was thinking what he could do with only a hundred dollars of that other man's money. He knew with no hesitation that he would run to Elmville, hire a carriage, take the distressed family back to Sanderson to their old house, pay the rent a month in advance, pay their debts, get the stored furniture, help them set it up, give them money to buy fuel and provisions for the month before the factory reopened. A hundred dollars of that money in his hand, which did not belong to him, meant respite for distress, which would be like a taste of heaven; it meant perhaps life instead of death; it meant perhaps more than earthly life, perhaps spiritual life, to save this family from the awful test of despair.

Carnes separated a hundred dollars from the rest. He put it in his own old wallet. He replaced the remainder in the minister's, and he went on to Elmville.

It was ten o'clock on Christmas-eve before Robinson Carnes, having left the Jarvis family reinstated in their old home, warmed and fed, and happier perhaps than they had ever been or perhaps ever would be, went to the vestry blazing with light in which the Christmas tree was being held. He stood in the door and saw the minister, portly and smiling, seated well forward. As he watched, the minister's name was called, and he received a package. The minister was a man with a wealthy parish; he had, moreover, money of his own, and not a large reputation for giving. Carnes reflected upon this as he stood there. It seemed to him that with such a man his chances of mercy were small. He had his mind steeled for the worst. He considered, as he stood there, his every good chance of arraignment, of imprisonment. "It may mean State prison for me," he thought. Then a wave of happiness came over him. "Anyway," he told himself, "they have the money." He did not conceive of the possibility of the minister taking away the money from that poverty and distress; that was past his imagination. "They have the money," he kept repeating. It also occurred to him, for he was strong in the doctrines of his church creed, that he had possibly incurred a heavier than earthly justice for his deed; and then he told himself again, "Well, they have it."

A mental picture of the family in warmth and comfort in their home came before him, and while he reflected upon theft and its penalty, he smiled like an angel. Presently he called a little boy near by and sent him to the minister.

"Ask Mr. Abbot if he will please see Mr. Carnes a moment," he said. "Say he has something important to tell him."

Soon the boy returned, and his manner unconsciously aped Mr. Abbot.

"Mr. Abbot says he is sorry, but he cannot leave just now," he said. It was evident that the minister wished to shake off the mendicant of his holy profession.

Carnes took the rebuff meekly, but he bade the boy wait a moment. He took a pencil from his pocket and wrote something on a scrap of paper. He wrote this:

"I found this wallet in your pocket in the coat which you gave me. I have stolen one hundred dollars to relieve the necessities of a poor family. I await your pleasure. Robinson Carnes."

The boy passed up the aisle with the pocket-book and the note. Carnes, watching, saw a sudden convulsive motion of the minister's shoulders in his direction, but he did not turn his head. His name was called again for a present as the boy passed down the aisle, returning to Carnes.

Again the boy unconsciously aped Mr. Abbot's manner as he addressed Carnes. It was conclusive, coldly disapproving, non-retaliative, dismissing. Carnes knew the minister, and he had no doubt. "Mr. Abbot says that he has no need to see you, that you can go when you wish," said the boy. Carnes knew that he was quite free, that no penalty would attach to his theft.

The snow had begun to fall as Robinson Carnes took his way out of Sanderson on the road to Elmville, but the earth had come into a sort of celestial atmosphere which obliterated the storm for human hearts. All around were innocent happiness and festivity, and the display of love by loving gifts. The poor minister was alone on a stormy road on Christmas-eve. He had no presentiment of anything bright in his future: he did not know that he was to find an asylum and a friend for life in the clergyman in the town toward which his face was set. He travelled on, bending his shoulders before the sleety wind. His heart was heavier and heavier before the sense of his own guilt. He felt to the full that he had done a great wrong. He had stolen, and stolen from his benefactor. He had taken off the minister's coat and laid it gently over the back of a settee in the vestry before he left, but that made no difference. If only he had not stolen from the man who had given him his coat. And yet he always had, along with the remorse, that light of great joy which could not be wholly darkened by any thought of self, when he reflected upon the poor family who were happy. He thought that possibly the minister had in reality been glad, although he condemned him. He began to love him and thank him for his generosity. He pulled his thin coat closely around him and went on. He had given the last gift which he had to give—his own honesty.

A Stolen Christmas

Harper's Bazar, December 24, 1887, 885, 890–91

"I DON'T S'POSE YOU air goin' to do much Christmas over to your house."

Mrs. Luther Ely stood looking over her gate. There was a sweet, hypocritical smile on her little thin red mouth. Her old china blue eyes stared as innocently as a baby's, although there was a certain hardness in them. Her soft wrinkled cheeks were pink and white with the true blond tints of her youth, which she had never lost. She was now an old woman, but people still looked at her with admiring eyes, and probably would until she died. All her life long her morsel of the world had had in it a sweet savor of admiration, and she had smacked her little feminine lips over it greedily. She expected every one to contribute toward it, even this squat, shabby, defiant old body standing squarely out in the middle of the road. Marg'ret Poole had stopped unwillingly to exchange courtesies with Mrs. Luther Ely. She looked aggressive. She eyed with a sidewise glance the other woman's pink, smirking face.

"'Tain't likely we be," she said, in a voice which age had made gruff instead of piping. Then she took a step forward.

"Well, we ain't goin' to do much," continued Mrs. Ely, with an air of subdued loftiness. "We air jest goin' to hev a little Christmas tree for the children. Flora's goin' to git a few things. She says there's a very nice 'sortment up to White's."

Marg'ret gave a kind of affirmative grunt; then she tried to move on, but Mrs. Ely would not let her.

"I dun know as you hev noticed our new curtains," said she.

Had she not! Poor Marg'ret Poole, who had only green paper shades in her own windows, had peeped slyly around the corner of one, and watched mournfully, though not enviously, her opposite neighbor tacking up those elegant Nottingham lace draperies, and finally tying them back with bows of red ribbon.

Marg'ret would have given much to have scouted scornfully the idea, but she was an honest old woman, if not a sweet one.

"Yes, I see 'em," said she, shortly.

"Don't you think they're pretty?"

"Well 'nough," replied Marg'ret, with another honest rigor.

"They cost consider'ble. I told Flora I thought she was kind of extravagant; but then Sam's airnin' pretty good wages. I dun know but they may jest as well have things. Them white cotton curtains looked dreadful kind of gone by."

Marg'ret thought of her green paper ones. She did not hate this other old woman; she at once admired and despised her; and this admiration of one whom she despised made her angry with herself and ashamed. She was never at her ease with Mrs. Luther Ely.

Mrs. Ely had run out of her house on purpose to intercept her and impress her with her latest grandeur—the curtains and the Christmas tree. She was sure of it. Still she looked with fine appreciation at the other's delicate pinky face, her lace cap adorned with purple ribbons, her black gown with a flounce around the bottom. The gown was rusty, but Marg'ret did not notice that; her own was only a chocolate calico. Black wool of an afternoon was sumptuous to her. She thought how genteel she looked in it. Mrs. Ely still retained her slim, long-waisted effect. Marg'ret had lost every sign of youthful grace; she was solidly square and stout.

Mrs. Ely had run out, in her haste, without a shawl; indeed, the weather was almost warm enough to go without one. It was only a week before Christmas, but there was no snow, and the grass was quite bright in places. There were green lights over in the field, and also in the house yards. There was a soft dampness in the air, which brought spring to mind. It almost seemed as if one by listening intently might hear frogs or bluebirds.

Now Marg'ret stepped resolutely across the street to her little house, which was shingled, but not painted, except on the front. Some one had painted that red many years before.

Mrs. Ely, standing before her glossy white cottage, which had even a neat little hood over its front door, cried, patronizingly, after her once again:

"I'm comin' over to see you as soon as I kin," said she, "arter Christmas. We air dretful busy now."

"Well, come when ye kin," Marg'ret responded, shortly. Then she entered between the dry lilac bushes, and shut the door with a bang.

Even out in the yard she had heard a shrill clamor of children's voices from the house; when she stood in the little entry it was deafening.

"Them children is raisin' Cain," muttered she. Then she threw open the door of the room where they were. There were three of them in a little group near the window. Their round yellow heads bobbed, their fat little legs and arms swung wildly. "Granny! granny!" shouted they.

"For the land sake, don't make such a racket! Mis' Ely kin hear you over to her house," said Marg'ret.

"Untie us. Ain't ye goin' to untie us now? Say, Granny."

"I'll untie ye jest as soon as I kin get my things off. Stop hollerin'."

In the ceiling were fixed three stout hooks. A strong rope was tied around each child's waist, and the two ends fastened securely around a hook. The ropes were long enough to allow the children free range of the room, but they kept them just short of one dangerous point—the stove. The stove was the fiery dragon which haunted Marg'ret's life. Many a night did she dream that one of these little cotton petticoats had whisked too near it, and the flames were roaring up around a little yellow head. Many a day, when away from home, the same dreadful pictures had loomed out before her eyes; her lively fancy had untied these stout knots, and she had hurried home in a panic.

Marg'ret took off her hood and shawl, hung them carefully in the entry, and dragged a wooden chair under a hook. She was a short woman, and she had to stretch up on her tiptoes to untie those hard knots. Her face turned a purplish-red.

This method of restriction was the result of long thought and study on her part. She had tried many others, which had proved ineffectual. Willy, the eldest, could master knots like a sailor. Many a time the grandmother had returned to find the house empty. Willy had unfastened his own knot and liberated his little sisters, and then all three had made the most of their freedom. But even Willy, with his sharp five-year-old brain and his nimble little fingers, could not untie a knot whose two ends brushed the ceiling. Now Marg'ret was sure to find them all where she left them.

After the children were set at liberty she got their supper, arranging it neatly on the table between the windows. There was a nice white table cover, and the six silver teaspoons shone. The teaspoons were the mark of a flood-tide of Marg'ret's aspirations, and she had had aspirations all her life. She had given them to her daughter, the children's mother, on her marriage. She herself had never owned a bit of silver, but she determined to present her daughter with some.

"I'm goin' to have you have things like other folks," she had said.

Now the daughter was dead, and she had the spoons. She regarded the daily use of them as an almost sinful luxury, but she brought them out in their heavy glass tumbler every meal.

"I'm goin' to have them children learn to eat off silver spoons," she said, defiantly, to their father; "they'll think more of themselves."

The father, Joseph Snow, was trying to earn a living in the city, a hundred miles distant. He was himself very young, and had not hitherto displayed much business capacity, although he was good and willing. They had been very poor before his wife died; ever since he had not been able to do much more than feed and clothe himself. He had sent a few dollars to Marg'ret from time to time—dollars which he had saved and scrimped pitifully to accumulate—but the burden of their support had come upon her.

She had sewed carpets and assisted in spring cleanings—everything to which she could turn a hand. Marg'ret was a tailoress, but she could now get no employment at her trade. The boys all wore "store clothes" in these days. She could only pick up a few cents at a time; still she managed to keep the children in comfort, with a roof over their heads and something to eat. Their cheeks were fat and pink; they were noisy and happy, and also pretty.

After the children were in bed that night she stood in her kitchen window and gazed across at Mrs. Luther Ely's house. She had left the candle in the children's room—the little things were afraid without it—and she had not yet lighted one for herself; so she could see out quite plainly, although the night was dark. There was a light in the parlor of the opposite house; the Nottingham lace curtains showed finely their pattern of leaves and flowers. Marg'ret eyed them. "'Tain't no use my tryin' to git up a notch," she muttered. "'Tain't no use for some folks. They 'ain't worked no harder than I have; Louisa Ely 'ain't never begun to work so hard; but they kin have lace curtains an' Christmas trees."

The words sounded envious. Still she was hardly that; subsequent events proved it. Her "tryin' to git up a notch" explained everything. Mrs. Luther Ely, the lace curtains, and the Christmas tree were as three stars set on that higher "notch" which she wished to gain. If the other woman had dressed in silk instead of rusty wool, if the lace draperies had been real, Marg'ret would hardly have wasted one wistful glance on them. But Mrs. Luther Ely had been all her life the one notch higher, which had seemed almost attainable. In that opposite house there was only one carpet; Marg'ret might have hoped for one carpet. Mrs. Ely's son-in-law earned only a comfortable living for his family; Marg'ret's might have done that. Worst of all, each woman had one daughter, and Marg'ret's had died.

Marg'ret had been ambitious all her life. She had made struggle after struggle. The tailoress trade was one of them. She made up her mind that she would have things like other people. Then she married, and her husband spent her money. One failure came after another. She slipped back again and again on the step to that higher notch. And here she was to-night, old and poor, with these three helpless children dependent upon her.

But she felt something besides disappointed ambition as she stood gazing out to-night.

"Thar's the children," she went on; "can't have nothin' for Christmas. I 'ain't got a cent I kin spare. If I git 'em enough to eat, I'm lucky."

Presently she turned away and lighted a lamp. She had some sewing to do for the children, and was just sitting down with it, when she paused suddenly and stood reflecting.

"I've got a good mind to go down to White's an' see what he's got in for Christmas," said she. "Mebbe Joseph'll send some money 'long next week, an' if he does, mebbe I kin git 'em some little thing. It would be a good plan for me to kind of price 'em."

Marg'ret laid her work down, got her hood and shawl, and went out, fastening the house securely, and also the door of the room where the stove was.

To her eyes the village store which she presently entered was a very emporium of beauty and richness. She stared at the festoons of evergreens, the dangling trumpets and drums, the counters heaped with cheap toys, with awe and longing. She asked respectfully the price of this and that, some things less pretentious than the others. But it was all beyond her. She might as well have priced diamonds and bronzes. As she stood looking, sniffing in the odor of evergreen and new varnish, which was to her a very perfume of Christmas arising from its fulness of peace and merriment, Flora Trask, Mrs. Ely's daughter, entered. Marg'ret went out quickly. "She'll see I ain't buyin' anything," she thought to herself.

But Marg'ret Poole came again the next day, and the next, and the next—morning, afternoon, and evening. "I dun know but I may want to buy some things by-an'-by," she told the proprietor, extenuatingly, "an' I thought I'd kind of like to price 'em."

She stood about, eying, questioning, and fingering tenderly. No money-letter came from Joseph. She inquired anxiously at the post-office many times a day. She tried to get work to raise a little extra money, but she could get none at this time of the year. She visited Mrs. White, the store-keeper's wife, and asked with forlorn hope if she had no tailor-work for her. There were four boys in that family. But Mrs. White shook her head. She was a good woman. "I'm sorry," said she, "but I haven't got a mite. The boys wouldn't wear home-made clothes."

She looked pitifully at Marg'ret's set, disappointed face when she went out.

Finally those animals of sugar and wood, those pink-faced, straight-bodied dolls, those tin trumpets and express wagons, were to Marg'ret as the fair apples hanging over the garden wall were to Christiana's sons in the *Pilgrim's Progress.* She gazed and gazed, until at last the sight and the smell of them were too much for her.

The evening before Christmas she went up to the post-office. The last mail was in, and there was no letter for her. Then she kept on to the store. It was rather early, and there were not as yet many customers. Marg'ret began looking about as usual. She might have been in the store ten minutes when she suddenly noticed a parcel on the corner of a counter. It was nicely tied. It belonged evidently either to one of the persons who were then trading in the store or was to be delivered outside later. Mr. White was not in; two of his sons and a boy clerk were waiting upon the customers.

Marg'ret, once attracted by this parcel, could not take her eyes from it long. She pored over the other wares with many sidelong glances at it. Her thoughts centred upon it, and her imagination. What could be in it? To whom could it belong?

Marg'ret Poole had always been an honest woman. She had never taken a thing which did not belong to her in her whole life. She suddenly experienced a complete moral revulsion. It was as if her principles, where weights were made shifty by her long watching and longing, had suddenly gyrated in a wild somersault. While they were reversed, Marg'ret, warily glancing around, slipped that parcel under her arm, opened the door, and sped home.

It was better Christmas weather than it had been a week ago. There was now a fine level of snow, and the air was clear and cold. Marg'ret panted as she walked. The snow creaked under her feet. She met many people hurrying along in chattering groups. She wondered if they could see the parcel under her shawl. It was quite a large one.

When she got into her own house she hastened to strike a light. Then she untied the parcel. There were in it some pink sugar cats and birds, two tin horses and a little wagon, a cheap doll, and some bright picture-books, besides a paper of candy.

"My land!" said Marg'ret, "won't they be tickled!"

There was a violent nervous shivering all over her stout frame. "Why can't I keep still?" said she.

She got out three of the children's stockings, filled them, and hung them up beside the chimney. Then she drew a chair before the stove, and went over to the bureau to get her Bible: she always read a chapter before she went to bed. Marg'ret was not a church member, she never said anything about it, but she had a persistent, reticent sort of religion. She took up the Bible; then laid it down; then she took it up again with a clutch.

"I don't keer," said she, "I 'ain't done nothin' so terrible out of the way. What can't be airned, when anybody's willin' to work, ought to be took. I'm goin' to wait till arter Christmas; then I'm jest goin' up to Mis' White's some arternoon, an' I'm goin' to say, 'Mis' White,' says I, 'the day before Christmas I went into your husband's store, an' I see a bundle a-layin' on the counter, an' I took it, an' said nothin' to nobody. I shouldn't ha' done such a thing if you'd give me work, the way I asked you to, instead of goin' outside an' buyin' things for your boys, an' robbin' honest folks of the chance to airn. Now, Mis' White, I'll tell you jest what I'm willin' to do: you give me somethin' to do, an' I'll work out twice the price of them things I took, an' we'll call it even. If you don't, all is, your husband will hev to lose it.' I wonder what she'll say to that."

Marg'ret said all this with her head thrown back, in a tone of indescribable defiance. Then she sat down with her Bible and read a chapter.

The next day she watched the children's delight over their presents with a sort of grim pleasure.

She charged them to say nothing about them, although there was little need of it. Marg'ret had few visitors, and the children were never allowed to run into the neighbors'.

Two days after Christmas the postmaster stopped at Marg'ret's house: his own was just beyond.

He handed a letter to her. "This came Christmas morning," said he. "I thought I'd bring it along on my way home. I knew you hadn't been in for two or three days, and I thought you were expecting a letter."

"Thank ye," said Marg'ret. She pulled the letter open, and saw there was some money in it. She turned very white.

"Hope you 'ain't got any bad news," said the postmaster.

"No, I 'ain't." After he had gone she sat down and read her letter with her knees shaking.

Joseph Snow had at last got a good situation. He was earning fifty dollars a month. There were twenty dollars in the letter. He promised to send her that sum regularly every month.

"Five dollars a week!" gasped Marg'ret. "My land! An' I've—*stole!*"

She sat there looking at the money in her lap. It was quite late; the children had been in bed a long time. Finally she put away the money, and went herself. She did not read in her Bible that night.

She could not go to sleep. It was bitterly cold. The old timbers of the house cracked. Now and then there was a sharp report like a pistol. There was a pond near by, and great crashes came from that. Marg'ret might have been, from the noise, in the midst of a cannonade, to which her own guilt had exposed her.

"'Tain't nothin' but the frost," she kept saying to herself.

About three o'clock she saw a red glow on the wall opposite the window.

"I'm 'maginin' it," muttered she. She would not turn over to look at the window. Finally she did. Then she sprang, and rushed toward it. The house where Mrs. Luther Ely lived was on fire.

Marg'ret threw a quilt over her head, unbolted her front door, and flew. "Fire! fire!" she yelled. "Fire! fire! Oh, Mis' Ely, where be you? Fire! fire! Sam—Sam Trask, you're all burnin' up! Flora! Oh! fire! fire!"

By the time she got out in the road she saw black groups moving in the distance. Hoarse shouts followed her cries. Then the church bell clanged out.

Flora was standing in the road, holding on to her children. They were all crying. "Oh, Mis' Poole!" sobbed she, "ain't it dreadful? ain't it awful?"

"Hev you got the children all out?" asked Marg'ret.

"Yes; Sam told me to stand here with 'em."

"Where's your mother?"

"I don't know. She's safe. She waked up first." The young woman rolled her wild eyes toward the burning house. "There she is!" cried she.

Mrs. Ely was running out of the front door with a box in her hand. Her son-in-law staggered after her with a table on his shoulder.

"Don't you go in again, mother," said he.

There were other men helping to carry out the goods, and they chimed in. "No," cried they; "'tain't safe. Don't you go in again, Mis' Ely!"

Marg'ret ran up to her. "Them curtains," gasped she, "an' the parlor carpet, hev they got them out?"

"Oh, I dun know—I dun know! I'm afraid they 'ain't. Oh, they 'ain't got nothin' out! Everything all burnin' up! Oh, dear me! oh dear! Where *be* you goin'?"

Marg'ret had rushed past her into the house. She was going into the parlor, when a man caught hold of her. "Where are you going?" he shouted. "Clear out of this."

"I'm a-goin' to git out them lace curtains an' the carpet."

"It ain't any use. We staid in there just as long as we could, trying to get the carpet up; but we couldn't stand it any longer; it's chock full of smoke." The man shouted it out, and pulled her along with him at the same time. "There!" said he, when they were out in the road; "look at that." There was a flicker of golden fire in one of the parlor windows. Then those lace curtains blazed. "There!" said the man again: "I told you it wasn't any use."

Marg'ret turned on him. There were many other men within hearing. "Well, I wouldn't tell of it," said she, in a loud voice. "If I was a pack of stout, able-bodied men, and couldn't ha' got out them curtains an' that carpet afore they burnt up, I wouldn't tell of it."

Flora and the children had been taken into one of the neighboring houses. Mrs. Ely still stood out in the freezing air clutching her box and wailing. Her son-in-law was trying hard to persuade her to go into the house where her daughter was.

Marg'ret joined them. "I would go if I was you, Mis' Ely," said she.

"No, I ain't goin'. I don't care where I be. I'll stay right here in the road. Oh, dear me!"

"Don't take on so."

"I 'ain't got a thing left but jest my best cap here. I did git that out. Oh dear! oh dear! everything's burnt up but jest this cap. It's all I've got left. I'll jest put it on an' set right down here in the road an' freeze to death. Nobody'll care. Oh dear! dear! dear!"

"Oh, don't, Mis' Ely." Marg'ret, almost rigid herself with the cold, put her hand on the other woman's arm. Just then the roof of the burning house fell in. There was a shrill wail from the spectators.

"Do come, mother," Sam begged, when they stood staring for a moment.

"Yes, do go, Mis' Ely," said Marg'ret. "You mustn't feel so."

"It's easy 'nough to talk," said Mrs. Ely. "'Tain't your house; an' if 'twas, you wouldn't had much to lose—nothin' but a passel of old wooden cheers an' tables."

"I know it," said Marg'ret.

Finally Mrs. Ely was started, and Marg'ret hurried home. She thought suddenly of the children and the money. But the children had not waked in all the tumult, and the money was where she had left it. She did not go to bed again, but sat over the kitchen stove thinking, with her elbows on her knees, until morning. When morning came she had laid out one plan of action.

That afternoon she took some of her money, went up to Mr. White's store, and bought some Nottingham lace curtains like the ones her neighbors had lost. They were off the same piece.

That evening she went to call on Mrs. Ely, and presented them. She had tried to think that she might send the parcel anonymously—leave it on the door-step; but she could not.

"'Twon't mortify me so much as 'twill the other way," said she, "an' I'd ought to be mortified."

So she carried the curtains, and met with a semblance of gratitude and a reality of amazement and incredulity, which shamed her beyond measure.

After she got home that night she took up the Bible, then laid it down. "Here I've been talkin' and worryin' about gettin' up a higher notch," said she, "an' kind of despisin' Mis' Ely when I see her on one. Mis' Ely wouldn't have stole. I ain't nothin' 'side of her now, an' I never kin be."

The scheme which Marg'ret had laid to confront Mrs. White was never carried out. Her defiant spirit had failed her.

One day she went there and begged for work again. "I'm willin' to do 'most anything," said she. "I'll come an' do your washin', or anything, an' I don't want no pay."

Mrs. White was going away the next day, and she had no work to give the old woman; but she offered her some fuel and some money.

Marg'ret looked at her scornfully. "I've got money enough, thank ye," said she. "My son sends me five dollars a week."

The other woman stared at her with amazement. She told her husband that night that she believed Marg'ret Poole was getting a little unsettled. She did not know what to make of her.

Not long after that Marg'ret went into Mr. White's store, and slyly laid some money on the counter. She knew it to be enough to cover the cost of the articles she had stolen. Then she went away and left it there.

That night she went after her Bible. "I declare I *will* read it to-night," muttered she. "I've paid fur 'em." She stood eying it. Suddenly she began to cry. "Oh dear!" she groaned; "I can't. There don't anything do any good—the lace curtains, nor payin' fur 'em, nor nothin'. I dun know what I *shell* do."

She looked at the clock. It was about nine. "He won't be gone yet," said she. She stood motionless, thinking. "If I'm goin' to-night, I've got to," she muttered. Still she did not start for a while longer. When she did, there was no more hesitation. No argument could have stopped Marg'ret Poole, in her old hood and shawl, pushing up the road, fairly started on her line of duty. When she got to the store she went in directly. The heavy door slammed to, and the glass panels clattered. Mr. White was alone in the store. He was packing up some goods preparatory to closing. Marg'ret went straight up to him, and laid a package before him on the counter.

"I brought these things back," said she; "they belong to you."

"Why, what is it?" said Mr. White, wonderingly.

"Some things I stole last Christmas for the children."

"What!"

"I stole 'em."

She untied the parcel, and began taking out the things one by one. "They're all here but the candy," said she; "the children ate that up; an' Aggie bit the head off this pink cat the other day. Then they've jammed this little horse consider'ble. But I brought 'em all back."

Mr. White was an elderly, kind-faced man. He seemed slowly paling with amazement as he stared at her and the articles she was displaying.

"You say you stole them?" said he.

"Yes; I stole 'em."

"When?"

"The night afore Christmas."

"Didn't Henry give 'em to you?"

"No."

"Why, I told him to," said Mr. White, slowly. "I did the things up for you myself that afternoon. I'd seen you looking kind of wishful, you know, and

I thought I'd make you a present of them. I left the bundle on the counter when I went to supper, and told Henry to tell you to take it, and I supposed he did."

Marg'ret stood staring. Her mouth was open, her hands were clinched. "I dun know—what you mean," she gasped out at length.

"I mean you 'ain't been stealing as much as you thought you had," said Mr. White. "You just took your own bundle."

The Gospel According to Joan

Harper's Magazine, December 1919, 77–88

"MY!"

"Don't you think I've done pretty well?"

"Sarah Bannister, you know as well as I do, it is wonderful!"

The two women stood in the best parlor, a long room, furnished with aggressive plush and mahogany, and onyx tables, and a marble Clytie drooping her head impudently in her out-of-place state in a New England parlor. The room was chilly in spite of the radiators, glaring with gilt in the most conspicuous wall spaces. Every piece of furniture—old-fashioned square tables, sofa, chairs, and piano—was covered with dainty things, large and small, of all colors and fabrics.

"To think you made everything here with your own hands!" commented Miss Lottie Dodd. She was a distant relative of Mrs. Bannister's, who lived with her a month at a time.

"Yes, and the worst of it is, it isn't quite a week to Christmas, and I haven't got the things done yet."

"Land! I should think you had enough here for the whole town."

"I'm giving to about the whole town this year. Then, you know all our cousins out West, and the raft of relations we never see except at our funerals, that live in Watchboro, and Center Watchboro, and South and North and East."

"I didn't know you remembered them Christmas."

"I don't every year, but this time I was so forehanded I thought I'd put them in with the rest."

"You don't mean to say you are remembering all the Rice family?"

"Yes, I am."

"Not all those children?"

"Oh, I've got the children's presents all ready; it's the older folks' I haven't got done. I have planned a lot of drawnwork."

"You do that so beautifully," said Lottie. She was a tiny woman snugged in a lavender wool shawl. The tip of her sharp nose was red. Her blue eyes were tearful, from cold and enthusiasm. Lottie was prey to enthusiasms, even petty ones.

"I've got a lot more to do. I sha'n't try any different patterns from these here; the same with the knitted lace. That will make it easier."

Sarah Bannister clipped the last word short with a sneeze.

"Sarah, you are catching cold in this room."

"Don't know but I am. It never will heat when the wind's northwest. It's bitter outdoors to-day, too. The snow hasn't melted one mite. Look at those windows all frosted up."

"Well, Sarah, we better be going back to the sitting room, where it's warm."

"Guess we'd better. I was going to look a little longer. I don't seem to see some things I know I've got. I do feel some as if I were catching cold. Hope to goodness I don't—just before Christmas, too. I'll get Henry to bring in some wood for the sitting-room hearth fire."

"I sort of wonder sometimes why you and Henry don't keep a man to fetch and carry," said Lottie Dodd, as the two entered the sitting room, meeting a gust of warm air, scented with geranium and heliotrope from the window plants. "Henry is quite some older than you, and it's beginning to show."

"Oh, Henry's perfectly able to do what little chores we have. Men want some exercise."

They sat down. Sarah Bannister began to crochet, a neatly rolled-up ball of finished lace bobbing as her fingers moved. Lottie worked laboriously on a blue centerpiece.

"It certainly is lucky you are so well off, Sarah."

"Yes, I realize it is. Henry never saved much, but I have enough for both, thanks to poor father. I never spend a cent but I think of him. He used to talk so much to me about not being extravagant."

"Oh, Sarah, as if anybody could accuse you of that!"

Sarah started, but she continued talking. "Poor father used to say—I remember as if it were yesterday—'Sarah, it's easy enough to get money, for those who have the right kind of heads, and work, but it takes more than heads to keep it. That's a gift.'"

Lottie Dodd, impecunious, who had never benefited much from Sarah's riches, except in the somewhat negative way of food and cast-off clothing, looked reflectively at the large, flat, rather handsome face.

Sarah stared sharply at Lottie, who did not speak. Silence and immobility make a fool inscrutable.

Sarah suspected. "Now, you wouldn't believe, Lottie Dodd, how little some of these things in there"—she shrugged her shoulders toward the parlor—"cost."

"You don't mean it." Lottie's voice was as blatantly innocent as a lamb's.

"Yes, I bought a lot at the Five-and-Ten-cent stores, and I had nice pieces of silk and satin and lace, and I mixed them in, and you'd never know. I thought of poor father every minute I was in these Five-and-Ten-cent stores."

"They would have just suited your dear pa."

Again the look of suspicion was in Sarah's eyes, to disappear before the other woman's innocent expression. Then the door-bell rang with a loud clang.

"Sakes alive! Whoever can that be, such a cold afternoon?" said Mrs. Bannister.

"Maybe it's a peddler."

"Well, if it is, he vamooses. I never will allow a peddler in my house." Sarah Bannister sneezed three times.

"Let me go to the door," said Lottie Dodd. "You have caught cold, sure as fate. Let me go, dear."

In Lottie's voice was the faint, very faint inflection in which she betrayed her consciousness that she was a year and a half younger than Sarah. To Lottie that meant, when she so desired, the feebleness of age for Sarah, juvenile agility for herself.

Sarah recognized that inflection. "I rather guess I'm as able to go to the door as you," she retorted. She thrust her face almost into the other's in a way she had when irritated.

"It was only on account of your cold, dear," protested Lottie, shrinking back.

"I haven't got any cold. If you're trying to wish one on me, you can just stop. Sneezing don't prove you've got a cold. Hm!"

"Why, Sarah!"

Sarah stepped majestically doorward as the bell rang again. She walked on her heels as she had a trick of doing when feeling unusually self-sufficient. Lottie peeked around the curtain over the pots of geraniums, but she could see nothing. She could hear voices, and the wind came in the cracks of the sitting-room door. The front door closed with a bang, and Lottie darted back to her chair. She expected to see Mrs. Bannister enter irate after turning away a peddler, but after Sarah entered a young girl, hardly more than a child.

"Go right to that hearth fire and sit down and get warm through," ordered Mrs. Bannister. She spoke in a stern voice, but her speech ended in a beautiful cadence. When the child was seated before the fire, which Sarah stirred to a higher blaze and piled with more wood, she gazed at the young face reflecting the red glow, and smiled in a way that made Lottie gaze wonderingly at her, and suddenly remember that years ago, so many years that she had forgotten, Sarah Bannister had lost a daughter about the age of this girl. Meantime Sarah Bannister was removing the girl's extraordinarily shabby hat, and pulling off gently her shabbier coat. The girl resisted the last a little, and her small, timid voice murmured something about her dress.

"Never mind your dress," said Sarah. "You will get warmer with these off."

As she spoke she laid the coat and hat on a chair, rather gingerly. Such rags as the coat disclosed, such rags of a red silk lining, and such a sinfully draggled feather decked the old hat. Sarah turned to look at the girl. Lottie was looking. Lottie had her mouth slightly open. Sarah gasped. The girl sitting there, meekly, almost limply, was a darling of a girl (judging from her little face). It was very pale now, but with the velvety pallor of a white flower. Her hair lay in soft rings of gold shading into brown about her small head. She wore her hair short, and it made her seem more a child. Her dress was torn about the sleeves and gaped where hooks were missing, unless pinned with obvious pins. Her little hands were stiff and red, and one continued to clasp cautiously the handle of an unspeakably shabby old bag. Suddenly she looked up, first at one, then at the other of the faces regarding her. She looked with perfect composure, so perfect that it directly made her seem older. Her great blue eyes had a womanly wise cognizance of the two women.

"How old are you?" demanded Sarah Bannister, suddenly.

"Thirteen last May," replied the girl. Her voice was charming, with a curious appeal in it. She seemed to be begging pardon for the fact that she was thirteen last May.

Sarah Bannister, her face working as if she were about to weep, went to a little china-closet, and presently came back with a glass of home-made wine, and a square of sponge cake on a pink plate.

"Here, drink this and eat this cake," said she. "It will do you good."

She set a small table beside the girl and placed the wine-glass and the cake on it.

"Thank you, ma'am," said the girl. She began to eat and drink rather eagerly. She was evidently famished, but very gentle about it. She still retained her hold of the bag.

Lottie spoke for the first time. "What have you got in that bag?" said she, rather sharply. The girl flashed her blue eyes at her in a frightened but defiant way.

"Things to sell," she whispered.

Lottie looked at Sarah. So she was a peddler, after all. Sarah did not return Lottie's glance. She spoke to the girl.

"When you have finished your cake and wine, and get real warm, I will look at the things you have to sell," said she, softly.

"Thank you, ma'am."

Lottie began to be aggressive. "What is your name?" she asked, peremptorily.

"Don't speak so sharp, Lottie," said Sarah. "You will scare her half to death. She's nothing but a child. She was half frozen. She was standing there on the door-step, shaking from head to foot, poor little thing, half dressed, too, on such a day as this." Sarah glanced at the heap of wool and red silk rags on the chair, and remembered a nice thick wool coat in the closet of a certain chamber.

Lottie asked again, but more gently, "What is your name, little girl?"

"Joan Brooks."

"Oh, I know her," said Lottie, with an accent of slight scorn. "Her father's that broken-down minister. He fills the pulpit sometimes when Mr. Whitman has bronchitis."

"He preaches very well, too," said Sarah, kindly.

"Father is not broken down. He stands up as well as you do," said Joan, unexpectedly. Then she began to rise. "Where is my coat?" said she.

"You sit right down, child," said Sarah. "She didn't mean a thing. Of course your father isn't broken down. We always speak that way of a minister who don't preach regularly."

"Father used to preach regularly," said the girl, eagerly, "but after we moved here the church he came to preach in burned down."

"That was the little Hyde's Corner church," interpolated Lottie. Sarah nodded.

"He preached regularly there," stated Joan, "until the fire."

"What does your father do now?" asked Lottie.

"He preaches for other ministers a great deal, and betweenwhiles he goes about taking orders for a beautiful book on the Holy Land."

Lottie looked at the geraniums, and her lips moved inaudibly: "Peddler."

"We don't have as much money as we did before the fire," stated the little girl, "and we don't have much of anything to give away. That is why—" She stopped.

Sarah caught up the bag, which Joan had placed on the floor beside her.

"Well, let us see what you have to sell," said she.

Sarah opened the bag and Lottie stood looking over her shoulder.

"My!" said Lottie, "what lovely drawnwork, and it's just the same pattern as that bureau-scarf you made for your cousin Lizzie, too!"

"And I wanted one like it for her married sister, Jeannie. How much is this, Joan?"

Joan mentioned a price. Lottie paled, and her mouth dropped when Sarah Bannister, so careful of money, said she would take it. She also bought for a large sum a beautiful table-cloth with embroidered corners for the minister's wife.

"That's just like the one you made yourself for Mrs. Lester Sears," said Lottie. She thought Sarah Bannister must be losing her wits. "There's that same cornucopia in one corner, and cluster of daisies in another," she mentioned, feebly.

"I know it," said Sarah, defiantly. "Why shouldn't it be the same? It's a common pattern. I made that table-cloth for Mrs. Sears because she was so good when I was sick with the grippe, sending in things 'most every day. I wanted to make something for the minister's wife just as nice, because she and Annie Sears are so thick, and because we all know the minister isn't very popular, and I feel sort of sorry for her, but I didn't have the time or strength to make it. This is a real godsend."

"You'll have to tell her you didn't make it," remarked Lottie, maliciously.

"I am not in the habit of either telling or implying a lie," replied Mrs. Bannister. Then she turned suddenly to Joan. "My dear, who made these pretty things?"

Joan crimsoned, then paled, but she lifted clear eyes of truth to Mrs. Bannister, "A lady."

"What lady?"

"A lady."

"But what is the lady's name?"

"I would rather not tell her name."

Sarah looked at Lottie and spoke with lip-motion: "Her mother."

Even skeptical Lottie nodded. What so likely as that the broken-down minister's wife might do this exquisite work, and send her little daughter out to sell it?

Sarah was examining the table-cloth. "I am sure it is a little different from mine," she reflected. "The bunch of daisies is larger."

Lottie nodded. "Looks so to me."

Sarah laid down the table-cloth and took up some knitted lace. "This is almost exactly the pattern of mine, and I did want to knit some for Daisy Hapgood. I am so glad to get this."

The more Sarah Bannister bought, the more the little girl's face beamed. Her cheeks flushed, her blue eyes gleamed. Sarah kept gazing at her with loving admiration. As she bought everything in the bag, Joan seemed fairly quivering with delight. She held her pretty upper lip caught between her teeth, lest she break into sheer laughter.

"I will take this handkerchief with the embroidered G," said Sarah. "It is just what I wanted to tuck in a letter to Ella Giddings."

"I thought I saw one in the parlor just like that," said Lottie.

"So you did, similar. Mine has a queer little quirk at the top of the G, and that is for Emma Gleason. I wanted to make another for Ella. Lottie, do you mind going up-stairs and bringing down my little black silk shopping-bag? My purse is in it. I don't want to go through that cold hall. I have got the grippe, I almost know it," said Sarah, when the bag was empty.

While Lottie was gone, Mrs. Bannister and the girl added up items rapidly on the back of an old envelope. Sarah was economical with paper. Sarah added with zeal, and her hand was over the sum total, and she had time to shake her head with finger on lips when the door opened. The girl nodded. She was only a child, but she understood. The other lady was not to know what the things cost.

Lottie cast a sharp glance at the gleam of white paper in Sarah's cautious hand. "Whatever made you hang that bag up in the closet, when you always keep it in the top bureau-drawer?" said she. "I had an awful hunt. Thought I never would find it."

"I remember hanging it there when I hung up my coat when I came home yesterday," replied Sarah, calmly.

Sarah loosened the strings of the bag. Lottie watched like a cat. Sarah took out her nice black leather pocketbook. Lottie craned her neck. Sarah bent over the pocketbook, hiding her proceedings, counted out money, folded it in a nice little roll, and gave it to Joan.

"There," said she, kindly. "That is right. Now you had better run and give it to your mother."

"I shall not take this money to mother," said she. "She will not expect it. It is my money. Father and mother wish me to be independent. I have this money for Christmas presents and I shall have to see to them myself."

Joan rapidly slipped into her ragged coat. Sarah thought of the warm one upstairs, but did not somehow feel like mentioning it.

"You mean to say you don't tell your mother about this?" said Lottie.

"Mother does not wish me to tell her everything," said Joan. "Father does not, either. They say I should lose my individuality."

"No danger, seems to me," said Lottie. When the girl had gone and was disappearing down the road, a red rag from the silken lining of her coat blowing back stiffly in the icy wind like an anarchist flag, the women stood at the window, watching her.

"She is a darling little girl," remarked Sarah, with an absent air.

Lottie looked at her. Directly there came before her mental vision the freckled face, the long nose, the retreating chin, the weak eyes and stiff, sandy hair of Sarah's departed daughter, long in her little green grave.

"She thinks this beautiful girl looks like her," Lottie reflected.

Directly Sarah spoke in a breaking voice, and tears rolled down her cheeks. "She is the living image of my Ida."

Lottie lied for the sake of her own heart. "Yes, so she is," said she.

"Then you saw the likeness?"

"How could I help it?"

"Want me to take these things into the parlor and put them with the others?" offered Lottie. "You mustn't go in there with such a cold as you've got."

"I'll put them in the secretary, here," said Sarah. "There's one drawer without a thing in it. I want to look them over again, and everything will have to be done up and addressed out here, anyway. Remind me to send to the store for some more Christmas ribbon tomorrow morning."

Sarah folded the dainty things she had bought and laid them carefully away in the secretary drawer, then she seated herself in her rocking-chair and took her pocketbook out of her black silk bag. She looked up and saw Lottie's sharp eyes turn away. She laughed and the laugh had a tang in it.

"Well, Lottie," said she, "if you want so much to know what I paid for the things, I am perfectly willing to tell you, although I cannot imagine why you want to know. I am not in the least curious, myself."

Lottie flushed suddenly. She tried to smile. "I ain't curious," she replied. "I never was. What makes you talk so, Sarah? It sounds sort of hateful."

Sarah paid no attention. "The things cost just twenty-three dollars and seventy-nine cents," said she, coolly.

"My goodness!"

"Yes, just twenty-three dollars and seventy-nine cents."

Very swiftly Lottie sped her own little shaft.

"Why, Sarah Bannister, I never knew you spent as much on Christmas presents in your whole life. You have never had the name of being as free as all that."

"I didn't deserve it," said Sarah. "All those things made up in the parlor there didn't cost fifteen dollars. I told you they didn't cost so much, and they didn't."

"And you laid out all that money on these things?"

"I didn't have to do the work on these, and the work means a good deal when you are tired out and coming down with the grippe. And, besides"—Sarah hesitated; then she finished with defiant accent—"when I saw that darling little girl, the exact image of my dear lost Ida, I felt almost ready to mortgage the place to buy her out."

"Well, all I can say is, I am beat," remarked Lottie. "If anybody had told me that you would spend twenty-three dollars and seventy-nine cents buying Christmas presents from a peddler, I should say if you did you had gone plumb mad."

"She wasn't a peddler, Lottie. That girl is the daughter of a minister of the Gospel."

"Minister of the Gospel! He ain't preaching. He's peddling books."

Sarah began to speak, but the door-bell cut her short.

"Who in the world is coming now?" she murmured, and smoothed her hair and straightened her apron-strings.

"Another nice peddler, maybe," said Lottie. "Don't put your pocketbook away, Sarah."

Sarah looked at her reproachfully, and coughed. "Will you go to the door?"

Lottie went, her head erect. Directly the door was opened Sarah heard a loud, very sweet, very rapid voice, and knew the caller was Mrs. Lee Wilson. Mrs. Wilson danced in ahead of Lottie, who followed her sulkily. She did not like Mrs. Wilson, who was so much prettier than she ought to have been, considering her years, and so much gayer and livelier, that it seemed to give grounds for distrust. Mrs. Wilson slipped back her handsome fur neck-piece, disclosing a deep V of handsome white neck, which Lottie glanced at, then openly sniffed. Then she spoke in a voice which seemed drawn out like thin wire. The voice had hissing sibilations.

"Don't you feel cold, Mrs. Wilson?" said Lottie.

Mrs. Wilson laughed. She understood. "Oh no," said she, sweetly. "I never catch cold with my neck exposed. Don't you think I am lucky to have a neck good enough to keep up with the styles? A woman does look so old-fashioned now, with a high collar."

Lottie flushed. "I care more about decency than I do about style," she snapped. Her animosity was no longer disguised.

Mrs. Wilson laughed again. "Well, it is nice to have a neck long and thin like yours in case the styles changed, and they are bound to, and I look like a freak with a high collar," she said, good-naturedly. "But, Sarah Bannister, and you, too, Lottie, I didn't come here to discuss low necks and high collars. I came here about that Brett family. You remember the talk when the father ran away and left those six children, after the mother died of quick consumption?"

"I thought an aunt came, or something," said Sarah.

"So she did, and stayed quite awhile, and then there was a report that she had gone away and taken the children. You know at first we thought the town would have to do something about it."

"Didn't the aunt take them away?" asked Lottie.

"Why, no, it seems she didn't. The minister's wife saw the oldest girl—she's a pretty little thing, you know—dragging a small one on a sled yesterday. She said both the children looked well dressed and well nourished, but the eldest girl wouldn't tell her who was looking after them."

"Guess the aunt came back," said Lottie, rather indifferently. Lottie was always indifferent when it came to large families of the poor. It had always vaguely seemed to her like something immoral.

Sarah looked interested. "Why, it seems as if the aunt must have come back," said she, "if they looked as well as you say. How old is the eldest girl?"

"Oh, they are all young. She can't be more than eight, a very pretty child with red-gold hair. They are all shy; won't talk. What I came about—" Mrs. Wilson hesitated a moment. She colored a little and laughed confusedly. "Well," she said, finally, "I suppose we have all been rather lax about those children. I had a letter from Mrs. S. Walsingham to-day, and how she had heard of the case I don't know, but she had, and—she reminded me very politely, but she reminded me all the same, that she was making an annual donation to the Ladies' Aid Society for just such cases. She said she presumed her letter was useless, for doubtless we had already looked into the case. She knew we hadn't. Somebody in this town has told her."

Lottie nodded her head in a sidewise direction. Mrs. Wilson laughed. "I dare say you are right," she agreed. "Emmeline Jay and her mother are always on the watch ever since they stopped going to church because they thought the minister before this one preached at them all. Well, anyway, Clara Walsingham wants to know, and, of course, she has a right."

"Just like Clara to write that sort of a letter," said Lottie. "Why can't folks come right out? I hate beating around the bush."

Mrs. Wilson giggled. "As for me, there never was a bush handy to beat around. I had to come right out and say my say. Well, the fact is not a woman of the society knows a thing about these Brett children, and who is going to begin? I would, but my little boy is sick, and I suspect measles. I can't carry measles into a poor and deserving family. The minister's wife says she would right away, but her sister with her four children has come to spend Christmas with her, and she has her own three and no help. She says after Christmas she can do anything."

"I'd go tomorrow," said Sarah, reflectively, "but I think I have taken cold, and—it seems selfish, but I must get my presents off. I got rid of working on more, for I bought a lot, but I have a quantity to do up."

The two women looked at Lottie. She sat with her chin high, gazing out of the window.

"Christmas is right here, next week Thursday," remarked Mrs. Wilson, helplessly.

"If my cold is better I will go and see these children to-morrow, presents or no presents," said Sarah, firmly.

Lottie looked over her shoulder at her. "'Twon't be any better. You've got fever now. Look at your cheeks."

As Sarah could not very well look at her own cheeks, and there was no mirror in the room, she gazed at Mrs. Wilson for confirmation.

She nodded. "Your cheeks do look pretty red," said she.

"I'll wait and see how I feel in the morning," she said as Mrs. Wilson rose to go.

In the morning Sarah was no worse and no better. The weather was severe. The wind was very high. Sarah decided to have Lottie bring the presents out from the icy parlor and see if she could not get them ready for mailing during the day.

"By doing that," said she, "I can have to-morrow to go and see those Brett children. Of course, something can be hung on the Sunday-school tree for them, anyway, and it can be seen to that they come, but I don't feel right to wait till after Christmas to do more than that. They may be suffering."

"Guess they're all right," said Lottie. "When there's such a tribe as they, somebody bobs up and looks after them."

Lottie deposited with care her first load of dainty things from the parlor. Sarah, muffled in a white wool shawl, sat out of the draught from the open door. Lottie went back and forth. She laid things on the table, the sofa, on chairs.

"Well, this is all," she said, finally.

"All?"

"Yes, I've brought out everything. You haven't things put away in other places?"

"No, only those I bought from the little girl yesterday. They are in the secretary drawer."

"Sarah Bannister, where is that beautiful embroidered table-cloth that we said was so much like the one you bought?" said Lottie, suddenly. "I don't remember bringing it out. No, don't you go to handling all these cold things. I'll look myself."

Lottie examined everything. Sarah watched. She was rather pale. Finally Lottie came forward and stood before Sarah with a determined air. "That table-cloth ain't here," said she.

"It must be."

"It ain't. When I look I look. It ain't."

Sarah stared at her.

"Some other things ain't here, too," said Lottie.

"What?"

"A lot of doilies, a lot of other things."

Sarah gasped. "Where do you think?"

"Sure you 'ain't put them away in other places?"

Sarah shook her head.

"Which drawer in the secretary did you put those things you bought from that girl?"

"Lottie!"

"Which drawer?"

"I don't see what you think that has to do with it."

"Which drawer?"

"Next to the top one," Sarah whispered, feebly.

Lottie crossed the room, her skirts swishing. She returned after two trips and laid the soft piles of dainty handiwork in two chairs before Sarah.

"These ain't cold," said she. "Now let's look over these things. Here's the table-cloth you bought."

"I don't see what you mean."

"Look at it; look real careful."

Sarah took the square of glistening linen, with its graceful embroidery, and examined it. She lingered long over one corner. Her lips tightened. She folded it carefully. "Lay it over on that other chair," said she.

Lottie obeyed. She looked a little frightened.

Sarah went on, examining one article after another. Lottie laid one after another on other chairs.

"There are still four more things missing," said Sarah.

"What?"

"That large centerpiece, really the best thing I had. I meant that for Clara Walsingham. She always sends me such beautiful presents. Then I don't see that blue sweater I knit for the Langham girl—Sally, you know—and I don't see the white Shetland shawl I crocheted for Grandma Langham. That was large and I couldn't fail to see it. And—I don't see the pink bedroom slippers I made for Cousin Emma's daughter Ruth."

Sarah's voice broke. She passed her handkerchief across her eyes.

"Don't you cry and get all worked up. It will make your fever higher."

"I haven't told you," moaned Sarah, weakly.

"What ain't you told me?"

"I haven't told you that the table-cloth I put in the secretary drawer, that I bought from that dear girl, who looks so much like my own daughter who passed away, is the table-cloth I made."

"You sure?"

"Yes, I found the place in the horn-of-plenty where I made a mistake and had to rip out something and work a leaf to hide it."

"Sarah Bannister!"

"I made all the other things I bought, too," said Sarah. "I had ways of telling."

"Are you sure?"

"I wish I wasn't."

"What are you going to do?"

"I don't know anything I can do."

Lottie, who had not received anything except a high-school education, but was usually rather punctilious about her English, forgot all caution. She sprang into a morass of bad grammar.

"She had ought to be took up!" she said, with decision.

"Lottie, that darling little girl!"

"Darling little limb of Satan!"

"She looked so—"

"If you say another word about her looking like your Ida I shall begin to wonder what your Ida really was. Likening your own flesh and blood to a thief and a liar!"

"Come to think of it, she didn't lie. She wouldn't tell the name of the lady who made the things."

"Oh, well, if she only stole, she ain't quite so bad. I shouldn't wonder," returned Lottie, sarcastically, "if there wan' goin' to be no question of brimstun' for jest plain stealin'."

"Why, Lottie, how you do talk! What has got into you?" Sarah said, weakly. Then she began to weep again.

The door-bell clanged. Lottie ran to the window and peeked.

"It's a man," she whispered. "Wipe your eyes, Sarah. It's the minister. I know him by his pants. He's the only man that don't go to the city to work that wears creased pants in the morning in this town. Wipe your eyes, Sarah. You don't want him to see you've been cryin'."

"I don't care," wept Sarah. "I'm going to tell him the whole story and ask for his advice. What's a minister for? He can offer up the question to the Lord in prayer."

"If he don't offer it up to his wife, it's all right," Lottie said in a loud whisper, on her way to the door. When she returned, the minister, Silas Whitman, followed her. He had removed his topcoat and appeared clad in clerical black, shabby, but tidy and beautifully kept. Silas Whitman's salary forced careful keeping and nearly prohibited expenditure. He was a very small man, fair, with high, light eyebrows, and light hair growing stiffly from his forehead. As a result, he had a gentle, surprised expression. He took a chair near Sarah Bannister, and she went on at once with her story. Silas listened, and his expression of surprise deepened to one of positive pain.

The minister was not exactly a success in this particular parish. He realized it forlornly, but saw no way out. He was a man whose genuine worth and attainments were dimmed by his personality. He was like a rather splendid piece of trained mechanism doomed to one track, which did not allow him to even use many of his abilities. He was overeducated for the little New England village, he was overinformed; mentally he towered among them like a giant among Lilliputians. There was not among them a man or a woman to whom he could betray his every-day thoughts of the great present of the world. Not one could have understood. During the war he had done his best to discharge his duty to his God and his country among a people whom the war, in spite of their Red Cross work and their contributions to the Expeditionary Forces, never reached. It came the nearest to reaching them when the profiteers hid the sugar and the scarcity began in the stores, when Mrs. A couldn't make currant "jell" and Mrs. B couldn't make peach preserve, and Mrs. C and all the rest of the alphabet could not bring sweet cake to the Ladies' Aid parties, when the men missed the sugar from their coffee; then it seemed to the minister as if through the fruit and pickle season his good New England people peered out and up, almost enough to smell powder and hear the roar of the cannon. At that time the minister preached two war sermons to full congregations, and had hopes. However, after the fruit season, the people settled back in their ruts of the centuries.

Silas, sitting there listening to Sarah's strange story, considered how she was shocked out of her tracks now, but how soon she would regain her step. It seemed a pity. Just now she was dramatic and interesting, and at the crucial moment of the tale, when Sarah had missed the four treasures, the door-bell rang, and Lottie, peering out of the window, announced, "It's her."

"I am so glad you are here," Sarah said to the minister; then, in the next breath, she plucked at his sleeve as the door opened, and begged in a whisper: "Better let me speak to her first. She's only a child."

The minister nodded, and Lottie re-entered, leading Joan, or, rather, pulling her, for the little girl seemed to resist.

"Come here, dear," said Sarah. "Don't be afraid. Nobody is going to hurt you."

The little girl, carrying her bag, which did not seem so full as yesterday, allowed Sarah to put her arm around her.

"Now, dear little girl," said Sarah, and her voice trembled, "I must talk to you, and—"

The child interrupted. "What is the matter?" she inquired, with the sweetest air of pity.

"The matter?" murmured Sarah.

"Yes, ma'am, the matter with you. You have been crying and look worried."

"So I am," said Sarah, stepping into the open emotional door. "I am worrying about you."

The child regarded her with great, blue, troubled eyes. "I am very well, thank you," said Joan. "Please don't cry any more about me. I haven't any stomachache, or toothache, and I said my prayers this morning, and there's nothing ails me, truly."

Sarah gasped. "Do you feel that you have done just right?"

"Yes, ma'am."

"Are you a little girl who loves God?"

"Yes, ma'am."

The minister's face twitched. He coughed quickly and drew out his handkerchief and blew his nose. Lottie eyed him sharply. Sarah looked bewildered. The minister looked from her face to the perfectly open, ready-to-answer one of the child, and he coughed again.

"What have you got in your bag to-day?" Sarah inquired, rather hopelessly.

"The other things to sell."

"What other things? Open the bag!"

The girl obeyed at once. She drew forth, one by one, the missing articles of Sarah's collection. She eyed them admiringly. "Pretty," she commented.

Sarah stared.

"Why don't you speak right up to her?" said Lottie.

The little girl stared at her and smiled sweetly. "If you please, ma'am," she said to Sarah Bannister, "I am very busy this morning."

The minister swallowed a chuckle. Lottie looked at him.

"Joan," said Sarah.

"Yes, ma'am," said the child, looking up brightly.

"I have found out that you had sto—taken all those things you sold to me yesterday from me. You sold me my own things."

The little girl gazed. "I am real glad you found out so soon," said she.

"My goodness!" said Lottie.

Sarah gasped. "Why?"

"Because I was afraid you wouldn't."

Sarah stared at her, quite pale.

"I would have told you this morning if you hadn't found out," said the little girl, calmly. She took up the centerpiece which she had brought and looked fondly at it. "This is real handsome and I think you must have worked real hard embroidering it," said she. She added, "This is five dollars."

"You aren't going right on selling me my own things?" gasped Sarah.

"I must sell them to you. I couldn't afford to give them to you, and I mustn't sell them to anybody else."

The minister spoke for the first time. "Why not?" he asked.

She looked wonderingly at him. "It wouldn't be right. Are you the minister?"

Silas replied that he was.

"Then I am surprised you didn't know it wouldn't be right, and had to ask me," remarked Joan.

"Why wouldn't it be just as right to sell to anybody else?" asked Sarah.

Joan looked as though she doubted her hearing correctly.

"Why, they are your own things!" she said simply.

Lottie came forward with a jerk of decision. "Now you look right at me, little girl," said Lottie. "Do you mean to tell me you don't know it was wrong for you to come here and sell Mrs. Bannister all this stuff?"

"It is hers," said Joan. She looked puzzled.

"Then, if it was hers, why didn't you leave it alone?"

"I wanted to sell it. I wanted the money."

"What for?"

"All those poor little Brett children."

"The Brett children?"

"Yes, ma'am. Their mother died and their father thought he'd like to go and live with another lady, so he got married and the other lady didn't want six children so in a bunch, and so he didn't worry any more about them, and they were all starving to death and freezing, and there are two just little babies. And so I have them to take care of, and I can't earn money, for I am not old enough, and this is the only way, I decided, and I have just begun, and it works perfectly lovely."

"Goodness!" said Lottie.

Now the Rev. Silas Whitman realized that he must enter the field or be thought a quitter by two of his parishioners.

"Come here, little girl," he said, pleasantly.

Joan went smilingly and stood at his knee.

"Now, my child, listen to me," he said. "Didn't you know it was wrong for you to do such a thing? Don't you know you ought not to take anything whatever that belongs to other people and sell it to them?"

"They are all hers."

"Then why ask her to pay for them?"

"I wanted the money for the poor little Brett children and there wasn't any other way."

"But why should she have to pay for her own things?"

"Because she hadn't given any money to the Brett children, and I didn't begin to ask what they are worth."

"Don't you know it is wrong?"

"No, sir."

"Do you realize what you have done?"

"Yes, sir."

"Tell me what."

Joan looked up in his face and smiled a smile of innocent intelligence. "I opened one of the long windows in her best room," said she, "and I took those things I sold her yesterday and these I brought to-day, and I hid them in the Brett house. Then yesterday afternoon I packed them very nicely in the bag. I couldn't get all the things in, so I had these left over, and I came and sold them."

"Do you think she is going to pay you any more, you little—" began Lottie, but Sarah hushed her.

"I am not going to pay her, but I am going to give her some more money to buy things for the Brett children," said she.

"And you don't think you have done wrong?" persisted the minister.

Joan looked at him wearily. "They are her own things and she has them back, and she has paid me the money, and you heard her say she was going to give me some more, and it is for the Brett children. I haven't done wrong. The lady didn't give the money in the first place to the Brett children, so, of course, I had to see to it. And now she has her presents all back and everything. I think I must go now or I shall have no time to buy some meat and cook the children's dinner."

Sarah opened her black silk bag and handed a bill to the little girl. "Kiss me, dear," she whispered.

Joan threw both arms around her neck and kissed her, over and over.

"Will you come and see me?" whispered Sarah, fondly.

"Yes, ma'am; I'd love to."

They all stood at a window watching the child go down the path. Suddenly Silas Whitman began to speak. He seemed unconscious of the two women. He watched the little girl, the red silk rag from her coat lining streaming, march proudly away with a curious air, as if she led a platoon, not as if she marched alone.

"There she goes," said the minister. "There she goes, red flag flying! Our problem is her truth, and who shall judge? It may be, all of this, the celestial prototype of Bolshevism. She may be the little advance-scout of the last army of the world, the child facing Pharisees, and righteous, and ancient evil, triumphant wisdom. There she goes, little anarchist, holy-hearted in holy cause, and if her way be not as mine, who am I to judge? It may be that breaking the stone letter of the law in the name of love *is* the fulminate which shatters the last link of evil which holds the souls of the world from God."

The minister caught up his coat, put it on, and went out. He did not look at the women.

They stared at each other.

"Lordamassey!" said Lottie.

Harriet Ann's Christmas

Alton (IA) Democrat, December 17, 1898, 5;
Bellows Falls (VT) Times, December 21, 1899, 10–11;
Fresno (CA) Morning Republican, December 24, 1909, 15

I WAS 12 YEARS old three weeks before that Christmas, but I was small for my age and looked no more than 10. There were four of us. I was the eldest. Then there was a girl of 10, one of 8½ and a boy of 7. In October we had moved to the house on the shore of Lonesome lake, which was very lonesome indeed. It was a solitary little sheet of water on the top of a hill, almost a mountain. There were no neighbors nearer than a mile. Father had moved to this farm on Lonesome lake because his father had died that fall, and the property had to be divided between him and his brother, Uncle William. Uncle William was not married, though he was older than father, and he and father and grandfather had always lived together and worked the home farm, sharing the profits.

After grandfather's death father and Uncle William had some difference. I never knew what it was about. One night after I had gone to bed I heard them talking loud, and the next morning father and Uncle William looked very sober at breakfast, and mother had been crying. That afternoon she told us that we were going to move because the property was to be divided, and were to have the farm on Lonesome lake, near Lebanon. Lebanon is a little village about ten miles from Wareville, where we were living then. Mother said she was sorry to go away because she had lived there so long, and she was afraid she would be pretty lonesome in the new home, but she said we must make the best of it. Uncle William was the eldest son and had a right to the first choice of the property, and of course since he was a bachelor it would be very hard for him to go to live at Lonesome lake.

We children rather liked the idea of moving and began packing at once. Flory and Janey had their dolls and their wardrobes all packed within an hour. Flory was the sister next to me, and I thought her rather old to play with dolls. I had given up dolls long before I was as old as she.

Two weeks after grandfather died we were all moved and nearly settled in our new home. There had been no one living in the house for several years, except when father and Uncle William went up there every year in haying time to cut and make hay. Everything seemed pretty damp and dismal at first, but when we got our furniture set up and the fires started it looked more cheerful. The house was large, with two front rooms looking on the lake, which was only about twenty feet distant. One of these rooms was our sitting room; the other was our parlor. Back of these rooms was a very large one, which was our kitchen and dining room. There were a dark bedroom in the middle of the house, a bedroom out of the kitchen, one where father and mother slept, out of the sitting room, and four chambers.

Thanksgiving came about a week after we had moved, and we had a rather forlorn day. We all missed grandfather and Uncle William. I am sure mother cried a little before we sat down to the table, and father looked sober.

When Thanksgiving was over, we began to think about Christmas. Mother had promised us a Christmas tree. The year before we had all had the measles and been disappointed about going to the tree at the Sunday school, and mother had said, "Next year you shall have a tree of your own if nothing happens." Of course, something had happened. Poor grandfather had died, and we had moved, and we wondered if that would put a stop to the tree. Mother looked a little troubled at first when we spoke of it. Then she said if we should not be disappointed if we did not have many presents and the tree did not have much on it except popcorn and apples she would see what she could do.

Then we children began to be full of little secrecies. Mysterious bits of wool and silk and colored paper and cardboard were scattered about the house, and we were always shutting doors and jumping and hiding things when a door was opened. Each of us was making something for father and mother, even Charles Henry. He was working a worsted motto, "God Bless Our Home." Then, of course, we were all making presents for one another.

It was a week and one day before Christmas. We had our presents almost done, and mother had promised to take two of us the very next day and go down to the village to do some shopping—we had been saving money all the year for some boughten presents—when the news about Uncle William came. A man rode over from Wareville quite late at night and brought word that Uncle William was dangerously sick and father and mother must come at once if they wanted to see him alive. Mother said there was nothing for it but they must go. She said if they had not come away just as they had, with hard words between father and Uncle William, she would have let father go alone and staid with us children; but, as it was, she felt that she must go too. She and father, though I can understand now that they felt anxious while trying to conceal it from us, did not think there was any real danger in our staying alone. They reasoned that nobody except the people in the village would know we were alone, and there was not probably one ill disposed person there, certainly not one who would do us harm. Then, too, it was winter and we were off the main traveled road, and tramps seemed very improbable. We had enough provisions in the house to last us for weeks, and there was a great stock of firewood in the shed. Luckily the barn was connected with the house, so I did not have to go out of doors to milk—it was fortunate that I knew how—and we had only one cow.

Mother staid up all that night and baked, and father split up kindling wood and got everything ready to leave. They started early next morning, repeating all their instructions over and over. We felt pretty lonesome when they had gone, I especially, not only because I was the eldest and felt a responsibility for the rest, but because father had given me a particular charge. I was the only one who knew that there was $583, some money which father had from the sale of a wood lot in Wareville a month after we had moved and had kept in the house ever since, locked up in the secret drawer in the chest in the dark bedroom.

Father had been intending to drive over to Wilton, where there was a bank, and deposit the money, but had put it off from one week to another, and now Wilton was too far out of his way for him to go there before going to see poor Uncle William.

Father called me into the parlor the morning they started, told me about the money and charged me to say nothing concerning it to the others. "It is always best when there is money to be taken care of to keep your own counsel," said father. He showed me the secret drawer in the chest in the dark bedroom, the existence of which I had never suspected before, though I was 12 years old, and he taught me how to open and shut it. If the house caught fire, I was to get the children out first, then go straight to the secret drawer and save the money. If there had been no possibility of fire, I doubt if father would have told me about the money at all, and I would have been saved a great deal of worry.

The money was on my mind constantly after father and mother were gone. I kept thinking, "Suppose anything should happen to that money while I have the charge of it." I knew what a serious matter it would be, because father had not much money and was saving this to buy cows in the spring, when he expected to open a milk route. I was all the time planning what I should do in case the house caught fire and in case the robbers came. The first night after father and mother went I did not sleep much, though the others did. We three girls slept in one room, with Charley in a little one out of it, and we were all locked in.

The next night I slept a little better and did not feel so much afraid, and the next day Samuel J. Wetherhed came, and we all felt perfectly safe after that. He came about 10 o'clock in the morning and knocked on the south door, and we all jumped. I don't suppose anybody had knocked on that door three times since we had lived there, it was such a lonesome place. We were scared and did not dare to go to the door, but when he knocked the second time I mustered up enough courage. I told Flory, who was as large as I and stronger, to take the carving knife, hide it under her apron and stand behind me. Of course I thought at once of the money and that this might be a robber. Then I opened the door a crack and peeped out. The minute I saw the man who stood there I did not feel afraid at all, and Flory said afterward that she felt awful ashamed of the carving knife and afraid that he might see it and be hurt in his feelings.

He stood there, smiling with such a pleasant smile. He did not look very old, not near as old as father, and he was quite well dressed. He was very good looking, and that, with his pleasant smile, won our hearts at once. He more than smiled—he fairly laughed in such a good natured way when he saw how we were all peeking, for the younger children were behind Flory, and I found afterward that Charley, who had great notions of being smart and brave, though he was so little, because he was a boy, had the poker, shaking it at the stranger. The man laughed and said in such a pleasant voice, pleasanter than his smile even: "Now, don't you be scared, children. I am Samuel J. Wetherhed."

The man said that as if it settled everything, and we all felt that it did, though we had never heard of Samuel J. Wetherhed in our lives. We felt that we ought to know all about him, and Janey said that night that she was sure she had seen his name in The Missionary Herald, and he must be a deacon who gave a great deal to missions.

Samuel J. Wetherhed went on to tell us more about himself, though I am sure we should have been satisfied with the name. "I have a married sister who lives in Wareville. She married a man of the name of Stackpole," said he, and we all nodded wisely at that and felt that it was an introduction. We knew Mr. Stackpole. He was the man to whom father had sold his woodland. "I went to visit my sister last week," said the man. "I haven't got any settled work. Yesterday my sister's husband saw your father, and he told him how he had left you all alone up here and felt sort of worried, and I thought as long as I was just loafing around and no use to anybody I might just as well come up here and look after you a little and stay till your folks got back and look out there didn't any wolves or robbers or anything get you." The man laughed again in such a pleasant, merry way when he said that, and then he went on to tell us that his sister's husband said Uncle William was better and the doctor thought he would get well, but he guessed father and mother would have to stay there for awhile. We asked the man in, and he made himself at home at once.

It seemed to me I had never seen a man so very kind as he was, and he was so quick to see things that needed to be done. He went out of his own accord and drew a pail of water, and he brought in wood for the sitting room fire. We children all agreed when we went up stairs to bed that night that there never was a man so good, except father. We had told him our plans for Christmas, and he was so much interested. He said of course we could have a tree. He would cut a fine tree, and if Uncle William was not well enough for father and mother to leave him on Christmas day he would go to Wareville himself and stay with Uncle William, so they could come home. He said, too, that he could go down to the village on foot, and if we would make out a list of the things we wanted he would go down and buy them for us. He went the very next day. We gave him all our money, and he brought back everything we wanted. We decided to make him some presents, too, and I began a little wash leather money bag, like the one I had made for father. Flory made a penwiper and Janey a worsted bookmark.

Samuel J. Wetherhed cut a beautiful tree for us, taking us all into the woods to pick it out. Then he set it up in the parlor so firmly that it did not shake. He rigged some sockets for candles and helped us string popcorn for decorations and make candy bags. He could sew as well as mother. Samuel J. Wetherhed was the most industrious man I ever saw. He was not idle a minute. He milked and did all the barn chores, he made the fires and drew water and swept the floors and washed the milk pails for me, and all his spare time he was at work upon our Christmas preparations as busily as we were. He found some boards and tools of father's and made some wonderful things with them. There was a nice box, which he showed us how to line with flannel, for mother to keep knives and forks in, a little boat for Charley and a number of other things.

I felt much easier in my mind about the money after Samuel J. Wetherhed came.

We had given Samuel the bedroom out of the kitchen to sleep in. He said he would rather have that, because it was so handy for him to build the fire in the morning, and I did not have the first suspicion that anything was wrong until the night of the day but one before Christmas. I had been sleeping well since Samuel came, through feeling so safe, though I had, as I afterward remembered, often started awake, because I thought I heard a noise, but that night I did not go to sleep as soon as usual. I was very much excited thinking about Christmas and father and mother coming home. Samuel had gone down to the village that morning and got a letter for me from mother in which she said that they were coming home Christmas morning, since Uncle William was well enough to be left. We were all delighted the more so because we thought that now Samuel could stay and have our Christmas tree with us. He laughed and thanked us when we said so, but in a moment afterward I noticed that he looked very sober, even sad. Well, thinking over everything made me very wide awake, and I guess it must have been as late as 11 o'clock when I was sure I heard somebody down stairs in the sitting room, which was directly under our room. I thought at once that it might be a robber and perhaps I ought to speak to Samuel in case he should not hear the noise. I waited till I heard the noise again very plain and was sure that I knew where it was—some one was trying to open the door of the dark bedroom, which stuck and had to be forced down before pulling. The children did not awake, and I made up my mind that I would not speak to them and get them scared to death. I thought that I would go down stairs very softly, steal past the sitting room door and go through the other way to the kitchen and wake up Samuel.

I got up and put on my dress. Then I went down stairs, and I don't believe I made any more noise than a cat. I saw a faint light shining from the dark bedroom, and I knew I had not been mistaken. Then all of a sudden I thought that father and mother might have come home and father be looking to see if the money was safe. I thought I would make sure before I called Samuel.

I went into the sitting room and crept across to the dark bedroom, keeping close to the wall. I peeked in, and there was Samuel rummaging in the chest where the money was. Then I knew that, however good Samuel might be in other ways, he could take things. It was an awful shock. I wonder why I did not scream and run, but I kept still. I went back up stairs and locked myself into the chamber and sat down on the edge of the bed to think. It did not seem to me that it was of any use for me to stay down stairs and watch Samuel. I did not think he could find the secret drawer without any help. I could not stop his taking the money if he was determined. Then, too, I reasoned that if he did not find it that night there would be time enough for me to hide it tomorrow, and father and mother were coming home next day.

I did not sleep any that night. I took off my dress and lay down. Before daybreak I had my plans all made. I tried to treat Samuel just as usual when I saw him in the morning, and I guess I did. After breakfast I carried a pitcher of water into the parlor as if I were going to water the plants. Then I lighted a match and touched it to one of the candles on the Christmas tree to make it appear as if I had only wanted to see how it would look, and then I touched it to the tree, and it blazed up. I waited until I dared wait no longer, and then I dashed on the water and screamed fire at the top of my lungs. They all came running in, Samuel first. He rushed for more water and the fire was out in a minute, but the tree was badly singed, and the children began to cry.

"Now, don't you cry," said Samuel "I'll go this minute and cut another tree."

So Samuel started off and Charley with him, and then I made Flory and Janey go up stairs. "You two have just got to go up stairs and stay there while I fix a surprise," said I. Surprises were a favorite amusement with us children. Flory and Janey laughed and ran off up stairs for a minute.

I set some molasses on to boil. Then I got the money out of the secret drawer and made six little parcels of it, rolled as tightly as I could and wrapped in letter paper. Then as soon as the molasses was boiled I made popcorn balls. Luckily I had enough corn popped. When I called the girls down stairs, I had two plates of corn balls. The balls in one were of extra size with strings attached all ready to hang on the tree, and in six of them were hidden the little rolls of money. The balls in the other plate were smaller, and those were to be eaten at once.

When Samuel and Charley came home, I gave them some of the little corn balls, and when Samuel had set up the tree I hung on the others. Then I thought the money was safe, but I wondered all the time what I should do if Samuel should come to me and ask me right out where the money was for I did not want to tell a lie.

That night we all went up stairs as usual, but I did not go to sleep. It was not very late when I heard Samuel moving about below, and presently he came to the foot of the stairs and called me.

I went to my door. My heart was beating so hard it seemed to choke me. "What do you want?" I made out to say as softly as I could, so as not to wake the children.

"Come down here a minute," said Samuel, and I went down to the sitting room. "I want to ask you a question," said Samuel. He tried to smile, but he was very pale and looked as if he was as frightened as I was. I was so afraid he would ask me right out, "Where is the money?" but he did not.

"I only want to ask if your father left some money in the house when he went away," said he, looking away from me as if he were ashamed.

"Yes, he did," said I. I had to or tell a lie.

"Well," said Samuel in a queer, shaking voice, "I would like to borrow that money for a little while. I need some money right away, and as long as your father ain't using it"—

"I would rather you waited and asked father," I said. "I don't think father would like it if I lent his money."

"I will make it right with your father," said Samuel. "Did your father tell you where the money was?"

"Yes, he did," I answered. I had to or tell a lie. I trembled for the next question.

"Where did he tell you it was?" asked Samuel.

"In the chest in the dark bedroom," said I. That was the truth, and it did no harm.

"Whereabouts in the chest?"

"In the secret drawer."

"Oh! So there's a secret drawer. Did you father tell you how to open it?"

I said he did.

"Well, you just come in here and show me how to open it," said Samuel.

I went with Samuel into the dark bedroom and showed him how to open the drawer. I could see nothing else to do. I stood back while he opened it. I wondered if it would be wrong for me to cry out as if I were astonished when he discovered that the money was gone. Then all of a sudden I heard a sound that made my heart jump with joy. I heard sleighbells and then father's voice shouting to the horse. "Father has come," said I.

Samuel made one leap and was gone, rushing through the kitchen and out the back door.

I ran and unbolted the south door, and there were father and mother come home sooner than I expected. When I saw their faces, I just broke down and sobbed and sobbed and told them all about it in such queer snatches that they thought at first I was out of my mind. Father said afterward that he never heard such a jumble of popcorn balls and secret drawers and Samuels. When father fairly understood what had happened, he lighted the lantern and searched out in the barn and the sheds to be sure that Samuel was not lurking about the premises, but he did not find him. Father said he knew the man; that he belonged to a good family, but had been sort of shiftless and unlucky.

When we were all settled down again for the night and I felt so safe and happy with father and mother at home, I could not help feeling troubled about poor Samuel out in the storm. I hope he would not die of cold and be found dead when the snow melted in the spring. There was quite a severe snowstorm. That was the reason why father and mother had reached home so late. They had been obliged to drive slowly on account of the gathering snow.

We were just sitting down to our Christmas dinner next day when we all stopped and listened. Then the sound came again, and we were sure that somebody was out in the storm calling faintly for help.

"It is the man!" said mother. "Do go quick as you can." Mother had been worrying about Samuel all day. She said she did not want him to perish if he had tried to wrong us, and father had been all around the farm looking for him. He thought, however, that he had gone down to the village the night before.

We opened the door, and we could hear the calls for help quite plainly. Father pulled on his big boots and started out. The storm was very thick. Soon we could not see father, but we could hear his shouts and the faint cries in response, and then we saw father coming back half carrying Samuel J. Wetherhed.

Samuel was pretty well exhausted, besides being frightened and ashamed when he saw where he was, back in the house of the man he had tried to rob. He tried to stop on the threshold of the outer door, spent as he was. "I guess you—don't—know," he began, but father interrupted him. "Come along in!" cried father in a hearty way that he has. "You have been good to my children and as long as you didn't do what you set out to there's no use talking about it."

Samuel was pretty well exhausted. He had spent the night in an old barn on the other side of the mountain and had been floundering about in circles all day, trying to find the road. However, he was able to eat some Christmas dinner with us, though he hesitated about that, as he had done about entering the door, and all of a sudden he dropped his knife and fork, bent his head down over his plate, and we saw that he was crying, though we tried to take no notice.

Samuel stayed with us that night and was present at the Christmas tree, though he seemed very sober and dashed his hand across his eyes a good many times when his name was called and he got his little presents.

The next day the storm had stopped, and father put the horse in the sleigh and took Samuel down to Lebanon to take the train. We never saw him again after he had shaken hands with us all and thanked mother in a voice that trembled so that he could scarcely speak and father had driven him off in the sleigh.

That day we girls pulled the corn balls to pieces and found the bills inside, not sticky at all. The next day father took the money to the bank, though he said he didn't know but corn balls were safer, since robbers knew that money was in banks, but he didn't think they had any suspicion of its being in corn balls.

We spent the next Christmas in our old home in Wareville, for father and Uncle William had made up and we had gone back there to live. We had a tree, and the day before Christmas a great box came by express with a handsome present for each of us. There was no name sent with them, but we always knew as well as we wanted to, and father and mother thought so, too, that they had come from Samuel J. Wetherhed, who, we had heard, had settled out west and was doing very well.

The Christmas Ghost

Everybody's Magazine, December 1900, 512–20

IN FRONT OF Jane White's house roared and surged, beating the rocky shores with unfailing tides, the great Atlantic. The waves floating an occasional fishing vessel, were all that passed before her front windows. From gazing all her life at such stern and mighty passers, the woman's face had gotten a look of inflexible peace. Jane White looked as if she would always do her duty, but as if she would spare neither herself nor her friends, if they came in the way; as if nothing could interpose between herself and her high tide mark, not even her own happiness nor that of others.

She was not an old woman, but she seemed to have settled into that stability of old age which comes before the final greatest change of all. Her days were absolutely monotonous. She lived alone, she kept her old house in order, she made her simple garments; always on Saturdays she harnessed her old horse into the wagon, and drove to the village three miles away for groceries; on Sundays she drove as regularly to church. These simple excursions for bodily and spiritual food were all that brightened her life. There were only two houses near hers. In one of them lived a bedridden old woman, and her elderly son and daughter; in the other, David Gleason. The bedridden old woman and the son and daughter had not been on friendly terms with Jane for years, and they had not entered each other's houses. Sometimes Jane used to look down the road to the gray slant of the Rideing house rising out of the hollow, with a scowl of dissent. She could hate with vigor, in spite of the severe peace of her expression. There was a mighty grudge between them. Once the son, Thomas Rideing, had paid attention to Jane White (that was in her mother's day), and Thomas's mother and sister had interfered, and broken off the match. They had told stories as to Jane's temper and poor housekeeping, and the young man had believed them. He had ceased courting Jane, and she had known the reason. Once afterward, coming home from church, she had stopped her wagon in the narrow, sandy road, beside the Rideing team, and taxed the mother and sister with it openly. Thomas had been driving his old gray horse. His mother and sister sat one on each side of him—that was before the old woman got the hurt which laid her up for life. Jane's mother sat at her left hand, quivering with resentment. She had been a wiry little woman, with a fierce temper.

"Whoa!" said Jane to her horse. Then she spoke out her mind once for all to Sarah Rideing and her mother. "I know just what you've said about me; you needn't think I don't," said she.

"And it's all lies, every word of it," said her mother, in a panting voice.

"We've got ears, and we've heard the loud talkin' when the windows were open and the wind our way!" Sarah Rideing had replied, with a vicious click of thin lips. Sarah Rideing was pretty, with a hard, sharp prettiness.

"And we've seen the clothes on the line," said her mother. Mrs. Rideing wore a false front, and that and her bonnet were grotesquely twisted to one side.

"We ain't never had a word in our family betwixt us, and as for our clothes, I'd be ashamed to hang such lookin' things as yours be out on the line!" panted Jane's mother.

"We've got eyes and we've got ears," repeated Sarah Rideing.

"Then I should advise your mother to look in the glass when you get home, and set her wig an' her bunnit straight," said Jane's mother, unexpectedly.

"Don't, mother," whispered Jane. Then she shouted g'lang to her horse, as did Thomas Rideing to his, but Jane passed him. Thomas had not spoken a word during the whole; he left the talking to the women. He had sat still, with his rather clumsy, good-humored face fixed on his horse's ears. He was a little flushed; otherwise he showed no sign of agitation. "Thomas Rideing is dreadful woodeny, anyhow; you ain't missed much," Jane's mother had observed, as they sped along the sandy road. Once she looked back and saw, with that glee over petty revenge which is often seen in an old woman who has lived a narrow life, old Mrs. Rideing trying to straighten her front piece and her bonnet, which was trimmed with tall, nodding purple flowers. "She'd better talk," said she. "She'd better get on her own bunnit and wig straight before she talks about other folks not being neat."

"I most wish you hadn't said that," said Jane.

"Why not, I'd like to know?"

"I wish you hadn't. It didn't have anything to do with it. It's like sticking in pins when folks have come at you with hammers."

"I hope you ain't goin' to get cracked because Thomas Rideing has jilted you," said her mother, sharply.

Jane laughed. "I ain't one of the kind to be cracked," said she. And she spoke the truth. She had taken the young man's attentions as a matter of course, very much as she had always taken the unfolding of the leaves in the spring. This was something which came to most women, and it seemed to be coming to her. When she saw that she was mistaken, she no more thought of questioning the justice of it, than she would have done if a cloud which promised rain had cleared away to fair weather, or the bush which budded last spring had failed to do so this. Matters of that kind she relegated entirely to a higher Power, and it was the easier for her to do so since Thomas Rideing was not a young man to awaken easily any girl's imagination. He was such a solid, incontrovertible fact of clumsy flesh and blood, and slowly, steadily working brain, that he could arouse only observation and acquiescence—never dreams. Jane was fully alive to the humiliation of being jilted, and wrathful as to the interference of Thomas's sister and mother, but in reality that, and the stigma cast upon her temper and her neatness, hurt her more at the time than the cessation of the young man's nightly visits. Ever afterward the clothes which flaunted from the White line shone like garments of righteousness, as, indeed, they had done before. Jane White's little domicile fairly shone with cleanliness, as did her person. Not a hair was out of place on her head; she was clean as one of the wave-washed pebbles on the beach. As for her temper, her mother died soon afterward, and there was no one for her to attack with a loud tongue, as she had been accused of doing, unless, indeed, she attacked that hard Providence in whose shaping of her destiny she believed. She was absolutely alone from one week's end to the other, since she and the Rideings never exchanged calls, and as for David Gleason, he was a single man, and many said an underwit, and he kept to himself, and never went into another house than his own, and Jane certainly could not call upon him. He was a small, fair-haired man, who had come to the place and built his little shack some ten years ago. Nobody knew from whence he came, nor anything about him. He seemed to be quiet and peaceable, and to have enough money for his simple needs, and the stigma of underwit had somehow attached itself to him from his secrecy. People argued that a man would be likely to tell something to his credit if there was anything to tell, and as nobody could imagine him to be a criminal with such a physiognomy, they concluded that he must be lacking in his intellects. He was commonly said to be love-cracked.

Sometimes Jane used to see this man going down the road, moving with a gentle shuffle and slight stoop, and wonder if he were love-cracked. Now and then she felt inclined to ask him to ride, when she passed him on the way to church—he kept no horse—but she never did. The man used to look after her, sitting up straight in her wagon, and disappearing between the scrubby pines of the coast country, with admiration, as any man might have done. The red coil of hair on the back of her head gleamed under her bonnet like a mat of red gold, she held her head and shoulders superbly. She was, in fact, a very handsome woman. The severe repose of her face had kept wrinkles at bay, and she had one of those rare complexions which the sea-air does not tan, and seam, and harden, but awakens to life and rosy color. People used to say that there wasn't a young girl that went to church who was any handsomer than Jane White; still, she had never had an opportunity to marry since Thomas Rideing deserted her. Everybody, in fact, believed her to be a slovenly housekeeper, and to have a bad temper. A fire of scandal is a hard thing to stamp out, and the sparks fly wide, and kindle afar.

Jane lived alone, with a sort of rigid acquiescence to the will of the Lord, and a smouldering hatred of the human instruments who had brought it to pass. In spite of her severe calm of demeanor, she had the natural weaknesses and longings of her kind. There were times, as the years went on, when she longed for Thomas Rideing to come again, as she had never longed at first. She was often afraid alone in her house, especially in the winter time. She confessed her fears to no one, hardly to herself. "What good does it do to be afraid? I know I've got to live alone, and there's no way out of it," she said. "I might as well get over it first as last." But she never was able to conquer her nervous fears. Often when the murmur of the waves on the shingle below the bank on which the house stood arose to a roar, and the winter wind was shaking the walls, this lonely human soul in the midst of it would light her candle, and peer about the house for the evil which she seemed to feel to be present; then she would extinguish her candle, and, shading her eyes, press her face close to the window, but she could see nothing except the wild drive of the storm outside. Then the saying in the Bible about the "Prince of the Powers of the Air" would come to her mind, and if she had been a Catholic she would have crossed herself. A vague fear, which was none the less terrible because it was vague, seemed to hold her as in a vise. However, Jane White's health, in spite of her sensitive nerves, was superb. She had never an ache nor ail until two days before Christmas, ten years after her mother died. Then she had a sudden attack of rheumatism, after a spell of damp, warm, unseasonable weather. It was all she could do to hobble about the house. When it came to going to the well for water, she thought at first she could never manage it. Finally she succeeded, fairly hitching herself over the ground, one step at a time. She thought of having the doctor, but she had no one to send for him, unless she could waylay some one passing. Both the Rideing and the Gleason houses were out of hailing distance, and had they not been, she would not have asked any of the dwellers therein to go for the doctor, unless it had been David Gleason. She thought that she might ask him, if she were to see him going by—he looked good-natured. But she did not see him nor any one passing that day. It was midwinter, and toward noon the snow began to fall. The lonely woman thought dejectedly that she didn't know what she was going to do. The stitch in her back was no better; she had no remedies to apply to it; she saw no likelihood of getting the doctor. It was much as ever she could do to keep up her fire and make herself a cup of tea at nightfall. A sense of utter loneliness, which was fairly desolation, smote her as she sat alone that evening. She heard the wind roar and the waves break, and the dash of the sleet on the window. She seemed to herself loneliness personified—one little human spark in the midst of an infinity of space and storm. At nine o'clock she went to bed. She slept upstairs. She had left the little bedroom on the first floor since her mother died. Her chamber was icy cold. She had heated a soapstone, and she rolled herself in an old flannel blanket, and clambered into bed with groans of pain.

It was a long time before she went to sleep; then she slept soundly for a few hours. It was perhaps four o'clock when she awoke with a shock of deadly terror. She *knew* some one was in the house. She was no longer *suspicious* that some one was in the house; this time she *knew*. The storm was still howling outside. She could hear the constant surge of the ocean, and the small drive of the sleet on the window. The room was absolutely dark; it must be still far from the winter dawn. She was *sure* that there was some one in the house.

She reached out for the matches which she always kept on the table beside her bed, and, as she did so, a cramp of pain seized her from the rheumatism. She nearly screamed, and the matches were gone. She usually moved them from the mantel-shelf when she went to bed, but she must have omitted to do so—it had been so difficult for her to get about the night before. Jane endeavored to rise. She thought she would grope her way across the room to the shelf and get the matches, but the pain in her back was so great that she dare not make the attempt. She said to herself, What if she should fall and break a bone out there in the dark? It seemed to her that she was safer in the bed. So she lay still, listening fearfully. She became more and more convinced that there was somebody in the house. She heard movements, soft and guarded, but plainly evident to a sharp ear, below. Once or twice she was sure that she heard a door open and shut. Later on she heard the pump out in the yard, which had a peculiar creak. She lay bathed in a cold sweat of terror, expecting every moment to hear steps on the stairs; and presently the first cold glimmer of dawn was in the room, and she heard a door shut below—then she heard nothing more. Everything was still.

It was late before Jane succeeded in dragging herself up, with groans and frequent pauses, and getting dressed and down stairs. She felt convinced that the visitor, whoever he was, had gone; but she thought of her mother's silver teaspoons, and the clock, and a gold watch which had belonged to her father and would not go, but was still an impressive gold watch, and very dear to her, and she thought of her table linen, and everything which was of any value; for she had no doubt then that the visitor was a thief.

But when she reached the kitchen, moving by slow and painful stages, she gasped, and stared, and stared again. A bright fire was burning in the stove (she had wondered if she could, by any possibility, make a fire with those pains like screwing knives in her back and shoulders), and the table was laid for breakfast, and the room was full of the aroma of coffee, for the pot was on the stove, and a pan of something covered with a towel stood on the back, and when she took off the towel fearfully, there were fresh biscuits. Then a nice little bit of beefsteak was in the frying-pan, all ready to cook, and the tea-kettle was full of hot water, and the water-pail in the sink was full. Outside the storm was still raging, but the kitchen seemed like a little oasis of warmth and comfort in the midst of it. Even the geraniums in the south window had been watered. She heard the cat mew, and opened the cellar door. The cat had been out when she went to bed, for she had called her in vain. Somebody had let the cat in and put her down cellar, lest she steal the beefsteak.

"Who let you in?" said Jane feebly to the cat.

She looked at the beefsteak and at the biscuits doubtfully, as if they might be fairy food, and have some uncanny property of harm. "I was out of meat, and to-day's Saturday, and I couldn't have got down to the store," said she; "and I didn't have a mite of bread mixed, and I don't know how I could have done it."

Finally Jane White cooked the beefsteak, poured out a cup of coffee, and ate her breakfast, though it was still with an unreasoning terror. It seemed a kindly deed, and yet it was so unexplained that it struck her with all the horror of the unusual. She ate suspiciously, almost as if she thought the food were poisoned. When she crept into the pantry to put away the dishes, she had another surprise, for she found on the shelf a little roasting piece, two pies, two loaves of bread, a piece of squash cut ready to boil, and some washed potatoes.

Jane looked at them, white as ashes. "My land!" said she. She staggered back to the warm kitchen, sat down, and reflected. She tried to think who could have done it, but she was entirely at a loss. For a moment she had a wild idea of Thomas Rideing and his old love for her, then she dismissed it. "He'd never get round to it," she said to herself. Then she thought of David Gleason, to dismiss that more peremptorily than the other. "There ain't anybody in creation who would do anything like this for me, and what's more, there wasn't anybody knew I had the rheumatism and couldn't do it myself," she argued.

She gave it up. She roasted her meat, and cooked the squash and potato, and remained alone all day. The storm continued until sunset. Then, when the west was a clear, pale gold, the flakes stopped falling, and the earth looked like a white ocean frozen suddenly in the midst of a tumult of rage. As for the real ocean, she could hear the boom of that louder than ever, for its fury does not subside so quickly as that of the earth. It cleared off very cold. Jane heaped her stove with wood when she went to bed (she burned wood from her own woodland), but she feared it would not last until morning, and she feared that she could not get down-stairs to replenish it. As night came on her rheumatism was worse, and then her fears arose to such a pitch that, had it not been for the cold and her illness, she would actually have gone over to the Rideings. She went to bed, and lay quaking with sheer terror for some time. At last all was still and she fell asleep, to awaken as she had done the night before, at the sounds below. This time her matches were in reach. She struck one and lighted a candle. Then she pulled up the blanket with painful efforts, and wrapped it around her; then she crept out of bed. Along with the woman's timidity was a spirit of investigation. Had she been a man she would have been afraid enough to make an excellent soldier. The battle would have been, for her, the only method of ridding herself of her panic. She could never have borne to cower behind breastworks.

She crawled down stairs, feeling as if she were a stiff lay figure instead of herself. She planted her feet rigidly as if they were wood; every step was agony, but she kept on. At that moment she was more terrified, if anything, to confront the stranger—because he had conferred benefits upon her—than if he had worked her harm. It would not have seemed so uncanny. In spite of her religious training the thought of the supernatural was strong in the woman's mind. She thought of her mother, of her father—how they would have felt to know she was all alone, sick with rheumatism in the winter storm, and God knew what she thought next.

When she opened the kitchen door her face was ghastly, peering over her candle. The kitchen was lighted; the fire burning; she smelled coffee; it was later than she had thought—five o'clock in the morning. She had only a vision of a figure swiftly moving out of sight into the pantry. Then she sprang, with a stab of pain, to the pantry door, and shot the bolt. She had a bolt on the pantry door, because the pantry window had no fastening; but she had never used it. After she fastened it she heard the person whom she had locked in trying to open that window, and said to herself grimly that he could not do it. That north window must be frozen down so hard that it would be impossible to stir it without hot water. The man, whoever he was—she was sure it was a man, there had been no flirt of feminine skirts on that flying figure—must have come in through the cellar. The bulkhead had never had a lock, for Jane and her mother, reasoning with the innocent fatuity of some women, had always said, "Nobody will ever think of coming through the cellar."

The person whom Jane had locked into the pantry did not pound or try to get out. Finally she took the carving-knife from the table—he had been slicing some sausage for her breakfast, apparently—and she went to the pantry door, and leaned her head toward it, curving her body at a careful distance. "Who be you?" said she.

There was no response.

Then she spoke again: "Who be you?"

"A well wisher," came in a feeble voice from the pantry.

Then a cold shiver ran again over the woman. Again the supernatural terror reasserted itself. It was much more alarming that a well wisher should come to her house, and do these kindly deeds for her on this wicked earth the night before Christmas—she remembered with an additional shiver that Christmas Day was dawning—than a burglar. She went over to the kitchen door, and stood there, all ready to run should the person in the pantry make a motion to escape. She kept her eyes riveted on the pantry door. She made up her mind that as soon as it was light enough she would go for the Rideings, no matter how they had treated her in times gone by. It seemed to her that the full day would never come; but at last the light broadened and deepened over the blue hollows and white crests of snow, and then she saw that a nice path was dug from her door to the well. "My land!" said she. She took a shawl off the peg, wrapped it around her, putting one corner over her head; succeeded, after many painful efforts, in getting into her rubbers, and was about to set out when she caught a glimpse of a man's figure going down the road. It was David Gleason going for his milk, which he got from a farmhouse two miles toward the village.

Jane crept out in the yard a little way and called. He heard her, and came shuffling toward her in a light spray of snow.

He had a mild, pleasant face; but Jane, after the prevalent report as to the state of his intellects, felt a little afraid to ask him into the house. "You go to the Rideings, and ask Sarah and Thomas to come right over here as fast as they can," said she. She was almost crying. David Gleason looked at her anxiously. "Anything the trouble, anything I can do?" he began, but she interrupted him. "Go as quick as you can," said she. She was almost hysterical.

It seemed to her an age before she saw David Gleason plod into the Rideing house, and presently he and Sarah, not Thomas, emerge. "Where in the world is Thomas?" she thought. "What good can a woman do?" She was glad to see Gleason returning with Sarah. She thought she would not be afraid of Gleason if Sarah were with him, and nobody knew what was in the pantry.

Jane met them at the door. Suddenly her rheumatism seemed better; she moved quite easily.

Sarah Rideing looked at her half alarmed, half indignant. "What is the matter, Jane White?" said she.

"There's something in the house," replied Jane in an awful voice, and the other woman turned pale.

"What do you mean?"

"There's something in the house. It came last night and made up the fire, and got breakfast, and got the water, and brought roast meat, and bread, and it came again to-night, and I came down and I locked it into the pantry."

"Did you see it?" asked Sarah, quivering. She grasped Jane's arm hard.

The two old enemies fairly clung together, drawn by mutual terror.

But David Gleason went close to the pantry door.

"It wasn't a woman, I know that," gasped Jane.

"Who's in there?" cried David Gleason.

There was no reply.

"It told me once it was a well wisher," said Jane, and Sarah Rideing trembled like a leaf. The reply struck her much as it had done Jane. Well wishers abroad in the deadly cold of a winter morning might well arouse terror.

"Oh, dear! Oh, dear! I wish Thomas was here," cried Sarah. "I couldn't find him nowheres. I don't know but something has got *him*. Oh, dear!"

"Who's in there?" demanded David Gleason. He had a firm voice for such a small, slight man.

"He ain't any more half-witted than I be," thought Sarah Rideing.

Then the voice replied again, but with a trifle more emphasis, "A well wisher." Both women started.

"It's Thomas," cried Sarah Rideing. Then she flew to the pantry door and unbolted it. "Thomas Rideing, what be you doin' here?" she demanded. "Be you gone crazy?"

Thomas Rideing, emerging from the cold, blue depths of the frozen pantry, looked at once shamefaced and self-assertive. "You needn't say a word, Sarah," said he. "I saw her having such hard work to get out to the well yesterday mornin', and I knew she'd got the rheumatism, and when the storm begun, and I thought of her all alone over here, I couldn't stan' it, an'," he went on, his voice gathering firmness in spite of an agitation which made him tremble from head to foot, "I—I know it was all a lie you and mother told about her not bein' a good housekeeper. There it was neat as wax here, and she laid up with rheumatism, too, and as for her temper, anybody that can get around at all with the rheumatism, and not say anything to be sorry for, hasn't got much temper, and—I wouldn't have minded one mite if she had."

"I should think you'd gone crazy," said Sarah scornfully, and yet her voice softened.

Thomas looked pitifully at Jane. "It don't seem as if I could stan' havin' you live here alone any longer," he said brokenly, as if his unhappiness over her loneliness were the only thing to be considered. It was the refinement of masculine selfishness, but Jane liked it.

"I didn't know you thought so much of me, Thomas," said she; then her face flamed.

"Well, I haven't got anything to say; you must suit yourself," Sarah said, still in that softened voice; then she and Gleason went out.

Thomas Rideing approached Jane, and put his arm around her. "Ain't you been afraid here all alone?" said he.

"Yes, I have; but I didn't suppose you cared."

"I did," said he. "There's no use in rakin' up bygones, but I know I've treated you mean."

"Yes, you have," admitted Jane impartially, but her eyes upon his face were tender.

"It wasn't so much because I was afraid you were a bad housekeeper, and bad-tempered, I didn't believe it; and I wouldn't have minded if you had been, but I backed out because mother and Sarah felt so. I guess mother will feel different now, but I can't help it if she don't. As for Sarah, I can't help it either. You ain't goin' to be left alone here any longer. How's your rheumatism, Jane?"

"I guess it's better; I haven't thought of it," replied Jane.

Then the outer door opened suddenly, and Sarah Rideing looked in. David Gleason's face showed over her shoulder. "Wish you a merry Christmas!" said Sarah. Her thin, pretty face was quite transformed by a sudden triumph of the best within her. The man behind her beamed with friendliness toward these people who were nothing to him.

It was suddenly borne in upon the consciousness of Jane White that love and kindness were not such strangers upon the earth as she had thought.

The Reign of the Doll

Harper's Monthly Magazine, January 1904, 285–96

THERE WAS A great storm. Fidelia Nutting was too frightened and excited to go to bed. It was eleven o'clock; three hours before, at eight o'clock, she had opened the door into her bedroom in order that the warmth of the sitting-room should temper the freezing atmosphere before she retired. She sat where she could see the peaceful white slope of the feather-bed; her head was heavy with sleep, but the strain of her nerves kept her awake. Fidelia was exceedingly timid, and even overawed, by any unusual stress of nature. Summer thunder-storms had always rendered her for the time a mild maniac; winds seemed to penetrate her soul, winter snows to enter and sift into the farthest crannies of her thoughts. This storm was sleet rather than snow. The wind raged. It seemed to pounce upon the house and shake it like a wild beast, then retreat, muttering, to some awful lair of storm, to return with a new gathering of fury.

Fidelia cowered and shivered, with a roll of fearful eyes. She was a large, elderly woman with the soul of a child. She was entirely alone in her little house; over across the street, in the large, old mansion-house of the Nuttings, her sister Diantha was also alone. Now and then Fidelia went to her window, that looked across the street, and saw with a thrill of half resentful comfort her sister Diantha's light. She reflected that Diantha also had always been afraid in a storm, though not as afraid as she—or not owning to it.

"She always used to keep her lamp burning when there was a thunderstorm and when the wind was high," reflected Fidelia. Diantha's lamp was set on a table in the centre of her sitting-room, in a direct line with Fidelia's window. A great beam of yellow light shone through the window—through the shreds of snow which clung like wool to the sashes, through the icy veil of sleet, through the foliage of the geraniums in Fidelia's beautiful window garden. Fidelia was a little afraid that the cold wind might injure her flowers, but she would not lower her curtain, because she was shamefacedly desirous of the company of Diantha's light.

Suddenly she heard a gathering flurry of sleigh-bells. They increased until they seemed in the room; then they stopped suddenly. Fidelia's heart leaped for fear.

"Something has stopped here," she gasped. It was unprecedented for anything to stop there at that hour and in such a storm. She shaded her eyes, and peered fearfully and cautiously from the window around her geraniums. She could see a dark shape at the opposite window, blotting out the lamplight, and she knew that Diantha was also looking. A man's figure, gigantic in a fur coat, lumbered slantingly through the drifts of the path to the front door. Fidelia put a little worsted shawl over her head, took her lamp, and crept tremblingly through the freezing front entry in response to the knock. Her bell was out of order.

"Who's there?" she asked.

"Express," he shouted, in an angry voice, and Fidelia turned the key and opened the door. The fur of the expressman's coat stood out, stiffly pointed with ice; his cap looked like an ice helmet. "Express, ma'am," he said, in a hoarse voice, and the package was in Fidelia's hand and he was gone. Then the wind came in a wild gust, and Fidelia fled before it with her streaming lamp. Back in the warm sitting-room she set the lamp safely on the table; then she stood gazing at her package. It was a long box, very nicely wrapped in thick paper and securely tied. Fidelia did not connect it with Christmas; Christmas presents were not within her present environments. She examined the package carefully, and saw that the address was correct—Miss Fidelia Nutting, North Abbot, and it was marked paid, with a blue pencil. She laid the package on the table, and seated herself near it in her rocking-chair. Another gust of wind came, and the bombardment of the sleet upon the window was frightful; it seemed as if the panes must be shattered. She looked at the package on the table, and a curious fear of it came over her. The unwontedness of that and the unwontedness of the storm seemed one, and instinct with terror.

"I'd like to know what's in that bundle," she whispered, with fearful eyes on it. She got up and gazed across the street at her sister's lamp, which still shone to comfort her. The dark figure, however, moved before it in a second. "She's looking out," she thought, with that curious mixture of timidity and anger and affection with which she always thought of her sister. She and Diantha had quarrelled over the distribution of the property after their mother died. Diantha had taken the old homestead and less money, and gone to live there alone. Fidelia had taken more money and the small cottage, and gone to live there. They spoke sternly when they met; they never exchanged visits; there was between them a sort of dignified hostility, to which they did not own. Although all the village knew that there was enmity between the sisters, none knew which of the two originated it, which had demanded the peculiar arrangement of property and the living part. Fidelia felt a certain sympathy with Diantha because of the express package. She knew how curious Diantha was, though she would not own to it. Curiosity at its extreme is like unslaked thirst. "Poor Diantha, she's just dying to know what is in that bundle," she said to herself. She, aside from her vague alarm over it, was loath to open it in the face of this eager, unsatisfied curiosity over the way. She watched her sister's light opposite. She had a desperate hope that she would keep it burning all night; but about half-past ten it went suddenly out. "Oh dear," groaned Fidelia. Loneliness went over her like a deep sea. New terror of the package seized her. She felt that nobody would send it to her with any good purpose. Her nervous terror had fairly for the time being unsettled her reason. Then she heard some one at the door. She waited, hoping that she might be mistaken, that it was the wind. But it came again. There was a sharp pounding on the door panels; it was impossible to think it was anything else.

Fidelia pulled her little shawl closely over her head, took up her lamp, and went forth into the cold front entry. The pounding came on the door with redoubled impetus. The caller had seen the lamp through the side-lights.

"Who is it?" cried Fidelia, in a voice which rang strange to her own ears. She was almost in convulsions of terror.

"Diantha," responded a shrill voice from outside. "Let me in quick; it's a terrible storm."

Then Fidelia set her lamp on the entry table, and fumbled in a tumult of surprise and delight with the bolt and the key and a chain. As the door opened, the lamp blazed high and went out. Diantha and Fidelia rushed upon the door, and together forced it back and locked it.

"Come into the sitting-room, Diantha," said Fidelia, in a trembling voice. "Look out you don't run into anything; it's very dark." Fidelia felt timidly for her sister's hand, and led her, feeling her way carefully, into the sitting-room.

Fidelia got a match and fumbled her way back to the entry, got the lamp and lighted it, and put it in its usual place on the sitting-room table. Then the sisters looked at each other. Each looked curiously shamefaced. Diantha was smaller than Fidelia, but more incisive. She was rather pretty, with a sharply cut, cameolike face framed in white hair, which was now indecorously tossed about her temples. She began smoothing it impatiently.

"I never saw a worse night," said she.

"It's a terrible storm," assented Fidelia. It was pleasant to find a common grievance. "Do you want a brush and comb?" asked she.

"Yes, I guess I'd better smooth my hair a little," said Diantha; and Fidelia got her brush and comb from the bedroom. She watched her sister standing before the sitting-room mirror, which hung between the front windows, and her whole face was changed. Whatever bitterness had been in her heart toward Diantha was lost sight of in her joy over companionship in this night of storm.

"It's a dreadful storm," said she.

"Yes, it is," assented Diantha. "I could hardly get over here. The telephone-wire is down, and the branches are crashing off the trees. There's a big maple branch right 'side of your front gate. I had to step over the end of it. It's awful."

"It's worse than it was," said Fidelia.

"Yes, it's worse than it was when the expressman came." Diantha looked hard at the package on the table.

Fidelia was slow to wrath, but all at once she had an impulse of indignation. So that was all her sister had come over there for,—just curiosity to see what was in that package, when she knew how frightened she was in a storm, how frightened she had always been. She sat down in the rocking-chair, and her large face took on an expression at once sulky and obstinate.

"Yes," she said, dryly, "I guess it is worse than it was when the expressman came." Then she said no more. She rocked slowly back and forth; a fierce rattle of sleet came on the window-panes. Diantha carried the brush and comb back to the bedroom; her white hair shone like silver; then she returned, and stood looking out at the black night pierced by the whiteness of the storm.

"Don't you feel afraid that your geraniums will get frozen, quite so close to the window?" she asked. "That Lady Washington lays right against the pane, and it is so cold that the window is frosting, beside the sleet."

Fidelia softened a little. "Maybe there is some danger," she said.

"Suppose we move them back a little?" said Diantha. "We can move them together, I guess."

Fidelia rose, and she and Diantha took hold of the flower-stand and moved it slightly away from the window.

"I guess that is safer," said Diantha. She looked at the package on the table again, but Fidelia was rocking back and forth with the old look of obstinacy on her face. Diantha also sat down near the stove. A great gust of wind shook the house; a tree crashed somewhere.

"It is an awful storm," remarked Diantha.

Fidelia felt such a thrill of thankfulness for companionship in the midst of that terrible attack of wind that she melted. "Yes," she said, "it is awful."

"It makes me think of stories I used to read of folks in a fort being besieged by Indians," said Diantha, looking at the package.

Fidelia's eyes followed hers. "Yes," she said, "it does."

"I suppose you don't want to go to bed yet?" said Diantha, rather formally. "I am not keeping you up?"

"No," said Fidelia.

"I thought you didn't use to go to bed in a hard storm," said Diantha, "and I felt kind of nervous alone, and I saw your light burning."

Fidelia's face lightened. So Diantha had not come over wholly for the sake of curiosity. Fidelia felt pleased to think her sister had felt the need of her, even selfishly. Her eyes and Diantha's both fell upon the package at the same time; then they met.

"I haven't opened it yet," said Fidelia, quite easily. She laughed.

Diantha laughed too. "You don't seem to be in much of a hurry to see your Christmas present," said she.

"Oh, I don't believe it can be a Christmas present."

"It must be."

"Who could have sent me one?"

"I don't know, but somebody must have."

"Perhaps I had better see what it is," said Fidelia. She rose, and Diantha hesitated a second; then she rose, and both women stood over the package on the table. Fidelia began carefully untying the string.

"Why don't you cut it?" asked Diantha.

"It's a very nice string," replied Fidelia, who was thrifty. Her thrift had made some of the difference between herself and her sister.

She strove hard with the knot, which was difficult. Diantha pushed her away, and untied it herself with firm, nervous fingers. Then she flung the string to her sister.

"Here's your string," said she, but with entire good-nature. She even laughed indulgently. Fidelia then wound the string carefully, while Diantha lifted the lid from the box. Both women gave little gasps of astonishment.

"Goodness!" cried Diantha. "Who ever could have?"

"I don't know," responded Fidelia, feebly. They both stared a second at each other, then again at the box. In the box, in a nest of tissue-paper, lay a large doll. The doll's eyes were closed, but she smiled in her doll-sleep—a smile of everlasting amiability and peace. Golden ringlets clustered around her pink and white countenance, her little kid arms and hands lay supine at her side, her little kid toes stuck up meekly side by side. The doll was entirely undressed, except for a very brief under-garment of coarse muslin.

"It's a doll," gasped Diantha.

"Yes, Diantha," gasped Fidelia.

"Who could have sent you a doll?" inquired Diantha, with some sternness.

"I don't know," replied Fidelia.

"There must be some mistake," said Diantha.

Fidelia's face, which had worn an expression of secret delight, fell. "I suppose so," she said.

Both women stared at the doll, as if under a species of fascination. The storm roared harder, the sleet beat against the window as if it would break the glass, another tree branch crashed, but they did not heed it. They continued to stare at the doll.

"She isn't dressed," said Fidelia, finally, with a tender cadence in her voice.

"No, she isn't," returned Diantha.

Diantha then lifted the doll very carefully and delicately by the middle of its small back. The doll's eyes immediately flew open, and seemed to survey them with intelligent and unswerving joy.

"Her eyes open and shut," remarked Diantha. She then pressed the small body a little harder, and there came a tiny squeaking cry. "It cries," proclaimed Diantha.

Fidelia simply stared.

Diantha looked speculative. "Most probably this doll belongs to the little Merrill girl that lives next door," said she.

"Perhaps it does," replied Fidelia.

"I guess you had better take it over there to-morrow morning and ask her mother."

"I suppose I had."

Diantha and Fidelia sat down after Diantha had placed the doll carefully back in the box, but she did not replace the lid. The two women rocked, and listened to the storm, which seemed to increase.

"There's no going to bed to-night, I suppose," said Diantha, with an angry inflection. She scowled at the storm beating at the windows.

The two rocked awhile longer. It was past midnight.

"That doll makes me think of that one I had when I was a child," said Diantha, in a tone of indignant reminiscence.

"It looks a good deal like mine, too," said Fidelia, in a softer tone.

"It seems," said Diantha, still in an indignant tone, "a pity to give away a doll to any child, not dressed."

Fidelia, looking at Diantha, blushed all over her delicate old face, and Diantha also blushed.

"Yes, it does," said Fidelia, in a hesitating voice.

"It's a shame," said Diantha.

"Yes," said Fidelia—"yes, I think it is a shame."

"I suppose you have a lot of pieces in the house?" said Diantha. She did not look at Fidelia then; she gazed out of the window. "It is a dreadful storm," she murmured, before Fidelia had a chance to reply, as if her mind were really not upon the doll at all.

"Yes, I have," replied Fidelia, with subdued eagerness.

"Well, I suppose the little Merrill girl would think a lot more of the doll if it was dressed; it would be a shame to give her one that wasn't, and if we've got to sit up for the storm we may as well do something. It wasn't ever my way to sit idle."

"I know it wasn't, sister," agreed Fidelia, falling insensibly into her old manner of addressing Diantha. "I've got a great many real pretty pieces," she said.

"Handy?"

"They are up-garret."

"Well, what if they are? I ain't afraid to go up-garret for them. You'd better light the lantern, that's all. I don't think we'd better carry a lamp up there; the wind blows too hard."

"I'll get it right away," said Fidelia, fairly tremulous with excitement.

"Have you got any pieces of that blue silk dress you had when you were nineteen years old?"

"Yes, I have some nice pieces."

"My green silk would make something handsome, but the pieces of that are all over at my house."

"I've got a big piece of that," said Fidelia. "You gave me some for patch-work years ago, and I did not begin to use it up; and I've got some of that pink satin I had when Abigail Upham was married; and I've got some dotted muslin, and some of that sprigged muslin, and plenty of old linen, and some narrow lace, and some ribbon."

"You'd better get the lantern, and we'll get the pieces and go right to work," said Diantha, rising with alacrity.

The two women went forthwith to the garret, stepping cautiously over the loose flooring, and peering timorously into the recumbent shadows beneath the eaves by the flashing light of the lantern which Fidelia carried. The pieces were in two old trunks and a blue cotton bag. They collected a quantity of remnants of silk and satin and linen, and went back downstairs to the sitting-room. Fidelia was trembling with the cold.

"You'd better sit close to the stove, or you'll catch your death," said Diantha, and she looked kindly at her sister.

"Yes, I will," replied Fidelia, gratefully.

"I'll set the lamp on the stand, and then you can see," said Diantha.

The two sisters, seated close to the warm stove, with the stand between them, went to work with half-shamed delight. They cut and made the tiny garments for the smiling doll, while the storm raged outside. They paid very little attention to it. They were absorbed.

"Suppose we make the pink satin just the way yours was made," suggested Diantha.

"With a crosswise flounce," said Fidelia, happily.

"And a little lace spencer cape."

"My old doll had one," said Fidelia.

"And so did mine."

"All our dolls used to dress alike."

"Yes, I know they did."

"We used to take a sight of comfort playing with them, sister."

"Yes, we did," agreed Diantha, harshly, "but those days are over."

Fidelia felt a little rebuked. "Yes, I know they are," she replied, meekly.

"We might make a dress of dotted muslin over the blue silk, like those our dolls used to have," said Diantha, in a softer voice.

"Yes, we might," Fidelia said, delighted.

As the two women worked, their faces seemed to change. They were tall and bent, with a rigorous bend of muscles not apparently so much from the feebleness and relaxing of age as from defiance to the stresses of life. Both sisters' backs had the effect of stern walkers before fierce winds. Their hair was sparse and faded, brushed back from thin temples, with nothing of the grace of childhood, and yet there was something of the immortal child in each as she bent over her doll-clothes. The contour of childhood was evident in their gaunt faces, which suddenly appeared like transparent masks of age; the light of childhood sparkled in their eyes; when they chattered and laughed one would have sworn there were children in the room. And, strangest of all, all rancor and difference seemed to have vanished; they were in the most perfect accord.

They worked all night, until the triumphant pallor of dawn overcame the darkness, and the window-panes were outlined in blue through the white shades. It cleared just before daylight.

"I declare, it's morning," said Diantha.

"We've worked all night," said Fidelia, in an awed tone.

"Better work than sit still," said Diantha. "You'd better put the lamp out."

Fidelia put out the lamp and pulled up a window-curtain.

"The storm is over," said she, "but it is awful! Just look, sister."

Diantha and Fidelia stood at the window and surveyed the ruin outside. The yard and the road were strewn with the branches of the trees; the trees, lopped and mutilated, stood cased in a glittering white mail over their lost members. It was a sylvan battle-field, where the victors had barely come off with their lives.

"It's dreadful; you can't get home yet a while," said Fidelia.

"I guess I can manage," said Diantha, suspiciously. She wondered if Fidelia wanted to be rid of her.

But Fidelia was looking at her with the expression of a child who wants to make up. "I thought I'd make some of those light biscuits you used to like for breakfast," said she.

"I don't see as I can get home before breakfast," said Diantha. Then she added, in another voice, "Yes, I always did like those light biscuits, sister."

"I've got some honey, too," said Fidelia.

"If there is anything I do like it is light biscuit and honey," said Diantha.

"We can finish dressing the doll after breakfast," ventured Fidelia, radiantly.

"Yes, we can. It's a shame to give a child a doll that ain't dressed."

The sisters worked until late afternoon on the doll's small wardrobe. Everything was complete, from the tiny stockings and slippers to the hat of drawn pink silk, after the style of one which Diantha's doll had owned a half-century before. When at last the doll was arrayed in her pink silk frock, her lace spencer cape, her pink hat trimmed with a fall of lace, under which her rosy face with its unswerving smile looked at her benefactors, they were radiant.

"I call that a very beautiful doll, sister," said Fidelia.

"She certainly is," agreed Diantha.

Fidelia looked at Diantha, and Diantha returned the look. A sudden cloud was over both faces.

"I suppose," said Fidelia, slowly, "we had better—"

"Yes, I suppose so," said Diantha, harshly.

"Before it gets any later," said Fidelia, with a sigh.

"Yes, I suppose so."

"To-morrow is Christmas. Maybe her mother wants to hang it on the tree."

"Very likely."

"Well, will you take it over, or will I?"

"I had just as lief."

"I will if you don't feel like it."

Still neither offered to move. Both regarded the doll, then again each other.

"That Merrill child is not nearly old enough to have a doll like that," said Diantha, suddenly.

"I don't think she is either," said Fidelia.

"No, she is not. It is strange people will buy such dolls for children who are no older."

"Especially since she has such handsome clothes."

"She would spoil the clothes in no time."

"Yes; she would let her wear that pink silk and her best hat every day."

"That little Merrill girl is not old enough to take care of that doll," said Diantha, with emphasis, and with much the same tone as if she had spoken of a baby. She gathered up the doll with determination.

Fidelia sighed. “Are you going to take her over there now?” said she. It was noticeable that both sisters now spoke of the doll as she and her.

“No, I am not. I am going to take her home,” declared Diantha.

“You are not going to take her over to the Merrills, sister?”

“No, I am not. That child is not old enough.”

Fidelia looked scared, and also aggrieved. “But,” she said, “that doll was left here; I don’t think you have any right to take her away, Diantha. If either of us is going to keep her, it ought to be the one to whom it was sent.”

Diantha surveyed her sister with an injured expression. “Fidelia Nutting,” said she, “you don’t think—you don’t really think—I would do such a thing as that? Of course I wasn’t going to take the doll away from you, although she does not really belong to either of us. Of course I know that you have the first claim. I was just going to take her to my house for a while, and I thought you would come over and have tea with me. I have some of that damson sauce you like, and the pound-cake and a mince pie, and I will make some of those griddle-cakes with butter and sugar and nutmeg on them. It’s lonesome for you here alone, with the roads not cleared enough so anybody can get in very easy, and it’s lonesome for me. I thought maybe you’d come over, but if—you don’t want to—”

“Oh, sister, I shall be very happy to come over, and I haven’t had any of those griddle-cakes since mother died. I never got the knack of making them myself. I’ll get my shawl and hood.”

“You’d better wrap up warm,” said Diantha; “it’s cleared off cold by the looks. And you’d better fix your fire so you can leave it. Maybe you’ll feel as if you could stay all night.”

When the two sisters crossed the road together, stepping among the débris of the storm, which had not yet been fully cleared away, the neighbors within range stared. In the Merrill house, next to Fidelia’s, the width of a wide yard distant, three faces were in the sitting-room window—Mrs. Merrill’s, her unmarried sister’s, and little Abby Merrill’s, round and rosy, flattened against the glass.

“Did you ever!” cried Annie Bennett, Mrs. Merrill’s sister. “There go the Nuttings across the street together. I wonder if they have made up.”

“They are going into Diantha’s house,” said Mrs. Merrill, with wonder. “I wonder if they have made up. I don’t believe one has been into the other’s house since their mother’s funeral.”

“Maybe they have,” said Annie Bennett.

"Mamma," said little Abby Merrill, "what do you spect Miss Nutting is carrying under her shawl?"

"I don't know, dear," said Mrs. Merrill.

"It looks like a dolly," said little Abby Merrill, wisely.

Mrs. Merrill and Annie Bennett laughed. "I guess Miss Diantha Nutting isn't going around carrying dollies," said Mrs. Merrill. "I guess you must be mistaken, darling."

Annie Bennett could scarcely stop laughing at the idea of Diantha Nutting carrying about a doll. But she suddenly remembered something. "Why, there's that parcel that came here for Fidelia by mistake last night," she said, chokingly. "Seeing her carry a parcel makes me remember that. I had quite forgotten it. She ought to have it, I suppose. Perhaps it is a Christmas present."

"Yes, she ought to have it," said Mrs. Merrill, turning away from the window as the door of the opposite house closed after Diantha's and Fidelia's shawled and hooded figures.

"I'll run over there and carry it," said Annie Bennett.

But little Abby interposed. She was wild to get out-of-doors after her imprisonment by the storm, and she was wild to carry a Christmas present. "Oh, mamma, let me carry it," she begged.

Her mother looked doubtful. "I don't know whether you can get over all those tree branches without falling and hurting yourself, darling," she said.

"Oh yes, I can," pleaded little Abby.

"I don't believe it will hurt her any if she wants to go," said her aunt Annie Bennett.

So little Abby Merrill, carefully wrapped against the cold, went across the street, picking her way among the fallen branches, with her mother watching anxiously, and carried the parcel to Diantha Nutting's door. "My mamma sent me over wif zis," said she—for Abby could not say "th"—"my mamma sent me over wif zis, zat was left at our house by a spressman by mistake last night." Little Abby Merrill never knew why Miss Diantha Nutting's face looked suddenly very strange to her, but she felt vaguely alarmed, and shrank back when Diantha spoke.

"Thank you, child," said she, in rather a deep voice, and she took the parcel.

Miss Fidelia Nutting's face was visible behind her sister's, and it wore a similar expression. "Oh, sister!" she gasped when little Abby Merrill had gone trotting, stepping high in her little red leggings, across the street. She was a stout little girl, and planted her little feet in a sturdy fashion. "Oh, sister!"

Diantha clutched her hard. "Come into the house," said she.

The two returned to the warm sitting-room, and then they looked at each other like two confederates in crime.

"Oh, sister, it is dreadful!" said Fidelia, faintly. "That doll must belong to little Abby Merrill, and this bundle she brought must be a Christmas present that somebody has sent me, and somehow the expressman made a mistake. She ought to have her, sister."

"Well," said Diantha, "go over there and carry her if you want to, then."

Fidelia hung her head. "She is a pretty small child to have such a doll, I suppose," she faltered.

"Then don't talk about it," said Diantha. "Why don't you open your parcel?"

Fidelia opened the parcel; inside the brown wrapping-paper was a nice white one tied with lavender ribbon. She untied the dainty bows, and unfolded a fleecy white shawl.

"Who gave it to you?" said Diantha.

Fidelia looked at the slip of paper pinned to a corner of the shawl. On it was written, "With Xmas greetings from Salome H. May."

"It's Salome May," she said.

"She always makes a sight of Christmas," said Diantha.

"I suppose she sent it because I gave her old-fashioned pinks out of my garden last summer," said Fidelia.

"It's a pretty shawl," said Diantha, with no enthusiasm.

"Yes, it is," said Fidelia; "but I never was in the habit of wearing a knit shawl in the house much." She laid the shawl on the table. "I suppose she sent the doll to the little Merrill girl," she added, after a pause.

"Very likely. She and Annie Bennett are intimate."

"Diantha, don't you suppose we are doing a dreadful thing?"

"No, I don't. I don't see why we are. We are not stealing that doll, are we?"

"No-o, I don't suppose we are stealing her," said Fidelia, hesitatingly.

"I am not stealing her, anyway. My conscience is clear. All I am doing is keeping her a little while, until the little Merrill girl is old enough to play with her and not destroy her."

"Oh, of course, that is all I am doing, too, sister."

Diantha Nutting prepared tea in the old dining-room, and she set the table with her mother's old blue Canton china and the best silver teapot and creamer. There were the griddle-cakes piled in a golden mound sprinkled with sugar and nutmeg; there was the damson sauce; there the pound-cake; but neither sister could eat much. The doll in her brave attire lay on the sitting-room table beside the shawl. Both felt, though they would not confess it to each other or herself, like greedy and dishonest children stealing another child's doll on Christmas eve. But they were yet firm. Fidelia remained with Diantha that night, and Fidelia occupied her old room out of Diantha's. Neither slept much. Often one called to the other in the darkness of the night: "Fidelia, are you asleep?" "Diantha, are you asleep?" Both were thinking of the doll and the little Merrill girl, and their consciences, which were their New England birthrights, never slumbered nor slept.

The next morning at breakfast—which they did not care for, although it was as desirable as the tea of the night before, being composed of hot biscuits and honey, and ham and eggs and coffee—they looked at each other.

"Sister, I can't do it. I can't keep it up any longer," said Fidelia, suddenly and piteously.

"Well, I suppose she'll have to have her, if she does destroy her," said Diantha, grimly. Then she took another biscuit.

"I guess I'll have another biscuit too," said Fidelia.

After breakfast Fidelia crossed the road to the Merrill house. She rang the bell, trembling, and Annie Bennett came to the door.

"Here is a doll," said Fidelia, trembling. She extended the doll in her pink silk hat and her spencer cape. "Here is a doll that was left at my house by mistake. My name was on the paper, but I guess she made a mistake on account of sending so many presents. Salome H. May sent me a shawl, and I guess she must have meant the doll for little Abby."

But Annie Bennett stared wonderingly at the doll. "Why, no," said she. "Salome sent a doll for Abby two days ago. She can't have sent this to Abby. Abby has five dolls this Christmas, anyway. It can't be Abby's. I don't know of any one else who could have sent her a doll. Was your name on the wrapper?"

"Yes, it was," admitted Fidelia, a great shamefaced hope in her heart.

Annie Bennett laughed. "Well," she said, "as near as I can find out, the doll is yours, Miss Fidelia. I guess somebody thought you and your sister needed a doll to play with."

Fidelia was aware of the friendly sarcasm, but quite unmoved by it. She blushed, but she smiled happily. “It is queer who could have sent it,” said she, “but I guess it can’t belong to little Abby.”

“No, I know it can’t,” said Annie Bennett.

Annie Bennett and Mrs. Merrill and little Abby Merrill, with her new doll from Salome H. May in her arms, all watched Fidelia Nutting cross the street to Diantha’s.

“She skips along like a child,” said Mrs. Merrill.

“She is a good deal spryer than Abby,” laughed Annie Bennett. “You ought to have seen how that doll was dressed; the funniest old-fashioned things. I wonder if she and Miss Diantha dressed it. I didn’t know but she would leave it for Abby anyhow.”

“I suppose they will give it to some child,” said Mrs. Merrill. “I suppose she thought Abby had dolls enough. I’d like to know who sent her that doll.”

“I know what I think,” said Annie Bennett. “I think Salome May had a doll left over, and sent it to Fidelia Nutting for a joke. It’s just like her.”

“Maybe she did,” said Mrs. Merrill, laughing.

But Fidelia and Diantha themselves were the children who loved the doll, and they could not spare her to another child. When Fidelia ran into the sitting-room of her sister’s house with the doll in her arms, Diantha stared.

“What have you brought her back for?” she asked, shortly.

“Oh, sister, the little Merrill girl has a doll from Salome H. May. This isn’t her doll. It must have been sent to me.”

“Fidelia Nutting, who do you suppose did such a silly thing as to send a doll to you?”

“I don’t know, sister.”

“Well,” said Diantha, “There’s one thing certain: if we don’t know whom she belongs to, there’s nothing to do but to keep her. If she wasn’t meant for you, it’s the fault of the sender.”

“Maybe we shall find out sometime about her,” said Fidelia. But they never did.

“Well, you had better stay to dinner,” said Diantha. “I hailed the butcher and got a chicken, and I’ve got pudding on boiling.”

When the two sat at dinner, casting stray glances at the doll on the sitting-room table, Diantha spoke.

“Look here, Fidelia,” said she. “I’ve been thinking. Suppose you rent that house you live in, and come and live with me. Nobody knows how much longer we've got to live, anyhow, and we can put our means together and have a girl to wait on us; we ain't either of us fit to live alone, and I guess we can get along. We used to get along well enough when we were children."

"Yes, we did," said Fidelia, cheerfully. "I'll come if you want me to, sister."

In the afternoon the sisters sat together in the sitting-room of the Nutting house. They were making some more clothes for a doll—a lavender silk frock from an old one of Diantha's, and a little black silk mantilla. They sat close to the window to catch the waning wintry sunlight—two old sisters, come together after years of estrangement, through the mediation of the universal plaything of childhood, which had come to them out of a mystery, and into a common ground of old love and memories.

"I suppose we ought to name this doll," said Diantha. "We always did name our dolls."

"Yes, I guess we had better name it," agreed Fidelia.

"We will keep her for little girls to play with if any happen in with their mothers," said Diantha. "And if a child asks what her name is, we ought to have something to say."

"Yes, I think so."

"Well?" said Diantha, interrogatively.

Fidelia blushed redly before her own sentiment; then she spoke. "I guess Peace would be a good name," said she, with a soft little shamed laugh at her sister.

"Well," said Diantha.

The two sisters continued sewing on the doll's clothes while the light lasted, their heads bent close together with loving accord, and the doll was between them, smiling with inscrutable inanity.

A Christmas Pastel

Boston Evening Transcript, December 19, 1891, 20

ON CHRISTMAS EVE a man and woman came down their house steps and went hurrying over the frosty pavement. Behind them the lights of the stately avenue converged like glittering processions, before them the lights of the Public Garden twinkled like flowers. The church stood on the corner, its dark network of vines spread like a shadow over its stone walls. High in the tower hung the silent bell that knew the Christmas chimes.

The woman's delicate chin was dipped deeply in rich fur, the furred edge of her gown swept the frosty pavement, red plumes trembled in her little bonnet. Her face shone out clear and rosy under a lamp-light. The man, as they passed, looked down at her, and there was love in his eyes.

"What shall I buy for Sister Grace?" said the woman.

"I know not, love, but here is my purse."

"And for Sister Maud?"

"Here is my purse, love, but I know not."

"And my million friends?"

"I know not, but here is gold enough. I have toiled for it all the month to give thee thy Christmasing."

"And the baby, and little Bess?"

"I know not, love, but here is the purse." High in the church tower hung the silent bell that knew the Christmas chimes.

Suddenly the woman stopped. She turned about. "What is following us?" said she.

"What mean you, love?"

"I heard little feet like a child's, pattering fast to overtake us."

"There is no child in sight, and you dream, love."

The man and woman went on. They entered the Public Garden. All around them over the frosty walks and the old flower-beds lay the shadows of the trees, clear and dark like silhouettes in the electric lights. Near them a stone sentinel stood guard on his stone pillar, over on the left a bronze horseman rode unceasingly on his bronze horse; a sheet of ice glittered with the cold white glitter of the moon.

"Sister Grace has jewels," said the woman. "She has laces and bronzes, there is naught now left in the world to give her."

"I cannot help that," said the man. "Here is the purse, love."

"And Sister Maud has all that, and also a lover. One cannot even give her love."

"I cannot manage that," said the man.

Before them lay the shadows of the tree-branches clear and black like silhouettes in the electric light.

"There is naught now left for the baby and little Bess," sighed the woman. "The nursery is full of toys, I know of naught that will please them for an hour."

Suddenly she faced about like a rose in a wind. "I hear little feet like a child's pattering fast to overtake us," said she.

"And so did I then," said the man.

"And I heard a little voice crying 'wait,'" said the woman.

"I heard not that," said the man.

They went on through the garden to the street. They crossed the street between the electric cars shooting past with flashes of fire from their wheels. They entered the old mall. "I would I could think of somewhat for the baby, and little Bess," sighed the woman.

"A little woolly lamb pleased me, when I was a child, and a stick of red and white peppermint candy," said the man.

"And a rag baby pleased me, but Bess has dolls from Paris. Oh, I hear again those little feet like a child's pattering fast to overtake us."

"And I," said the man.

"And I heard that little voice crying 'wait.'"

"And I too," said the man, "but there is no child here."

Behind them on the street shot the electric cars with sharp hisses like scythes, with fire flashing from their wheels. The man and woman went on. An old woman with a shawl over her head slunk by them muttering;

the man took out his purse, and held something toward her—"Here, take this for Christmas," said he. There was a gruff, shamed note in his voice, he cleared his throat. The old woman stood motionless; suddenly a hand was thrust forth from under her shawl like a claw from a cage. The old woman stood motionless as they went on, then the electric light shone on her withered old face looking after them.

"Now the patter of little feet is close at our heels," said the woman, and they both turned, but no child was there.

"I heard that little voice crying 'wait,' louder," said the woman.

"And I," said the man.

They came to the border of the mall. Before them shot the electric cars, up and down the street with sharp hisses like scythes, with fire flashing from their wheels.

They crossed the street and came into the midst of the great throng pressing up and down under the glare of the white lights. The eyes of the people were eager, and their breaths went before them in clouds. The footsteps of the people rang out on the frosty pavement, but the man and the woman turned ever as they went on, for they heard above all the others the fast pattering footsteps of the child.

A wrinkled hand stretched out in their faces from a street corner. The man opened his purse. "It is a cold night, though he be an impostor," he said as they went on. Then they turned again, for the child's footsteps sounded nearer.

Fir trees, laden with wax candles and sugar angels, stood in the shop windows; the shop doors held the faces of crowding people like picture frames. A woman stood looking in a window, and the light from the Christmas tree within fell on her face. The man opened his purse. "She has children and no money," his wife said, as they went on; then she turned to see the child whom she heard following.

The eager-eyed people pressed up and down under the white lights, the very candles and the sugar angels shone in the shop windows, and the man and woman went homeward across the mall.

"We have bought nothing but a little wool lamb and stick of red and white peppermint candy for the baby, and a rag baby for little Bess, and nothing at all for sister Grace and sister Maud, and the million friends," said the woman.

"We have given the money all away to strangers," said the man. The child's footsteps rang out in their ears like music.

"The child is here!" the woman cried out, and knelt down and made a ring with her arms. "See you not, I have him fast?"

"Yes, I see," said the man, and he stopped over her.

"The child has wings," said she.

Printed in the USA
CPSIA information can be obtained
at www.ICGtesting.com
JSHW022010040923
47680JS00002B/102